Praise for *The Homewreckers*

"Mary Kay Andrews is the queen of beach reads. This one combines our love of romance, HGTV shows, and murder mysteries. What more could you want?"   —*Country Living*

"A frothy combination of a hectic old-house-renovation story and a cozy mystery with a hint of romance centered around a likable heroine who has been holding too many feelings at bay. A perfect summer escape."   —*Booklist*

"Andrews (*The Newcomer*) sparkles in this fast-paced tale. . . . The author skillfully navigates the various threads—there's sexual tension between Hattie and a slew of suitors, and a twisty third act involving Lanier's fate. Andrews's fans will eat this up."   —*Publishers Weekly*

"Mary Kay Andrews has done it again, produced a feel-good book with just the right mix of tension, mystery, and human drama to satisfy almost any reader."   —*Mystery & Suspense*

"Seamlessly combines romance and mystery."   —*PopSugar*

"Imagine if HGTV and a murder mystery met, fell in love, and unexpectedly produced a rom-com."   —*E! Online*

"Bestselling author Mary Kay Andrews has penned twenty-six novels with heartfelt plots—and her latest follows suit."   —*Woman's World*

"Mary Kay Andrews is having her moment. . . . She's a great, great writer and [*The Homewreckers*] is a lot of fun."   —NBC's *Today* show

"What could be a better setting for romance than a house renovation? . . . No spoilers, but I can tell you you'll have fun finding out."   —*Tampa Bay Times*

"What makes a great beach read? There's no better person to ask than Mary Kay Andrews, an author whose name is synonymous with the genre."   —*Greenville Journal*

"Why all of Andrews's books haven't been made into TV movies yet, I'll never know. This one sounds like an ideal candidate. Are you paying attention, Hallmark Channel?"
—*The Atlanta Journal-Constitution*

"I went into *The Homewreckers* expecting a home-improvement-themed romance, and I got a bonus gift: a cozy mystery! . . . If you're looking for a romance that is a whole lot more, definitely try *The Homewreckers*!"
—*Jen Ryland Reviews*

"Once again, Mary Kay Andrews delivers a solid summer read I would recommend . . . hands down!"
—*A Southern Girls Bookshelf*

"Heartfelt and humorous."   —*The Bitter Southerner*

"Mary Kay Andrews is one of the queens of beach reads, and she's back again this year with this touching and funny novel."   —*LifeSavvy*

"Centered around finding love and flipping houses, *The Homewreckers* delivers a tale for both romantics and cold-case lovers."   —*Deep South* magazine

By Mary Kay Andrews

The Homewreckers
The Santa Suit
The Newcomer
Hello, Summer
Sunset Beach
The High Tide Club
The Beach House Cookbook
The Weekenders
Beach Town
Save the Date
Christmas Bliss
Ladies' Night
Spring Fever
Summer Rental
The Fixer Upper
Deep Dish
Savannah Breeze
Blue Christmas
Hissy Fit
Little Bitty Lies
Savannah Blues

The Homewreckers

A NOVEL

Mary Kay Andrews

St. Martin's Paperbacks

This is a work of fiction. All of the characters, organizations, and events portrayed in this novel are either products of the author's imagination or are used fictitiously.

Published in the United States by St. Martin's Paperbacks, an imprint of St. Martin's Publishing Group.

THE HOMEWRECKERS

Copyright © 2022 by Whodunnit, Inc.
Excerpt from *Summers at the Saint* copyright © 2024 by Whodunnit, Inc.

All rights reserved.

For information, address St. Martin's Publishing Group, 120 Broadway, New York, NY 10271.

www.stmartins.com

Library of Congress Catalog Card Number: 2022002309

ISBN: 978-1-250-34182-2

Our books may be purchased in bulk for promotional, educational, or business use. Please contact your local bookseller or the Macmillan Corporate and Premium Sales Department at 1-800-221-7945, ext. 5442, or by email at MacmillanSpecialMarkets@macmillan.com.

Printed in the United States of America

St. Martin's Press hardcover edition published 2022
St. Martin's Griffin edition published 2023
St. Martin's Paperbacks edition / May 2024

10 9 8 7 6 5 4 3 2 1

In Memory of Katie, My Warrior Princess,
with a heart full of love

PROLOGUE
A Dark and Stormy Night

The wind howled and shrieked and the waves slapped angrily against the seawall, huge, looming masses of clouds all but blotting out the pale yellow crescent moon. Rain was blowing in now too, razor-sharp shards slashing at her bare legs.

"It was a dark and stormy night." She picked her way down the concrete abutment. Funny but not so funny. She'd told the girls in her advanced placement English class that it was a cliché. Yet here she was, a living, breathing cliché, in more ways than one.

The last time. That's what she'd told herself nearly an hour ago as she slipped out of the house without a backward glance.

In the confessional that week—the first time she'd gone to confession in years and years—she'd promised Father she would put an end to this madness.

"It's adultery. You know that," he'd said, sharply. "And you know this has to stop."

Her face still burned with the shame of his words. She'd wept and promised to end the affair. To be the kind of woman everyone believed her to be; her family, her friends, and yes, all those impressionable girls who looked up to her, adored her as "the cool teacher."

She'd been so careful. Never a hint to anyone. No one could know. She'd stressed that to him a hundred times. There was so much at stake. They had taken every precaution. And yet . . .

Her wet hair whipped around her face. She'd look like a drowned rat by the time she got there. But she knew he wouldn't care. Within a minute of her arrival, he'd be tearing at her clothes with a ferocity that both amused and terrified her.

But tonight would be different, she promised herself. Tonight was goodbye.

Up ahead, two hundred feet away, she spotted the flickering light in the dock house, the only light on the storm-blackened horizon. All the beach houses along here were vacant this time of year, silently waiting for their absentee owners to return again in the spring. Distracted, she stumbled on a deep crack in the concrete and nearly pitched sideways into the waves, but somehow managed to right herself. Her breath was coming in hoarse gasps, her heart pounding in her chest as she stopped to regain her bearings.

And what if she had fallen? What then? Cruel irony, right? After the deal she'd cut with God? Make things right at home, quit dropping so many f-bombs, be nicer to her coworkers, cut her mom some slack, go back to church? To die on the way to a breakup with her lover, definitely smashed on the rocks, probably drowned, or worse, her bloody body chewed on by sharks? It would be the ultimate reverse God-wink. Like being flipped off by the universe.

Shake it off, she told herself, with a ragged laugh. Stop being such a drama queen. This last stretch of seawall was treacherous, battered by the last hurricane to slam against the coast. She stepped carefully onto the weedy embankment, her shoes slipping a bit on the wet grass. Ahead, the light was flashing off and on. Semaphore code. He'd taught himself from an old navy handbook he'd found somewhere, and he got off on signaling her all kinds of dirty phrases when he arrived early and knew she was approaching. She thought of it as his version of foreplay.

God, she was going to miss him. Miss the fun, the spontaneity, and yeah, the sheer excitement, the terror, the thrill of crossing the line and stepping outside the good-girl façade she'd spent a lifetime constructing. But not the sex. He actually wasn't a skillful lover, but then it had never really been about that. Had it?

Just ahead she saw the familiar clump of oleander bushes that marked the boundary line of the property and jutted out onto the seawall. There was no going around that thicket. She ducked her head and reached up to push a branch out of her way. Her hand slipped and the branch whipped back, slapping her hard across the face. She screeched, more in surprise than pain, but the cry died in her throat as an arm clamped around her windpipe.

The last thing she saw, right before she blacked out, was the flashing light at the end of the dock spelling out a word. H-U-R-R-Y.

1

Do Drop-in

- - - - - - -

As she inched along on her back beneath the rotting foundation of the Tattnall Street house, Hattie Kavanaugh was already having second thoughts. About her insistence on inspecting the corroded cast-iron pipes herself, instead of taking her plumber's word. About all the money Kavanaugh & Son had already sunk into this 157-year-old magnificent wreck. About not owning one of those wheeled things auto mechanics used—what were they called? Creepers? But mostly, she was having second thoughts about that second cup of coffee she'd gulped just before being summoned to the house they were restoring in Savannah's historic district.

The call had come from one of their subs, reporting the unhappy news that scrap bandits had struck overnight, stealing the copper tubing from three brand-new air-conditioning compressors. An eleven-thousand-dollar hit to their already wildly out-of-control construction budget. And now this.

"Uh, Hattie?" Ronnie Sewell, Hattie's plumber, was lounging against the bumper of his pickup truck when she and Cassidy Pelletier, her best friend and construction foreman, arrived at the Tattnall Street house that steamy Saturday morning. "We got issues."

She and Cass followed the plumber around to the rear of

the house, where she found a freshly dug trench leading beneath the home's brick foundation.

"I had a feeling something wasn't right," Ronnie said, pointing to the trench. "I decided to get under the house and take a look."

Hattie swallowed hard. "Just tell me, Ronnie. What's the problem?"

"The problem is, you got a hunnerd percent crappy old cast-iron pipes under there. And you know how it floods on this flat street, right? And it all drains to the back of this lot. Water's been collecting under there for no telling how long. Well, it's all ruint. Rusted, busted, ruint."

"Oh God," Hattie moaned. She eyed her plumbing contractor. He was in his late fifties and built like a fire hydrant, with a huge belly that lapped over his belt. "Are you sure? I mean, you went all the way under the house?"

Ronnie shrugged. "I got as far as I could go. It don't take a rocket scientist."

Without a word, Hattie walked away. When she returned, she was zipping herself into her own baggy white coveralls. She pulled a bandana from her pocket and tied it around her hair, then fastened plastic goggles over her face.

"What?" Ronnie said, his face reddening with indignation. "You calling me a liar? Hattie Kavanaugh, I been doing business with your father-in-law since before you were born. . . ."

"Calm down, Ronnie," Hattie snapped. "I had this house inspected before we made an offer on it. Nobody said anything about bad pipes. I'm not calling you a liar, but I need to see it with my own eyes. Tug would tell you the same thing if he were here."

"See for yourself then." He turned and stalked off in the direction of his truck, muttering as he went. "Goddamn know-it-all girls."

Cass bent down and peered at the trench beneath the foundation, at the pool of mud and brick rubble, then looked back at her friend. "For real? You're crawling down into that swamp?"

"You wanna go instead?"

"Who, me? Oh hell, no." Cass shuddered. "I don't do mud."

Hattie went over to a tarp-covered stack of lumber, selected a pair of two-by-fours, and slung them over her shoulders. She shoved the boards under the house, considered, then went back for another pair, laying them beside the first two boards.

Cass handed Hattie her flashlight.

"Pray for me," Hattie said, flattening herself on the boards. "I'm going in."

Mo Lopez pedaled slowly along in the bike lane. The neighborhood he was passing through was clearly in transition. On one side of the street, brick or wood-frame Victorian-era homes boasted signs of recent restoration, with sparkling new paint jobs and manicured landscapes. There were smaller homes, too, modest Craftsman cottages with bikes chained to wrought-iron fences, porches bristling with fern baskets and potted plants and weedy yards. As he pedaled, an idea began to form in his head.

Savannah, he reflected, was a pleasant surprise. He'd accepted the invitation to speak to television and film students at the Savannah College of Art and Design strictly as a favor to Rebecca Sanzone, the assistant head of programming at the network. One of her former classmates now worked in the SCAD admissions office. Becca, of course, had been much too busy to make the trip herself, and had forwarded the invite to Mo.

"You should go," she'd urged. "Why sit around town and wait for these network idiots to make up their minds?"

The idiots were Rebecca's immediate bosses at the Home Place Television Network. The former president of programming had been abruptly fired two months earlier, and the new guy, Tony Antinori, was said to be taking a long, hard look at the HPTV lineup.

Mo was understandably anxious. *Killer Garage*'s first season was considered a success for a new show, but this second season, viewers weren't quite as fascinated with watching motorheads spend obscene amounts of money building garages equipped with everything from video-gaming consoles to elevators to full kitchens. The numbers, Rebecca had pointed out, weren't awful, but they weren't awfully *good* either.

He needed a new idea, and he needed it fast. His thoughts drifted back to what Tasha, the SCAD administrator, had told him; that Savannah had the distinction of being the largest intact contiguous trove of original nineteenth-century architecture in the country. This town was a beehive of restoration and renovation activity.

His mind worked as furiously as his legs. On a street called Tattnall, he spied a trio of vehicles parked in front of an imposing three-story Queen Anne Victorian. As he got closer, he saw two pickup trucks that had KAVANAUGH & SON, GENERAL CONTRACTING stenciled on the door.

Mo paused at the curb and looked up at the house. A full-scale restoration was obviously under way. Scaffolding had been erected on the east side of the house, where some of the old wooden siding had been replaced, and other sections had been scraped down in preparation for paint. Piles of lumber were stacked around the yard, and pallets of roofing shingles had been unloaded on the porch.

The roof and the porch overhang were both covered with

blue tarps. The eaves and porch of the house dripped with elaborate wooden gingerbread trim.

He leaned the bike against a sawhorse and climbed a set of temporary wooden steps leading to the porch. The front door, a period-perfect confection of hand-carved detailing inset with a leaded-glass window, was ajar.

Mo paused in front of the door, edging it open with the toe of his shoe. "Hello?"

His voice echoed in the high-ceilinged foyer. No answer. He shrugged and stepped inside. The interior of the house was a marvel of Victorian excess. Several different decades' worth of wallpaper layers were in the process of being stripped away to the bare plaster walls. Overhead, an enormous chandelier dripping with dusty crystals and frosted glass globes swung from a ceiling decorated with crumbling but intricate plaster ornamentation.

"Place is a money pit," Mo muttered, but the contrast between the before and after could be amazing. He walked toward the back of the house. Looking up, the view was of ceilings with gaping holes; underfoot were floors of oak parquet laid in a herringbone pattern, nearly obscured with decades of blackened varnish.

"Nice." He kept walking, passing what had obviously once been a bathroom. The old penny tile floor was filthy, and the only remaining fixture was a claw-foot bathtub filled with fallen plaster fragments. Exposed pipes poked up through the floor.

At the end of the hallway he spied the wide opening to what would obviously be the kitchen. He stood in the doorway, studying the scene. It had high, water-stained ceilings and walls that had also been stripped to the studs. The floor featured layers upon layers of linoleum, some of which had been peeled all the way down to the subfloor.

Mo took a couple of steps into the kitchen and suddenly,

the world seemed to crumble beneath his feet. He heard wood splintering and reached out, in vain, to try to break his fall. Then, darkness.

The last thing he remembered hearing was an outraged voice screeching, right in his ear, "What the hell?"

Hattie scooted on her butt as far under the house as she could, looking for the source of the broken pipe. She thought she was now directly beneath the kitchen, but it was damp and dank, and her flashlight beam picked out a maze of corroded cast-iron piping that had been dug out to expose the line.

She heard footfalls overhead.

"Cass?" But these footsteps were too heavy to be coming from skinny-as-a-rail Cass. Maybe Ronnie had a change of heart? Surely he'd know better than to walk into the kitchen where termites had laid waste to those floor joists.

Thunk. Chunks of rotted wood and linoleum and more than a century's worth of unspeakable debris rained down onto her face. Followed by a body. A large, living body, which landed directly on top of her.

"What the hell?" she shrieked.

In the dim light she could see that the body was a man.

"Uuuhhhh," he moaned. His face was beside hers, and he looked dazed.

"Get offa me," Hattie said through clenched teeth. With effort, she managed to roll him sideways, until he was lying flat on his back in the muck beneath the house.

She heard footsteps again. "Hattie?" Cass's head poked through the hole in the kitchen floor. She pointed the beam of the flashlight at her friend, and then at the prone body of the intruder, who was groaning and also trying to sit up. "Who's the guy? And what the hell is going on down there?"

"Damned if I know," Hattie said. She held out a hand to her best friend. "Come on. Get me outta here. Ronnie was right. The pipes are toast." She pointed at the stranger. "And so is this guy. Call the cops. Looks like we trapped us a scrap bandit."

2
The Proposal

- - - - - - -

Hattie looked down at the guy sprawled on the kitchen floor. Some women might have found him attractive. He wore black designer jeans and a black open-collared shirt, which told her he wasn't local, because nobody with any sense wore all black in the sweltering heat and humidity of a Savannah summer. Currently he was splattered with muck *and* scowling up at her like *she* was the intruder instead of vice versa.

Cass prodded Mo's leg with the toe of her boot and glanced over at Hattie, who was brushing chunks of gunk out of her hair. "Doesn't look like my idea of a scrap metal thief."

"You're right," Hattie said. "For one thing, it looks like he's got all his own teeth. For another, he's dressed too nice." She played the flashlight over Mo's ruined tennis shoes. "Dayum, girl. Check it out. These Nikes cost like, six hundred dollars."

"Maybe he stole them," Cass mused.

"Cute," Mo said, suppressing a groan as he got back on his feet. "Hilarious. You two must be a smash hit at the comedy clubs around here."

He glanced down at himself and sighed. Both arms sported jagged, bleeding scratches. His clothes were filthy and the Nikes were caked in mud. Or something like it. He groped the back of his head with his fingertips and felt a knot raising. Maybe he was concussed? It was that kind of day.

"The front door was standing wide open," he lied. "How was I supposed to know this place is a death trap? I could sue you for maintaining a criminal nuisance."

"And we could call the cops and have you locked up for trespassing," Cass shot back. "Right, Hattie?"

But Cass's best friend was studying the guy's face. She'd definitely seen him before, the dark hair brushing his shirt collar, the olive complexion that went with the hair and eyes, aggressively thick eyebrows, and one of those trendy not-beard beards. He'd been staring down at his phone, but she was sure he had been listening to her conversation with Tug.

Hattie snapped her fingers. "Hey. You were sitting at the table next to ours at Foxy Loxy this morning. And obviously eavesdropping on my conversation."

"Not eavesdropping," Mo insisted. "Minding my own business, having breakfast. Not my fault that you talk so loud everyone in the place could hear you."

"Hmm. And then you show up here less than an hour later. At this house we were just discussing. Obviously a co-incidence."

Mo made another snap decision.

"Okay, not a coincidence," he said. "I did overhear you and—your dad?—talking at that café. And I was intrigued." He reached into his hip pocket and brought out a slim leather case. He plucked a business card from the case and handed it to her.

Hattie's eyebrows drew together as she read the card. "Mauricio Lopez. President, executive producer, Toolbox Productions." She handed the card to Cass. "This doesn't tell me why you followed me over here, and then trespassed on my work site."

"Toolbox is a television production company. I create original reality shows, currently for the Home Place Television Network. While I was biking around the historic district this morning, I got an idea for what I think could, potentially, be a new reality show. So, what, you and your dad are flipping this house? And I gather it's not going well." He looked pointedly around at the gutted kitchen, then down at the man-size hole in the subfloor.

Cass and Hattie exchanged a look.

Hattie flicked the card back in the direction of Mo's chest and it fluttered to the floor. "First off, Tug is my father-in-law, not my dad. Secondly, not that it's any of your frickin' business, but the house is coming along just fine."

Mo shrugged. "So you're not over budget? The banks actually *do* want to loan you enough money to finish? And you were crawling around under this house just for shits and grins when this rotted floor collapsed beneath me?"

Hattie's face blushed a dull red. "You should go now, before you really piss me off."

"Do *not* piss her off," Cass warned. "Seriously, dude, just go."

"Don't you even want to hear my idea?" Mo countered. "An original, unscripted show. You and your crew would be the stars. Rehabbing an old house as a flip."

"Oooh!" Cass deadpanned, nudging Hattie with her elbow. "He wants to put us in the movies. Hollywood, here we come."

"Not the movies. Television. And not Hollywood," Mo said. "That's the point. Savannah is the perfect setting for a reality show. All this history, these old houses. Plus, labor and material costs have gotta be way cheaper down here. What did you have to pay for this place, anyway?"

"None of your business," Hattie said.

"Eighty-two thousand," Cass volunteered. "Squatters

were living here. It was a bank foreclosure. So, what? You'd buy this house for the show?"

"Cass!" Hattie shot her a warning look.

"No. That's not how it works. You invest your own money in the real estate, and you earn all the profits off the house when it sells. Of course, we negotiate a standard performance fee for you and your crew and line up some sponsors to trade their product in return for exposure on the show. Just how much have you sunk into this money pit already?" he asked.

"We're done here," Hattie said. She pointed toward the back door. "Go. Away. Now."

Mo shook his head in disbelief. "You know how many people would sell their soul for an opportunity like this? To star in a new network reality show? I passed half a dozen historic houses being rehabbed while I was riding over here."

"Go trespass on their job sites then," Hattie said. "Fall through their floors." She took his elbow and gave him a not-gentle shove. "Move along."

When he reached his bike, Mauricio Lopez turned, whipped out his cell phone, aimed, and clicked off a series of photos. The two women stood in the driveway watching him speed away on the fat-tired bike. "You think that guy's for real?" Cass asked.

"Don't know, don't care," Hattie said. She unzipped her coveralls, stepped out of them, and reached for her cell phone. "I gotta make nice with Ronnie, apologize, and get him back over here to start replacing all those cast-iron pipes."

Hattie gazed up at the house. She'd been so thrilled when she'd seen the address on the county tax assessor's list of foreclosures. She'd been watching this street for two years, riding past this particular house on an almost daily basis, stalking it like a jealous lover.

Her secret name for the house was Gertrude, after Gertrude Showalter, an elderly woman who'd lived across the street from Hattie's family when she was growing up.

She'd seen the busted-out windows, the piles of empty liquor bottles and trash strewn around Gertrude's porch, watched with dismay as a summer storm sent a huge tree branch crashing through the roof, knowing that the rain pouring in would further deteriorate the structure.

When the foreclosure listing was finally published, she'd been the first to show up on the courthouse steps, two hours before the bidding started, determined to win at any cost, to save this elegant old girl, polish her up, and sell her for a handsome profit.

Tug tried to warn her about buying a house without ever stepping foot inside, but she'd been determined to prove him wrong.

She'd driven directly from the courthouse to her new old house on Tattnall Street with the key clutched tightly in her fist.

Nothing about Gertrude fazed her. Not even the pigeons that had taken up residence in the attic or the petrified possum carcass she found under a rotted kitchen cupboard gave Hattie pause.

It wasn't just money and sweat equity Hattie had invested in Gertrude. She'd poured her heart into this house. But now, damn it, she was seeing it through the eyes of the ballsy television guy.

The realization dawned on her suddenly, like a cold hand gripping her throat. She'd broken Tug Kavanaugh's first commandment of real estate investing, the one he'd preached to her since she'd scraped up the down payment for her first flip. "A house is just a bunch of lumber and nails, Hattie. It's just a thing. Never fall in love with anything that can't love you back."

She'd had one great love in her life, and lost it in the blink of an eye. When would she learn? Tug was right, she knew. No amount of love, creativity, or good vibes was going to turn Gertrude into the peacock she'd envisioned. Her shoulders slumped as she thumbed through the contacts on her phone.

She found the plumber's number, tapped it, and waited. The phone rang once, twice, three times. He picked up after the fourth ring.

"Yeah?" He was still pissed.

"Ronnie? Look, I'm sorry. You were right, but I had to see it with my own eyes. All that pipe under the house is shot. What's it gonna cost to replace everything?"

"Minimum?" The number he quoted was way north of what Hattie's gut told her. "Hattie? You there?"

"I'm here," she said grimly. "Never mind."

Tug's footsteps echoed through the high-ceilinged rooms. It was early evening, and a slight breeze was blowing through the open windows. Hattie trailed after him, resolute in her determination to bite the bullet.

He was muttering numbers as he walked, shaking his head, rolling his eyes. When he got to the kitchen he stared down at the jagged hole in the floor before looking up at his daughter-in-law.

"There's a couple of guys I met at the lumberyard last month. They're investors. Buying up houses in Midtown. We got to talking while I was waiting for my stuff to get loaded. I told the younger one about this house. He said he'd been watching our progress. Likes this street. Thinks it's got great potential. He gave me his card. Name's Keith. Said if we were interested in selling . . ."

"We are." Hattie bit off the words.

"They're paying wholesale. Not retail. We'll lose a bunch of money on this one. You know that, honey, right?"

She nodded, unable to speak.

Tug went on. "You're doing the right thing. It hurts, I know, but hell, we all make mistakes. It's not the end of the world."

Hattie swallowed hard. "What about the bank?"

He patted her shoulder. "I'll talk to the bank. We've done business with those SOBs for nearly forty years. They've never lost money on me before. It'll be okay."

Hattie touched his hand. Tug's skin was tough, wrinkled, crisscrossed with scabs and scars. "I'm sorry, Tug. You tried to tell me, but I wouldn't listen."

"Don't be sorry, little girl," he said, his voice gruff. "Be smart. Take what you've learned from this and walk away, knowing you did your best, but this time, it just wasn't enough."

3

And the Bike You Rode in On

Mo went back to the hotel, showered and changed clothes, then climbed back on the bike to continue his tour of the historic district. But he couldn't manage to get Hattie Kavanaugh off his mind.

Truthfully, he'd noticed her as soon as he sat down at the café table next to hers earlier that morning. In her early thirties, he guessed, and she had that fresh-faced girl-next-door thing going on, her hair in a careless ponytail. Slender, but curvy in the right places.

Her personality at the house was confrontational, obnoxious even. He liked that she wasn't intimidated by having a strange man suddenly fall on top of her. Liked that she didn't back down easily. Even in mud-caked work boots, grimy coveralls, with her head wrapped in a bandana, this woman had presence. And with her hazel eyes, and full lips, the upper one of which bore a slight scar, he could already tell the camera would love her. The hair would need to be blonder, that was a given.

By four that afternoon, Mo was sweat-soaked and exhausted. The skies were darkening, and the air so heavy with humidity you could almost wring it out.

But for reasons he couldn't explain, he found himself pedaling past the Tattnall Street house again. The only vehicle present was the Kavanaugh & Son pickup, which was still parked at the curb. He spied the girl he'd met earlier, sitting on the porch steps, holding her head in her hands, her shoulders shaking.

A for-sale-by-owner sign had been planted in the grassless yard. This was new.

He approached slowly. A few yards from the porch, he gave a discreet cough.

The girl raised her head. Her face was red and tear-streaked. She'd stripped off the coveralls and was dressed in the same pair of faded jeans and light blue tank top she'd worn earlier that morning at the café.

"What?"

"Hey," Mo said. "So? You're selling the house now? Before you finish it?"

"What do you care?" She used the back of her hand to swipe at a snot bubble.

He'd never been good with women who cried. He should go, but something, her sudden vulnerability maybe, drew him closer.

Mo sat down on the step beside her, leaving a couple of feet of sunbaked brick between them. "I'm sorry," he offered.

She snuffled and looked away. "Tug's right. It's a money pit. I bit off more than I could chew. He's got a couple of investors who are interested, but we thought we'd go ahead and put it on the market. Maybe some other sucker like me will bite."

Hattie rested her chin on her knees.

"You'll be losing money?" he guessed.

"Yeah. Money we don't have. That I don't have. Like an idiot, I sunk all my savings into this venture."

"What'll you do after you sell this place?"

She shrugged. "We've got a kitchen addition on Wilmington Island, a rooftop deck at a town house over on Jones Street. What Tug calls our bread and butter."

"No more house flipping?"

"Not unless I hit the lottery," she said. "No bank will touch us after this fiasco."

"That's too bad," Mo said. "This show I was telling you about . . ."

"No!" She shook her head vehemently. "I told you before. Not interested. Go find some other dumb blonde. Savannah's full of 'em. Everyone wants to be a celebrity. Everyone but me."

"I don't want someone who wants to be a celebrity. I want someone who has a passion for what they do. Somebody with a vision. Who's fearless."

"You don't know me," Hattie said. "Deep down inside, I'm a total chickenshit. I'm afraid of heights. And of dying broke and alone. Which is looking more and more likely these days."

"Alone?" Mo raised an eyebrow. "You said this Tug guy is your father-in-law. Where's your husband?"

"Dead."

Mo winced. "Oh. God, I'm sorry."

"It's okay," Hattie said. She exhaled slowly. "Nobody expects someone my age to be a widow. People don't know what to do with that kind of information."

"Can I ask . . ."

"No," she said, standing abruptly. "This pity party is officially over. I'm gonna go home, hit the shower, and drown my sorrows in a bottle of beer. I'm not usually this rude, Mauricio . . ."

"It's Mo. Nobody calls me Mauricio."

"Okay, Mo. I'm fixing to lock up here, so gonna have to ask you to leave."

"You never even told me your name," he protested. "I was thinking maybe you'd give me a do-over on the introductions?" He stuck out his hand. "Hi. I'm Mo Lopez. Intrepid intruder. Admirer of old homes, in search of a hit show."

Her upper lip twitched a little. He wanted to reach out and touch that scar, ask what had happened, but he didn't dare. She looked down at her own hands. They were grimy, the short nails caked with mud, but she wiped the palms on the seat of her jeans and shook. "I'm Hattie Kavanaugh. Dog lover, licensed, failing contractor. Not looking for a career in show business."

"Nice to meet you," Mo said. "Tell me about your friend."

"Cass? We've been best friends since parochial school, and we both work for Tug. I guess you'd call her construction foreman. Er, forewoman. We're not really big on titles at Kavanaugh and Son."

"So your husband was the son in Kavanaugh and Son?"

"Actually, my husband, Thomas Henry, was the third generation to work in the business. Tug's dad started the company, so he was the original son in Kavanaugh and Son." Her expression softened. "That's how Hank and I met. I got a job cleaning up construction sites for his dad while I was still in high school, and eventually I talked Tug into letting me learn the trades. I started out as an apprentice carpenter."

"Kind of an unusual job for a young woman," Mo said. "You didn't go to college?"

"I took some classes at Georgia Southern—you can actually major in construction management there—but after a while, I didn't see the point in paying to sit in a classroom and get lectured about stuff I already knew how to do," Hattie said.

Mo hesitated, but decided to take one more stab at winning her over.

"See, you'd be perfect for this show I'm creating. It's an

entirely new concept. If the network bites, and I don't see why they wouldn't, we'd film on location, right here in Savannah."

"Thanks, but the answer is still no. I screwed up this house in a major way. No more house flipping. From now on, I keep my head down and stay in my lane." Hattie went to the front door, pulled a ring of keys from her pocket, and locked the door. She ran her hand longingly over the intricately carved molding of the door, as though she were bidding goodbye to an old friend.

"See you around, Mo," she said.

After she was gone, he walked over to the for-sale sign, took out his phone, and snapped a photo of the number posted at the bottom. He heard a rumble of thunder, glanced up, and saw a silvery crack of lightning piercing the black clouds boiling overhead. He ran for the bike. He was half a block from the Victorian on Tattnall Street when the skies opened up, huge, warm bullets of rain pelting him as he pedaled furiously back toward the hotel.

4

Saving Savannah

Mo called Rebecca during his layover in Atlanta on the way back to L.A. "I've got something for you," he said, trying to sound cool, despite the rising excitement he'd felt while banging out his pitch back in his Savannah hotel room. "The concept for my next show. Something really different."

"That's nice," she said, her tone noncommittal.

"When can we meet? Tomorrow?"

"I've got a huge meeting with Krystee and Will's people first thing tomorrow morning, and then I'm having their agent over in the evening, nothing fancy, just drinks and sushi so we can hash out some issues. . . ."

He swallowed his disappointment. "Okay, then dinner?"

"It's wall-to-wall meetings. All day. Why don't you call Asha tomorrow and tell her I need her to schedule us for breakfast—no, scratch that, I've got a breakfast thing Wednesday. Let's say coffee, mid-morning. Can you do that?"

Mo sighed. Asha Singh was Rebecca's longtime assistant. Getting past Asha was like getting into Fort Knox. "Yeah. I'll call her."

"Great. See you then."

He dozed fitfully on the flight from Atlanta to L.A. Two

hours into the flight, he gave up, retrieved his laptop from the seatback pocket, and went back to the pitch.

He rubbed his face wearily, rolled one shoulder, then the other. He actually liked working on planes, enjoyed the forced solitary confinement. He donned his noise-canceling ear-phones and read back what he'd written.

Saving Savannah. Definitely. It was a solid concept. He'd downloaded a dozen of the best photos he'd shot around the Savannah historic district, and he now attached them as a slide show at the top of the document. The arching live oaks dripping with Spanish moss, the rows of nineteenth-century town houses, front stoops and window boxes exploding with colorful flowers, and yes, the Tattnall Street house, along with the series of shots featuring Hattie Kavanaugh and her foreman, Cass.

He'd gone back to the house early this morning, and waited, with two cups of iced coffee, until the construction foreman, er, forewoman, arrived.

Time was short. He handed her one of the cups. "Cass, right?"

Cassidy Pelletier looked down at the coffee, which was in a Foxy Loxy cup. She tasted it. Her exact order. Iced mo-chaccino, extra cinnamon.

She eyed Mo warily. "How did you know?"

"Lucky guess. Anyway, can we talk? My flight leaves in a couple of hours. Your friend turned down my offer to work on this new show of mine, but I think maybe you could change her mind."

"If you think that, you really don't know Hattie," she said.

"She's in financial trouble, right?" he pressed.

"Yeah."

"This show could change all that. She'd get a regular pay-check. You would, too. And once the show airs, Kavanaugh and Son will be on everyone's radar, and business will take off. You'll have more work than you can handle, and you'll be able to name your own price. No more crappy bathroom renos, excuse the pun."

Cassidy Pelletier didn't seem impressed. "So you say."

"It'll mean jobs," Mo went on. "We hire at least twenty people during a typical taping cycle. Camera operators, audio engineers, assistants, drivers, hair and makeup people, set dressers, catering. A nice boost to the economy."

"Sounds good to me, but if Hattie says no, she usually means no."

"Maybe you could help me change her mind," Mo said.

"Why would I do that?"

"You're best friends, right?"

"Right."

He gestured at the Victorian. "She's losing money on this place, the company too. She takes that personally, right?"

"You don't even know. Tug and Nancy, they're not just the company. They're her family. She feels responsible. Tug's getting close to retirement age. Already had a mild heart attack. It's killing Hattie."

"They're actually her in-laws, right? What about her own family? Where are they?"

"Down in Florida. Her mom, anyway. Don't know about her dad. Her parents split up when we were in high school. Her mom packed up and left, but Hattie wanted to stay and finish out the year at St. Mary's. She moved in with my folks; it was supposed to be just 'til summer, but she ended up staying two more years. After graduation, she got a little bitty basement apartment all on her own. She worked days for Tug and took night classes at Georgia Southern, paid her own way, all the way. That's Hattie. She's hard-core."

"And her husband? How did he die?"

Cass gave him a sharp look. "She told you about Hank?"

"Just that he was dead."

"He was killed in a motorcycle accident. Almost seven years ago."

A truck pulled up to the house and beeped the horn. Cass looked at her phone. "Look, my crew's here. I can't stand around talking to you all day."

He handed her another business card. "I'm headed back to L.A. and I'm going to sell this show concept to the network. But it won't work without Hattie. And you. Can you try to talk to her? Make her understand that this is a way to turn things around? If not for her, for Tug?"

"You haven't even told me what kind of show you're talking about," Cass said.

"It'll be called *Saving Savannah*," Mo said. "We'll focus on preservation, and how important it is to a community, to its history, to save these old houses. We'll follow along as Hattie and you and your crew take an old wreck like this one and bring it back to life."

Cass turned and pointed at the Victorian. "But not this house?"

"No," he said succinctly. "The format will be find it, fix it, flip it. This house is too far along in the cycle. And frankly, from the look of things, mistakes have been made here."

"I never liked this place," Cass murmured.

"Why's that?"

"Too big. It's not our brand. In the past, we've stuck to smaller houses." She waved her hand dismissively. "This thing was too high stakes for me. My idea of gambling is buying a five-dollar scratch-off ticket at the Gas-n'-Go. I couldn't believe it when Hattie insisted on buying it. Tug didn't like it either."

"Then why go ahead with the flip?"

"She had her heart set on it," Cass said. "In the end, she convinced Tug it was a good deal. I mean, she got it at a good price, I'll say that, and now we know why. Bad roof, water damage, bad pipes. You name it, this dump has it."

Mo let that thought sink in. If—no, when—they started taping, the house would need to be smaller, more relatable to viewers like Cass Pelletier. A few problems with a house were okay, preferable actually, because it showed viewers even experts could get things wrong when there were challenges. But for the first season, they'd need a house that was a home run.

He checked his watch. His airport pickup time was only fifteen minutes away. "Will you talk to Hattie? Convince her you guys need to do this show?"

"I can try."

Asha was on the phone when Mo strolled into the tiny reception area, but her eyes flicked toward Rebecca's closed office door. She put her hand over the receiver. "Careful. She's in a mood."

"What's going on?"

Asha shook her head. "I'm supposed to tell you she's only got fifteen minutes. In fact, I was *supposed* to cancel your coffee date, but I convinced her to squeeze you in. Don't make me regret it."

"Thanks for the heads-up."

Rebecca was pacing around the office, shouting at someone on the speakerphone.

"No, you listen to me! This is unacceptable. I don't give a flying fuck about some fucking moratorium on building in the flood zone. Call someone at the state, for God's sake. Tell them if you don't get that permit, you'll have to close down the project. Permanently. Remind them what's at stake. Just get it done, Byron. Or I'll fucking find someone who can."

Mo pulled a chair up to Rebecca's desk, a sleek white lacquered Art Deco number whose surface was uncharacteristically littered with folders, papers, empty Pellegrino bottles, and half-empty takeout containers.

Rebecca finished the call but kept pacing around the room.

"Assholes!" she muttered, crossing to the desk and sitting down. "I'm surrounded by assholes and incompetents."

"What's wrong?"

"My entire Wednesday night lineup is going up in flames."

The door from the outer office opened and Asha entered, carrying a Lucite tray with two cups of espresso. She set the tray on the console behind the desk and hurried away, shooting Mo a sympathetic look before closing the door again.

"Wednesday?" Mo wrinkled his brow in confusion. "But that's what, *Building Bridgehampton* and *Buyer's Remorse,* right? And *Going Coastal.* I thought you were meeting with Krystee and Will's people yesterday. Drinks and sushi?"

"That was Byron from *Bridgehampton* on the phone just now. He says the county won't issue a permit for the swim spa. *Someone* in the neighborhood narced him out to the code enforcement Nazis, and they've totally shut down construction."

"That sucks," Mo said, feigning sympathy. Byron Atkinson's B-Reel Productions was the creator of *Building Bridgehampton,* and he seemed to have some magical ability to come up with shows that Rebecca adored.

"You haven't even heard the worst of it," Rebecca replied. She took a sip of the espresso and paused for dramatic effect.

"Krystee is pregnant. With twins!"

"But that's great, right? After all that infertility drama last season? Twins should be a huge ratings boost. Not that they need it."

"It would be a ratings boost. Except that her idiot doctor has put Krystee on immediate enforced bed rest. She's only at ten weeks! Alan and Shayla wanted to give me the news in person. They've shuttered the show."

"Really? How awful. Can't they just let Will take over for the rest of the season and do some establishing shots of Krystee on the phone, discussing the house with him?"

"I wish," Rebecca said. "But let's face it, Will has the personality of boiled brussels sprouts. We all know Krystee is what puts the sparkle in *Going Coastal*. Our viewers don't want to see her staring at her swollen ankles, chewing prenatal vitamins, and knitting baby booties."

"So what's gonna happen?" Mo asked. "Reruns?"

"Not if I can help it," Rebecca said. "We need fresh content, and we need it now. I've been going over some stuff we've had kicking around in development . . ."

"What about my new idea?" Mo broke in. "Becc, I swear, you're gonna love it. Just let me show you."

"I got your email. *Saving Savannah*?" She wrinkled her nose. "Doesn't sound very sexy. In fact, it sounds totally granny."

Mo took out his phone and thumbed through the photos until he came to the shots he'd surreptitiously taken of Hattie Kavanaugh at the coffee shop, along with the ones he'd taken of Hattie and Cass outside the Tattnall Street house. He passed the phone over to Rebecca. "Does she look granny to you?"

He'd captured Hattie mid-sentence. Her hair was held back with a bandana, her cheeks sprinkled with freckles. She wore not a speck of makeup as far as Mo could tell, but some kind of light seemed to emanate from those hazel eyes of hers. She didn't have the glamour of a Krystee Brandstetter, who managed to look sexy even in a hard hat and welder's goggles, or the exotic appeal of Hayden Horowitz, the glamorous real estate host of *Building Bridgehampton*, but to Mo, that was a selling point.

"Cute," Rebecca said, handing the phone back.

"Look again, Becc," Mo said, thumbing over to the next photo of Hattie, taken as she climbed into her pickup truck. "This girl really has something. She's fresh as buttermilk, absolutely no phoniness about her. And she's fierce. Won't back away from a challenge. Viewers will eat her up. The women will want to be like her, the men will want to sleep with her. And she's got that southern accent—not that grits-and-gravy, syrupy one—more like the tour-guide-at-the-museum southern. Kinda refined. Educated."

Rebecca thumbed through the rest of the photos, stopping at a shot of the Tattnall Street house. "This is the house she's rehabbing? It's gawd-awful."

"That's the project she's about to finish," Mo said, taking the phone back. "Of course, we'd start the show with a new house. Something smaller, more relatable."

"What's her story?" Rebecca asked. "I mean, who is she? How did you find her?"

"I was having breakfast at a place down the street from my hotel and I overheard her and her father-in-law talking about this house they were working on. I was intrigued, so I rode around until I found the house. And her."

He deliberately omitted the whole falling-through-the-kitchen-floor anecdote.

Rebecca wrinkled her nose again. "So this girl is married? I don't want another Krystee and Will situation."

"Not married. Widowed," Mo said. "According to her best friend, she married her high school sweetheart, but he was killed in a motorcycle accident a few years ago."

"A widow. Hmm. I kind of like the possibility. Plucky young widow . . . rehabbing old houses. That's a story line our viewers could sympathize with."

"Right?"

Rebecca tapped the phone. "Who's this woman she's talking to in front of the house?"

"Her best friend, who's also the construction foreman."

"I like that," Rebecca mused. "She's Black, so we get built-in diversity right there. Tony would love that, all right."

Mo pulled his iPad from his messenger bag, opened the pitch document for *Saving Savannah,* and gave it to Rebecca.

"The real star of the show would be Savannah," he told her. "The place oozes atmosphere. And it's got great creative energy because of SCAD. Tons of talent living there, and every place you look, a camera crew is shooting a film or television project."

"Georgia's a right-to-work state too," Rebecca said, tapping her pencil on her desktop. "So super cheap labor costs, plus the tax incentives the state offers filmmakers."

"That was my next point," Mo said. He could feel Rebecca's mood lightening. She was into this idea, totally into it.

She'd tabbed back to the photo of Hattie now, the pencil tapping a mile a minute.

"Well?"

"I need a sizzle reel, obviously, so we can see if this girl can walk and chew gum. And the house, the one you'd rehab for the first season."

"That's no problem at all," Mo lied. "How soon?"

"Now." She handed him the iPad. "*Going Coastal* is going on hiatus. So your little Savannah show, if you can pull it together, can be our fall replacement."

Mo felt his mouth go dry. "But . . . this is May."

"I'm aware," Rebecca said. She picked up a folder and leafed through it. "Byron sent this over last night. Somehow, he'd already heard about Krystee and Will. It's freakish how he always seems to know what's going on in this town. And of course he just happens to have a new show already in development."

"Of course he does," Mo said. "Just out of idle curiosity, what kind of low-budget crap is he trying to sell you now?"

Rebecca arched an eyebrow. "Jealousy doesn't suit you at all, Mo. It's actually very intriguing. Each week he's pairing an up-and-coming designer with a client just emerging from a bad divorce, to totally redesign their master bedroom. *Suite Revenge*. Don't you just love it?"

"I guess it's okay," Mo admitted.

She tossed the folder onto the desktop. "I told him I'd think about it. So. My sizzle reel? When can you have it ready for me? Tony is already breathing down my neck about a replacement for Krystee and Will."

He took a deep breath. "I'll need a couple weeks."

The door opened and Asha stepped inside. "Rebecca? Your car's here."

Rebecca jumped up and grabbed her jacket. "Talk soon. Ciao, Mo."

5

Hattie Hears Him Out

- - - - - - -

Ribsy met her at the door of the bungalow. Hattie collapsed onto one of the Adirondack chairs on the front porch. Hank had built the chair as a birthday gift for her from plans she'd showed him on Pinterest.

It was just the one chair. He'd had the pieces for its mate all cut and laid out on his work bench in the garage. And then one muggy August night, right after dinner, he'd decided to take his vintage Kawasaki out for a ride, after a long day working on a remodel at Isle of Hope. The client was a wealthy lawyer, and every morning, the lawyer's wife met him at the job site with a long, frustrating list of change orders.

Hattie was at the kitchen sink washing up the dinner dishes when Hank came in, his helmet under his arm. "Just gonna take a ride out to Tybee," he'd told her. "Maybe watch the sunset over the Back River."

"Let's drive out there," Hattie had suggested. "Let me finish the dishes and I'll . . ."

"Nah. I just wanna feel the wind in my face. I'll be back in an hour." He'd kissed her on the cheek. And then he was gone. The pieces of the second Adirondack chair were still on the work bench, just as he'd left them, but now covered with cobwebs.

Hattie unlaced her boots and peeled off her socks. An early evening quiet had settled over the street. She reached around, unsnapped her bra, and slithered her arms out of it, pulling it off from beneath her grimy T-shirt. She dropped the bra to the weathered floorboards, stretched her legs out, and sat back in the chair.

Ribsy sat down beside her, putting his muzzle on her lap. She scratched his silky ears and heard his feathery tail thump enthusiastically on the wooden floor. In those awful, endless months following Hank's death, Cass had insisted she needed something in her life to care about. One day, she showed up at Hattie's front door with a small, wriggling brown-and-white ball of fur in her arms. A pound puppy, she'd called him.

"He's yours now," Cass had said gruffly. "A rescue. I already paid for his shots, so you can't take him back."

Hattie closed her eyes and willed the tension to leave her body. But it seemed to Hattie that every muscle in her body was clenched tight. She looked over at the dog, who was now flopped down on the floor, blissfully unaware of the situation she'd placed them both in.

"Oh Ribsy." It came out in one long breath, a cross between an exhale and a sigh. "We are so screwed."

They had an offer on the Tattnall Street house from one of the investors Tug knew. It would leave them in the red, but her father-in-law was adamant that they get out from under the financial burden. Hattie had begged him to wait. Just a week. Let her finish painting the exterior, get the roof finished, get the house polished enough to beckon a buyer just as naïve as she'd been, who'd pay something close to retail.

"Not one more penny," Tug had vowed. "We sell it as is and count ourselves lucky."

"Lucky" was not a word Hattie would use to describe her current financial status. Unbeknownst to Tug, she'd staked everything on Tattnall Street. And not just her savings.

The knot in her stomach felt like a boulder right now. She could lose the house. This house, the wood-frame bungalow in Thunderbolt, a former fishing village just east of the Savannah city limits, had been a bank foreclosure that she and Hank had bought for $32,000, right before their wedding. They'd fixed it up over two years, using leftover lumber and materials scrounged from the company's job sites, working nights and weekends, sleeping on pallets on the floor. She'd paid off the mortgage with the insurance settlement from Hank's accident.

It's what he would have wanted, she knew. But she hadn't had the time, or so Hattie told herself, to finish any of the projects they'd started together. The wooden shingles on the front of the house still bore a dozen different swatches of paint, because she couldn't decide which was the right color. The kitchen countertops were still plywood, even though the granite slabs were right there in her backyard. And the lumber for the second bathroom they'd planned to build was still stacked beside the driveway, where it had been sitting for seven years.

Hattie stared out at the street, tears blurring her vision. One by one, the other houses on this block had been bought up and rehabbed over the past few years. She'd been terrified when Hank found the derelict house on Bonaventure Road hiding behind massive overgrown azaleas. The seller had run an unlicensed tattoo parlor here and rented out rooms by the week.

What would Hank think of the mess she'd gotten herself into? Of the very real possibility that she would lose this house because she'd gotten, as he would have put it, "so far out over your own skis."

The streetlights were blinking on now. She should go in, shower, and eat something. Maybe, standing in the claw-foot tub they'd rescued from the dumping ground of the backyard, the cool water sluicing over her body, she'd come up with some realistic solution to her predicament. Or maybe she'd just wash her hair, put on clean clothes, and fall into bed. Maybe she'd finally get some sleep.

She glanced over at the dog and scratched his ears again. "Come on, buddy," she said softly. "Let's go inside."

"Hattie?" Cass cleared her throat.

They were sitting at their usual table at Foxy Loxy.

"Hmm?" Hattie was jotting down numbers on a legal pad, scratching through them, consulting her phone, and reading incoming text messages.

Cass gently removed the phone from Hattie's hand.

"Hey! I'm in the middle of something here. I might have found a buyer for all those damn kitchen cabinets."

"Great. That can wait for a minute. Something I need to talk to you about. And I need your full attention."

"Please don't tell me any more bad news. I really can't take one more thing right now."

"It's not bad news. In fact, I think it's a way we can come out of this whole Tattnall Street deal smelling like a rose. But you gotta promise to hear me out."

"Oh-kay." Hattie sat back in her chair. "Hit me."

"It's about that television producer. The one who fell through the floor?"

"Mauricio?" Hattie rolled the name off her tongue.

"Mo-reese-ee-oh? Please. Like I'm gonna believe some dude who walks in off the street and tells me he wants to make me a star."

"No, listen." Cass pushed aside the plate with the remains of her muffin and placed her own cell phone on the table. "I checked him out. There's this website? IMDb? It stands for Internet Movie Database. It's got everything about everybody even remotely connected to show business. Mauricio Lopez is for real. His company, Toolbox Productions, has made a bunch of actual television shows. Look here." She tapped the phone screen and read off the names.

"*Fresno Flip. Beach Dreams,* and this garage one, I've seen that one."

"I remember *Beach Dreams,*" Hattie said. "I couldn't believe the crazy prices people pay for waterfront houses on the West Coast. Anyway, it doesn't matter that he's real. I told him no. Tattnall Street is sold. Like Tug said, I gotta move on."

"Mo Lopez came to see me Monday, and I think you should listen to his idea."

"No." Hattie crossed her arms over her chest.

"You promised to hear me out," Cass said.

"So I lied."

"You can't lie to me. I'm your best friend. We promised each other, in eighth grade, remember? We'd never lie to each other."

"You lied when you told me you were still a virgin," Hattie pointed out. "Senior year."

"That was different. Also, you lied when you told me you thought those yellow-and-red-striped pants I wore to the Cardinal Mooney homecoming game didn't make my butt look big. You let me walk out of the house looking like a friggin' circus tent."

"I didn't want to hurt your feelings," Hattie said.

"Enough ancient history. You're going to listen if I have to tie you to that chair," Cass said. "He wants to do a show called *Saving Savannah*. About preserving old houses and saving Savannah's history, one house at a time."

"Still a no."

"Would you listen? We'd buy another smaller, more manageable house. Start from scratch. That's what the show would be about. And we'd get paid. To do the show. It would be incredible publicity for Kavanaugh and Son. Mo says it'd mean jobs, and not just for our subs. Camera operators, sound people, all that kind of stuff."

"Mo?" Hattie gave her a look.

Which Cass ignored. "He's flying back here today. We're meeting with him. . . ."

"I'm not meeting with anybody," Hattie cut her short. "Except this builder from Hilton Head who wants to meet me at the storage unit this afternoon."

"Great. But in the meantime . . ."

"Ladies?"

Hattie looked up. Mauricio Lopez stood to the right of their table. He had two iced coffees in hand and was gesturing to an empty chair nearby. "Is this seat taken?"

Hattie Kavanaugh was laughably easy to read, Mo thought. Her previously animated expression vanished the minute he sat down at the table, replaced by pursed lips and a jaw set at an angle between grim and enraged. She regarded him as she would a large, dead rodent, as he handed her the Styrofoam cup with a quivering mountain of whipped cream.

"You're welcome to sit down, but I was just telling Cass I have no intention of being part of any 'alleged' television show," Hattie said.

"Alleged?" Mo put his hand to his chest. "I'm hurt."

Cass giggled and Hattie rolled her eyes. "Look," she said. "I've seen some of those HPTV shows. They're ridiculous. The one where you plop two strangers down on an island and challenge them to build a house together out of palm fronds and driftwood?"

"*Castaways*? That wasn't one of my shows, but it was a huge ratings hit. And if that tsunami hadn't come out of nowhere, it would still be on the air."

"Didn't I read somewhere that the woman, Penny, I think her name was? Didn't Penny end up suing your network?"

"That case was dismissed. Her contract with the production company specifically said they were not liable for any relationship issues arising from the show."

Cass snapped her fingers. "I remember that show. Axel? Was that the guy's name? Total stud, but dumber than a box of rocks. And also, I thought he was secretly gay."

"Not so secretly," Mo said. "Except to Penny. But could we get back to the reason why I wanted to meet with you two? First off, *Saving Savannah* is not an 'alleged' show. I have a commitment from the network, and an incredibly tight deadline. So what's it gonna be?"

"Thanks for the coffee, but I'm still a no," Hattie said.

"Can I ask why you're so dead set against my proposal?"

"I'm just not interested. I'm a contractor, not a character in some made-up quote 'reality' show. I take my work seriously, even if you don't. I believe in fixing up old houses, finding their souls, making them shine again, and giving them new life."

"I'm giving you the opportunity to do that, and more," Mo said. "This is a chance to recoup your losses—not just your own, but your father-in-law's losses, too. I'm guessing he also had a sizable investment in that house, right?"

"Yes. And I'm determined to make that up to him."

"Doing this show could help you do that. You'd get paid

and the publicity for Kavanaugh and Son would be priceless. Clients will be lining up to hire your company. It's a surefire deal."

Hattie still looked dubious. "Surefire? For real?"

"Yes," Mo said. "If we get the sizzle reel shot, like, right away, and the network gives us the green light."

Cass tapped Hattie's hand. "Now will you listen?"

"What's a sizzle reel?" Hattie said.

Mo smiled. "I thought you'd never ask."

6

Hattie When She Sizzles

"What we're doing today isn't a sizzle, it's more like a talent reel," Mo explained. "I'll film you, just with my phone, ask you some questions about yourself, your experience in the business, that kind of thing. Very informal. It's just so the network can get an idea of who you are. As a person."

"Like an audition?" Hattie didn't like the sound of it. She didn't like the sound of any of this. It felt weird. "This feels too personal," she complained. They were sitting in the living room of her bungalow in Thunderbolt. It had been Mauricio Lopez's idea. "Why can't we just do this at the office?"

"We're not just selling you," he said. "We're selling your personality, your aesthetic. You renovated this house, right? So it's full of your personality. Your look."

He'd had some misgivings when he pulled up to the house. The clapboard siding bore a patchwork of paint colors, there were stacks of lumber and building materials in the driveway, and the yard looked shaggy and neglected.

She gave him a quick tour of the bungalow, noting his raised eyebrow at the unfinished state of the kitchen. "You know how it is," Hattie said. "The cobbler's children . . ."

The living room was a different story. The plaster walls

were painted a warm white, and all the original walnut woodwork gleamed in the late afternoon sun. There was a fireplace with an unusual arched firebox, but instead of firewood, it was filled to the top with large, bleached-out conch shells. Built-in bookshelves on either side of the fireplace were crammed with books, mostly paperbacks, interspersed with bird's nests, deer antlers, chunks of coral, framed bird prints, and more seashells. And was that a cow skull?

He was seated in an armchair with a white slipcover and threadbare arms. An old blue-and-white quilt had been tossed over the seat. The sofa was white too, come to think of it, and the cushions were mashed down, almost misshapen with age. Paintings were hung on all the walls, and all of them were seascapes.

"You can tell a lot about a person by the things they surround themselves with," Mo said. "That's what the network wants to see. Your authentic personality."

"I'm not sure I want them to know that much about me," Hattie shot back. "Why can't I just do what I do? Fix up old houses? Why does this need to be about me?"

Mo sighed. He'd been trying to get Hattie to relax and open up for the past forty minutes. Frankly, he'd never worked with such unenthusiastic talent. Most of the people he encountered in his line of work were dying to get into show business, falling all over themselves to be stars of the small screen. More than one woman had actually offered to sleep with him. Men, too. Hattie Kavanaugh was the complete opposite.

"I could go to any construction site in town and get any random yahoo with a tool belt and a contractor's license to show me how to fix up a house," Mo said. "But I chose *you*. Because you've got something. You're passionate. You're smart. You've got attitude. Too much attitude. And it doesn't hurt that you're damned attractive. The camera is going to love you."

"Me?" Hattie seemed taken aback.

"You've done something different with your hair today, right?"

She blushed. Cass had bullied her into getting a blow-out at the salon down the block from their office. Now her stick-straight hair was soft and shiny and fell in waves to her shoulders. All morning she'd been fighting the urge to bunch it up into a ponytail. She was wearing makeup, too. Not a lot. Just some blush and mascara and lipstick.

"I had a blowout," she admitted.

She wasn't just attractive, Mo thought. She was, well, lovely. Maybe what made her so lovely was the fact that unlike most of the beautiful women he'd ever met, this one was completely unaware, or even indifferent to how she looked.

She'd ditched the baggy Carhartts, faded T-shirt, and work boots. Today she wore jeans that showed off her slender body, some kind of flowery cotton peasant top with a drawstring that revealed just a hint of cleavage, and newish, white Chuck Ts.

"Okay, let's get going," he said, reluctantly dragging his thoughts back to business. "Ready?"

"As ready as I'm going to get."

He'd clipped his iPhone to a tripod with a remote trigger and placed the tripod behind the chair he was sitting in, because he thought she might feel less self-conscious if he wasn't pointing a phone at her as they talked.

"I'll count to three, and nod. And we'll go."

She nodded and he could feel the tension from where he sat. She was sitting ramrod straight, her spine pressed to the back of the sofa, her mouth stretched in an unflattering death rictus of a smile.

"Try to relax," he said. "This isn't the parole board. It's just you and me. Talking about fixing up old houses. Right?"

"I guess."

Mo threw his hands up, exasperated. "Look. Do you want to do this or not?"

"I said I'd do it." Hattie stared down at her hands. For the first time he noticed the slender gold wedding band on her left hand.

"Why the change of heart? I mean, you'll make money, yeah, but you won't get rich off this show, so if you're only agreeing to do the show for the money . . ."

"It's not just about the money. I mean, okay, yeah, some of it's about the money."

"Then why did you agree to do this show? Seriously, Hattie. I need to know."

She jumped up from the sofa, pacing the room, gesturing wildly with her hands. Mo clicked the remote to start recording, but Hattie didn't seem to notice.

"Maybe I need to prove something to myself. That I'm good at what I do." She glared at him. "I'm really good at what I do. I know you probably don't think so, because of how I screwed up Tattnall Street. But I am. I'm a woman on a job site. I'm the boss, but nobody wants to believe that. Do you know what that's like? Every time a new sub comes on the job, every time an inspector shows up, they look right past me and ask to see the boss. Every. Freakin'. Time. They see me, and it's like, whoa, who's the cute chick in the hard hat? They hit on me, but they never believe in me. When we have a client, like for a kitchen or bath or deck addition? It's Tug who goes out to meet with the client and give them an estimate, because they don't actually believe a mere girl knows what she's talking about. So it's not enough for me to be as good as a man. I gotta be better than them. And I gotta prove it. Every. Damned. Day. So maybe that's why I'm doing your damned show."

He ignored her glare. "See? That's what I'm looking for

from you. The camera needs to see it. Give me some of that 'fuck off' attitude."

She blinked. "Did you just film that?"

"You bet your sweet ass I did." Mo grinned. "I'd say you're warmed up. Now sit down and answer my questions."

"My name is Harriet Kavanaugh, but everyone calls me Hattie. I live in Savannah, Georgia. I've lived here all my life. I fix up old houses. Sometimes I buy 'em, fix 'em, and sell 'em, but in this current real estate market we mostly just fix them up for our clients. Our company is called Kavanaugh and Son. My father-in-law's father, Thomas Senior, started the company, and then Tug—that's my father-in-law, it's a nickname for Thomas Junior—took over, and my husband, that is, my late husband, Hank, he came into the company and so did I."

Mo interrupted. "How long have you been renovating old houses?"

"Most of my life, I guess. I started working for Tug when I was in high school, cleaning up around job sites. Eventually, I started bugging the guys to show me how to do stuff. And that's how I learned all the trades. I can do framing, finish carpentry, electrical, and basic plumbing, in a pinch."

"Did you tell me you went to college and majored in construction management?"

"I took classes for a year or so, but it was expensive. I figured I could learn more on the job than I could sitting in a classroom. Later on, I took the exam for my professional contractor's license. I passed on the first try." Hattie beamed at the memory.

Mo nodded his approval. "What's your favorite part of what you do?"

"Honestly, what I love best about my job is walking through an old house. Touching it, wondering about its past, listening to it, then figuring out how to bring it back to life again for a new family."

Mo nodded and gave her a thumbs-up. "What's it feel like, when you've finished restoring an old house?"

Her face lit up with enthusiasm. "It's just the best. Sometimes we work months and months on a house, slogging through the nasty stuff, replacing old pipes, ripping out knotty pine paneling from the sixties and gross bathrooms, and it feels like you'll never get it all done. Then, one day, the plaster's patched and painted, and we switch on a crystal chandelier I found in a junk shop, and bam! It feels like I've won the lottery. And I forget about all the sweat and tears and rat poop. Maybe it's like childbirth? Like, once you see the baby you fall in love and you don't even care about what it took to bring that kid into the world."

Mo flashed two thumbs up. "More," he mouthed.

"What else can I say?" Hattie asked. "I'm not all that interesting."

He rolled his eyes. "What do you do when you're not working? Hobbies? Interests?"

She laughed. "I'm always working. When I'm not on the job, I'm thinking about the job. Lately, I've been on the hunt for another old house to rehab. I drive all over town. I check the monthly foreclosure notices, talk to real estate agents about what listings they might have coming on the market. And then, for the houses themselves, I'm always on the look-out for salvaged building materials. I've even been known to dumpster dive if I spot a good-looking old mantel sticking out of a trash pile."

"Where do you keep all that stuff?"

"I've got a shed out back."

"No hobbies at all?" Mo looked doubtful.

"I hang out with friends. I read a lot." She gestured at the bookshelves. "I like those old paperback mysteries."

"So, you're really into murder?" Mo asked.

"Not the gory stuff. I'm interested in why seemingly decent people cross the line."

"What else do you like to do?"

Hattie had to think about that. "I take Ribsy for walks. And he rides shotgun when I'm out scouting for a house to save."

"Ribsy?"

"My dog." She whistled, and after some scratching at a door at the end of the hallway, the dog, a furry brown-and-white blur, came hurtling into the living room, nearly knocking over the tripod with Mo's phone on it. He lunged at Hattie, who laughed and wrapped her arms around him, while he proceeded to slobber all over her face.

"This is my main man."

"We talked about this a little bit, before the interview started, but tell me why you're interested in doing this show," Mo said. "*Saving Savannah*."

She scrunched up her face while she thought about it, choosing her words slowly.

"Every day, I drive past old houses in this town that are just sitting there, slowly deteriorating. Once a house is empty or abandoned, nobody is there maintaining it. The roof goes bad, you get water damage, rot, termites. Squatters move in. They set fires in the winter to keep warm, strip off anything they can sell to get money for booze or drugs. At some point, it becomes too late to save a house. And that makes me sad. It's such a waste." She placed the palm of her hand on her chest. "It hurts my heart to see that. It's our history, you know? The history of our community."

"And?" he prompted.

"Maybe, with a show like this, I can inspire people to do what I do. Take a look at their community, find a house that needs some love, and fix it up. Or just appreciate the house they live in. I'd like to do a show where I could show people the proper way to prep and paint woodwork. Or to tile a bathroom, or re-glaze an old window. And maybe I'd talk about the wrong way to do stuff. I'd want to be— approachable? Is that the word for it?"

"And relatable." Mo was coaching her now. "What else? Do you want to say something about Savannah?"

"Like what?"

"Like, maybe, you want to show off the beauty of your hometown, give something back to a town that's given you so much? Preserve a vanishing piece of the community."

Now it was Hattie's turn to roll her eyes. "Didn't I already say that? Like, when I talked about how it hurts my heart?"

He clicked the remote to stop the video.

"Okay, yeah. You did sorta say that. For now, let's try this. I want you to look right at me. Smile. And say something like this: 'I'm Hattie Kavanaugh. And I'm saving Savannah. One old house at a time.'"

She shook her head. "That's dumb. I'm just one girl. How am I going to save Savannah?"

"Do you have to question everything I say? Just do it, okay? It's like, a metaphor. What we call a tag line. These network execs are looking for personality more than anything. You might feel like it's over the top, but the viewer needs to sense your energy. Your enthusiasm. You gotta sell it, lady."

Hattie gave a long, belabored sigh. She posed herself in front of the fireplace, fluffed her hair, and wet her lips. "Go," she told him.

He clicked the remote, then counted down with his fingers. *Three. Two. One.*

"I'm Hattie Kavanaugh. And I'm helping to save my hometown of Savannah. One old house at a time."

"Perfect!" Mo said. "See, you're really good at this when you want to be."

Hattie collapsed onto the nearest chair. "I need a cold beer."

7

Tybee Time

- - - - - - -

"It can't be done," Hattie told Cass, closing the lid of her laptop computer. "There's absolutely nothing on the market in this town in our price range. Nothing that qualifies as even remotely historic with a price under our budget."

Cass sat at the desk facing Hattie's in the cluttered, no-nonsense offices of Kavanaugh & Son. It was a small, crowded space, less than a thousand square feet, with a glass storefront facing Bull Street. There were three battered army surplus metal tanker desks in the main office, one each for Cass, Hattie, and the office manager, Zenobia, who also happened to be Cass's mom. Tug had his own tiny space.

"Where are you looking?" Cass asked.

"The usual places, Zillow and all the local real estate companies' websites."

Zenobia Pelletier looked up from her own computer. "Did you check the list of foreclosures on the county website? Maybe we could find a cute little fixer in Parkside or maybe Live Oak."

"Yes'm," Hattie said. "I checked. It's slim pickings. The only thing that fits our budget are some sixties split-levels on the south side, and some seventies ranch houses way out in the county. Nothing Mo Lopez would consider even remotely historic, or—what's that word?"

"Telegenic," Cass said helpfully. "What about Thunderbolt?"

"Are you kidding? My little shrimping village is all of a sudden trendy. As soon as something comes on the market, it gets snatched up. One of my neighbors has this dumpy little circa-1930s cottage—completely unrestored, no central air. He planted a for-sale-by-owner sign in his yard last week and before the end of the day he had six buyers in a bidding war."

Zenobia removed her red-framed reading glasses and pinched the bridge of her nose. She was in her early fifties, with short, carefully coifed streaky blond hair, a sprinkling of freckles across her light brown cheeks, and long, perfectly polished acrylic nails.

"What about Tybee?"

"What about it?" her daughter asked. "If we can't afford something in town, we sure as hell can't afford a house out at the beach."

"You know, as I was leaving church Sunday, I heard old Mavis Creedmore ask Father Mike to pray for her, because she and her cousins are fixing to lose their beach house on Chatham Avenue."

Hattie stopped scrolling through the real estate listings and perked up. "Is that Katie Creedmore's grandma? She graduated from St. Mary's a year behind us. And Holland Creedmore played on the Cardinal Mooney football team, a couple of years ahead of us. He was quite the stud, as I remember."

Cass rolled her eyes but said nothing.

"Mavis never married. I think those must be her brother's grandkids," Zenobia said. "There was a whole slew of

Creedmores running around town when I was a girl. Anyway, Mavis is the oldest, and I'mma tell you, she rules the roost. Two of her brothers died young, some kind of cancer. She outlived everyone, so now she's, like, the matriarch."

"But Chatham Avenue?" Hattie scoffed. "Come on, Zen. Those houses are all on the Back River, with docks and boathouses. Even a shack would be way out of our price range."

"Maybe not," Zenobia said. "Hang on. Let me look it up in the county records." Her long acrylic nails flew across her laptop keyboard, clicking with each keystroke.

"Mhmm. Here it is. Fifteen twenty-three Chatham Avenue. Owners are listed as Mavis Creedmore, Reeves Creedmore, and Holland Farrell Creedmore. This isn't one of those big ol' beach houses you're thinking about, Hattie. Built in 1922. Only eighteen hundred square feet. Okay, two stories, wood frame. Four bedrooms. One bath."

"Must be some hobbit-sized bedrooms," Cass observed. "And only one bathroom for four bedrooms?"

"It's a beach house, baby," Zenobia said. "Back in my day, when you went to stay at the beach, you *stayed* on the beach. All you needed in your room was a bed, maybe a nightstand, and some hooks to hang up your clothes."

"What else does it say about the Creedmores' house, Zen?" Hattie asked.

"Mmm. I see a tax lien. Oooh. They really are fixing to lose their house. Latest appraisal is $425,000. All the value's in the lot, not the house. Here's the survey. Looks like there's some kind of outbuilding. Maybe a boat shed, something like that?"

Hattie fiddled with a paper clip, bending and twisting it as she thought. "Can't believe a lot on Tybee isn't worth way more than just that. Zen, are you friends with Mavis Creedmore?"

Zenobia shrugged. "We've served on altar guild together at Blessed Sacrament for a long time. We're not friends, but we been knowing each other for years."

"What's she like?"

"She's in her eighties. Cranky, and opinionated. You know that generation. They always think their way is the only way."

"Huh," Cass said, grinning at her mother. "Who does that sound like?"

Zenobia picked up a plastic Kavanaugh & Son promotional flyswatter and flicked it at her daughter. "Remember who writes the paychecks around here, little girl."

Hattie pushed her chair away from the desk and it made a screeching noise on the worn linoleum tile floor. "Come on, Cass. Let's take a ride out to Tybee and check it out."

"But that house isn't even for sale," Cass protested.

"Yet," Hattie said. "Anyway, we can cruise around and check for new listings or for-sale signs that aren't on the Zillow radar yet."

Hattie was quiet on the long drive out to Tybee Island. The tide was out. Traffic was light. It was late spring, and the marsh grasses on either side of US 80 were a brilliant chartreuse green. Cass glanced over at her.

The temperature was mild for Savannah, mid-eighties, but Hattie's face was pale and beaded with perspiration and she seemed to have a death grip on the steering wheel.

Hank's accident had happened on this stretch of what all the locals called Tybee Road. The highway narrowed to two lanes after you left Whitemarsh Island, and anytime there was a wreck, especially on one of the four bridges you crossed to reach Tybee, traffic could be tied up for hours.

"Hey," Cass said softly. "You okay?"

Hattie nodded.

"We don't have to do this," Cass pointed out.

"I have to," Hattie said. A pink blotch bloomed on her cheeks. "It's stupid. I mean, it's just a dumb bridge. The bridge isn't what killed Hank."

She had a point. A drunk driver, coming from a day-long binge at one of the numerous bars on the island, was the cause of Hank Kavanaugh's death. The drunk, a teenager, had veered into the oncoming lane of traffic to avoid hitting something on the roadway, and struck the motorcyclist head-on. As soon as he saw what had happened, the kid took off running, abandoning his car—and the mortally wounded Hank—in the middle of the Lazaretto Creek bridge span.

A physician's assistant, who happened to be approaching the scene when the crash happened, called 911, then ran from her car to try to help. Hank was still breathing, she later told police. But it had taken more than an hour for emergency responders coming from Savannah to weave through the snarled traffic to reach the accident site. And by then, Hank Kavanaugh, age twenty-nine, had succumbed to his massive head and chest injuries.

"I can drive if you want me to," Cass offered, but Hattie shook her head.

"How come you're suddenly hot to trot on this *Saving Savannah* thing? I thought you hated the idea."

Hattie drummed her fingers on the pickup's steering wheel. "I did. Still do. But I'm the one who put the company—and Tug—in the red on the Tattnall Street house. So it's up to me to fix it, and I don't know any other way to try to recoup our losses."

They were almost to the top of the humpbacked Lazaretto Creek bridge. If you looked to the right, you saw the shrimp boats and dolphin tour boats tied up to the docks there. If you looked to the left, you might spot one of the massive container ships, some longer than a city block, gliding by on the way to or from Savannah's port facility.

Hattie felt herself involuntarily holding her breath. Get a grip, she told herself.

She slowed the truck as they passed the Tybee Island city limits sign, laughing at the spectacle of a family of four having their photo snapped in front of the giant resin replica of a sea turtle, and she followed the highway as it made the curve at the ocean and turned east, becoming Butler Avenue, which was the town's main drag.

"Tell me the house number we're looking for?" Hattie asked.

Fifteen twenty-three," Cass said, glancing down at her phone.

Hattie rolled the truck windows down and inhaled the salt air. She glanced around at the passing scenery, at the houses and shops lining both sides of Butler. "Wow, it's a lot more fixed up than I remembered."

Cass sniffed. "If by 'fixed up' you mean they added some new T-shirt shops and renamed the hotel, I guess it is. Tybee ain't Hilton Head. And it ain't St. Simon's Island, that's for sure."

"You are so damned bougie, Cassidy Pelletier," Hattie said, laughing. "I like Tybee. It's like, the last unspoiled beach town. No outlet malls, no high-rise condo towers, no fast-food joints . . . well, except for Arby's. I mean, Arby's is still here, right?"

"When's the last time you were out here?" Cass demanded.

Hattie's laugh trailed off. "You know . . . now that you say that, I guess it's been awhile."

"This is a waste of time," Cass muttered. "I know you feel snake-bit by Midtown, but I bet if we made some calls to some real estate agents, we could find a hip-pocket listing. You know? One that hasn't gone online yet?"

"Maybe. But as long as we're here, let's take a look."

They drove past Tybrisa Street, with its one-block-long strip of bars, souvenir shops, and ice cream parlors, following Butler until it dead-ended into Chatham Avenue at the far south end of the island.

Hattie peered out the window as she rolled slowly up the street. She pointed at a real estate sign posted at the gate of a rambling wood-frame house. "Damn. Look at the size of this place. Cass, can you look it up?"

"On it," Cass replied, scrolling through the Tybee Island real estate listings on her phone. She laughed. "This one's a cool $2.3 million. The lot's over an acre and the listing says it can be subdivided into four lots."

"Obviously not the Creedmores' house," Hattie said.

Half a block away, Cass pointed at a weather-beaten wooden sign nearly obscured by a clump of palmettos.

"Can you make out what that sign says?"

Hattie pulled the truck onto the weedy shoulder of the road.

"Um, I think maybe it's something with a *C* and an *M*?"

"This has to be it," Cass said. "The house across the street is fifteen twenty-four. I guess this is what used to be the driveway?"

A narrow sandy path was barely visible through the screen of overgrown scrub pines, palmettos, and wax myrtles. Hattie stepped over a rotted tree branch and into a tunnel of green. She glanced over her shoulder at Cass, who was standing, motionless, with both hands on her hips.

"You gonna just stand there?"

"Who, me? Do I look like a girl who wants to go hiking back in some godforsaken, snake-infested jungle like that there?"

Hattie shrugged. "Okay, I'll go by myself." She set off through the underbrush, kicking at morning glory vines creeping across the path and batting away low-hanging branches.

"Damn it," she heard Cass mutter. "Hold on, okay? Let me just cut me a snake stick."

8

This Property Condemned

- - - - - - -

Hattie picked up a snake stick of her own and the two women moved slowly through the thick tangles, using their sticks to push aside the greenery.

"There's gotta be a house back here somewhere, right?" Hattie asked, brushing a cobweb from her face.

"I mean, unless Mom gave us the wrong address. Who knew a lot could be this deep?" Cass said.

When they were a hundred yards from where they'd parked the car, they emerged from the path into a clearing. The house, or what was left of it, loomed before them.

"Holy shit," Hattie breathed.

The house had once been white, but over the years the wind, salt air, and time itself had wiped away all but the faintest traces of paint. It was two stories, as advertised, but the second-story roof was topped with a faded blue plastic tarp. A screened porch was wrapped around the second floor, but the screens were shredded and flapping in the mild afternoon breeze.

"It's like that Edgar Allan Poe story they made us read in high school," Cass said. "'The Fall of the House of Usher.' I guess this is 'The Fall of the House of Creedmore.'"

"Make that Creepmore," Hattie said. She took a few steps

toward the house and stopped in her tracks and pointed. "Uh-oh."

A stout-looking two-by-four had been nailed across the rickety-looking steps to the front porch. Nailed to the board was a sign with black lettering on a yellow background.

NO TRESPASSING, CONDEMNED PROPERTY—POSTED, CITY OF TYBEE ISLAND.

Cass touched her arm. "Okay, that's enough for me. This house isn't a teardown, it's a fall-down. Let's go. I saw a gelato shop back there on Tybrisa. Seaside Sweets. My treat."

Hattie stood her ground. "It has a certain kind of shabby charm to it. Don't you think?"

"No," Cass said. "Absolutely not. Shabby is not charming. We've already been down this road. *Hello?* Tattnall Street? Does that ring a bell with you?"

"That was different. We should have known better than to pour so much money into such a big house. I should have known better. This house is only about a quarter of the size of Tattnall Street. I mean, how bad could the place be?"

"How bad? Do you see that tarp on what's left of the roof? Hell, there isn't even a front door. God knows what kind of critters have taken up residence in there. Or people. Could be axe-murdering squatters."

Hattie kept walking toward the house, but Cass stayed where she was.

"Do not go in that house, Harriet Kavanaugh," Cass warned. "Do not. I am not following you inside that house of horrors. No, ma'am. Just stop where you are."

Hattie was ducking under the two-by-four. "Don't be such a scaredy-cat. Come on. It won't hurt to just take a look around."

* * *

The porch floorboards groaned with each halting step Hattie took. "Don't collapse," Hattie whispered. A sheet of plywood had been nailed across the spot where the front door should have been.

She peered through a salt-caked window to the left of the door and got a dim glimpse of a front room with a jumble of furniture.

Over her shoulder, she yelled to Cass, "I can't hardly see anything from here. I'm gonna go around to the side of the house."

Cass crept closer. Right up to the edge of the porch. "I don't like this place."

Hattie walked carefully around to the west side of the porch, stepping over the rusted skeleton of a bike.

On this side of the house a twisting green wisteria vine had breached the crumbling wooden railing and snaked across the floor and up the clapboard siding. Panicles of pale purple flowers dripped artistically down the wall.

"Wisteria. Ugh." Hattie had seen the damage the invasive vine could wreak on trees and outbuildings in her own yard in Thunderbolt. She continued around to the back of the house, keeping her eyes focused on the sagging porch floorboards.

"Wonder what these foundation piers look like," she muttered to herself. She glanced backward and saw Cass, clambering over the wisteria vine. "There you are. I thought maybe a snake got you."

Cass shot her the middle finger. "What's it look like back here? Can't be any worse than the front of the house, right?"

"I think there's definitely foundation issues," Hattie said, pointing at the floor.

"The river's back here somewhere," Cass said, gesturing. But a thick screening of bamboo, palmetto, and scrub pine completely blocked out any view of the water.

Cass walked over to the far edge of the porch, testing each step with the toe of her sneaker, and stopped when she came to a doorway with a window.

"Hey," she called, pressing her face to the dusty glass. "C'mere. If this doesn't convince you this house is a loser, then I give up."

The first thing Hattie noticed was the kitchen ceiling. Most of the plaster from it was now arrayed across the countertops and floors.

"Uh-oh," she said. "What do you wanna bet there's a leaky bathroom upstairs, right above this kitchen?"

"I never bet on a sure thing," Cass said. "But what about the rest of this horror show?"

The room was lined with knotty pine cabinets. Most of the warped cupboard doors hung open, exposing shelves bristling with dishes, glassware, and canned goods. The countertops were harvest-gold laminate. The floor was a checkerboard pattern of avocado green and harvest-gold roll vinyl. The stove and refrigerator were avocado green and spotted with rust.

"If they had a contest for fugliest kitchen, this one would win first place," Hattie said.

"We've wasted enough time here," Cass replied. "You saw the sign. It's condemned. Let's just go back to town, and see if Mom came up with any serious contenders."

Hattie reluctantly followed Cass around to the front of the house. She took one last look over her shoulder before starting down the driveway toward the truck. "There's something about this house, Cass. It's a hundred years old. It's crying out to be saved."

"Not by us," Cass said.

*   *   *

Cass's phone rang just as they were about to climb into Hattie's truck. "It's Mom." She tapped the speaker button and answered.

"Hey, Mom, what's up?"

"Are y'all still out at Tybee?"

"Just getting ready to leave," Hattie said.

"Did you find the house?"

"What's left of it," Cass said. "It's a wreck. The city's condemned it and it's all boarded up. Guess you better go back to cold-calling real estate agents."

"Maybe not. I been doing some snooping around. Talked to a lady who's known Mavis Creedmore for years. That house was left to Mavis and her two younger cousins by their grandma. One cousin lives way up north and hasn't been home in years, and the other, Holland Senior, lives in Ardsley Park. I guess his son is the boy who played football at Cardinal Mooney. Holland Senior was some kind of stockbroker, but he's retired now.

"Mavis claims she had no idea about the liens, or that the house had been condemned, until one of the Tybee neighbors called her recently and asked why the family had let things go so bad out there. She's hopping mad about the whole thing."

"I'm surprised none of the family living in town ever asked her the same thing," Hattie put in.

"Those Creedmores are bad to feud. Did y'all go in the house?"

"There's a big no-trespassing sign nailed to the porch," Cass protested. "But we looked in the windows. Ugh. The place is a teardown."

"Hold on, now," Zenobia said. "I called out to Tybee City Hall. Talked to a nice lady there named Carol Branch. The city condemned the property because neighbors were calling and complaining about it being an eyesore and a public nuisance."

"What exactly does that mean?" Cass asked.

"In this case, it means the city just got some federal grant money to incentivize private investment in historic but distressed properties," Zenobia said. "They're gonna auction that house off through sealed bids. Starting price is twenty-eight thousand and change, which is the amount owed for back taxes and delinquency fees."

"What?" Hattie shouted into the phone. "That's crazy! A beachfront house on Tybee for under thirty thousand?"

"There's a catch," Zenobia cautioned. "More than one, actually. The buyer has to conform to all kinds of historic preservation regulations. The house has to keep to the same footprint, which means no additions. All changes to the exterior of the house have to be 'sensitive to the historic nature of the original home,' whatever that means."

"We've done houses within Savannah's historic district and dealt with those kinds of regs before," Hattie said. "The rules are a pain in the butt, but it's not impossible."

"All work on the house has to pass city inspections. And the work has to be completed within twelve months," Zenobia went on.

"What else did this Carol Branch say, Zen?"

"The feds require that the city advertise the house on their website for a month and the time's up this week. Buyers have to submit a sealed bid to the city, with a certified check by noon this Thursday."

"That's the day after tomorrow," Cass said. She looked over at Hattie. "Even if you were interested, where would you get that kind of money that fast?"

Hattie jingled her truck keys, a nervous habit she'd picked up from Hank. "Zen, how soon could we get into the house to take a look around?"

"You can't. House is being sold as is."

Cass waved a finger in Hattie's face. "No. Do not do this. I know you think you've got something to prove, but this house is not the one. It's got bad vibes."

"There's no such thing as bad vibes." Hattie cranked the truck's ignition.

9

The Other Rebecca

Mo paced around the tiny living room of the carriage house he'd rented on Charlton Street. He'd found the place online, attracted principally by the location, in the downtown historic district, price—cheap by L.A. standards—and the fact that the place came with an off-street parking space.

He'd been alarmed when Rebecca called late the night before to say she'd be arriving in Savannah—today.

"Don't worry. It's all good news," she'd assured him. "Tony loves your idea. In fact he loves it so much we want to fast-track everything. Can you set it up for me to meet your star? Tomorrow? She doesn't have an agent, right?"

"Okay, that's great," he said, too startled to ask any more questions. "I should be able to set up a meet with Hattie. And no, I'm pretty sure she doesn't have an agent."

"Perfect," Rebecca said. "Shoot me the address where you're staying. I'll text you when my plane lands. Don't worry about picking me up. I'll just grab a cab."

He heard a car pull into the lane behind the carriage house, went to the back door, and opened it.

Rebecca looked impossibly fresh for someone who'd just

gotten off a red-eye flight from L.A. with a stop in Atlanta en route to Savannah. She was wearing a relaxed version of her power suit in chocolate brown, along with her signature oversized Jackie O tortoiseshell sunglasses.

"Look at this place," she exclaimed, admiring the pocket-sized walled garden. "It's like a storybook."

"That's Savannah for you," he said. "Come on inside. Can I get you something to drink? I've got Pellegrino in the fridge."

"Perfect," she said, following him through the kitchen and into the main living space. "Ooh. This is super cute. Maybe your Hattie can flip a house and make it look like this?"

"Doubtful," Mo said. "This house, unrestored, sold for $1.2 million three years ago. Just guessing, but I'm thinking my landlords probably sunk another half a million into it."

"So, out of our girl's price range," Rebecca said.

"Not just that. Historic properties like this one, which was built in 1848, are subject to review by the historic preservation commission. You can't change out a doorbell in the historic district without having approval from them. Which can take months."

"We certainly don't have the time or budget for anything like that," Rebecca reminded him. "That's one of the reasons I flew out here. Tony wants you to start shooting immediately."

"That's impossible. You know what kind of preproduction timetable I need, Becca. Six weeks is the absolute minimum, and I'm not sure I could even do it that fast."

"You'll have to, if you want that Wednesday night slot," Rebecca said, blithely ignoring his protest. "Another thing. We're going to tweak your concept. Just a bit."

"Tweak it how?"

She sipped the Pellegrino. "First off, Tony's not fond of the name *Saving Savannah*."

"But that's what the show's about," he protested.

"Now, don't get all defensive on me," Rebecca said. "You can still save or preserve an old house. That doesn't change. But we need the show itself to be more exciting, more high concept, high risk, high drama."

He sighed, waiting for the inevitable.

"So!" she said brightly. "I had this thought. Why not do something really daring? And original? Even . . . provocative."

"You're not talking about doing a nude flip or something crazy like that, right?"

"Nude flip!" She laughed giddily. "That's cute, Mo. No. Okay. Get ready. I think you're gonna totally love this. *Homewreckers*!"

"*Homewreckers*? I mean, what does that even mean?" Mo asked. His gut churned, because he knew what was coming. Something diabolically awful.

"Picture this: We've got your girl Hattie. She's cute as a button and wholesome and southern-fried freckles. And then we bring in this gorgeous L.A. designer. He's a blond, big-city drink of water with tons of published projects. His name is Trae Bartholomew, by the way, and your viewers are going to go literally nuts over him. He's done television too."

Mo grabbed his iPad and tapped the IMDb tab, typed in the name Becca had just mentioned, and stared down at the photo. "He looks like a male model," Mo said. "And according to his bio, he's the biggest loser in one of your design competitions."

"He came in second," Rebecca said. "But that's beside the point. Trae is talented, he's experienced, and best of all, he tests great with our target audience."

"I'm still not grasping this concept, Becca. And if I don't, our viewers won't either."

She gave him the death stare. "You're being deliberately

obtuse. Okay, I'm going to dumb it down for you. *Homewreckers* is at the space where a dating show meets a flip show. Think mash-up of *The Bachelorette* and *Flip or Flop.* Get it?"

"So . . . Hattie buys a house to flip, and we bring in a designer to tell her how to do it? And what? They fall in love and fall into bed? Are you serious with this shit, Becc?"

"You know me better than that, Mo. I never joke."

This, Mo reflected wryly, was possibly the truest thing she'd ever said. He'd never known Rebecca to tell a joke, or even a vaguely funny anecdote.

"I'm serious," she went on. "And so is Tony. *Homewreckers,* or this 'shit' as you call it, is the show he wants. And if you want to sell it to HPTV, that's the show you're going to deliver."

Mo glared across the table at her and she glared right back. The doorbell broke up the staring contest.

"That should be Hattie, correct?" she asked. "Can't wait to meet her in person. And, Mo? Let's make sure we're both on the same page with this show. The clock is ticking. We don't have time for mistakes."

As Rebecca's eyes traveled over her, Hattie felt her cheeks burn, felt herself shrinking inside her own clothes, the designer jeans Cass had insisted on loaning her, her own blouse, carefully ironed early that morning, and stack-heeled suede booties, because they made her feel taller and more powerful.

But under the microscopic stare of the network executive, who wore an outfit that probably cost as much as her first truck, Hattie was already reevaluating her appearance. She should have worn more makeup, earrings, a nicer top.

She should have gotten a manicure, a blowout, a facial. She should have been born blonder, and taller, and definitely with a flatter butt and higher cheekbones.

"Hattie," Rebecca cooed. "Our newest star in the HPTV firmament. It's great to meet you. Mo's been telling me all about you!"

"Good to meet you, too," Hattie said. She looked over at Mo, unsure of the next step.

"Let's all sit down," Mo said, gesturing to the dining room table. He'd placed yellow legal pads at all three chairs, and his laptop was open. "Hattie, Rebecca's just been telling me about some, uh, modifications of our original concept for *Saving Savannah*."

Rebecca cleared her throat and shot Mo a barely perceptible warning signal. "I've also been telling Mo that the reason I flew out here today was to expedite and accelerate this whole preproduction process. As you might have heard, we've had an unexpected blip in our programming lineup."

"A blip?" Hattie repeated.

"Krystee Brandstetter is pregnant, with twins, but there are complications, and her doctor has her on strict bed rest. We were in the middle of filming her fourth season, but now *Going Coastal* is shut down for at least six, maybe seven months. Or longer."

Hattie wracked her brain. Was she supposed to know this Krystee person?

Mo must have sensed her cluelessness. "*Going Coastal* is the network's biggest hit show. Krystee and her husband, Will, restore old houses up in North Carolina. Krystee started a blog about fixing up an old farmhouse they bought near Wilmington, and it went viral. Their show is the tentpole for the Wednesday night lineup. Which is where you come in."

"And how lucky for us that Mo found you," Rebecca said cheerily. "Everyone at HPTV is so excited about the possibilities for this show."

Rebecca Sanzone was all business. She opened a slim leather folder and handed Hattie a sheaf of papers and a pen. "This is our standard contract for talent, with the compensation schedule attached. You'll see your per-episode fee here." She pointed at a tiny yellow arrow sticker on the document.

"And here," Rebecca went on, pointing to a neon orange sticker, "is your statement that the property you'll be working on is owned by you, or your corporate entity, that you and your corporate entity assume all responsibility for debts incurred by your project, and that you and you alone are liable for any damages or injuries arising from this property, and that in the instance of any such damages or injuries, the network will be held harmless."

Hattie nodded numbly, scanning the contract. The fee structure, even though Mo had already explained it earlier, still seemed like a shockingly paltry amount of money for something involving so much investment and risk on her part.

She hesitated. "Mo didn't say anything about signing contracts today. I thought this would be more of a meet-and-greet-type situation. Shouldn't I have a lawyer look at this?"

"That's completely up to you," Rebecca said. "I'm so sorry Mo didn't make the nature of this meeting clearer to you. Again, time is of the essence, but if you really feel the need to have an attorney review what's merely a standard contract . . ."

Hattie glanced over at Mo, who was silently gnashing his molars, both at the indignity of being casually thrown under the bus, and at the ethical bind Rebecca had placed him in.

She'd never even hinted that the network was ready to sign Hattie to a contract, and if she had, he'd have advised her to get a lawyer to review the paperwork.

Now though, it was too late to pump the brakes. He nodded at Hattie. "I think it's okay."

"I'm assuming you've already bought the house you'll be working on for the show, correct?" Rebecca went on. "I'd love to see some photos. Exterior and interior, so I can give my boss a feel for the scope of the work."

"No," Hattie said, surprised. "I mean, there hasn't been time. I only agreed to do the show, like, two days ago. The real estate market here is incredibly tight. Finding the house is going to take some time."

"Time is a luxury we don't have," Rebecca said sternly. She pointed out the living room window of the town house, toward Charlton Street, with its row of elegant town houses. "This town is absolutely crawling with old houses. I saw tons of possibilities just from the window of my cab this morning. Surely there must be at least one old house you can scoop up for a song."

"You might have seen a lot of old houses, but what you didn't see were for-sale signs," Hattie retorted. "No offense, but I do this for a living. Finding the right property at the right price—it's like looking for a needle in a haystack. And I'm not the only one looking. As soon as something does come on the market, invariably there are half a dozen offers from other investors—all cash, and over asking price within hours, if not minutes."

Rebecca's smile was patronizing. "I do this for a living too. Let me give you a tip. Savannah has a film and television commission, or something. Call those folks and let them know you've signed to do a network show that will potentially bring millions of dollars' worth of jobs and prestige to

Savannah. I'm sure they'll bend over backwards to help you find the right property."

"I'll keep that in mind," Hattie said. "But what happens if I can't magically conjure up a house by—when did you say was the deadline?"

"The deadline is now," Rebecca said. "Or no later than the end of this week. And, to be blunt, if we don't have a house to flip, we don't have a show. Which would be so unfortunate, because, Hattie, we really, really like you. We like the look of Savannah, the idea for *The Homewreckers.* . . ."

Hattie blinked. "*Homewreckers*? I thought the show was called *Saving Savannah.*"

"Change of plans," Rebecca said. "Mo can explain." She slid two more pieces of paper across the table to Hattie. "But in the meantime, here are the last two documents you'll need to sign." She tapped a neon pink arrow on one page and a neon green one on the next document. "Here, and here."

Hattie picked up the first page and read silently until she came to what seemed like the most important sentence in a page full of eye-glazing legalese.

She read the paragraph out loud. "The network shall have the unilateral right to terminate this agreement or take punitive action against the individual named herein in the event that such other party engages in reprehensible behavior or conduct that may negatively impact his or her public image and, by association, the public image of the contracting company." She looked over at the network executive. "Reprehensible behavior? Like, me promising not to get arrested? Or knocked up?"

"It's a morals clause," Rebecca said, waving aside her concerns. "Standard boilerplate to protect the network from potential embarrassment. It simply says you are who and what you represent yourself to be. Nobody likes a skeleton-in-the-closet-type surprise."

Hattie felt the blood drain from her face. Surely the network wouldn't care about her father's embezzlement conviction and the resulting scandal. It was old history. Her legal name was Harriet Laing Kavanaugh. She'd taken her mother's maiden name after her parents' split, and of course, Hank's name when they married.

"Right." Hattie scribbled her name beside the neon-colored arrow and turned to the next page.

Rebecca anticipated her next question. "And that's a non-disclosure agreement. Also standard in the industry. It just says that any dealings you have with the network or its employees are to remain strictly confidential. So, no leaks about any on-set drama, no tell-all stories in the tabloids."

Hattie signed on the line next to the arrow and handed the documents back to Rebecca.

Mo exhaled slowly. "Great! What do you say I take you two ladies out to lunch to celebrate the start of a beautiful relationship?"

"Thanks, but I'd better not," Hattie said, standing up. "I've got Tug out cruising the neighborhoods looking for houses to flip, and Zenobia and Cass are scouring the real estate listings trying to come up with some possibilities."

"I can't stay either," Rebecca said, gathering all the documents into her briefcase. "My car should be here any minute."

"Car?" Mo said dumbly. "You're not staying over?"

"I wish!" Rebecca said. "I've got to get back to L.A. Lots of meetings, as always. But I've met and signed our new star, so my work here is done."

Rebecca's cell phone pinged. "Damn. There's my car." She gave Hattie a brief hug. "Can't wait to get busy on *Homewreckers*. You're going to be amazing!"

10

With This Ring

Davis Hoffman lifted the lid of the velvet box and held the jeweler's loupe to his eye and peered down at the large diamond solitaire, which was mounted between a pair of perfectly matched sapphires. "Nice," he said under his breath. "Beautiful cut and clarity." He ran his index finger over the delicately chased and engraved platinum band. "Beautiful workmanship here too. It's exquisite."

Hattie tried to swallow the lump in her throat. She wiped sweaty palms on her jeans.

"Davis? I . . . I really don't want to sell it."

"Hank gave you this?"

Davis and Hank had been friends all through prep school at Cardinal Mooney Catholic. After high school, Davis had gone off to college up north, to study architecture at Princeton. But after his father's death, his mother had prevailed on him to come home to work in the family business, Heritage Jewelers, whose storefront on Broughton Street had been a Savannah landmark for as long as Hattie could remember.

She nodded, tears stinging her eyes. "It was his grandmother's ring. According to Tug, your grandfather made this ring himself."

"I should have recognized this swirling magnolia blossom

pattern," Davis said, running a fingertip over the elegant chasing. "It was Granddad's signature design. This kind of old-world craftsmanship is a thing of the past."

"I know," Hattie whispered. "It's just . . ."

"You need cash." Davis gave her a kind smile. No pitying, just understanding.

"I do." Her cheeks flushed with embarrassment.

She filled him in on the HPTV show, and the dilemma she was facing. "I'm strapped for cash. Our last flip didn't really work out and we had to sell it for a loss. The only way I can dig myself out of this hole I'm in is if I do this show. But I can't flip a house I don't own."

"Have you found a house to buy?"

"We're working on it. I don't want to jinx the deal by talking about it."

Davis twirled the ring on his finger. "Estate jewelry is hot right now. Our millennial brides love the idea that they're getting something with a history. They even have a word for this style—grand millennial. I could probably get seventy-five thousand for this ring, with the right customer."

Hattie gasped. "That much? I had no idea. I haven't worn it since Hank died. My work has me crawling around under houses all the time and I'm terrified I'll lose one of the stones."

"Tell you what," Davis said, leaning across the glass-topped counter. "I'll loan you forty thousand cash, using the ring for collateral. Will that help?"

Hattie swallowed hard. She looked down at the engagement ring, now glittering in its satin-lined nest, and thought about the night Hank had given it to her.

They'd been working all day on the house in Thunderbolt, tiling the new shower stall. She was hot and hungry and exhausted, and wanted to order a pizza and collapse into the bed, but Hank insisted they drive out to the beach and watch the sunset. They parked the truck and used the Eighteenth Street walkover to cross the dunes with a painter's drop cloth for a picnic blanket.

Hattie had managed to step on a piece of glass and cut her foot and she was in a foul mood. As the sun slid toward the horizon, she was still griping about idiots who ignored the signs forbidding glass on the beach when Hank leaned over and planted a kiss on her lips.

"Could you please shut up? I'm trying to do something here." Then he reached in the pocket of his jeans and handed her the velvet box.

She'd gasped when she saw the ring. Her hand was shaking uncontrollably when he took the ring from the box and slid it onto her left hand. "Well?"

"Is it real?" Hattie had never seen anything more beautiful. The sapphires were bluer than Hank Kavanaugh's eyes, which were very, very blue. And the diamond was the biggest she'd ever seen.

"Hell yes, it's real. Do you think I'd give you a fake ring?" He'd pretended to be hurt.

Hattie had thrown her arms around his neck and blubbered out a string of insane sentences. "Oh my God! Hank, it's amazing. Where did you get this? Can we afford it? So, what? We're getting married?"

They'd stayed on the beach, laughing, drinking wine, and kissing and talking and doing other things that, although not specifically forbidden by city ordinance, probably would have been frowned upon by the local authorities.

She was thinking about that night now, standing at the counter at Heritage Jewelers, while Davis Hoffman patiently waited for the answer to his question.

"Yeah," she said finally. "That would be a huge help." She touched the ring box. "And . . . you won't sell it? Because I'm going to pay you back, Davis. I swear, I'll pay you back."

"I won't sell it," he promised. "Stay right here while I get the paperwork squared away."

He left the ring box on the countertop and walked to the back of the store. She touched the ring, then closed the lid of the box.

Five minutes later, Davis was back. He handed her a printed-out form and a pen. "That's a detailed description of your ring, and my appraisal of its worth. I'm a certified gemologist in case you're wondering. And there are the terms of our arrangement."

Hattie looked up. "I trust you, Davis." She scribbled her name on the line at the bottom of the document and handed it across the counter to him. He took the bottom copy of the document, folded it, and placed it in an envelope. "Your check is in here," he said.

"So that's it? We're good?"

"We're good. I'll put the ring in our safe. What else are you up to these days?" he asked casually. "Have you dated any, since . . . Hank?"

"Not much. I, um, was sorry to hear about you and Elise."

He shrugged. "Not as sorry as my mother. I think Elise got custody of her in the divorce."

Hattie laughed. "I hope they'll be very happy together."

"Doubtful. Unfortunately, I don't think Elise is capable of happiness. Come to think of it, neither is my mom."

"You've got a daughter, right?"

His long, serious face brightened. "Ally. She's four, going on forty." He pulled his phone from his pocket, scrolled through the camera roll, and held the phone out for Hattie to see.

The little girl was seated in an office chair, holding a kitten in her lap. She had dark blond hair and huge dark eyes.

"Adorable," Hattie said. "Do you get to see her much?"

"You just missed her. She loves 'helping' play store here."

"Lucky you." Hattie took the envelope and tucked it in her pocketbook. She held out her hand, and he took it, closing it between both of his.

"Davis . . . I . . ." She bit her lip. "Anyway, thank you."

"Glad I could help out." He released her hand. "And if you ever want to grab a bite of dinner, or have a drink? I'm your guy. Totally."

"Okay," she said.

Davis plucked a business card from an ornate gold container on the display counter and scribbled on the back of it. "Here's my cell. Give me a call. Let me know if you get the house."

11

Daddy's Girl

She felt her jaw muscles clenching as she pulled off the paved highway and onto the bumpy dirt road that led to her father's place. Sensing her anxiety, Ribsy, who'd been happily riding shotgun with his head sticking out the passenger window, stretched across the bench seat and placed his muzzle in her lap.

"Good boy," Hattie murmured, scratching his ears. His tail thumped the vinyl upholstery. At least someone was enthusiastic about this mission.

She'd called Woodrow Bowers late in the evening, after an agonizing session of number crunching, when she'd realized even the funds from her pawned engagement ring would not be nearly enough to buy and rehab the Creedmore house.

He'd seemed happy, if surprised to hear from her, and readily invited her to the cabin for lunch the next day.

"You cook now?"

"Hell yeah, I cook. How do you think I've been eating all these years?"

"You never cooked before. . . ."

"Before I went to prison," Woody finished the sentence for her. "It's okay to say it, Hattie. Prison. When you get to the gate call me, and I'll ride up on the golf cart and let you in."

Hattie rehearsed her proposal on the thirty-minute ride from Thunderbolt to the camp. She hadn't slept much the night before, already second-guessing her decision to turn to Woody for money. But she was out of options. Her father was her last resort.

She put the truck in park when she reached the cattle gate and reached for her phone. There were no-trespassing signs tacked to trees on either side of the gate, and a utility pole nearby bristled with security cameras.

"Hey, Dad. I'm here," she said when he picked up.

"Be right down."

She hadn't been to her grandfather's old fish camp in decades. She'd visited here often while the old man was alive. It was PawPaw who'd gifted her with her own set of tools, so that she could hammer and saw in the barn right alongside him as he tinkered with woodworking projects. Back then, Woody had been too busy to spend much time at his father's camp, always impatient to get back to town for meetings, or fundraisers, or work.

PawPaw died when she was fourteen, and the visits to the fish camp abruptly ended. It wasn't until Woody's release from prison that he announced his plan to restore the camp and live there full-time.

She heard the golf cart's near-silent approach on the road. Woody's English cockers, Roux and Deuce, sat beside him on the front seat, and they began barking when they caught sight of her.

He parked the cart, gave her a nod in greeting, then unlocked the gate and swung it inward to allow her to pass. She drove through and he relocked the gate, testing to make sure the lock held.

Woody had gotten paranoid since his release from prison. He never elaborated on who or what he thought was threatening him, but he changed his cell phone number often, and had his mail sent to a post office box in town. Except for the times he ventured out to pick up mail, groceries, and supplies, as far as Hattie could tell, he rarely left the grounds of the fish camp.

She followed behind the golf cart as it wound through a half mile of heavy woods, then past a fenced pasture where a graying donkey and a chestnut-brown horse grazed, and finally, down the narrow dirt road to the camp.

He waved her to park next to the cabin, and when she got out of the truck, he gave her a brief, awkward half hug. Ribsy jumped down from the truck and the cockers circled him, sniffing the newcomer and wagging their stubby tails in approval.

"Cabin looks nice, Dad," Hattie said. She'd remembered it as a primitive wood hut, with a sloping roof over a covered front porch where a stray cat or two always lounged. But now it was a snug cottage, with real windows with dark green–painted frames and shutters.

"I've been making improvements," her father said. "Keeps me busy." He leaned down and scratched Ribsy's head. "You got a dog."

"Yeah," she said. "After Hank died, it got kind of lonely. Ribsy's good company."

"Dogs are the best company there is," Woody said. "Come on inside. I got lunch ready."

They ate in front of a window looking out at the river. The place was a bachelor's paradise. There was no sign of a woman's touch.

She wondered about that. She and her father had an

unspoken pact. He never mentioned Amber—the other woman who'd been the recipient of all Woody's ill-gotten gains—and Hattie never asked about her.

He'd made ham salad sandwiches on rye bread. There were bread-and-butter pickles, and potato chips, and iced tea.

Hattie took a bite of the sandwich, chewed, and pointed at the bread, which didn't look store-bought. "Did you take up baking, too?"

He shrugged. "It's not that hard. You just read the recipe and do what it says to do. The kneading is my favorite part. You get to pound the hell out of it, and it doesn't talk back." He tapped the jar of pickles on the table. "Made these, too."

"Never thought you'd turn into a baker, gardener, and pickle-maker, Dad. After all those years working at the bank. Mom used to say you'd burn Kool-Aid."

He cracked a smile. His face had gotten leathery, lined with wrinkles. His hair was streaked with silver and he wore it longer these days. Woodrow Bowers had always been a handsome man, but now, in his sixties, he looked like he could model hiking gear, or be a host for one of those outdoor shows where everyone wore plaid shirts and fly-fishing vests.

"How is your mom?"

"Okay, I guess. We don't talk a lot."

"Does she know about this television show you're fixing to do?"

Hattie had explained about *Homewreckers* in her call to him the night before.

"Not yet. I wanted to wait until I get the house under contract."

"Tell me about the house," her father prompted. "It sounds like you're going to have to pump a hell of a lot of money in it. And right after you lost your shirt on that place on Tattnall Street. You sure you'll make back your investment?"

She bristled at his blunt reminder of her most recent failure, and realized that in Woody's eyes, she was still the same age she'd been when he'd been sent to prison.

"You know, Dad, I've been doing this for a living since I was eighteen. I've run all the comps on Tybee waterfront houses sold in the past eighteen months. The lot alone, without the house, is worth half a million dollars, easy."

"Come on. Tybee Island, half a million?"

"It's not like it used to be, Dad."

"Okay, let's talk numbers."

She'd brought along a yellow legal pad with her rough estimate of what she'd have to spend to buy the house, and an even rougher number for the renovation. "This is all just based on eyeballing it," she explained, tapping the paper with her pen. "The Creedmores have basically let the house rot since the last hurricane."

"Hard to believe Holland Creedmore is just going to sit back and let that house get bought out from under him. You want to watch out for that character. Back in the day he always had some kind of shady back-room deal cooking."

Hattie stared at her father.

"What? You think your old man is the only one who ever committed a crime? Listen here, Hattie. The only difference between me and Holland Creedmore and at least half the movers and shakers in Savannah is that I got caught and went to prison for what I did."

She doodled on the legal pad. Sketches of houses and trees and birds and bunnies. Anything to avoid meeting her father's eyes.

"Look at me, young lady," her father said sternly, in the same tone of voice he'd used when she was a child, berating her for a less than perfect grade in school.

She lifted her chin and coolly met his gaze. Once his eyes

had been a deep, piercing brown. Now they were lighter, almost greenish-hazel.

"I made mistakes a long time ago. But I paid back that money. I've been a model citizen since I got out, and I don't appreciate being judged all over again by my own daughter."

He hadn't really changed, Hattie realized. Woody Bowers, at his core, would always be Woody Bowers. He'd survived prison and he would survive everything life threw at him because the only person he really cared about was himself.

"Go ahead and say what's on your mind," he challenged.

"You paid back the money you stole from orphans and widows and kids with cancer. You think going to prison erases all that. But what about what you stole from me, and Mom? You destroyed our family, and you have never once acknowledged, let alone apologized, for that. The stink from what you did settled on me, and on her."

"You haven't done so badly," Woody protested. "You got to stay in that expensive private school. I saw to it that you had money for what you needed. And now, when you come to me because you need money, do I turn you away?"

She got up and looked out the window, toward the river, and changed the subject. "What are you afraid of, Dad? Why all the security cameras and locked gates? Why all the secrecy?"

"There are people out there who don't like the fact that I'm out of prison, and I'm making money again. I got to watch out for myself."

He began clearing the lunch dishes. "You want something else to eat? Some cookies?"

"No, thanks. I better get back to town."

He pulled out a binder of checks and placed it on the table, scratching numbers on the paper so furiously the pen pierced the check in a couple of places. He ripped it from the book and held it out to her.

"So that's it, huh? You show up here, ask me for a loan, get your check, and then leave?"

Hattie didn't flinch. "What did you expect? A teary-eyed family reunion? You want to hold me up with emotional blackmail? That's not gonna work on me anymore, Dad. I finally figured it out. Everything is a transaction to you. Okay, fine. I don't need your love, or your approval, or even your respect anymore. But I'll take a loan. And I'll pay you back. Because, just like you taught me, I know now that a clean balance sheet is the key to happiness."

She took the check, folded it, and put it in her pocket. She opened the back door and whistled for Ribsy. "Come on, boy. Time to go home."

12

Mo's Wakeup Call

Mo awoke suddenly, jerked upright into a state of semiconsciousness by the persistent dinging from his phone. He'd fallen asleep at the dining room table, facedown on the budget spreadsheets he'd spent the evening composing and revising. A still-damp puddle of drool had blurred the ink on the printouts.

He found his phone, buried under a greasy takeout pizza box. "Christ," he mumbled. It was 2:15 A.M. There were four recent text messages, all from Rebecca.

Trae's agent has been putting me through the wringer, but I think he's on board. Call me as soon as you get this.

"Trae?" Oh. Right. The designer-slash-catalog model Rebecca had recruited for his show. *His* show.

Mo was too tired to trudge up the stairs to bed. He picked up the phone and collapsed onto the sofa. Two more texts from Becca had landed in the five minutes since he'd taken a piss, washed his hands, and kicked off his shoes.

What are you hearing about the house? When can I see it?

He held the phone an inch away from his face, talking to himself as much as Rebecca. "I don't know. It hasn't even been a day. Jesus, gimme a break."

Tony doesn't like the girl's hair. He thinks it looks mousy. I agree. Can she go lighter? Darker? Extensions?

"Her name is Hattie. Hattie Kavanaugh," Mo said. Anyway, there was nothing wrong with Hattie's hair. It looked fine to him. More than fine. Thick and shiny, falling softly around her face.

How's the crew shaping up? Who is your showrunner?

He yawned and closed his eyes again. Most of his regular L.A. crew had already been hired away by other production companies, but since so much film and television work was being done in Georgia these days, he'd managed to lock down what he thought was a pretty credible crew of locals. The showrunner was another matter.

Taleetha Carr, his showrunner for *Killer Garages,* would be a natural for *Homewreckers.* She was smart, funny, hardworking, knew reality shows inside out and upside down. Everyone loved Taleetha. Everyone except Rebecca, who had taken an instant dislike to her.

"Don't you worry 'bout it, baby," Taleetha told Mo, patting his cheek, after the first time she'd locked horns with Rebecca in a postproduction meeting. "It's not like I'm guacamole. Not everyone's gonna love me."

Taleetha had been his first phone call after he'd gotten the green light for what he was still stubbornly, insanely, calling *Saving Savannah.*

"Momo!" she'd exclaimed, picking up on the first ring. "What up?"

He'd forgotten how much he'd missed the unsinkable Taleetha Carr. "I might have a job for you, that's what's up."

Taleetha hadn't missed a beat. "Not HPTV, right? You know I love you, but I am not working for Rebecca Sanzone again."

"You'd be working for me," he'd protested.

"And you're working for her."

"I work for myself," Mo had said. "Anyway, can we talk business for a minute? I'm on this crazy-fast time track, and I really need you, Leetha. Just hear me out before you say no."

"I'll listen, but that's not gonna change my mind," she'd relented.

He'd explained about meeting Hattie Kavanaugh, and how he'd gotten the spark of an idea for a show set in Savannah.

"Have you ever been here?" he'd asked. "It's hauntingly beautiful. The history, all these incredible pre–Civil War homes, the flowers and the trees and the Spanish moss . . ."

"And the rednecks waving all those Confederate flags? Did you forget about them?"

"No. I mean, yeah, I admit there's still some of that, but Savannah's so much more than that. Anyway, we need to start shooting by early next week. I need you, Leetha."

"Next week? Baby, this might come as a news flash for you, but I've got a job."

"Taleetha Carr, are you cheating on me?"

"Hell yes. A girl's got to work, you know. Cole Ryder's got a development deal for a show he's calling *Dumpster Divas,* about a group of L.A. chicks who make a living picking up trash and recycling and reselling it."

"In development," Mo had said. "Has any network said yes?"

"Not in so many words," she'd admitted.

"In the meantime, I've got a sure thing. A signed contract with HPTV, and a crew, and we're ready to start filming as soon as you get your sassy ass down here."

"No. Nuh-uh," Taleetha had said. "Not even for you."

"I'm gonna email you the talent reel I shot. You'll love Hattie. Drives a pickup truck, runs the construction company with her father-in-law. She's the real deal."

"The answer is still no, Mo. But what's the big rush with this new show?"

"I finally got a lucky break," he'd said. "Krystee from *Going Coastal* is pregnant with twins and she's on strict bed rest, which means the show is on hiatus for at least six months."

"And that Wednesday night slot is up for grabs. Temporarily," Taleetha had said thoughtfully.

Mo had seen an opening and jumped on it. "You know you want to do this show with me, Taleetha. You miss me. You miss us."

She hadn't denied it. "What about Becky the Bitch? What's she gonna have to say about you hiring me?"

"Leave her to me," Mo had said. "How soon can you get here?"

"To Savannah? I'm not even sure I know where that is."

"You fly to Atlanta, then you get on a flight to Savannah. I'll book your flight tonight. You can be here by Friday."

She had let out a long sigh. "Okay, send me that talent reel and everything else you've got."

The phone buzzed again, like an angry fly trapped against a window screen. Mo sighed.

Dealing with a workaholic like Becca sucked up all the oxygen in the room.

His phone buzzed again.

WHERE ARE YOU? WHAT'S GOING ON? WHY HAVEN'T YOU ANSWERED ME?

He yawned and typed.

It's only 3 A.M. here. All good with the show. Talk tomorrow.

He lifted one hip and shoved the phone under the sofa cushion and fell instantly back to sleep.

13

Winner Takes All

- - - - - - -

"Uh, hi. I'm here for the Creedmore house?"

A heavy plate-glass window separated her from the clerk who sat at a desk in the lobby of the Tybee City Hall. He was an older man, wearing a white polo shirt and a sour attitude. He looked up at Hattie over black-rimmed half-moon glasses that perched on the tip of his nose.

"What's that?"

Hattie raised her voice. "The Creedmore house!" Two people who'd been loitering nearby, studying the notices on a large bulletin board, looked up, startled.

"What about it?"

"The city condemned that house, and I placed a sealed bid to buy it this morning. I was told that the bids would be unsealed at noon," Hattie said.

"Back there. In the conference room." He pointed to a door at the far end of the hall.

As Hattie started down the hall she noticed that both the people who'd been standing in the lobby were following her. One was a powerfully built man, late-thirties, she guessed, with blond, slicked-back hair and a thick mustache. He wore jeans and a light blue, rumpled oxford-cloth dress shirt, and he walked with a slight limp. The other man was much older, dressed in the same kind of work clothes Hattie wore on the job, a faded T-shirt, tan Carhartts, and steel-toed work boots.

Today, though, Hattie was dressed in black capris, and a black-and-white-striped blouse. She was even wearing lipstick. She wanted to make a good impression, as if to show city officials that she would be a good caretaker of that crumbling house a few blocks away.

The younger guy hurried past her, reached the door to the conference room, and went inside. Hattie pushed through the door and the older man followed suit.

A woman in her fifties sat in a padded swivel chair, with a pile of envelopes and a clipboard on the conference table in front of her. Were all of those bids on the Creedmore house? Hattie's heart sank.

"Sit anywhere," the woman said, without looking up from a file folder she was leafing through. Hattie chose a chair at the end of the right side of the table. The blond man was seated directly across from her, and the other stranger sat closer to the clerk.

"Okay," the woman said, glancing down at her phone. "I'm Carol Branch. It's noon, and I'm going to go ahead and unseal these bids." She nodded at the three people in the room. "I'm assuming all of you are here because you've placed bids?"

"That's right," the blond said.

"Yeah," the older man responded.

The clerk took a letter opener and slowly slit a manila mailing envelope, removed a piece of paper, nodded, wrote something on her clipboard, and reached for the next bid.

By the time the clerk was done, Hattie counted eight bids. The clerk's expression never changed. When she'd opened the last envelope, she took her pencil and ran it down the list on her clipboard.

The waiting was agony. The blond man drummed his fingertips on the tabletop until Hattie thought she'd lose her mind. The older man stared up at the ceiling, seemingly fascinated with the beauty and symmetry of acoustic tile.

Hattie's phone buzzed with an incoming text from Cass.
Any news?

Hattie quickly silenced the phone, just as another text from Mo Lopez arrived.
Did you get the house? Call me ASAP

Finally, the clerk nodded and looked up, acknowledging the three strangers in the room with a curt nod.

"Is one of you Harriet Kavanaugh?"

Hattie's heart thudded. "That's me."

"Congratulations. You're the high bidder and the owner of the property at lot twelve, subdivision thirty-six, otherwise known as fifteen twenty-three Chatham Avenue."

"Shit!" The blond man pounded the tabletop with the flat of his hand. "How much was the winning bid?"

The clerk pursed her lips and looked down at her clipboard.

"Come on, man! It's a matter of public record."

"Twenty-nine thousand, seven hundred twenty-eight dollars," the clerk said. "All the pertinent information will be posted on the city's website."

She stood up. "Miss Kavanaugh? If you'll come to my office, we'll start the paperwork on your closing documents." She gave the two men a curt, dismissive nod.

"Something ain't right here," the blond exclaimed loudly, shoving his chair away from the table. "This thing was rigged. She can't buy my family's house out from under me like that."

"Sir?"

"Holland Creedmore," the man said. He took a menacing step toward the clerk, who stood her ground. "The city has no business selling off my family's property like this. It's not right, and you know it."

Hattie had been trying to figure out why this man looked so familiar. Now she had her answer. Back in the day, Holland Creedmore Jr. had been the pride of Cardinal Mooney. He was Mr. Everything, Mr. All-State football this, baseball that. His handsome, square-jawed face was splashed across the sports page of the Savannah newspaper on a weekly basis.

He was jowlier now, the blond hair receding from his wide forehead, and the muscled physique of his youth seemed to have softened.

The clerk's voice was calm. "Mr. Creedmore? All legal procedures were strictly followed. The property owners were notified when the condemnation action was initiated, and given the required amount of time to mitigate the deteriorating condition of that property, which had become a public nuisance."

"Bullshit! You people sent some kind of mumbo jumbo letter to my senile cousin who thought it was an overdue light bill."

"The owners of record were informed, by registered letter, at each step of this process, and the city posted the condemnation proceedings in the county's legal organ, which is the *Savannah Morning News*."

"Nobody reads that rag!" Holland Creedmore shouted. "How the hell was the rest of my family supposed to know what was going on in this fuckin' banana republic you people are running out here?"

The clerk remained unruffled. "The condemnation signs were posted, as required by law, on your family's property a year ago. If, at any point, any member of your family had initiated any kind of maintenance of that property, or paid the property taxes, the city would have halted the condemnation process."

"My crazy cousin had the locks changed," Holland said. "She and my father had some kind of feud. They haven't spoken in years."

"Unfortunate as that is, it doesn't change the property owners' responsibilities or their tax liabilities," the clerk said. "I'm sorry, Mr. Creedmore, but the matter is out of my hands."

Holland Creedmore cursed under his breath and stormed from the room. For the first time, Hattie noticed that the older man seemed to have already slipped away.

"If you'll follow me, we'll get this paperwork started," the clerk told Hattie.

She signed forms and documents for what seemed like hours, but in real time only amounted to forty minutes. Each time she signed a document, the clerk stamped it with her heavy metal notary seal.

When it was over, the clerk slipped copies of the documents into a gray plastic envelope and handed it over to Hattie.

"Well, congratulations."

"Thank you," Hattie said, clutching the envelope to her chest.

"And you realize that, starting today, the clock is ticking on this transaction. Correct? The conditions of this federal grant are very specific. You have twelve months to complete the restoration of your property. I've given you the historic preservation guidelines your project will be required to meet. You'll have to submit plans for your restoration within a week, before your building permit can be issued, and of course, after that, call for inspections at every phase of construction. The city's code enforcement officer will be monitoring your progress."

"I understand," Hattie said.

The clerk handed her a key. "Good luck."

Hattie climbed into the driver's seat of the truck, her heart beating wildly.

What the hell did I just do? Did I really hock my engagement ring to buy a condemned house I've never stepped foot inside of? Did I actually just sign my life away in there, and promise to basically rebuild something without the slightest idea of how I'll do that? Where the hell am I going to get the money?

Her phone vibrated, and she realized she'd forgotten to switch off the silent mode.

"Oh my God, Cass," she said after picking up. "We got it. I was high bidder. I just bought a beach house for less than thirty thousand dollars!"

Cass was silent for a moment. "Jesus, take the wheel."

Hattie unfastened the flap of the envelope holding the closing documents. "I know. You can't believe all the paperwork I just signed. I had no idea there'd be this much red tape."

There was a polite tap on the passenger side window. Holland Creedmore Jr. crossed around to the driver's side window, with an apologetic smile.

"Hey? Can I talk to you for a minute?"

"Call you back in a minute, Cass," Hattie said. She ended the call.

"Hi," she said, hesitantly. "What's up?"

"Look, I realize I was, uh, kind of a horse's ass in there and I just wanted to apologize."

"That's okay."

He wrinkled his ruddy forehead as he studied her. "Hey, uh, I went to high school with a guy named Hank Kavanaugh. Any relation?"

"He was my husband."

"Oh. Well, shit. I think we played Little League together. Wow. That was a damn shame. About the accident, I mean. Sorry."

"Thanks." Hattie started the truck. "Nice to meet you."

"Hang on," he said, keeping his hand on the door. "The thing is, that house never should have been sold. It was all a big mistake. Creedmores have owned it, like, forever."

"But your family didn't pay the taxes," Hattie pointed out. "The lot is like a jungle. You can't even see the house from the street. And the house is falling down. Like the clerk said, your family had a year to do something about it."

"Yeah, well, you don't know my family. It's complicated. Because my granddad, when he died, left the house to my dad and his two cousins, one of which I've never even met. From the time I was a little kid, while my grandparents were alive, my whole family, all the cousins and aunts and uncles, we used to spend every summer at the Tybee house. But Mavis and my dad never got along, and she super hated my mom. There was a big fight about the house, because she was too cheap to spend the money to keep things up. Like, wouldn't even allow us to put central air in the place, after my dad offered to pay for it. Then, after Hurricane Irma hit, and the roof got blown off, it turns out she hadn't kept up the insurance. It was gonna cost, like, forty thousand to put a new roof on the place. The up-north cousin refused to pony up for it, and Mavis and my dad got into a huge fight. That's when she changed the locks, and that's when the house went to shit."

Hattie was at a loss for words. "Sorry, but that's not my

problem. If your family wanted to save the house, they could have. But you didn't. You could have bid more money to buy it, but you didn't."

She put the truck in reverse, but Holland Creedmore didn't move. His big, meaty hands were clamped on the truck's window. "You're right," he said. "Absolutely right. Look, I'm willing to buy the house back. Right now." He dug into the back pocket of his jeans and brought out a checkbook. "Okay? Say, forty thousand? That's a sweet ten-thousand-dollar profit right there."

"No, thanks," Hattie said. "I bought the house fair and square and I plan to restore it. Gotta go now." She began to slowly back out of the parking space. He loosened his grip on the door, but kept walking right beside her.

"Okay, fifty thousand. I'll write you a check right here."

"Not interested," Hattie repeated. She pulled onto Butler Avenue. When she looked in the rearview mirror, Creedmore was standing in the middle of the street, shouting at her. She sped away.

14

Buyer Beware

- - - - - - -

Shortly after noon on Thursday, Mo Lopez's phone dinged. He looked down at the incoming text photo.

It was a house. A huge, half-dead palm tree obscured the front of the wooden structure. There was definitely a front porch. Two stories, with the remnants of a screened porch on the second floor. Boarded-up windows and doors and a sign that read NO TRESPASSING, THIS PROPERTY CONDEMNED.

The message was from Hattie Kavanaugh.

Is this enough of a fixer-upper for you? Hope so because I just bought it.

His fingers raced across the keyboard.

Awesome. It'll be the ultimate BEFORE. Where is it? Are you there now? Don't touch a thing. Have you been inside? Send me the address.

Fifteen minutes later he was on the road to Tybee Island.

Hattie and Cass sat in the truck's cab, parked in the sandy driveway. The bed of the pickup was piled with tools. Tug's truck was parked on the weedy shoulder of the road.

He'd been appalled when Hattie called to tell him what she'd done.

"A condemned house? Are you out of your ever-loving mind? Sight unseen?"

"It was the only house I could afford," Hattie told him. "Please don't be mad at me, Dad. I know we can turn this into something. Think about it—a hundred-year-old house on the Back River. How many original houses are there on that stretch of Chatham Avenue? Think of the sunset views. Of porches, looking out on Little Tybee? It's gonna be magical, I swear."

"Think of the sunsets?" Tug retorted, with a snort of disbelief. "Think of the termites. The rot, the decay. The bad wiring, crappy plumbing. I bet it doesn't even have heat, let alone air-conditioning. Mother of God, Hattie! Think of the money it'll cost. Thirty thousand's no bargain if we have to sink another five hundred thousand just to bring it up to code. And no bank's gonna touch a project like this. Not with a ten-foot pole. Not with a twenty-foot pole."

Hattie had anticipated his reaction.

"Mo says the network's advertisers will give us product in return for on-air plugs. So, like, we'll get all the HVAC equipment donated by the manufacturers. Same with the kitchen cabinets and appliances, the hardwood flooring, and the insulation. And the paint and the roofing material . . ."

"And our subs? You think they're gonna work for free too?"

"I think they'll at least cut us a break because it'll be great advertising for them. And Mo says the network will kick in some money for labor and materials. . . ."

"Some? Do you really believe this television guy is gonna live up to all his promises?"

"I have to," Hattie said softly. "Are you coming out here to see the house, or no?"

"I don't like it, but I will," the old man said.

Hattie changed clothes in the truck, slithering out of her dressy pants and into a pair of jeans. She pulled a long-sleeved T-shirt over her head and laced up her work boots.

Cass, with a sullen expression on her face, had already fired up the chain saw and was savagely attacking a fallen scrub pine whose branches were blocking the driveway. Hattie donned her work gloves and began hauling the cut branches out of the way, while Tug whacked at the encroaching undergrowth with a sling blade and a pair of loppers.

Mo spotted the teetering mountain of limbs and branches from half a block away. He pulled onto the shoulder and parked behind the Kavanaugh & Son trucks. Hattie and Cass were in the process of dragging a huge oak limb down the driveway toward the street.

He jumped from the car, grabbed his camera, and pointed. "Stop right there," he called to the two women, aiming the camera at them.

"Hell no!" Cass yelled. "You can't take my picture looking like this. Sweaty and nasty with leaves and shit hanging outta my hair?"

"You're supposed to look like that," Mo replied. He pointed the camera at Hattie, whose sweaty T-shirt clung to her body. She'd jammed a baseball cap over her hair, and her forearms were dirty and crisscrossed with small cuts and scrapes.

"Look into the camera and tell me what you're doing," he coached.

"I'm trying to clear this driveway. Right now it's impassable," Hattie said.

"Keep telling me what you're doing and why. We'll use this for social media. Give people a sneak peek at what they'll be seeing once *Homewreckers* goes on air."

She rolled her eyes.

"Just say something like, 'Hi, I'm Hattie Kavanaugh and I'm a homewrecker. Wait until you see the house at the end of this driveway we're clearing. I can't wait to get started.'"

"I hate that name," Hattie said. "It makes me sound like I'm trying to steal some other woman's husband. Makes me sound slutty."

"Get over it," Mo said. He looked over at Tug, who'd been watching this interchange and shaking his head. "Come on, Mr. Kavanaugh, you get in there too. Okay?"

"Who, me? You don't want a fat old geezer like me in your pictures. Take a picture of these beautiful young ladies right here."

"It's a reality show, Mr. Kavanaugh," Mo said. "If you'll just sort of move in between Cass and Hattie, act like you're helping them move that tree limb, that'd be great."

"If it's reality, why do you want us to act?" Hattie grumbled, as she shifted positions to allow Tug to shoulder part of the weight of the limb.

They stood in a small semicircle, facing the Creedmore house.

"Jesus, Mary, and Fred," Tug exclaimed, wiping his sweaty brow with a handkerchief. "Hattie, what have you gotten us into?"

But his daughter-in-law wasn't listening. She was unloading tools from the bed of the truck, and now advancing on the porch and the boarded-up front door with a crowbar, while Mo trained his camera on her.

"Don't actually do anything," Mo called. "I want to save the drama for when our crew gets here."

"I'm not waiting for a camera crew to get into this house," Hattie said.

"We could go around the porch to the kitchen door," Cass suggested. "Did they give you anything like a key at city hall?"

Hattie brandished the crowbar. "This is all the key I need. Watch out for these rotten floorboards," she called, as the group trailed along the side of the house.

They clustered around her as she examined the back door. The wood was rotted and swollen from the damp. Hattie gave the door a kick, and the bottom panel splintered in half. Another kick and what was left of the door swung open with a creak from the rusty hinges.

"Gonna need a new door," Cass said.

"This is gonna be awesome," Mo said, following Hattie inside.

He'd meant to film the kitchen, but he was drawn to Hattie's expression, her face alive with authentic excitement, her energy a palpable presence.

"Awesome, my ass," Tug muttered.

Hattie wasn't listening. She felt the familiar rush that came from starting a new project, the mixture of anticipation and dread and excitement. Hank always said she was an adrenaline junkie, and he wasn't wrong.

He'd known her better than anybody, better than she knew herself. Hank had always been the quiet one, the planner, the plotter. And Hattie? She was always ready to kick in the door of a new project and plunge in headfirst. As much as she loved starting a new job like this one, she was reminded that she was starting another project without him. It had been almost seven years, and the missing him was still there.

Now, it wasn't the knife-sharp anguish she'd felt that first year, the despair of waking up without him in bed beside her, or fixing a sandwich for one instead of two, or pushing his clothes aside in the tiny bedroom closet to get to her own.

The pain wasn't like that now. It was more like a dull ache, like the pain of a scar that never quite healed. She would never stop missing Thomas Henry Kavanaugh, but in the meantime, this old house needed her.

"It looks like the Creedmores just walked away one day, locked the doors, and never came back," Cass said, pointing at the kitchen cabinets. "They even left dirty dishes in the sink."

It was true. The sink was full of grease-clotted dishes covered with a thin film of cobwebs.

"Do you know the family that owned this house?" Mo asked.

"Savannah's a small town, son," Tug said. "Almost everybody knows everybody else."

"The matriarch of the family, Mavis Creedmore, goes to church with my mom," Cass explained. "That's how we found out the house might be up for sale."

Hattie picked up the narrative. "Holland Creedmore was a couple years ahead of us at Cardinal Mooney, that's the boys' Catholic prep school here. He was a big deal back in the day."

"More like a big dickhead," Cass muttered.

"You're talking about Creedmore Junior. His dad, Big Holl, was in my class," Tug said.

"Holland Junior was at Tybee City Hall today," Hattie said. "He was totally pissed when he found out I'd outbid him. Yelled at the city clerk and threatened to sue. Then he actually followed me out to the truck. He offered to buy the house from me for fifty thousand."

"You should have taken the money and run with it all the way to the bank," Tug said.

"This kitchen's a decent size," Hattie said, ignoring her father-in-law. She pointed at the low ceiling, with its water-logged plaster. "Job one in here is ripping out the dropped ceiling. Let's hope there are some cool old beams behind that crap."

"Let's hope the whole damn thing doesn't fall in on our heads," Tug said.

"Is this a bathroom? In the kitchen?" Cass poked her head into a doorway to the right of the kitchen door, then backed quickly away, both hands pressed to her nose. "Gaaaah! Mildew city!"

Hattie took a look for herself. The room in question was long, spanning the back of the house, and narrow. Somehow, a washing machine and clothes dryer had been shoved in there, along with a toilet, a sink, and a prefab fiberglass shower stall. The floor was covered with what looked like dark green artificial grass.

"Good news is this bathroom isn't original to the house. Probably added in the seventies, and of course, without being permitted." She turned and gestured to Mo. "Take a photo of all of this. It comes out day one."

They moved toward the front of the house, with Mo snapping photos to document the "before" condition of the house, and Hattie dictating notes into her phone.

"Big living room–dining room combination up here. Great fireplace, but the tile surrounding is all wrong. And we're gonna need a new mantel."

Tug, grunting, knelt on the hearth and shone his flashlight up the chimney. "I don't like the looks of this flue. It's stuffed with old newspapers. And what looks like an old squirrel's nest."

"What's wrong with the flue?" Mo asked.

The old man heaved himself upright. "Too narrow to build a proper fire without burning the joint down, which is why they stuffed the papers up there, to keep out the drafts. We either rip it out, or we leave it alone and just call it decoration. Or spend five thousand dropping a new fire-rated liner in there."

"We can't rip it out," Hattie said. "Part of the terms of the sale was that everything we do here has to meet historic preservation standards."

"Seriously?" Cass shook her head. "That's gonna be a major pain in the ass."

"Save that thought," Mo interjected. "When we do the walk-through with Trae, you can discuss that on-camera. It'll make for great conflict."

"Who's Trae?" Cass asked.

"Oh. Yeah. That's another format change the network wants. As part of the *Homewreckers* concept, they've hired a designer, super talented guy, his name is Trae Bartholomew. He'll be, like, your partner, in the restoration of this house. You'll meet him next week, along with the rest of the crew who'll all be here by then."

"Partner? I don't need a designer partner," Hattie said. "I'm the designer on all our projects."

"Except this one," Mo said firmly.

Hattie stood with her back against the fireplace, arms crossed over her chest. "Nope. I bought this house with my own funds. Nobody said anything to me about a partner, or a designer. So if that's the deal the network wants, I quit. Deal's off."

Mo sighed. "You're aware that you're contractually obligated to do this show, right?"

"So sue me." Hattie's jaw was set, her eyes flashing.

"That could happen," Mo said. "But here's the other thing. If you walk away from this deal, you're also walking away from all the building materials our sponsors were set to donate, plus your salary, plus the money the network budgeted for labor."

"I'll still have this house. And my independence," Hattie shot back.

"Good luck with that," Mo said. He nodded at Cass, and then Tug. "Nice to meet you, folks. Wish things had worked out."

15

A Change of Heart

Tug watched the producer's departure. "That's settled then. You'll call Little Holl and sell him back the house. At a handsome profit. And we'll be done with this television nonsense."

"Right," Cass agreed. "Think about it, Hattie. That's a twenty-thousand-dollar profit. We can find another house, in way better shape."

But Hattie wasn't listening. She'd wandered into the living room and was perched on the arm of a harvest-gold sofa with arms pocked with cigarette burns. The original ceilings in the room were high, with heavy beams. She was picturing the room as it could be, with hardwood floors, curtains at the windows that lifted in the breeze, maybe a card table set up near the windows, with a pair of armchairs drawn up to it for a game of Scrabble, or cards.

She picked up the machete she'd abandoned on the porch and headed toward the backyard. Tug and Cass stood on the back porch, talking quietly. "Hattie?" Tug called.

Hattie picked her way through the underbrush, swinging the machete to clear her way. She smelled the river before she saw it, passing a tumbledown boat shed flanked by the hull of a long-abandoned johnboat. Finally, she spotted the remains of a cracked concrete walkway and followed it until she caught the flash of sunshine on gently lapping waves.

She was surprised by how much waterfront footage the lot commanded, possibly two hundred feet. It was low tide now, and a set of wooden steps led down to an exposed stretch of sandy beach. A dock stretched out into the river, and at the end was a covered dock house. The silvery planks were worn and splintered in places. She wouldn't dare walk out on it until her carpenters had a chance to replace some of the planks.

"Damn." Cass had followed her down to the water's edge and was standing beside her.

Hattie pointed across the river, toward a spit of tree-lined sand. "Great view of Little Tybee, huh?"

"If you like that kind of thing."

A curved dorsal fin and silvery-gray back broke through the surface of the water, and then another, and then a pair of smaller fins.

"Sharks," Cass said hopefully.

"Those are dolphins and you know it," Hattie said. "A whole pod of 'em."

"You're not going to sell this house back to Creedmore, are you?"

"Nope," Hattie said, shaking her head. "This house is special, Cass. I'll do whatever it takes to keep it. Even if it means making a fool of myself on television."

Her best friend let out a long, aggrieved sigh.

"You're just gonna have to trust me on this," Hattie said, reaching for her phone to call Mo Lopez. "We can make it work."

Two days later, Trae Bartholomew sat in the front seat of the producer's car, staring at the scene unfolding in front of him.

Air-conditioned trailers had been trucked in, a tent had been erected for craft services, and rented trucks full of lights and camera equipment were lined up along the rutted oyster-shell driveway. A trio of RVs was parked in the front yard. But it was the house that held his attention.

He looked over at Mo Lopez. "You're kidding me, right? We're going to restore this thing? To what? It was hideous when it was built, and now it's hideous *and* decrepit."

Mo's smile was tight. "Think of the inherent drama of the before and after. Think of the beyond-belief *OMG* moment during the reveal in episode six. Most importantly, Trae, think of a Wednesday night prime-time slot. Didn't *Design Minds* air on Saturday mornings?"

Trae's oversized, mirrored aviators slid down his outsized nose as he reconsidered. "It's a good-sized lot."

"Waterfront lot," Mo added.

"And maybe it's just as well that people haven't been mucking it up with a lot of unfortunate eighties additions." He tilted his head to the right. "Okay, I'm getting some clarity. And I'm dying to meet my costar."

"She's dying to meet you too," Mo lied.

Hattie's "trailer" was really a rented Winnebago. She'd been pacing around for an hour, alternately annoyed and nervous about having to deal with this celebrity designer. She'd Googled Trae Bartholomew, seen the splashy *Architectural Digest* layout on his ski lodge project, and other magazine pieces about his less well-known projects.

Finally, there was a light knock on the trailer door. "Hattie? You decent?"

"Come on in," she called.

Trae Bartholomew filled the doorway. He was taller than

she'd expected, probably six-four. Separately, his features weren't extraordinary. He had toffee-colored hair, startling, deep-set blue eyes, a golden California tan, a long face, and a pronounced, square jaw that was bristling with just a stylish eighth-inch of stubble. But taken together, he was startlingly, head-turningly gorgeous.

He wore white jeans and a silk shirt stretched across a chest so taut and muscled that Hattie instinctively tucked in what little tummy she possessed.

"Hattie!" he exclaimed, stepping forward and taking her hand in both of his. "At last!"

"At last," she murmured. "So nice to meet you."

"I can't wait to see this house of yours," Trae said. "Mo's been telling me all about the potential."

"It's got potential, all right," Hattie agreed. "Along with lots and lots of problems."

Trae rubbed the palms of his hands together. "Let's go."

He stood in front of the house, studying it. "Kind of a weird little place, isn't it? I mean, is it even two thousand square feet? I find it odd that it takes up so little room on what's obviously a very large, waterfront lot. The first thing I'm seeing is wings, jutting out from either side of this porch, maybe with some board and batten siding. Then, on the second floor, we'll do some dormers. . . ."

"No." Hattie shook her head. "Absolutely not."

"But it's so dinky and stunted. So . . . insignificant," Trae protested. "It's crying out for some kind of grand gesture." He whipped a pen and a rolled-up sketchbook from the back pocket of his jeans and began drawing.

"Did Mo mention that we're on an incredibly tight budget?" Hattie asked, an edge creeping into her voice.

"Yes, but . . ."

"Grand gestures cost grands. Hundreds of grands, and we

don't have that kind of money. Plus, we're operating under strict historic preservation guidelines. We can't expand the house's footprint. At all."

"We've only got six weeks to shoot," Mo added.

"Guidelines," Trae said dismissively. "They're just that. A guide. I've never met a set of regulations that I couldn't ease around."

"Code enforcement officers are gonna be watching us like hawks," Hattie said, bristling. "If they catch us 'easing around' their regs, they could shut us down."

"*If* they catch us," Trae said.

She led him through the house, trying not to take his criticisms personally.

"Well," he said, standing in the living room, "at least the proportions in here are workable."

He stuck his head in the doorway of the downstairs bedroom. "A king-size bed won't fit in here. And what's with that toy sink in the corner?"

"This is typical vernacular beach cottage architecture of the twenties, when the house was built. The sink's there because there's only one bathroom, so folks could brush their teeth and wash up before bed," Hattie told him.

Trae looked stunned. "You're telling me there's no en suite bath for the master bedroom?"

"That's right." Hattie walked into the room and pulled open a narrow closet door. "This room backs up to a sort of mudroom on the back porch. But I was thinking, we could steal some square footage from that, and do with this closet. The bathroom on the second floor is directly above here, so there's that. We squeeze in a shower stall, commode, and sink, and voila, that gives us a master suite."

"No closet?"

"It's a beach house," Hattie told him. "We'll put a row of

pegs on the wall. And if absolutely necessary, I bet we can find an antique armoire to fit between those two windows."

"I guess that could work," Trae said. "Let's see the other bathroom."

Mo and Hattie exchanged a meaningful glance that didn't escape notice from the designer. "What?"

"It's uh . . . pretty bad," Hattie said. "Don't say we didn't warn you."

Trae backed slowly away from the bathroom, squarely bumping into one of the kitchen counters. "Who puts a bathroom in a kitchen?" he sputtered. "And then decides, 'hey, let's put the washer and dryer in there too.'"

"Don't worry, it's all going away," Hattie assured him. "We'll move it to a new laundry room on the back porch and bump the kitchen into this space."

Mo sensed Hattie's growing impatience. "Any thoughts about the kitchen, Trae? We've got an advertiser that's a cabinet manufacturer. They'll supply all the cabinetry as a trade-off, and we'll get the appliances from Build-All. They're a big chain of building suppliers in the Southeast. So we've got a little room in the budget in here."

"Offhand?" Trae flicked a bit of plaster from the yellow Formica countertop. "A stick of dynamite and a match is the only thing that can help."

"That's it," Hattie huffed. "Mo, you can show him the rest of the house. You two don't need me."

She was picking at a salad in the craft services tent when one of the carpenters appeared at her side. "Hey, Hattie, there's a guy here from the city who wants to see you."

"What about?"

Joey, the carpenter, pointed toward the front of the house. "I think he's a code cop."

"Shit."

She hurried out of the tent. Sure enough, an older white man was pacing back and forth in front of the front porch, a clipboard tucked under one arm, visibly agitated.

"Hi," she said. "I'm Hattie, the owner of this property. Is there some kind of issue?"

"Howard Rice, Tybee Island code enforcement." He tapped the badge pinned to the front of his starched uniform shirt. He had one of those tiny Charlie Chaplin mustaches. "Yes, there's a problem. Who's responsible for cutting down all those old-growth trees out here?"

"Old growth? They were palmettos and scrub pines and a couple of scrawny magnolias and half-dead crape myrtles."

"No. I saw for myself. I saw the photos before you people hauled away the evidence, plus you left the stumps. There were at least three protected tree species that you people cut down. In clear violation of the city's tree ordinance."

"We didn't haul away any 'evidence,'" Hattie protested. "We didn't even know the city had a tree ordinance. The whole driveway was blocked with a bunch of trash trees. We had to cut our way through just to reach the house."

"Ignorance is no excuse," he said, shaking a finger in her face. "The city's tree ordinance is posted on the Tybee Island website. I suggest you familiarize yourself with it, before I issue you another citation."

He ripped a piece of paper from the clipboard and thrust it at her. "That's a thousand-dollar fine. Payable by cash, cashier's check, or credit card at city hall."

"What!" Hattie stared down at the citation. "That's insane. You people condemned the property because neighbors complained that it was overgrown. Now you wanna penalize me for cutting down the overgrowth?"

"Those were mature trees," he repeated. "I saw the photos. I saw the tree stumps and measured them for myself. And you should know, if I find another code violation like this one, I won't hesitate to issue a stop-work order. Television show or no television show."

16

Hammer Time

Hattie stood in front of the downstairs bathroom wall, a sledgehammer resting on her shoulder, waiting for direction from Mo.

"Okay, now look at Trae, offer him the sledgehammer, then take a step back."

"Hold on," Trae protested. The cameraman glanced over at Mo, who motioned for him to stop filming.

"That's the dumbest thing I've ever heard," Trae said. "I'm a designer, not a construction worker. Nobody's going to believe I'd ever actually wield a sledgehammer."

"Then make a joke about that," Mo said sharply. "It's called banter, for God's sake. Deliver the line, hit the wall, and let's move on." He looked at his watch. "We've only got another hour of daylight, and I need that wall down so Hattie's people can get started with the insulation and wallboard."

"The point is, me pretending to use a sledgehammer makes me look ludicrous," Trae said. "And I'm tired of being the punch line to your lame jokes." He yanked off the Kavanaugh & Son hardhat he'd been wearing and threw it aside, nearly hitting the gaffer with it. "Screw it. I'm done for today." He stalked out of the kitchen, scattering the small knot of crew members who'd been standing around, waiting for the actual action to begin.

Hattie rolled her eyes. "Hey, Mo? This sledgehammer ain't getting any lighter here."

Mo turned back to her. "Go ahead and give it a whack. Pretend it's Trae's skull." He pointed at the cameraman. "Okay, let's roll."

Hattie swung the sledgehammer, slamming it into the wall with all the pent-up frustration of a day spent sitting around waiting for something to happen, sending plaster and lathe flying.

She glanced at Mo, who silently signaled her to repeat. She did, relishing the sound of splintering wood.

When she finally lowered the sledgehammer, she'd managed to take out a roughly four-foot-square patch of wall. With her gloved hands, she pried away more of the lathe.

"Oh crap," she muttered, poking a finger in one of the exposed wall studs. The wood crumbled into dust, like stale cake. "This isn't good." She pulled away more of the plaster and lathe and pointed. "Termites."

Mo motioned for the cameraman to zoom in for a closer shot.

"Now explain why this is such bad news," he told Hattie.

She pulled a screwdriver from her toolbelt and stuck it into the damaged stud. "This two-by-four is like Swiss cheese. There's a high probability that the rest of the studs are in the same condition." She pointed toward the point where the wall met the ceiling line. "See how it sags like that? I was hoping maybe this was just a matter of an old house settling, but that was me being optimistic. We'll have to reframe this whole exterior wall. And because it's termite damage, we'll have to tear up at least part of the floor here, because it could mean that we have foundation issues, too."

She glanced over at Mo, who was signaling for her to finish her explanation.

Hattie's shoulders sagged as she looked directly into the camera.

"We run into these kinds of problems all the time on the coast here in Georgia. Heat and humidity are like a playground for termites. In an old house like this one, that hasn't been lived in or maintained in years, once your structural integrity has been compromised, you're screwed." She made a sweeping gesture at the wall behind her. "Let's just hope the ceiling joists are still intact. Because if not . . ." Her voice trailed off.

Mo signaled for her to continue.

"We didn't have the luxury of inspecting this old house before we bought it. The place had been condemned. So we're kind of flying blind here. We might have foundation issues. We might have a problem with the ceiling beams. Our budget for the project, all in, is $150,000, but if we have to pour a new foundation and reframe this whole back wall, as well as the ceiling, that could put us tens of thousands of dollars in the hole. And we won't really know the extent of any of that until we tear down these walls and get a peek at what's behind them."

She picked up the sledgehammer and slammed it into the wall again. "Hammer time."

"Hey, Hattie, take a look at this." Cass held out a small blue billfold. The leather was faded and stiffened with age.

Hattie was sitting on the back porch, sipping from a bottle of cold water, while the camera crew was repositioning to shoot the next sequence. Mo sat nearby, reading his email.

Hattie took the wallet and turned it over. "Where'd you find this?"

"Donnie, one of the carpenters, found it in the bathroom wall," Cass said, pointing toward the back wall, which was now completely open to the back porch. "Beneath that big razor blade slot, on top of, like, hundreds of old rusty razor blades."

Mo looked up. "Razor blade slot?"

"You find them all the time in old houses," Hattie explained. "Usually in the back of those old-timey metal medicine cabinets that were recessed into bathroom walls. I noticed the slot in there was unusually large, but I really didn't think much about it."

"I wonder how the hell a wallet got stuck in that slot," Cass said. "Let's see if there's anything in there."

Hattie opened the billfold. "Well, we're not gonna get rich off this thing." She pulled out three faded one-dollar bills and two fives, along with two tiny plastic-encased woolen squares attached by a narrow green ribbon. Inside each of the plastic squares was the image of the Virgin Mary, with an image of a heart in flames on the reverse.

"Is that a scapular?" Cass asked, leaning closer to examine it.

"You lost me," Mo said. "What's a scapular?"

"It's like a religious icon," Cass said. "Catholics have different ones for different things. You get them blessed by a priest and then they're supposed to protect you from evil, I guess. I got one when I was confirmed. Zenobia has one like this that my grandmother gave her when she had me, in her billfold. It's pretty old-school. What else is in there, Hattie? Is there any ID?"

Hattie plucked a driver's license from one of the billfold's credit card slots.

"Holy shit," she whispered. Wordlessly she handed the license to Cass.

"Oh my God," Cass murmured. "Lanier Ragan. That's gotta be our Lanier Ragan, right?"

"Look at the photo," Hattie said. "That's absolutely her."

The two women stared at each other, and then down at the driver's license.

"I guess that scapular didn't work so good for Mrs. Ragan," Cass said. "'Cause if we found that wallet in the bathroom wall out here, something evil definitely happened to her."

"I never believed she'd just up and leave her little girl like that," Hattie said.

Hattie was still going through the billfold. She plucked out a small photo, a picture-perfect studio portrait; the vivacious young mother, the tall, broad-shouldered husband, beaming down at his wife, one hand resting lightly on her shoulder, the other resting on the shoulder of a little girl, maybe three or four years old, a blonder version of her mother, dressed in an identical white blouse and red plaid jumper.

"Look at this," she said, showing Cass the portrait. "Is this the saddest thing ever?"

"Slow down," Mo said. "Who is this woman? What are we talking about here?"

"Lanier Ragan. She was an English teacher at our high school, St. Mary's. Everyone loved her. We all wanted to be her, you know? And one night, she just disappeared," Hattie said.

Mo's eyes widened. "Tell me more."

Cass was looking down at the family portrait. "It happened when, junior year?"

Hattie snapped her fingers. "Sophomore year. I remember it was wintertime. We had a candlelight vigil for her, out in the school courtyard, and it was so cold I thought I'd freeze to death."

Mo grabbed his laptop and opened his search engine. "Tell me the woman's name again? And the year she supposedly disappeared?"

"Lanier Ragan." Hattie spelled out the last name. "Not supposedly. She did. Disappear. I guess that would be winter of 2005."

Mo's fingers flew across the keyboard. He pulled up a story from the *Savannah Morning News,* datelined February 9, 2005.

BELOVED LOCAL TEACHER
BELIEVED MISSING

"Here it is." He read the first paragraph of the story aloud.

"'Savannah police are searching for Lanier Pelham Ragan, a popular St. Mary's Academy English teacher, 25, who disappeared the night of February sixth.'"

Cass sighed. "She was only twenty-five back then?"

Mo continued reading.

"'Mrs. Ragan, a petite blonde and the mother of a young child, was last seen by her husband around midnight Sunday.

"'Frank Ragan, the missing woman's husband, said he and his wife attended a neighborhood Super Bowl party on Sunday night, and walked back to their home together at around 11:30 that night. Ragan, who is the head football coach at Cardinal Mooney Catholic prep, told authorities that after the couple's babysitter drove away from their home, he went immediately to bed, but his wife stayed up to clean the kitchen and fold laundry.

"'When he awoke at six o'clock Monday morning, he found his wife missing. Their three-year-old daughter was still asleep. Lanier Ragan's car, a white Nissan, was not in the home's driveway. Ragan said he called his wife repeatedly, but all phone calls went immediately to voicemail. After searching his home, and calling neighbors, friends, and coworkers to ask if they'd seen his wife, he asked a neighbor to look after his child while he drove all the streets in the vicinity, trying, unsuccessfully, to spot the Nissan, or his wife.

"'Savannah police spokesman Carey Filocchio said Ragan called authorities around 12:30 P.M. Monday to report his wife missing.

"'We are asking the public to assist in the search to return this beloved wife and mother home to her family,' Filocchio said. 'The subject is five-foot-two, weighs 92 pounds, and has dark blond hair and blue eyes. Last seen wearing jeans and a New England Patriots football jersey and white Nike tennis shoes. Her vehicle, a 2001 silver Nissan Altima, Georgia license plate PCH-678-3420, has a dent in the right rear bumper and a St. Mary's Academy faculty parking sticker affixed to the front windshield.'

"'Filocchio declined to say whether police believe foul play could be involved in the disappearance.

"'Frank Ragan was not available for comment.

"'According to a close family friend, Lanier Ragan moved to Savannah three years ago, from Fairhope, Alabama. A graduate of the University of Mississippi, she met her future husband in college, where he was an athletic trainer. The two married in 2001.

"'This is not the Lanier I know,' her friend said. 'She would never just up and leave her husband and little girl at home. She just wouldn't. We are all praying for her safe return.'"

Mo thought for a moment. "So. This Lanier woman was never found?"

"No," Cass said. "At the time there were all kinds of

rumors floating around. Hattie, her little girl would be about eighteen or nineteen now. Do you remember her name?"

"Her name was Emma," Hattie said promptly. "Mrs. Ragan was a total Jane Austen freak. She made us all watch the movie, and then she brought in her DVD of *Clueless*. Remember, Cass? Mrs. Ragan made everything so much fun."

Mo smacked his forehead with the palm of his hand. "Okay, hold that thought. Cass, go put the billfold back where it was found. I'll get the cameras set up again, and we'll reenact. You'll pull out the billfold, Hattie, you'll look at it—and be just as shocked that it belongs to the mysteriously disappeared Lanier Ragan. Tell that story all over again—you and Cass talking about how nice she was, all of that."

"Shouldn't we call the police or something?" Cass asked.

"Because we found an old wallet? It might not mean anything," Mo said. "She disappeared, what? More than seventeen years ago?"

"Or it could mean a lot, especially to her family," Hattie said. "We can film the segment in the kitchen, Mo, but as soon as it's done, I'm calling the cops. I own this house. There has to be a reason we found that billfold in the wall. It's my responsibility to find out what it means."

"Great," Mo muttered, walking away. "Call the cops. They'll probably shut down my set, which will mean complications and delays. Just what I need right now."

17

Too Many Cooks

"Can I see that?" Trae asked. He'd been standing on the sidelines, watching with a bemused expression as Hattie and Cass reenacted the discovery of the billfold in the wall for the cameras. Filming had halted so the lighting could be readjusted.

Hattie hesitated. "It just occurred to me—this might be evidence from a crime scene. The police might want to fingerprint it or something." She was still holding it, but had donned a work glove on her right hand.

"Amazing to think that thing has been hidden in that wall for, how long?" Trae asked.

"She disappeared in 2005. It's probably been in there at least since then," Hattie said.

"Maybe she's been here since then too," Trae said, lowering his voice. He looked around the now gutted kitchen. "What if we literally found her skeleton in a closet? Mwu-hahahahaha!"

Hattie looked away and grimaced. "Please don't make a joke about this, Trae. Lanier Ragan was a great teacher. She was somebody's wife. A mom."

Trae shrugged. "Just trying to lighten things up around here. I didn't know I'd touched a nerve."

"Well, you did," Cass shot back. She'd taken an instant dislike to the California designer.

"Folks?" Mo walked up with a very tall, very bald Black woman. "Want you to meet your showrunner. Taleetha Carr. She's the best in the business. Leetha, meet our homewreckers, Hattie Kavanaugh and Trae Bartholomew." He nodded at Cass. "And this is Cass Pelletier, Hattie's wingwoman and site foreman."

Taleetha wore shredded jeans and an oversized Lakers jersey. She shook hands all around, and Hattie noticed, when she shook hers, that the showrunner had a distinctive tattoo of a coiled snake on her right forearm. She felt instantly intimidated. For about thirty seconds.

"Hi, y'all," Leetha said, "Momo here has been sending me the video to keep me up to speed on your progress. Sorry it took me so long to get out here from L.A. But I'm here now, so we gonna churn and burn and get this mutha fixed up. Am I right?"

She nudged her star. "Hattie Mae, okay if I call you that?" Leetha didn't wait for a response. "I like this place. I mean, right now, it's a dump, but that's where we come in."

Leetha turned in a slow circle, taking in the deconstructed kitchen. "Wow. This is some shitshow, huh? Heard y'all had some drama today."

"But seriously, it's better to know now, right? If we have structural issues," Trae said. "Wait until you see what I've designed for this kitchen. It's going to be fabulous."

Leetha's laugh was loud and raspy. "No, Ashtray, I'm not talking about the termites. I'm talking about the wallet in the wall."

Trae's face darkened. "Please don't call me that."

She gave him a playful poke in the arm. "Aww, now don't go getting your feelings hurt, TraeTrae. I got nicknames for everybody. Like Mo here? He's Momo."

Leetha studied Cass for a moment. "Hmm. I think you're gonna be Cash. As in Cash Money, because you look like the lady who watches the bottom line around here."

Cass laughed. "Am I that obvious?"

"All right," Leetha said, clapping her hands. "Let's get rolling." She pointed at Trae. "I need you to unroll your plans on that table over there, describe the drawings to Hattie Mae, then walk around the kitchen and demonstrate where everything is going to go."

"Ready when you are," Trae said.

"Just let me blot out the shine on their foreheads, and give Trae's hair a spritz," said Lisa, the hair and makeup girl, darting in from the other side of the room with a crossbody bag and a toolbelt that contained, instead of hammers and screwdrivers, hairbrushes, combs, lipsticks, and blushers.

"Don't make 'em too pretty," Leetha cautioned. "We're trying to keep it real. And speaking of real, y'all don't need to be so polite. Hattie, I know you're a nice southern girl and all, but try to push back when Trae here gets out of line. Gimme some drama, y'all!"

Trae walked around the gutted kitchen with Hattie at his side. "Right here," he said, pointing at the back wall, "we'll put a bank of lower cabinets with a double sink under a custom casement window looking out at the water."

"I love that idea," Hattie said. "Whoever's doing the dinner dishes here will have the best view in the house."

Her thoughts strayed to the paragraph she'd read in the newspaper story, about how, on the night of her disappearance, Lanier Ragan had stayed up late to clean up the kitchen after her husband had gone off to bed. Had she looked out her own kitchen window that night? If so, what did she see?

Was there danger lurking out there in the darkness? Or had Mrs. Ragan—their funny, smart English teacher—been plotting her own disappearance?

"Hattie?" Trae was looking at her, waiting for her to deliver her next line, which they'd already discussed.

"Right," Hattie said, snapping back to attention. "A custom window? Why don't we use stock windows framed out to fit? It'd be much cheaper."

Trae's upper lip curled. "It'll look cheaper, that's for sure. No, I've already priced out a custom window for the space. And the manufacturer is going to give us a great deal on it."

"I guess." Hattie looked dubious. "What kind of countertops were you thinking? Our budget already took a major hit with all the termite damage in here."

"Granite," Trae said promptly. "I picked out a beautiful piece at a boneyard here in Savannah." He showed her a sample. "Isn't this gorgeous? It reminds me of the interior of a conch shell. I think I'll have it done in a slightly matte finish. It'll be stunning."

Hattie shook her head. "Pink granite? Are you serious? This isn't Versailles, Trae. It's a simple, period beach house, at Tybee Island. Anyway, we can't afford granite."

"It's definitely not pink," Trae snapped. "This granite will absolutely make this kitchen. With plain, out-of-the-box white cabinets, and not-custom windows, I've got to do something to salvage my design."

"We are *not* doing granite," Hattie said emphatically. She looked over at Cass, who was off-camera.

"Cass—can you explain things to Trae?"

"Gladly." Cass still felt awkward on camera. She didn't know what to do with her hands. But Leetha gave her a gentle push, and now Cass was in the middle of the scene.

"Look, Trae," Cass started. "We can do a nice quartz that

looks like granite for way less money. You said it yourself—
the view out the kitchen window is the real star in here."

"Fine." He walked back to the work table—really just a
sheet of plywood set atop a pair of sawhorses, and pointed to
the plans unrolled there. "Here's the cabinet layout."

Hattie pretended to be fascinated. She'd seen them earlier
in the day, of course. "I really like this butler's pantry," she
said, tapping the drawings. "And I like your idea of painting
these cabinets a contrasting navy."

He held up a miniature cabinet door. "I'm keeping it super simple with the cabinets. Plain, Shaker-style doors and
drawers in white."

"About the island," Hattie said. "I've got an antique haberdashery cabinet that came out of an old store in downtown
Savannah. It'll have room for four barstools like you've
drawn here. Everyone likes a place to sit and hang out in the
kitchen at the beach. And wait 'til you see what I've been
hoarding to hang above it."

She reached into a wooden crate and triumphantly held
up a bulky hanging brass lantern. The chain rattled and
clanked. "These are lanterns that were salvaged from some
old Liberty ships down at the port. I've got a pair of them.
What do you think?"

"They are pretty fabulous," Trae admitted. "And the nautical look is perfect for a beach house. Now, about the tile. I
plan to make a real splash with the backsplash." He chuckled at his own joke.

"How much of a splash?" she asked.

With a dramatic flourish he held up a square of mottled
greenish-teal tile. "Is this the most gorgeous thing you've
ever seen? Hand-blown and imported, and it'll look just like a
piece of sea glass you might find on the beach right outside
the windows here."

Hattie examined the tile, pretending it was her first time

seeing it. "Pretty," she admitted. "But how durable is it? I've used glass tile twice in kitchens in the past, and if something knocks against it, it breaks. Also, what's the cost?"

"Immaterial," he said. "Because it'll be the focal point in here."

"No, no, no. We don't have the budget for that. Trae, I know you're used to doing million-dollar kitchens out in California, but this is Tybee Island. Find something cheaper."

He slapped the tile down onto the table. "Fine. You win. We'll do basic, boring, generic white subway tile—the kind you find in every mediocre kitchen in America."

"What about this?" Hattie said, relenting. "You can use your glass tile as an accent above the range. And for the rest of the space, a good-looking white subway tile. Now, about the floor," she prompted. "Please tell me you weren't planning marble."

"Nope," he said. "There's wood under this old vinyl. I want to paint the floors—in a big diamond pattern. White and sort of a jadeite green, finished with a matte poly."

"Finally a cheap and relatively easy fix," Hattie said approvingly.

"Finally something we can agree on," Trae said, rolling his eyes.

"Cut!" Leetha yelled. She clapped her hands together and checked her watch. "We're losing light. Tomorrow, we need to move into that living-dining room situation. So, Hattie Mae and Cash Money, I need y'all to get all those windows out there unboarded and move all that nasty old furniture and get rid of that carpet. Your call is for eight."

"See you tomorrow," Trae said as he walked off the set.

Hattie and Cass looked at each other. "There must be a dumpster load of furniture out there," Hattie said.

"That oak dining room table probably weighs a ton," Cass

added. "And what about that gross gold shag wall-to-wall carpet? Who's ripping up all that stuff?"

"Have all the guys already gone home?" Hattie asked, walking out to the porch. "Tug? Are you still here?"

There was no answer. The tech crews were busy loading up their equipment. Trae waved as he got in his rental sedan and drove away.

"Looks like it's you and me, sis," Cass said.

"Left with all the heavy lifting. Again. Also, I forgot to tell you. We had a visit from the Tybee code cop earlier. He issued us a ticket for a thousand dollars for cutting down those trees that were blocking the driveway."

"Seriously? How'd he even know? I had the guys haul a lot of that stuff to the dump."

"He said he had photos. I think someone must have narced us out."

"Probably one of the same neighbors who complained to the city about the lot being overgrown," Cass exclaimed. "Why are people so pissy?"

"Don't know." Hattie pulled her cell phone from her pocket.

"You calling College Hunks Hauling Junk?" Cass asked.

"That's a good idea, but no. I'm calling the cops to tell them about finding Lanier Ragan's wallet."

18

Blue Light Special

- - - - - - -

Hattie was on her third trip to the dumpster when she saw the police patrol car rolling slowly down the driveway, blue lights flashing. She tossed the armload of mildewed and water-swollen books into the trash, dusted her hands on the back of her jeans, and waited.

The cop parked next to her truck. He got out and looked slowly around at his surroundings. He was white, in his mid-fifties, nearly bald, with the exception of a fringe of graying hair and a matching neatly trimmed mustache and goatee. He wore the Tybee police uniform, khaki pants and a navy polo shirt with the city logo. A gold badge was clipped to his belt.

"Hi," Hattie said, walking over to him. "I'm Hattie Kavanaugh."

"Al Makarowicz," the cop said, not removing his aviator-style sunglasses. "You the one who called in about finding the wallet?"

"Yes."

"Wanna show it to me?"

"It's inside the house," she said.

He looked around and shook his head. "How old is this place?"

"It was built in 1922, and remodeled a couple of times."

She started walking toward the house, with the cop matching her stride.

"How long have you owned the place?"

"Just a week. It was condemned, and I bought it from the city. We're just starting work on it and we're taping a reality TV show about the renovation." They were standing just inside the front doorway.

"We got a briefing about that. Hear there's gonna be a lot of cars in and out here."

Cass trundled into the living room with a wheelbarrow full of lathe and plaster chunks.

"This is Cass Pelletier. She's the one who actually found the wallet. Cass, this is Officer Mak . . ."

"Detective Makarowicz," he said. "Don't bother trying to pronounce it. People just call me Mak. Or Al Mak. Or Detective Mak."

"Hi," Cass said. "The wallet's out in the kitchen."

"It gets worse," the cop said, following the women into the gutted space. "You really think you can make this place livable?"

"It's our job," Hattie assured him. "Rescuing old houses and bringing them back to life."

"You ask me, this one's DOA," Makarowicz said.

"There's the wallet." Cass pointed to the sawhorse table.

"How many people have handled it, since you found it?" he asked, donning a thin pair of latex gloves.

"Just me and Hattie," Cass said.

He picked up the wallet and began examining it. "I understand you knew the woman this belonged to? Lanier Ragan?"

"She was our teacher, at St. Mary's Academy," Hattie said. "But she went missing in 2005."

He plucked the driver's license from the wallet and studied it. "So young," he said under his breath. He put the license back, then dropped it into a paper evidence bag.

"Show me where you found the wallet, please," he said, addressing Cass.

Cass walked to the back wall of the kitchen. She'd tacked a blue tarp to the exterior of the wall.

"This was an old bathroom, which we were demolishing," she said. "At one time, there was a sink right here, and a medicine cabinet. Beside the medicine cabinet, there was a sort of slot in the wall, where people would put used razor blades. We were knocking out the old plaster and lathe when we found the wallet, sitting back here, between the wall studs."

"My grandma's house had one of those slots in the medicine cabinet," he mused, kneeling down on the floor. "Any idea how that wallet could have gotten back there?"

"Only way we can figure is that someone shoved it through that slot," Hattie said.

Makarowicz stood up slowly. "Do I wanna know what happened to the slot?"

"It's gone," Hattie said apologetically. "I kinda sledgehammered it. What's left of it is out in the dumpster."

"Under a couple dozen loads of debris," Cass added.

"Figures." He gestured toward the back door. "What's outside?"

Hattie opened the door and the three of them walked onto the back porch. "See for yourself. I'm not sure when was the last time anybody lived in this house. But beyond all this jungle, there's a little beach, and of course, the Back River. There's an old dock and boathouse, too, but I haven't walked out onto it, because I don't know how safe it is."

"Oh. Right. I forgot this is waterfront." Makarowicz shot her a rueful smile. "I'm kind of new to Tybee. Still getting my bearings."

"Really?" she asked.

"Moved down here six months ago, after I retired from

the Atlanta Police Department. I did twenty-seven years. Detective the last eighteen, but the stress and Atlanta traffic were getting to me. High blood pressure. It was my wife's idea to come down here to Tybee for some peace and quiet."

"You retired and then went right back to work again as a cop?"

"Not at first. Hell of a thing. We moved down here for my health, and damned if Jenny wasn't the one . . ."

Hattie saw the haunted look in his eyes. She waited.

Mak looked off toward the river. "Up and died on me. Heart attack." He snapped his fingers. "Gone. Just like that. Suddenly, I had way too much time on my hands."

"I know how that is," Hattie said, touching his arm. "I lost my husband in a motorcycle accident seven years ago."

"Jesus!" he exclaimed. "You're so young. Not even thirty, right?"

"I'm thirty-three," she said. "But Tybee must be pretty boring after Atlanta."

"Oh no, lots of excitement. Already today I picked up a punk for taking a piss in some old lady's front yard on Jones Street, and then I took a stolen bike report from a college girl who, it turns out, was so drunk she forgot the rental company came and picked it up last night."

"A regular crime spree," Hattie said.

Makarowicz held up the evidence bag. "Tell me this. Was she ever found?"

"Not that we know of," Cass said. "And we probably would have heard."

"St. Mary's is the Catholic girls' high school, right?" he asked.

"Yes," Hattie said. "My mother and grandmother graduated from there."

"My mom did too," Cass added.

"I've got a daughter who's about your age," Makarowicz

said. "I remember when Lorna was in high school. Lots of gossip. Lots of drama. At the time, what did all you girls think happened to this Mrs. Ragan?"

"Some people thought she ran away with a man," Cass said.

"So, a married woman runs off with another dude. Not a very original concept."

"I never believed that," Hattie said. "Her husband was the hot football coach at Cardinal Mooney, that's the Catholic boys' prep school. They were really a cute couple."

"And she had a little girl," Cass added. "She talked about Emma all the time in class."

He'd taken a small notebook from his pocket and was jotting down notes. "Did she have any ties to this house that you know of?"

"Maybe," Hattie said. "The family that owned this house—the Creedmores? Their kids all went to St. Mary's and Cardinal Mooney, and I think Holland played football for Coach Ragan. He was a couple years older."

"Creedmores? Do any of them still live in the area?"

"Yeah," Cass said. "Mavis, kind of the matriarch, goes to church with my mom."

"Holland Junior lives here too," Hattie said. "I had a run-in with him last week, at city hall."

"What was that all about?" Makarowicz asked, still taking notes.

"He wasn't happy that I was able to buy the house. After the family basically abandoned it, the city condemned the property and put it up for sale, with sealed bids. It was all perfectly legal, but he was furious. Threatened to sue the city, then yelled at me, then offered fifty thousand to buy it from me outright."

"Why was it abandoned?"

"According to Holland, the roof was damaged after a

hurricane, and nobody could agree on who should pay for the repairs, so the family just walked away and quit paying taxes."

Makarowicz looked dubious. "Looks like a lot of work."

"We'll finish the ground floor restoration in six weeks," Hattie told him, sounding more confident than she felt.

"If you say so." He handed his notebook over to Hattie. "Write down your contact information there, please. And hers. And the name of the guy you ran into at Tybee City Hall. Holland . . ."

"Creedmore," Hattie said.

She scribbled her number and Cass's on the notepad and handed it back to him.

"Okay, I'm gonna call this in to the Savannah PD. Somebody will be in touch. In the meantime, if you happen to find anything else of hers . . ." He took a business card from his pocket. "Gimme a call."

19

Alert the Media

- - - - - - -

"Well, this is certainly a first for me," Molly Fowlkes said. They were sitting in a scarred wooden booth at Pinkie Masters', a dive bar in downtown Savannah. She was drinking Pabst Blue Ribbon, Al Makarowicz was drinking ice water.

"Being in a bar?" Mak asked.

Her laugh was gravelly—incongruent with the appearance of a delicate-featured woman, in her late forties, with short, light brown hair, and a fringe of bangs that brushed the frames of her tortoiseshell-rimmed glasses.

"No. I'm a reporter. Bars are like church for people like us. I mean, having a cop call me with a story. That doesn't happen. Especially in Savannah."

"Tell you the truth, I've never called a reporter before, so it's a first for me too," Al said. Makarowicz had found Fowlkes's byline on a newspaper clipping from the case file a Savannah detective had let him borrow long enough to make an under-the-table copy.

"I checked you out, you had quite a career with the Atlanta PD," she said. "How'd you end up out on Tybee Island?"

"Fed up with Atlanta crime and Atlanta traffic," he said. "A buddy told me there was an opening, I applied, and now here I am, living the dream."

"So, Detective Makarowicz, you said you had some news? About the missing English teacher?"

"Just call me Mak. Yeah. Lanier Ragan. Did you know her?"

"Not personally. I've only been at the paper twelve years."

"Only," he said pointedly.

"In Savannah, that makes me a newcomer," she said. "You know how it is, if you're not a native Savannahian," she said, making quote marks with her fingers, "you're an outsider. But I've had an obsession with that story ever since I got here. So don't keep me in suspense. What's the news?"

"We found Lanier Ragan's wallet this week."

She leaned across the table, her eyes wide with excitement. "Where?"

"In an old house that's being renovated, out on Tybee. The contractors found it behind the old plaster walls, stuck in between the wall studs."

"Any idea how it got there?"

He shook his head. "They said there was an old razor blade slot in the wall, the kind people used to dispose of used blades, and they think somebody shoved it in there."

"Oh. My. God." She was scribbling in a steno pad she'd whipped out of her purse. "Who're the people who found the wallet?"

"The woman's name is Hattie Kavanaugh. She just bought the house last week, and they're filming some kind of do-it-yourself television show there. One of her crew members found it. This girl, well, she's probably in her early thirties, so not really a girl. This woman, she graduated from St. Mary's Academy. She actually had Lanier Ragan for an English class."

"Interesting," Molly Fowlkes said. "Tell me about this television show. They're filming out at Tybee? That's kind of weird in itself."

"I don't know that much about it," Mak admitted. "They said it's called *Homewreckers*. My wife used to watch all those shows." He smiled slightly. "And she never missed your column."

"Past tense?" Molly asked.

"Yeah."

"Oh. Sorry. So. *Homewreckers*. What's that about?"

He shrugged, and his whole body went into the effort. "Fixing up an old house. Here's another coincidence for you. The family that used to own the house, for like, the last sixty years? The son played football at Cardinal Mooney for Lanier Ragan's husband."

"Frank Ragan," Molly said promptly. "What a douche. He was so heartbroken by his wife's disappearance he started shacking up with one of his neighbors less than a year later."

"Really? How do you come to know something like that?"

She twirled the beer can on the tabletop. "Told you I was obsessed. What else do you want to know? Last I heard, Frank was selling real estate in Orlando. He and the neighbor lady broke up awhile ago."

"And the daughter?"

"Emma. Now that's a sad story. She dropped out of high school, went to rehab. Last time I checked, she was working in a local tattoo parlor."

"She didn't move to Florida with her dad? What's up with that?"

"Don't know. She won't talk. I've reached out a couple times, but no luck."

"Do you have the name of the tattoo place?" Now it was Makarowicz's turn to pull out a steno pad.

"Inkstains," Molly said. "Want me to text you the number?"

"Yeah, that'd be good. What else do you know?"

She gave him a look. "That's not how this works. You're supposed to tell me stuff so I can write a great column. Maybe win a Pulitzer, or at least get a raise."

"Honest to God. There's nothing else to tell. The wallet was found. Eventually it'll be sent to the state crime lab, but after sitting in a moldy wall for all these years, you can imagine how much help that'll be."

Her pen was poised above her notepad. "What's the name of the son who played football for Frank Ragan?"

He considered holding it back, but relented. "Holland Creedmore. I think he does something in sales."

"Creedmore. That sounds familiar." She typed the name into the search bar on her phone. "Oh yeah. This town is crawling with Creedmores." She held the phone so he could read the search engine results.

"Holland Creedmore Senior was president of the Rotary Club, on the Savannah Board of Aldermen. . . ."

She raised an eyebrow. "President of the Cardinal Mooney Alumni Association." She laughed. "And Mavis Creedmore. That's how I knew the name. A real crank. She writes indignant letters to the editor about unleashed dogs pooping in the city squares. Typewritten, in all caps. Like on a monthly basis. Once got arrested for chasing down a tourist whose chihuahua shit in front of the cathedral. Assaulted the poor guy with her cane."

"Sounds like quite a distinguished family," Mak said. "I think I need to talk to Holland Junior. Maybe Senior, too."

"What's your theory about Lanier? Usually it's the husband who did it, am I right?"

"It's too early for me to have a theory," Mak said. He looked down at his notes and what he'd copied from the incident reports in the old police file.

Frank Ragan states he was reluctant to contact police when he initially discovered his wife missing because he thought she might have left "because she was pissed at him for drinking too much at a Super Bowl party the night before." Ragan said he asked a neighbor to watch their young daughter, who was still asleep, while he drove around looking for his wife's car, a white 2001 Nissan Altima. After he returned home, he called his wife's closest friends, as well as her mother to ask if they'd seen Lanier. His mother-in-law then urged him to call the police, as it was unlike her daughter to go off and leave like that.

"I haven't had a chance to talk to the husband yet," Mak said. "We'll see."

"Any chance she might still be alive?" asked Molly.

"You say you've been following this story for years. Tell me what you think."

"Definitely dead," Molly said. "I've talked to some of her former students at St. Mary's, a couple teachers who worked with her at the school, even her college roommate at Ole Miss. Everyone agreed, even if the marriage was in trouble, she never would have walked off and left her little kid like that."

"*Was* the marriage in trouble? Lanier's mother said in the statement I read that Frank spent too much time with his team and drank too much, but had never gotten violent."

"I don't think it was perfect. Frank was this macho, alpha male type. Lanier, from what I hear, was sort of a dreamer, loved books. They were an unlikely couple, and she was barely twenty-two when they got married." She started to say something else, but stopped.

Mak pounced on it. "What?"

"The last time I wrote a story, I think it was on the tenth anniversary of her disappearance, I got a phone call at the office. This was before our phones had caller ID. It was a woman, she wouldn't tell me her name. She said she was sick of hearing everyone talk about Saint Lanier. That's what she called her. She hinted that Lanier was running around on Frank. I asked her flat out—who was she running around with? And she laughed and said I wouldn't believe it, but it was her boyfriend. Her *high school* boyfriend."

"Lanier's high school boyfriend?" Mak asked, confused.

"No. This anonymous woman's boyfriend. Who was in high school at the time, and played football for Frank Ragan."

"And you never passed that along to the Savannah cops? Or wrote about it?"

"You might find this hard to believe, but I don't write stories based on rumors or anonymous tips," Molly said. "I asked around, couldn't verify it."

"Do you think it could have been true, even considering the source?"

"I didn't think that much about it at the time, but you know? Back in the spring I did a story about a production of *Little Women* that was put on by a local theater group. I was chatting with the director, a woman named Deborah Logenbuhl, who used to be the drama teacher at St. Mary's. As soon as she told me that, my ears perked up. I asked her if she knew Lanier, and she looked like she might cry. Turns out she and Lanier were best friends."

"And?"

"She was pretty cagey when I asked her if the rumor about Lanier could be true. She said Lanier changed in the last few months before she disappeared. She was moody, secretive even."

Molly leaned forward. "They used to have a standing Saturday morning coffee date. But she said Lanier no-showed a couple times that fall."

"There's nothing like that in the Savannah PD files," Makarowicz said. "Why didn't she tell that to the cops working the case?"

"She was on maternity leave at the time, her baby was very preemie, spent six weeks in the ICU, and nobody ever contacted her to ask her about Lanier."

"Some investigation," Makarowicz said, shaking his head. He tapped his pen on his notepad. "Do you have contact information for this drama lady?"

"Deborah Logenbuhl," Molly repeated, taking out her phone again. "I'll text you her contact info."

"Good," Mak said. "That's a pretty decent start for me. You got what you need?"

"Are you kidding? Lanier Ragan's billfold turns up in an old beach house on Tybee, seventeen years after her disappearance? Yeah, that's front-page stuff. Guess I better get back to the office and start working the phones."

She put a five-dollar bill on the table and stood to leave. "Hey, uh, Mak? Thanks."

"No problem. You'll call me if you get any more of those anonymous tips, right?"

"As long as it's a two-way street, yeah."

20

Breaking News

It was still dark when Hattie left her cottage in Thunderbolt, but the first streaks of pinkish purple lit up the sky as she drove east toward Tybee Island.

Her mind was on the day's task—rebuilding the staircase at the Creedmore house. The original was impossibly narrow and steep and awkwardly placed just a few steps inside the front door.

It had been Trae's idea to relocate the stairway to the hallway outside the downstairs bedroom and to add a small powder bath in the space beneath. The move would open up the living room, give better access to the second floor, and add a second bath downstairs. She'd been forced to (secretly) admit Trae was right.

As she crossed the Lazaretto Creek bridge she felt the familiar twinge, a sense memory, of Hank, on his Kawasaki, riding away from their cottage that night, with only a fleeting, backward glance in her direction. She blinked back the inevitable tears, forcing herself to consider the challenge at hand.

The network had given them only five more weeks to finish work on the house. It seemed impossible. She and Cass and her framing crew had worked on the house until 11 P.M.

the night before, punching a hole in the hallway ceiling so that work could begin this morning to erect the new stairs. Her painters were working from sunup to sundown, scraping, priming, and patching the old clapboard siding, and sometime this week, the plumbers would begin replacing all the old ductile iron piping.

Even Trae had been enlisted to pitch in with the manual labor. He'd spent the early part of the week peeling layer after layer of old wallpaper from the upstairs bedroom walls, all the while entertaining Mo's crew with his running commentary on which wallpaper was the most heinous.

"This," he'd said, holding up a strip of wrinkled seventies-era paper with a design of neon orange sunbursts superimposed over eye-popping purple stripes, "is a crime against humanity. Someday, I hope the designer of this atrocity will be jailed for this visual abuse."

"Keep it up, Trae," Leetha had encouraged. "Viewers love this outrageous shit."

Hattie couldn't decide if she'd just gotten immune to Trae Bartholomew's abrasive personality or if he had, somehow, actually started to grow on her.

As she approached the house, Hattie was startled to see half a dozen vehicles parked on the shoulder of the road at the entrance to the driveway. There were two Tybee police cruisers and television vans from all three local network affiliates with roof-mounted satellite antennas.

Hattie steered the truck down the driveway, which had gotten even more rutted from all the trucks and machinery coming in and out of the construction site. It would have to be repaved, and soon. More money.

Her cell phone rang and she saw that the caller was Cass.

"Where are you?" Cass demanded.

"Just pulling up to the house. What's going on?"

"Obviously you didn't see the paper this morning," Cass

said. "There's a big story splashed across the front page, about us finding Lanier Ragan's wallet. That Tybee cop we talked to—Makarowicz—has reopened the investigation."

Hattie was a couple hundred feet from the house when she spotted the small knot of people standing at the edge of the porch. "I'm here now. Where are you?" she asked.

"Walking toward you." She spotted Cass, cell phone in hand, approaching the truck.

She put the truck in park and hopped out. Cass trotted over.

"Welcome to crazy town," she greeted Hattie and gestured toward the gathering near the porch. "Mo is actually giving a press conference. We've been waiting for you to get here."

"Me?"

"You're the star of *Homewreckers*. All these reporters want to hear from you."

Hattie took a step backward. "Come on. I didn't even find the wallet. I don't want to be on TV. I just want to do my job and fix up this old house."

"News flash, Hattie. You *are* on TV. That's why they want to talk to you. The sooner you talk to them, the sooner they'll go away and let us get back to work."

"What do you think happened to Lanier Ragan? Could she be here? In this house?"

Hattie recognized the reporter from WTOC, the local CBS network affiliate. He was tall and slender, with dark, slicked-back hair, and he had a television camera aimed directly at her. Aaron something.

"I don't know . . ." Hattie started to say.

"Is this house haunted?" another reporter called out.

"What? No," she shot back. "There's nothing sinister going

on here. It's an old house, and we're trying to restore it. Families lived here once, people laughed and danced and watched the sunset and blew out the candles on birthday cakes. Babies took their first steps on the beach back there, and couples fell in love and got engaged. For almost a hundred years."

"But what about Lanier Ragan?" Aaron something persisted. "Could something bad have happened to her here? Why else would her wallet be here, hidden in that wall all these years?"

"I can't answer that," Hattie said, shaking her head. "But I hope the police find some answers. I'm sure her family wants that too."

"Did you know Lanier Ragan?" This time the question came from a petite Black woman with cascading braids whom Hattie recognized as Nya Davies, from WSAV, the local NBC affiliate.

Hattie felt herself flush. "Yes, Mrs. Ragan was my favorite teacher at St. Mary's Academy. She was amazing. All the girls loved her."

Mo clapped his hands and elbowed his way through the crowd of reporters. "Okay, folks, we need to wrap this up. The police are investigating, and we, of course, are giving them our full cooperation. We want this mystery solved, too, but in the meantime, we've got a very short deadline to finish work on this house. *Homewreckers* will debut this fall, on HPTV."

He put a hand on the small of Hattie's back and steered her firmly, and quickly, away from the reporters who were still calling out questions for her. He unlocked the front door of the house and they stepped inside.

"Thanks," she said, her voice shaking. "That was . . . intense."

"You handled it just great," he said. "Like a seasoned pro."

His voice echoed in the empty, high-ceilinged room. "You gave 'em as much as you had, and you were convincing."

"Are the bosses at the network . . . like Rebecca . . . are they worried about this wallet thing?" Hattie asked. "I guess it's bad publicity, huh?"

"You don't know much about the entertainment business, do you? The newspaper story mentioned *Homewreckers* and the network. It's gone viral. All publicity is good publicity as far as HPTV is concerned."

"That's pretty heartless," Hattie said flatly.

"It's a pretty heartless business," Mo agreed. "By the way, the reporter from the newspaper wants to talk to you."

"I hope you told her no. I literally have already said everything I know about that wallet." Hattie gestured at the scaffolding she and Cass had erected in the hallway leading to the bedroom. "We've got to get the new staircase roughed in today. And I thought you wanted to shoot me with Trae, discussing paint colors."

"The camera crew is heading to town with Trae to shoot his paint-shopping expedition. He'll bring back samples, you'll paint swatches on the back porch, and we'll film that. In the meantime, I promised the reporter you'd give her ten minutes of your valuable time."

"When's that supposed to happen?"

"No time like the present," Mo said. He pointed toward the back of the house. "She's waiting for you in the kitchen. Be nice, okay?"

21

Twenty Questions

- - - - - - -

She found the reporter kneeling down against the back kitchen wall, running her fingertips over the newly taped and mudded wallboard, almost as though she was trying to divine what was hidden beneath that surface.

"Hattie Kavanaugh, meet Molly Fowlkes," Mo said, backing out of the room. "I'll, uh, leave you two alone, but Hattie, we're gonna need you in makeup in about fifteen minutes."

"I'll be there," Hattie said.

Molly tapped the wall. "Is this where you found the wallet?"

"Approximately," Hattie said. "It was stuck down there between the studs."

"Okay if I take a photo?" The reporter didn't wait for permission. She pulled a bulky black camera from her shoulder bag and started clicking frames. "Could you stand over by the wall?"

Mindful of Mo's admonition to play nice, Hattie shrugged, ran her fingers through her hair, and dutifully posed.

"Tell me about Lanier Ragan," Molly said. "What was she like?"

Hattie stalled, walking over to the makeshift worktable,

unrolling a set of plans that had been left out and bending over to examine them, while she mentally composed a response.

"You know how it is in high school—you always think your teachers are really old, even though now, I look back and realize they were mostly in their thirties and forties. But Mrs. Ragan was different. She was like *us*."

"How so?"

"She dressed and acted young. Like, she always wore cute outfits, not some old-lady sweaters and skirts and orthopedic shoes, but the kinds of stuff we wished we were allowed to wear to school instead of those dopey plaid uniform skirts and knee socks and saddle shoes. She listened to the same kind of music we did—like, she knew every word to every pop song. She was just . . . fun."

"Fun, how?"

Hattie didn't hesitate. "I remember for our AP English class, she said if everyone in the class aced this test, she'd come to school dressed as Britney Spears and act out the whole 'Baby One More Time' video."

Molly looked impressed. "Catholic schools must have changed a lot since my day."

"It was awesome," Hattie said. "She had her hair in pigtails, and the whole slutty uniform thing going on. She lip-synced it, and I swear, you'd have believed she actually *was* Britney."

"She must have been really popular with the girls."

Hattie let out a long, soft sigh. "Yeah. She was the kind of teacher who actually listened. Who was interested in what was going on with her students. You could tell her stuff, and you knew she wouldn't judge. She was compassionate, you know?"

"Can you give me an example?" the reporter asked. She studied Hattie's expression. "I won't write about it—if it's too personal. I'm just trying to get a feel for who she was, and what she meant to her students."

Hattie felt the blood rushing to her cheeks. "I don't know . . ."

"I swear."

"Okay," Hattie said, taking a deep breath and exhaling slowly. "My sophomore year, my parents broke up, and there was a scandal. My mother moved down to Florida, but I wanted to stay in Savannah. So I moved in with my friend Cass's family. It was an incredibly painful time for me."

"I'll bet."

"I had kind of a rough time of it. Some girls that I thought were my friends, not Cass, but some others—they just turned their backs on me. And Mrs. Ragan got what I was going through. I'd stop by her classroom after school, while she was grading papers, and we'd talk. A couple times, we walked over to the 7-Eleven—the one on Drayton Street— and we bought Cokes and sat in the square and talked."

"And that helped?"

Hattie nodded. "She told me everybody goes through bad stuff. Every family has secrets—ugly secrets. And she told me it wasn't my fault. Here's the thing she said to me that I've never forgotten. 'Don't look over your shoulder. The past is past. Just try to get through it, and give yourself some grace.'"

Molly tapped her pen thoughtfully. "I wonder what kind of secrets Lanier had?"

"I wonder now too. At the time, I was too self-involved to ask. I guess I thought she was so cool, she must have her own life all figured out."

Molly nodded and wrote something in her notebook. "Did she talk to you girls about her personal life?"

"She had a picture of her husband and her little girl on her desk. She'd tell us cute stories about the stuff Emma said."

"What about her husband? The football coach. Did she talk about him a lot?"

Hattie smoothed the plans out with her hands. "Sometimes. I'm guessing you've heard those old stories about her having a secret boyfriend? There were all kinds of rumors back then—that she'd run away with another man, that Coach was having an affair and she found out so he killed her and tossed her body in the marsh. You wouldn't believe all the gruesome stories repressed Catholic schoolgirls came up with."

"Sure I would. I went to an all-girls parochial school in Baltimore, and then to college at Holy Cross." Molly chewed on the cap of her pen for a moment. "I practically lettered in sexual repression. Let me ask you this. Did you ever hear any rumors that Lanier was having an affair with a high school kid?"

"What?" Hattie's hand shot out and knocked over a half-full Styrofoam cup of coffee, spilling the tepid liquid onto the plans. She grabbed a painter's rag and began mopping up the mess. "Where'd you hear something like that?"

"I did a piece for the paper about the tenth anniversary of the disappearance, back in 2015, which prompted an anonymous call from a woman who claimed that at the time she vanished, Lanier was sleeping with the woman's high school boyfriend—who was on Frank's football team."

"Oh my God," Hattie said. "That's just . . . so gross. I mean, yeah, I guess it was believable that she could have been sleeping with another man—but a high school kid? No. I never got that cougar vibe from Mrs. Ragan. No. Definitely not. Yuck."

Molly laughed. "Now you really do sound like a Catholic schoolgirl. But stop and think about it for a minute. Lanier Ragan was only twenty-five. If she *was* having an affair with a high school kid, it wouldn't have been that big an age difference. Maybe only six or seven years, if the guy was a senior. I've done my research. Frank Ragan was ten years older than Lanier. They met and started dating while she was a junior at Ole Miss and he was an athletic trainer."

"I never knew that," Hattie admitted. "Back in the day, we all thought he was incredibly hot. They were so cute together."

"And he was married when they met," Molly said. "He and Lanier got married the week after she graduated from Ole Miss."

"So much for Mr. and Mrs. All America," Hattie said with a sigh. "I don't know why, but this makes me so incredibly sad all over again."

"It might not be true," Molly cautioned. "The caller wouldn't give me her name, or the boyfriend's name. I made some cautious inquiries at the time, but nothing ever came of it, which is why I dropped it. But now . . ."

"Hattie?" Lisa popped her head into the kitchen doorway. "We need you in makeup."

"Okay. Coming." She shot the reporter an apologetic smile. "Sorry. I really hope you find out what happened to Lanier Ragan. Selfishly, I really hope it's not connected to this house."

"About the house," Molly said quickly. "I know Holland Creedmore's family owned it up until a couple weeks ago. And that he played football at Cardinal Mooney for Frank Ragan. Could there be more of a connection?"

"Maybe? Holland was older than me, and he ran in a whole different crowd."

"What kind of crowd was that?" the reporter asked.

"You know. Rich kids, jocks, stoners."

"And who did you run with?" Molly asked, smiling.

"Mostly just Cassidy Pelletier—maybe you met her, she works with me, and we've been best friends since parochial school. And a few other girls."

"Hattie!" Mo bellowed from outside the back door. "Now!"

"Gotta go." Hattie made a quick exit.

22

Up on the Roof

- - - - - - -

Hattie was sitting in the makeup chair as Lisa fussed over her hair. "I think we should maybe do it in a French braid, or something different. The network honchos saw the video from earlier in the week and they want you to look more feminine."

"More feminine?" Hattie stared in the mirror. Lisa had already spent thirty minutes spackling, powdering, and contouring her face. She barely recognized herself beneath the thick fringe of extensions Lisa had painstakingly glued to her own stubby lashes. "What next? Do they want to dress me in a tube top and a pair of Daisy Dukes?"

Jodi, the wardrobe assistant, bustled in just then with a garment bag draped over her arm. "Not quite." She laughed, unzipping the bag and holding up a pair of distressed cut-off overalls and a hot pink sleeveless crop top. "But close."

"Noooo," Hattie moaned. "I can't work in that getup. And it's not my style. Does Leetha know about this?"

"Don't know," Jodi said. "But your call is in five minutes, so we need to get you out of that chair and into your duds before she starts screaming for my hide. And also, I'm supposed to tell you to ditch the work boots."

* * *

Mo and Leetha were huddling with one of the cameramen when Hattie slunk into the living room.

"Gurrrrl," Leetha said, taking in Hattie's newfound glamour. "Did somebody forget to tell me we're shooting a pole-dancing sequence today?"

"Lisa said she got orders from the network to tart me up, and then Jodi handed me these crap clothes and said she'd been told I needed to ditch the Carhartts." She pointed a finger at Mo. "Was this your idea?"

"Nope. That came from Rebecca. She and Tony watched the video and came up with this. And just to be clear, I'm as appalled as you."

"I feel ridiculous," Hattie said. "These damn overalls are all up in my Kool-Aid, and every time I move I'm afraid one of my boobs will come flopping out."

"Would that be such a bad thing?"

She turned to see Trae standing in the doorway. "Might be a ratings booster," he drawled. "We're gonna start calling you Hattie the hottie."

"Never mind that," Leetha said, glancing down at her notes. "Let's talk about today. We need to reshoot that back porch sequence from yesterday."

"But the new floorboards are already nailed down," Hattie protested.

Leetha's smile was grim. "Not anymore. But don't fret. I only had the guys pull up a small section. You'll stand in the hole they made, point out where y'all rebuilt the old crumbling brick pilings with concrete block, and that's it."

"What about me?" Trae asked.

"Downstairs bathroom. Tiling, sink vanity, shower enclosure, mirror," Leetha told him. "Check in with Jodi. She's got a different shirt for you to wear, since you'll be demonstrating your tiling skills today."

"Me?"

The wardrobe girl waved a blue denim work shirt at him.

"No fair," Hattie said. "If I have to wear a crop top, he should at least have to wear a wife-beater."

A slow smile spread across Leetha's face. "Great idea. Let's let the viewers at home get a look at Ashtray's guns. Jodi, we're gonna need a pair of scissors."

Trae stood in the new bathroom shower holding up a piece of subway tile in one hand and a trowel in the other, while Hattie coached him in the finer points of the job. His face was dripping with perspiration and his biceps, now exposed since the sleeves of his work shirt had been hacked off, gleamed in the bright glare of the camera lights. He looked hot, literally and figuratively.

"Okay, now you want to spread a thin layer of the mortar mix on the wall with the flat side of your trowel. Think of it like icing a cake."

"I've never iced a cake," Trae said. "I don't do carbs."

Hattie rolled her eyes. "Why am I not surprised? Okay, think of it as peanut butter, which is protein, right? You have made a peanut butter sandwich at some point in your life, right?"

"No. Our housekeeper made the peanut butter sandwiches and the butler served them," he said, his voice dripping with acid. "Yeah, Hattie. I get the picture."

He glared at her for a moment, then flicked a glob of mortar mix at his tormentor, which landed squarely on her nose. "Is that too thick, Hattie Mae?"

23
Tool Time

They were seated in a corner booth at an Italian restaurant not far from Mo's carriage house. Rebecca waited until after the waiter brought their drinks; an Aperol spritz for her, bourbon for Mo.

"Mo, I wish you hadn't hired Taleetha Carr. You know how I feel about her."

Ever since she'd texted him that she was on her way to Savannah, he'd halfway expected a confrontation like this. And one look at Rebecca told the story. Her face had that tense, aggrieved look he'd come to know all too well. He took a long sip of his drink, welcoming the icy burn that slid down his throat as he mentally plotted his response.

"Well, I wish you'd let me know you were flying out here today. You kind of threw me for a loop. Is that what this ambush is about? Leetha? She's great at what she does. That's what I care about. She's established a solid rapport with Hattie and Trae, and the crew loves her. Maybe you can just forget your personal differences. For the good of my show."

Rebecca tapped the side of her glass with her fingernail. "Ambush? It's not an ambush. I had business in New York, and I thought, since I'm on the East Coast . . . Let's talk about the show. What do you think of the chemistry between Hattie and Trae? I think it's really working."

"Too soon to tell. They're already knocking heads over budget and design choices."

"That's great. Build that conflict. It gives our viewers something to keep coming back for. They can take sides. Anyway, who doesn't love a slow-burn romance?"

Mo laughed in disbelief. "What are you talking about? There is zero chance these two will get together."

"I disagree. Trae has incredible magnetism. I think Hattie is going to fall for him, and hard. In fact, I'm counting on it."

He stared at her as the reality of Rebecca's vision sunk in. "Are you telling me you told Trae to try to seduce her? Jesus, Becca. That's . . . vile."

"Who said anything about seduction? They're both adults. I was just pointing out that Trae is a very attractive man. And Hattie's cute. And single. Look, we both know this show is only ten percent about fixing up an old house. The rest of it? People love the idea of love. They're intrigued with watching the dance. So that's what we give them. The dance. All I'm saying is, don't stand in the way of that. Encourage it. Play it up. If they're bickering on camera, show that. And when the spark happens . . . fan the flame."

Mo took another gulp of the drink.

"As far as I'm concerned, this show actually *is* about fixing up an old house. I'm a little worried about this missing woman angle. The last thing we need is for the cops to show up and shut down production. We're already going to be stretched incredibly tight now that we've got structural issues."

She listened intently while he listed all the work the house needed.

"You've only got five weeks," Becca reminded him. "Marketing is already working on the promotional campaign, Mo. There's no going back now. Does Hattie understand that the house absolutely has to be complete by the end of the shoot?"

"She gets it," Mo said wearily. "We all get it."

"Need a hand?" Hattie didn't hear his car pull into the driveway, didn't even hear his footsteps echoing in the now empty living room. She'd been concentrating on the old wall-to-wall carpeting in the living room, first scoring it with a box cutter, then yanking it away from the floor.

Trae Bartholomew had ditched his pristine white jeans and designer tee. He wore Carhartts like Hattie's, a paint-spattered tee, and grungy tennis shoes that had lost their laces, and, she thought, he looked damn fine.

"Really? You came back to help?" She straightened and stretched out her aching back.

"Why wouldn't I?" He looked around the living room. All the old furniture and the piles of debris were gone. The dated seventies brass chandelier that had hung over the dining room table had been pulled down and work lights now illuminated the cavernous living and dining room spaces.

"Man. You and Cass managed all this?"

"Cass called a local company and they sent out a couple of college kids to haul away all the furniture and junk to the dump. We never could have done it without them."

"Where's Cass now?" he asked, looking around.

"Pizza run. We ordered from Lighthouse, but they're slammed and we're starved, so she went to pick it up."

"Wish I'd known," Trae said. "I would have brought something from town."

She eyed him warily. "Really? Why would you do that?"

He laughed. "You mean, why would a snooty, demanding L.A. designer lower himself to actually act like a decent human being?"

"Well, yeah."

"I'm not really an asshole in real life, Hattie. I just play one on television. We're in this together, you know. If this project isn't amazing in every way, and *Homewreckers* tanks, my career and reputation go with it. Now, tell me what you need me to do."

She pointed at the dining room, where the carpet had already been removed. "If you're serious, all that nasty carpet padding was so old and damp, patches of it stuck to the floor. We'll come back and sand everything later, but first we've gotta scrape up the rubbery patches, plus pull up all the tack strips. You up for that?"

"Let me just grab my tool belt," Trae said.

"You own a tool belt? For real?"

"I'm a man of many talents," he told her.

By the time Cass returned to the house with a large pizza and a six-pack of beer, Trae was using a putty knife to pry up the last of the tack strips in the dining room.

She set the pizza box on the work table they'd dragged into the living room. "What's he doing here?" she said, nodding in the designer's direction.

"I came back to help," Trae said. "Why does everyone find that so hard to believe?"

Cass popped the top on a bottle of beer, ignoring him, and handed it to Hattie. "Maybe because he's been acting like a dick so far?"

"He's not as bad as we thought," Hattie said, taking a long pull from the bottle. "Plus he has his own tools."

"I'm standing right here," Trae protested. "Come on, ladies. Cut me some slack."

24

Little Girl Lost

Makarowicz was sitting in his cruiser, looking over his notes when Dawna Gaines, the TPD dispatcher, radioed him. "Hey, Mak, there's a girl been calling here all afternoon, asking to speak to you about that article in the newspaper. Her name's Emma Ragan."

"Give me her number, please." He grabbed his phone and typed the number into it as she called it out. "Any other calls?"

"Just the usual assorted wingnuts," she said cheerfully. "I left their numbers on your desk, but this girl sounds legit. And frantic."

"Hello?" She picked up on the first ring.

"Miss Ragan? This is Detective Makarowicz, at the Tybee PD. I understand you'd like to talk to me."

"Yes," she said, a little breathlessly. "Only I'm at work, and I don't get off until nine. Could we maybe meet after that?"

"I'm off at six, but yeah, tonight will work," he said quickly.

"Could we meet downtown at the Crystal Beer Parlor?"

she said. "I'll tell my boss something important came up. Is eight okay?"

He spotted her at a two-top in the corner of the main dining room. Her hair was chopped short and silvery white with purple tips. She was studying a menu, and despite the sleeves of tattoos covering both forearms, she looked about twelve years old.

"Emma?"

She looked up. Her bright blue eyes were rimmed with black eyeliner and she had one of those little silver rings in her nose, and she was so petite he was tempted to ask the hostess for a booster seat for her. What was the word he was thinking applied to her? Waifish. Yeah. She looked like one of those waifs from a Dickens novel.

"Detective . . . I'm not sure how to say your last name."

"Makarowicz, but just call me Mak."

Their server appeared. He ordered a burger and a Diet Coke. She asked for a salad and herbal iced tea. "No cheese on the salad, please. I'm a vegan." She had her hands folded in front of her on the table.

"I'm glad you reached out to me, Emma," he said. "I'm sorry the article ran before I could contact you."

"So it really is her wallet? You're sure?"

"Looks like it. The driver's license photo checks out, as do the credit cards. Her St. Mary's faculty ID is in there too. And there's a family photo of you, and her, and your dad. And one of the two of you. And another one of you, maybe a preschool picture?"

"Ohhhhh." She picked up a paper napkin from the dispenser on the table and twisted it.

She started shredding the napkin. Her nails were short

and painted black, and the cuticles were reddened and raggedy, like she chewed on them.

"Why was her wallet in that house?" Emma asked.

"That's what I'm trying to find out. Does the name Creedmore mean anything to you? That's the name of the family who owned the house at the time your mom went missing."

"No, not really. But I looked them up, after I saw that piece in the newspaper. They had some connection to Cardinal Mooney, the school where my dad used to coach, right?"

"That's right. Have you asked your dad about the connection?"

"We don't really talk. I don't even have his phone number."

"I understand he's living down in Florida. Orlando? Does that sound right?"

"Maybe?"

"Was there some kind of argument? I'm only asking, Emma, because I'm trying to get a fix on your family dynamics."

"An argument?" Her laugh was brittle. "Like, just one? No. Me and my dad, we just see things different. Like, always. After Mom went away, things were bad. My grandma was real sick with cancer, and she couldn't help babysit me anymore. After Grandma died, he kinda hooked up with this chick who lived down the street. Rhonda. She was divorced, and her kids lived with their dad. So, Rhonda moved in with us."

Emma smirked. "One big happy family. I got out of there just as soon as I could."

"How did you do that?"

"Dropped out of school, moved in with my boyfriend, got a job at Taco Bell, but the pay sucked, so then I got a job waitressing at a bar down on River Street. By then I was sixteen."

"That's a lot of responsibility for a sixteen-year-old," Mak observed.

"I was basically on my own way before that," Emma said, shrugging. "You know what life is like for a high school football coach in the South, right? Like, *Friday Night Lights* but on steroids. All he cared about was football. Winning the game, winning the region, winning the state. Getting his players signed to play in college. He didn't give a rat's ass about me."

Mak blinked. "That sounds pretty harsh."

"I'll admit, I didn't make his life easy. Me and Rhonda didn't get along. I got in trouble for cutting school, smoking weed. The usual. I think he was relieved when I left."

Their food arrived. He slathered mustard on his burger and ketchup on his fries. She looked down at her salad and sighed, painstakingly removing the cubes of cheese. "They never remember to leave off the cheese," she mumbled.

"Emma . . ." he started. "I know you were only three, but did it seem to you that your parents had a happy marriage? I mean, do you remember any arguments, things like that?"

"I was four. No. I don't remember them fighting. I remember my mom's laugh. Tinkly, you know? She liked to sing. She'd sing while she was fixing supper, and she'd sit me up on the kitchen counter and teach me songs, and she'd do this dance. Way later, I saw some YouTube video and I realized, she was doing that Britney Spears song, 'Baby One More Time.' I bet I've watched that video a thousand times, because it reminds me of her. It's even the ringtone on my phone."

"It's good you have nice memories like that," Mak said. "Did the police talk to you, after she disappeared?"

"I don't think so," she said. "Everything from that time . . . I was so little, you know? My grandma died pretty soon after that, and all I can remember is being sad. I kept asking my dad to take me to her house, and he said he couldn't, 'cause Grandma went to live with Jesus."

She snorted. "What a pile of shit! Like he ever believed in Jesus."

Mak chewed his burger, and she continued sorting out her salad.

"What do you think happened to your mom?" he asked.

"I used to think he killed her," she said, those blue eyes unblinking. "That's part of the reason why I got out of there as soon as I could. I blamed him."

"Do you still?"

"Maybe? When I was in rehab the first time, I had a pretty cool therapist. We talked a lot about why I was so angry. At my mom. At my dad. At Rhonda. My therapist said I had abandonment issues. Well, duh." She leaned forward, across the table. "Maybe he didn't actually kill her. But I do know this: She loved me. And she loved my grandma. If she were going to leave, she would have taken us with her, or sent for us. But she didn't."

"Did your dad ever talk to you about what he thought happened to your mom?"

"Never. Well, there was this one time—we had a huge fight because I'd stayed out all night with my boyfriend, and he caught me sneaking in through my bedroom window. It was a Saturday morning and he was in a foul mood because Cardinal Mooney had lost the night before, to a team that wasn't even that good. I knew he'd been drinking, because his eyes were all red and bloodshot. And he grabbed my arm and pinched it really hard. So hard, it scared me. I'd never been scared of him before. I hated him, but I wasn't afraid of him, you know?"

"He'd never gotten physical with you before?"

"No. He'd yell or he'd give me the silent treatment, but

he wasn't a hitter. Anyway, that morning, like I said, he was pretty wasted, and really worked up. He called me a slut, said I was just like my mom, sneaking around, whoring around. . . ."

Emma's eyes teared up and a thin stream of black eyeliner trickled down her cheek.

"I lost it. I started punching him and kicking him and told him if Mom did sneak around it was probably because he was such a dickhead. His face—I've never forgotten the expression on his face. I really thought he was gonna hit me when I said that. Instead, he told me if I didn't straighten up, I was headed for jail. A couple weeks after that, Rhonda told him I'd been stealing her Xanax, and that gave him an excuse to kick me out, which was fine by me."

Mak dipped a french fry into a puddle of ketchup. "Emma, this is kind of a tough question, but it seems to me, you're a pretty tough kid. Do you think what your dad said was true? About your mom running around?"

"I've always wondered," Emma admitted. "Once, a couple years ago, I even tried to talk to one of Mom's best teacher friends from St. Mary's, Mrs. Logenbuhl. She was always nice to me. Like, she'd take me out for ice cream on my birthday, and that kind of stuff. That night, I out-and-out asked her if she thought my mom was having an affair, and she acted totally shocked, and then she changed the subject."

"That's interesting," Mak said. "Anything else you can tell me? Any other thoughts about any connection she might have had to that house on Tybee?"

"Not really. But if you find something out, you'll tell me, right?"

"I promise," he assured her.

He motioned for the server, who brought their check.

"Where are you living now?" he asked.

"I actually moved back home last year."

"With your dad?" He didn't bother to hide his surprise.

"As if! No, I mean I'm living in our old house. I bought it," she said proudly.

"Good for you," Mak said. "How did that happen?"

"When my grandma died, she left some money for me. It was supposed to be for college, like that was ever gonna happen. But when I turned eighteen, I got my inheritance. So I bought our house back."

"I bet that's a good feeling."

"I hired a private detective, too. To try to find her. He sent away hair from her hairbrush to one of those DNA matching places. You know, in case someone had . . . found her body."

"I'm guessing nothing ever came of it?" Mak asked.

"No. Pretty sure the guy ripped me off."

Makarowicz scowled. What kind of a scumbag ripped off a grieving kid?

"I used to sneak back there, you know? After my dad sold it? At night, I'd climb the fence, and I'd sit in this swing my grandpa hung from a big tree in the backyard. Some nights, I swear, I thought I could hear my mom singing in the kitchen again. I told my therapist about it and she said that was actually a good self-soothing technique."

Emma nodded and stood up. She started to walk away, but then came back to the table.

"Hey, Mak? Would it be possible to get those pictures? From her wallet? I don't hardly have any pictures of me with my mom. Please?"

Her voice was so wistful, it cut right to his hardened cop heart. "Right now, we're keeping the wallet and everything in it because it's evidence, but since you're her next of kin, I'll make sure it gets returned to you."

25

Gadget Returns

- - - - - - -

Monday of week two, Hattie and Cass were standing on the front porch of the house, checking on the progress of the new floor. "Looks great," Hattie said, running her hands over the planking.

"It should. The framing crew was out here 'til almost midnight last night. The camera crew rigged them up stage lights so they could see. I told the guys not to come in until ten this morning. I'm afraid we'll burn 'em out if we keep working them this hard."

Hattie walked to the edge of the porch and shaded her eyes as she searched the morning clouds for some good news. When she heard the crunch of tires on the driveway, she turned her head to see a city-issued white pickup rolling slowly toward the house.

"Uh-oh." Cass stood by her side. "Is that the code cop again?"

"Inspector Gadget, defender of trash trees," Hattie confirmed. "Now what?"

Rice was obviously worked up. His mustache was twitching as he marched toward the porch, his hand extended with another slip of paper.

"Miss Kavanaugh?"

She nodded. "Is there a problem?"

"Your neighbors certainly think there's a problem. We've had multiple calls and complaints about you people, hammering and sawing, operating power tools and carrying on until all hours of the night. And those klieg lights, or whatever you call them, shining in people's windows. Are you aware that the city has a noise ordinance?"

"Um, I'm not sure," Hattie said.

"I suggest you check the city website. Quiet hours are to be observed from 10 P.M. until 7 A.M.," he said, handing her the citation. "That's a two-hundred-dollar fine." He looked around the porch with interest.

"That reminds me. I don't see your filming permit posted anywhere. Do you even have one?"

"We have one," Cass volunteered. "It's taped on the door of our construction trailer."

"It's supposed to be prominently displayed at the entrance to the project," Rice snapped. He turned and stalked back to his city vehicle.

Hattie squinted, trying to read the tiny print on the citation. "I wonder who keeps siccing the cops on us?"

"Like he said, the neighbors," Cass said. "Most of these houses on this street have been in the same family for generations. These folks are old and set in their ways."

"Or maybe it's not just the neighbors," Hattie mused. "Maybe Little Holl is still pissed at me for buying this place. Maybe he's making trouble to get even with me."

"Entitled white assholes like Junior are used to getting their way."

Hattie folded the citation and tucked it in her pocket. "Whoever it is, we can't afford to keep getting these citations. The first time he was out here, Inspector Gadget threatened to close us down if we don't toe the line. Tell the crews, Cass. No more working past ten. And in the meantime, I guess I'll walk up and down the block and try a little fence-mending."

26

A Shift in Attitude

"Hattie!" Davis Hoffman pulled alongside her as she was walking into Chu's convenience store to pay for gas.

It was early morning, not even eight. "Hi, Davis," she said, walking over to his car, a black Mercedes convertible. "Are you slumming out here on Tybee?"

"Checking on the house for my mom," he said, rolling his eyes. "Hey, I saw that article in the newspaper about you finding Lanier Ragan's wallet. You didn't tell me you were buying the old Creedmore place. Wow! If I'd known it was going on the market, I would have bought it myself. It's only two doors down from ours. I guess we're neighbors now."

"Be careful what you wish for," she told him. "The place is a disaster. And speaking of neighbors, we're in hot water with them. Someone has reported us, twice, to the city code inspector's office."

"Oh man, what'd you do?" Davis asked, leaning out the car window.

"It's all just nit-picky bullshit stuff," she assured him, "but the fines are killing me."

"Anything I can do?" he asked. "I know most of the folks on the block."

"That's okay. I apologized and dropped off gift baskets.

In the meantime, I better go. We've got a tight shooting schedule today."

"Can't wait to see what you're doing with the place," Davis said. "I'd love a tour."

"I'll call you," Hattie promised. "Soon."

Trae was sitting in the makeup chair, a plastic cape tied around his neck, when Hattie arrived in the trailer. He was simultaneously scrolling through the emails on his phone, flirting with Lisa, and critiquing her work as the hair and makeup artist skillfully applied highlighter to his cheeks and chin, and patted tinted concealer under his eyes.

"Hey, gorgeous," he said, flashing Hattie one of his hundred-watt smiles.

"Be right with you, Hattie," Lisa said. She picked up an electric razor. "I just want to sharpen up these sideburns a little."

"Not too sharp," Trae cautioned. "I kinda like that natural look."

Hattie guffawed. "Natural? You're currently wearing more makeup and hair product than I wore to prom."

"Yeah, but who wore it better?"

"All done!" Lisa whisked the cape from his shoulders and gestured to Hattie. "Next."

Trae vacated the chair but not the trailer, leaning against the wall with his arms crossed over his chest as he watched Lisa start work on Hattie's hair. He was dressed in artfully faded jeans and a white cotton T-shirt just tight enough to show off his toned physique, and had a rolled-up newspaper tucked under his arm.

"Another story in today's paper about the wallet-in-the-wall lady," he said.

"What's it say?"

Trae unrolled the paper and tried to hand it to her.

"Just tell me what it says, okay?"

"It's about that Tybee cop who came out here the other day. Says he's officially taken over the investigation from the Savannah cops. Nice mention of us in here, too. They even spelled my name right. Yours too."

"I guess that's a good thing," Hattie said.

"How did your interview go with the reporter?" he asked.

"Okay. It wasn't like there was a lot I could tell her about finding the wallet."

"But you were with her for quite awhile," he commented. "I'm just curious why this is such a big story, what? Sixteen years later?"

Hattie watched her reflection in the mirror as Lisa deftly wove her hair into French braids, loosening some strands, then using the end of her comb to pick out some wispy bangs.

"Seventeen years. Lanier was special to a lot of people. Yeah, it's been years since she vanished, but that makes it all the more puzzling. Where did she go? What happened to her?"

"Well, you knew her. What do *you* think happened?"

"Like Cass said, nothing good. I don't believe she ran off and left her little kid behind. Molly, that's the reporter, has heard all the rumors—that Lanier was having an affair. Which was the rumor going around way back when we were still in high school . . ."

The trailer door opened and Cass stepped inside. "Hey, Lisa, Mo says you want to jazz me up for my scene this morning?"

"Yup," Lisa said. "I'll get to you as soon as I finish with Hattie. Your outfit's over in wardrobe if you want to get dressed first."

"Nooo," Cass protested. "What's wrong with what I'm wearing?" She was wearing a faded olive-green T-shirt, baggy cargo shorts that fell just below her knees, and high-top Converse sneakers.

Trae shot Hattie a look. "Where shall we start? First off, Cassandra . . ."

"It's Cassidy."

"Okay, *Cassidy*. No offense, but there's a homeless woman hanging out at the gas station on the corner who wants her clothes back. What you're wearing is aggressively ugly."

Hattie cleared her throat. "Ignore Trae. I *think* what he means is, that outfit, while comfortable, and practical, doesn't exactly play up your best assets."

"Cass, don't worry," Lisa said. "Jodi showed me your outfit. It's just skinny jeans and a T-shirt. You've got a cute butt on you. So why not play it up?"

"Maybe I don't want to play it up because I don't want any of these pervy subs getting the wrong idea," Cass said, still pouting.

"I promise, it's nothing provocative or revealing," Lisa said.

Cass was back in five minutes, wearing the slim-fit jeans and a short-sleeved coral-colored T-shirt with a V-neck.

"That's what I'm talking about," Trae said, appreciatively. "Pants that actually fit, plus that color's great on you, whereas that putrid green? Not so much."

"So now you're a fashion expert, too?" Cass asked.

"Just a designer with an innate color sense," he said.

"He might be obnoxious, but he's right," Hattie said. "Sorry."

The trailer door opened and Gage, Mo's assistant, stuck

his head inside. "Hattie? Trae? We're ready for you inside the house."

With the cameras rolling, Trae dipped a brush in the first can of paint and applied it to a section of siding on the front of the house. He looked over at Hattie. "What do you think?"

She shook her head. "Too bright. That aqua would be great on one of the mid-century concrete block cottages on the island, but it's not right for a house this old."

He nodded and opened the next can, but Hattie stopped him. "Ew. No."

"But it's a historic color," he protested. "Swiss mocha."

"Tastes great in coffee, but who wants brown at the beach? Definitely not."

He held up the next can. "White. I've noticed a lot of wood-frame houses from this era are painted a stark white. This shade is a little softer, and we can do something interesting on the trim and shutters. Maybe a dark Charleston green."

She watched as he brushed the paint onto the siding, then stood back and studied it.

"Technically, it's right for the period, but it's sort of boring, don't you think?"

"I agree," Trae said. "And that's why I saved the best for last."

He popped the top of the last can of paint with a dramatic "Ta-da! I give you Tybee Beach Glass!"

Without waiting for her comment, he painted a wide swath of clapboard siding.

The paint was a soft, grayed-down blue-green.

"I like it," Hattie said, taking a step backward, then tilting her head.

"I was down by that shed near the beach and I noticed

this old wooden boat with the most gorgeous faded, salt-glazed blue-green. It reminds me of a piece of beach glass. I scraped a bit of the paint off it and had it color matched at the paint store this morning."

"Perfect!" she beamed. "Tybee Beach Glass it is."

"White trim? Doors painted orange-pink?"

Hattie looked dubious. "Orange-pink?"

He picked up a smaller can of paint and popped the lid, holding it up for her to see, then brushed a small square of coral paint onto the siding. "This reminds me of a hibiscus blossom."

"I never would have picked that color for the door, but actually, I'm kind of loving it," she said.

"Wait!" Trae said, feigning shock. "Are we actually agreeing on a design decision?"

"I'm as surprised as you," Hattie said. She took the brush and painted a narrow coral stripe down the bridge of his nose.

"Cute," Trae said, after the cameras stopped rolling. He rubbed at his nose with a towel.

"That was great, y'all," Leetha said. "Finally I'm seeing some chemistry between you two. Don't you agree, Mo?"

The producer was sitting on the sidelines, watching the video from earlier in the day on his laptop. He didn't look up. "Yeah. Big improvement. Seemed more natural, less contrived. Hattie, we need to reshoot some of your stuff with Cass from this morning. The lighting was shit, and you seemed to be mumbling half your lines."

Hattie bristled. "I was *not* mumbling."

"Okay, so maybe you had a mouth full of grits or something. Whatever. We still have to reshoot. Lisa needs you and Cass so she can touch up your faces. I've got the guys setting up in there, and we'll be ready for you in twenty minutes."

Mo walked back inside the house.

"So," Trae said. "It isn't just me he hates. It's me, and you."

"Don't take it personally," Leetha advised. "Mo don't like nobody during a shoot."

Cass was already sitting in one of the makeup chairs when Hattie arrived in the trailer. Lisa was brushing powder across her cheeks, immune to Cass's complaints.

"I don't look like myself with all this war paint."

"On camera, it looks completely natural," Lisa assured her. "And you have amazing skin. What kind of moisturizer do you use?"

"Bacon grease!" Cass said. "And I throw in some corn-meal to exfoliate."

Lisa recoiled in horror.

"Not really," Cass said, laughing. "I use what my mom and grandma use. Pond's." She stood up and swapped chairs with Hattie.

"Hey, did you see there's another story about us in today's paper?" Cass asked, picking up an old issue of *People* magazine. "Must be a slow news day."

"When we talked the other day, that reporter, Molly Fowlkes, told me she's obsessed with Lanier Ragan. But here's a new wrinkle. She asked if I'd ever heard rumors back then that Lanier was having an affair with one of her husband's football players."

"Huh?" Cass stopped leafing through the magazine.

"Crazy, right? But Molly said that a few years ago, after she wrote a column about the ten-year anniversary of the disappearance, she got an anonymous phone call from a woman who claimed that her boyfriend at the time, who was a Cardinal Mooney football player, was sleeping with

Lanier. She said she wanted Molly to know that Lanier wasn't a saint."

"And she had no idea who the woman was?" Cass asked.

"No. They didn't have caller ID on their phones. She said she never wrote about it for the paper because she could never confirm the woman's story. I told her I'd never heard anything like that. Have you?"

Cass was studying a magazine photo of Jennifer Lopez in a tight-fitting satin dress and held it up for Hattie to see. "You believe this chick is in her fifties? Wonder how much time she spends in the gym?"

"No telling. But it's her job. She gets paid a bajillion dollars a year to look like that. You haven't answered my question. Did you ever hear any rumors about Lanier Ragan sleeping with a high school kid?"

"Don't think so," Cass said. She picked up a pen and began working on the celebrity crossword puzzle at the back of the magazine.

"Look this way, Hattie," Lisa said. "I need to re-glue those eyelashes."

At the end of the afternoon, Hattie was slumped in a folding chair on the front porch of the house, guzzling from a cold bottle of water. A late afternoon rainstorm had set in, and thunder boomed ominously off to the east. Trae collapsed on a chair next to her.

"Damn," he said, pulling his damp shirt away from his chest. "How do you people live in this climate? I feel like I'm living in the rinse cycle of a dishwasher."

"Welcome to Savannah," Hattie told him. "But wait until October. The humidity lifts, and it's still plenty warm enough to hit the beach. Christmas is chilly, but the skies—oh God, they're so blue, and the air is crisp, and the camellias are amazing. I bet they don't have camellias like ours in L.A. And then in February, right around Valentine's Day, the azaleas start to bloom. Every downtown square looks like something out of a postcard. I've got this one azalea in my yard—actually, the color is really close to that coral you want to paint the front door here. . . ."

"Okay, I'm sold," Trae said, laughing. "Where do you live? Here on Tybee?"

"No. I've got a little bungalow in Thunderbolt."

"Thunderbolt? That's a real place?"

"Very real. It used to be a fishing village, with all the shrimp boats tied up along the Wilmington River. We bought it before we got married, and I've been fixing it up ever since."

Trae looked surprised. "I didn't know you were married. So, what, you're divorced?"

"No. I'm a . . . God, I hate this word. Widow. Married young, widowed young."

His face colored. "I'm sorry. For assuming, and for your loss. I know it's none of my business, but what happened?"

"Hit-and-run by a drunk teenaged driver on the Lazaretto Creek Bridge," Hattie said. "Hank was on his motorcycle."

"Jesus," Trae whispered. "I'm sorry, Hattie. Tell me they caught the little shit and threw his ass in prison."

"I wish," Hattie said. "It's been seven years now. The officer who worked the case still calls to check in with me. And every time I get that call, it feels like a fresh stab in the heart."

Trae reached over and squeezed Hattie's hand. He let his hand linger there, for just a second longer than necessary. His hand was warm, and she realized she felt comforted.

"Hey," he said, breaking the awkward silence. "I'm starved. And I am not eating any more craft service food today. How about dinner? Is there a place on this island where I could get a decent martini?"

"Sundae Café," Hattie said promptly.

"What do you say we both clean this pancake makeup off our faces and head over there?"

"Okay," she said, surprising herself. "Let me see if Cass wants to come too."

"Swell," he said, but his tone gave him away.

"Never mind," Hattie said, laughing. "Give me ten minutes and I'll be good to go."

27

What's for Dessert?

Trae rolled his eyes in disbelief when he saw where the restaurant was located—in a small strip shopping center, wedged between Chu's convenience store and XYZ Liquors. "Really? Are we having barbeque, or pizza, or barbecued pizza?"

"Don't be such a snob," Hattie said. "The food here is as good as anything you'd find in downtown Savannah, or Charleston."

They found a table in the small front room, ordered drinks—a dirty martini for Trae, a glass of chardonnay for Hattie—and were about to order dinner when a woman, middle-aged, sunburnt and excited, edged toward them.

"I told my friends," she pointed at a table of five women, "I know that's him. That's gotta be him. You're Trae Bartholomew, right? From *Design Minds*?"

Trae flashed a blinding smile. "That's me."

She clapped her hands. "Yay! I knew it. We all thought you should have won. That girl that did win, Jovannah? Her room was the tackiest thing I've ever seen. I mean, who glues aluminum foil to a wall? Ugh! Anyway, your room was the best. And we're all big fans, we follow you on Instagram, and we're dying to know about your new show!"

The women at the table all waved in unison and lifted their wineglasses in a toast.

"Well, thanks," Trae said, trying and failing to appear humble. "*Design Minds* was a fun show, and I got a lot of business out of it, so I guess, in the end, I really did win."

"We saw the photos of the new project you're working on," she said. "That kitchen is the worst!" She glanced meaningfully at Hattie. "Is the project in Savannah? Is this your, like, assistant?"

"My costar!" he said hastily. "Hattie Kavanaugh." He lowered his voice. "We're shooting a new show for HPTV. But keep that on the down-low, okay?"

"Really!" she shrieked. "Right here on tacky old Tybee?"

"Tybee's not tacky," he said. "It's charming. Quaint. Unassuming. And wait until you see the transformation. It'll be the most gorgeous beach cottage you've ever seen."

"Where is the house? When will the show air?"

Trae held up his hands in surrender. "I can't give you the address, but I can tell you it's a historic waterfront house, and the show will air on Wednesday nights starting this fall."

"I can't wait!" the woman said. She produced a menu and a pen. "Would it be rude of me to ask for an autograph?"

"I'd consider it rude if you didn't ask," he said, scrawling his name across the menu. "Now, how about a photo?"

"Oh my God!" she trilled, and nodded at Hattie. "Would you?"

"Of course," Hattie said, but when she stood up, instead of inviting her to pose, the fan handed her the phone.

Trae got up from the table and draped his arm across the woman's shoulders. "Say '*Homewreckers*'!" he prompted, beaming down at the stranger.

Hattie clicked off three or four frames and handed the phone back.

"That was awkward," Trae said, when the woman returned to her friends. "Sorry. Sometimes these hard-core fans can be pretty insensitive."

He picked up the menu. "What's good here?"

"Locally caught seafood," Hattie said. She looked over her shoulder at the table of women, who were chattering and pointing toward them. "Does that happen to you often?"

He grimaced. "Now and again. That *Design Minds* show was shot three years ago, but it lives on in the world of reruns. Which means that I get to keep reliving the fact that Jovannah, a dog-groomer-slash-designer from Terre Haute, beat me out of the fifty-thousand-dollar grand prize."

"Ouch," Hattie said.

"It's okay. They gave her a show and only aired six episodes before the network pulled the plug. That's showbiz, right?"

"I wouldn't know," Hattie said. She leaned forward with her elbows on the table. "What do you think the chances are that our show will do okay?"

"I think we've got a winning combination," Trae said. "Mo and Leetha are good at what they do. The house is gonna be fabulous when we get done with it." He winked. "And you can't deny our chemistry."

Hattie blushed and sipped her wine.

"Listen. Rebecca Sanzone wants our show to work. There's a reason they gave us that Wednesday night slot, and I'm not just talking about Krystee Brandstetter's twins. Not to sound like an immodest jerk, but I've got six hundred thousand fans on social media, like that lady and her friends at that table over there. So just between us—we're a lock."

"Really?" She swept a strand of hair behind her ear as she considered the ramifications of having a hit television show.

Trae reached over and touched her hand. "Cheer up.

Maybe we'll tank. Or the house will burn down. Or we'll find that schoolteacher's mummified body in the attic."

She yanked her hand away. "Not funny."

"Sorry." He shook his head. "You're right. Bad joke. Bad taste. Blame it on the jitters."

Their server appeared. "Why don't you order for us?" Trae suggested. "Seafood sounds good."

Hattie ordered the crab cake appetizer and crispy fried flounder for both of them. And another glass of wine.

"Jitters?" she said, when the waiter was gone.

"Yeah. You know, boy-girl jitters."

"Oh, please. Save that kind of flattery for your fans," she said.

"I'm being completely honest with you," he insisted. "Trying to win you over isn't an easy task."

"Why do you feel the need to win me over? We got through a whole segment today without me wanting to brain you with the sledgehammer. I call that progress."

He laughed. "Is it that you don't like me, or don't trust me, or both?"

She felt the heat rising in her cheeks. "I like you just fine."

"'Fine' is not a ringing endorsement."

The waiter slid a basket of warm bread onto the table, alongside a dish of olive oil. Hattie helped herself to a slice, tearing off a bit and dipping it into the herb-flecked oil.

She chewed the bread and sipped her wine. He raised one eyebrow. "That's it? That's all you got for me?"

"Okay," she relented. "Maybe you're growing on me. A little bit."

"Like mold? Is that supposed to be good?"

"Trae? I think we've got a good working relationship, and it seems like Leetha and Mo are pleased. I honestly don't know what more you want from me."

He leaned across the table and kissed her gently on the

lips. "This," he murmured in her ear. "This is what I want from you. For starters."

Hattie's eyes flew open just in time to catch camera flashes going off at the table of fans. The women were giggling and nudging one another.

She drew back from him, and her face felt like it was in flames. "Shit."

He glanced over his shoulder at the women, then returned his focus on Hattie. "Ignore them, please. This is about us."

She took a gulp of wine. "Us? I don't know what to say."

"You could start by saying you enjoyed the kiss."

"Wow," she said, stumbling to phrase her reaction. "You took me totally off guard. That was sort of a hit-and-run kiss, wouldn't you say?"

"Not really. You asked me what more I want from you, and I responded with a demonstration. On impulse. You admitted we have good on-screen chemistry. So I wanted you to realize that we could be good together off-screen, too. Very good." He raised an eyebrow. "Unless that's repugnant to you? I mean, God forbid you would find my attentions unwelcome, or think I'm sexually harassing you."

"Sexually harassing? No!" she said quickly. "And you're not totally repugnant."

There was that smile again. He'd used it on those fans, of course, but this one, she told herself, was different. It was genuine. And totally disarming. She could feel her defenses melting.

Now their server was at the table with their appetizer, and she offered up a silent prayer of thanks for the welcome distraction.

Trae took a bite. "Hey! This is great." He dipped the crab into the bright red puddle of sauce on the plate. "What's this? I like the spice."

"Hot pepper jelly. It's a southern thing, mixing the sweet with the heat."

"The sweet with the heat. If that's a metaphor for southern girls, I approve."

She shook her head. "You're incorrigible."

"I think that's the nicest thing you've said to me tonight."

When their entrees arrived, Hattie managed to steer the conversation away from any discussions of chemistry by asking Trae about his favorite projects.

"The big-budget ones are the most fun, of course," he said. "These Silicon Valley tech bros who have money to burn are up for the most audacious, over-the-top interiors I can come up with. And they all want to outdo each other. I did an actual freestanding multiplex movie theater for one guy, complete with a full-service concession stand with a wood-fired pizza oven."

"That's crazy," Hattie said.

"What about you? What's your favorite historic restoration?"

"Hmm." It didn't take Hattie long to come up with a response.

"Two years ago, a friend of Tug's sold us his late mother-in-law's house in Ardsley Park. That's a very desirable in-town neighborhood that was Savannah's first streetcar suburb. It was a rundown 1920s Georgian Revival on a gorgeous double lot. The family never listed it with a real estate agent."

She smiled at the memory. "It had hundred-year-old live oaks and boxwood hedges, set back off the street, and it was big—almost four thousand square feet, with an incredible solarium with a fireplace and original leaded-pane windows and Cuban tile floors."

"Tell me more," Trae prompted.

Hattie's face lit up as she described the transformation. "We completely reworked the kitchen space, took out most of the walls. At the time, we had a really talented cabinet-maker working for us. He copied some glass-fronted cabinets that were in the breakfast nook, and we did all the upper cabinets in that same look. We stripped a dozen layers of old paint off the butler's pantry, down to the original oak, and dropped a copper bar sink into it. Best of all, our electrician figured out how to remove the guts of a 1920s-era walk-in fridge and install a new working compressor and motor."

She sighed. "That's the dreamiest kitchen I've ever done. The rest of the remodel was pretty cut and dried. We made a downstairs master suite from what had been a den and the servants' quarters, and then we took the four upstairs bedrooms and made them into three en suite bedrooms. There was an old carriage house on the property too. We converted the downstairs garage into a pool-house-slash-playroom, and made the upstairs a guest cottage."

"I'm impressed," Trae said. "And how did you make out, when you flipped it?"

"Not as well as we should have," she said ruefully. "I did what Tug always accuses me of doing. I fell in love with the house and spent too much. We bought it for $235,000, and spent another $200,000 on the remodel, which at the time was the most we'd ever spent out of pocket on spec like that."

"Doesn't sound like that much to me. All in, around $435,000, right?"

"Not a lot to you, but it was for us. We probably could have made more if we'd installed the pool and backyard landscaping I'd designed, but Tug put his foot down, so we listed it at $779,000 and sold it for $750,000, and I was completely thrilled."

"You nearly doubled your investment," Trae said. "Well done."

"Not as well done as the guy we sold it to," Hattie admitted. "He put in the pool, probably spent around fifty thousand, and flipped it six months later for $1.2 million."

She sighed. "Every time I drive by that house, I'm tempted to knock on the door and ask the new owners to give me a tour."

"If you love your darlings, you have to let them go," Trae said. "I agree with your father-in-law, by the way. Never fall in love with something that won't love you back. It's just a house. And there's always another project, right around the corner."

"Easy for a man to say," Hattie said. "Not so easy for someone like me, with a tendency to fall too hard."

He studied her face, illuminated by the candle lantern on the table. "I wouldn't have guessed that about you. But it's good to know."

Trae clasped her hand in his, and this time she let him. He leaned across for another kiss.

"Ahem."

Their server was back, with a plate containing a huge chocolate brownie topped with ice cream, fudge sauce, and whipped cream, which he placed on the table in front of Trae.

"We didn't order that," Trae said, clearly annoyed at the interruption.

"Compliments of your fans," the server said, nodding in the direction of the table full of women, who were all watching gleefully, camera phones pointed.

Trae stood and did a half bow. "Thanks, ladies!" he called, amid a burst of camera flashes.

He took his seat and forked up a chunk of the confection. He aimed the brownie, dripping with melting ice cream and fudge sauce, directly at Hattie's lips.

"Open wide," he commanded.

"But, I don't want . . ." she protested, and then did as she was told.

More camera flashes.

Flustered, Hattie dabbed at her mouth with her napkin.

"You missed a spot," Trae said. He touched his fingertip to her bottom lip and left it there for just a second longer than was absolutely necessary.

He looked up at their server, who was hovering nearby, enjoying the spectacle. "We'll take the check now."

"The ladies already took care of it," the server said.

"If I'd known they were going to do that, I would have ordered a bottle of wine," Trae told him. He waved at the women, took a tiny bite of the dessert, then laid aside his napkin.

"Let's get out of here."

28

Smoke Gets in Your Eyes

- - - - - -

"How about a nightcap?" Trae asked, as she slid into the front seat of his rented Lexus.

"It's after nine," Hattie pointed out. "Anyway, as far as I know the only place to get a drink at this time of night on Tybee is one of those tourist bars where they serve glow-in-the-dark frozen drinks."

"We could ride into Savannah," he said. "My hotel has a rooftop bar with a great view of the river. And plenty of normal-colored cocktails."

"I don't think so," Hattie said. "It's thirty minutes to downtown from here, then I'd still have to drive back to Thunderbolt, and I've got a seven o'clock call time tomorrow."

"You could take a Lyft. Or maybe we could just have a quiet drink at your place? Thunderbolt? Every time I pass through it on the way out here I wonder why it's named that."

"Oh no," Hattie said, instinctively drawing away. Her place? A kiss was one thing; inviting him back to her home, and possibly her bed, if she was reading him right, was taking things entirely too fast.

Trae smelled delicious, like a dangerous combination of

sandalwood and leather and bergamot, and it would be so easy to allow herself to be seduced by him. But not tonight.

"Just take me back to Chatham Avenue so I can pick up my truck, please. I really do have to get home. Ribsy's been cooped up in the house all day. I promised him a walk when I get home. And like I said, it's an early day for me tomorrow."

"My call time's not until nine," Trae said, backing the car out of the lot, then turning onto Butler Avenue.

"That's because you're a man. All you have to do to get camera ready is comb your hair and make sure your fly is zipped. I, on the other hand, have to submit to Lisa's flatiron and contouring brushes. And let's not even talk about wardrobe."

"We both know that's not accurate," he said grumpily. "How about a raincheck?"

"We'll see," Hattie said.

He glanced over at her. "Is that southern-lady speak for 'we should just be friends'?"

She yawned widely. "No, it's Hattie saying I've been on my feet for fourteen hours today, and right now, I just want to go home, shower, and pass out."

They rode the next few blocks in silence. Trae swung the Lexus onto Chatham Avenue and slowed as he approached the driveway.

They were still rolling down the driveway toward the house when Hattie pointed her nose in the air and began sniffing. "Do you smell that? Something burning?"

"Maybe someone's grilling?"

She rolled the window down. "Definitely not."

"Was any of the crew burning trash today?" Trae asked.

"No. Everyone's gone home for the night." She pointed to a plume of white smoke spiraling from the rear of the house.

"Stop right here." She was out of the car and running, even before Trae had put the Lexus in park. "Call nine-one-one," she yelled over her shoulder.

Orange flames shot out of the top of the dumpster, and now the white smoke had turned black and oily. Panicked, she ran to the edge of the porch to look for the hose the workers usually used to clean up with, but the intense heat drove her back.

Eyes stinging, choking from the fumes of smoke, she could only stand helplessly by, watching as the flames from the dumpster, which had been pulled close to the house, licked at the newly stripped wooden siding.

She heard the blare of the fire engines approaching, and turned to see Trae racing toward her. "Hattie, get away from here," he yelled, tugging at her arm, but she was frozen in place, unable to look away. "Come on," he insisted. "It's not safe." He pointed toward the flashing red lights reflecting off the front of the house.

A moment later, a tanker engine rolled slowly toward them, and one of the firemen, dressed in protective gear, hopped out of the cab and approached.

"Is there anyone in the house?" he called.

"No, not that we know of," Hattie said. "It's under construction."

"What's in there?" he asked, pointing at the dumpster. "Any chemicals?"

Coughing violently, Hattie nodded. "Painters have been working back here," she said, between gasps. "And construction debris. The roofers have been throwing the old shingles and tar paper in there."

Three more firemen emerged from the truck and began laying hose.

"You two need to clear this area," the fireman said. "And move those vehicles."

A crowd of rubberneckers had already gathered at the entrance of the driveway. Half a dozen cars were pulled alongside the shoulder of the road. Bicyclists clustered together, chatting and pointing. A pickup truck was parked on the other side of Chatham Avenue, with gawkers piled into the truck bed. A bare-chested teenager had positioned himself in the middle of the driveway, cell phone held in the air to video the conflagration.

Hattie beeped furiously at the kid, who turned and flipped her off before slowly ambling out of the way. She drove past and parked on the shoulder a few yards away from the nearest car. Trae parked the Lexus behind her, got out, and joined her in the front seat of the truck.

"Are you okay?" he asked.

Tears streamed down her smoke-blackened face. She nodded, then buried her face in his shoulder. "If I lose the house . . ."

He patted her back. "You won't. It's literally just a dumpster fire. I think we got there just in time. Five minutes later . . ."

She sniffed and nodded, wiping at her runny nose with her sleeve. "Oh my God. Maybe if we hadn't had dessert—"

"Shh. There's no telling when that fire started. It could have been smoldering for hours."

Someone was tapping on the driver's side window. Hattie looked up and was momentarily blinded by a camera flash. A twenty-something woman grinned and held up her phone. "I knew that was you, Trae!"

"Get the fuck away from here," he growled. "Just go!"

The woman backed away slowly.

"Unbelievable," Trae muttered. "People are unbelievable."

They heard a distinctive *whoop whoop whoop* of sirens, followed by a pair of Tybee police cruisers, blue lights flashing.

"What now?" Hattie craned her neck to watch, as one cruiser sped down the driveway toward the house. The other cruiser stopped, backed up, and parked diagonally across Chatham Avenue. A uniformed cop got out of the cruiser and began walking up and down the roadway, motioning to the onlookers. "Come on now, move along," he yelled.

There was another knock at the window. Hattie rolled it down. "Officer . . ."

"Y'all need to go on home now," the cop said, bending down to look inside the truck.

"It's my house," Hattie blurted. "That's my house that's on fire."

"Oh." The cop shrugged. "Sorry about that. I guess it won't hurt if you stay. Just keep your vehicle pulled completely off the roadway, in case we need to get an ambulance in here."

"We will," Trae said, leaning forward. "Is there any news? Why were the police called?"

"SOP for a house fire," the cop said.

"Have you heard anything? Is the fire out yet?" Hattie asked.

"I'll radio the other officer and let you know what I hear," the cop said. "Hang tight."

The cop reappeared what seemed like hours later to Hattie. "Ma'am? The fire has been extinguished, but y'all can't go back there yet. They're soaking the dumpster and the ground around it. My captain's on his way here, and he'd like to speak to you."

"Okay," Hattie said. "We're not going anywhere."

Ten agonizing minutes passed. "I can't stand not knowing

what's happening," Hattie said, opening the door and hopping out of the truck.

"But the cop said . . ."

"I don't care," Hattie said. "I'll stay out of the way, but I have to see for myself if my house is still standing."

Trae let out a long, annoyed sigh.

She was halfway down the driveway when she finally caught sight of the house, backlit in the flashing red lights of the fire truck, visible in a haze of grayish-white smoke.

Hattie coughed and rubbed at her eyes. It wasn't a mirage. The house was intact.

She spotted the first firefighter, who was leaning against the trunk of an oak tree in the front yard, guzzling from a bottle of blue Gatorade. He'd removed his heavy protective gear and was dressed in a sweat-soaked T-shirt and gym shorts. He looked up at her and nodded, guessing her next question.

"We got it out," he said. "My guys are just wrapping things up back there. All things considered, you got damn lucky."

"How bad?" she asked.

"Not as bad as it could have been. You've got some smoke damage to that wooden siding and the back porch, but we knocked it back pretty quick."

"Thank you. Thank you so much," Hattie said.

"Looks like it could be a cool old house," he said, looking over his shoulder. "I ride my bike past here all the time, but I had no idea something this nice was way back in here, what with all the weeds and junk out front."

"It's nearly a hundred years old," Hattie said.

"Somebody said y'all are shooting a movie or something here?"

"It's a television show. About fixing up an old house. It's called *The Homewreckers*."

He laughed, turned his head, coughed, then spat something into the grass.

"Y'all need to talk to your contractor, ma'am. They ought to know better than to throw those oily rags and stuff into an open dumpster like that. If we'd gotten here ten minutes later than we did, you'd be looking at a big old pile of cinders right now."

"I'm the contractor," Hattie said. "And I'll definitely speak to my crew about that."

She heard the crunch of tires on the drive and turned to see a red SUV rolling toward them. "That's our chief," the firefighter said, taking one last gulp of Gatorade. "He's gonna need to talk to you for his report."

Hattie was still giving the fire chief her contact information when the Tybee police cruiser came bumping down the drive.

The chief waved and the police car pulled alongside them. The window of the cruiser lowered and she recognized the driver. It was Makarowicz, the detective she'd met the previous week, after they'd discovered Lanier Ragan's wallet in the wall.

"We meet again," he said. "Everything okay?"

"Dumpster fire," the fire chief said. "My guys are about ready to roll out." He nodded at Hattie. "We'll be in touch if we need anything else from you. I'll send an investigator out tomorrow, just as a formality."

"Want to take a look?" the cop asked.

"I do, but I'm dreading what I'll find," Hattie admitted.

"We got company," Makarowicz said, shielding his eyes from the headlights of an approaching car.

"Trae," she exclaimed. "I completely forgot he was still here."

The white Lexus came to a stop a few yards away. She reached the car just as he was getting out.

"How's the house?" Trae asked. "I was starting to get worried."

"See for yourself," Hattie said, pointing toward the house. "Still standing. The firemen said the blaze was mostly contained in the dumpster. Sorry. The fire chief needed my info for his report, and then Detective Makarowicz, from last week, just got here and wants to talk to me."

Trae shifted uneasily from one foot to the other.

"You should go ahead and head back to town," Hattie urged. "There's nothing you can do here tonight."

"You sure?"

"I'm sure. Sorry to end the night on such a sour note. I'll see you in the morning."

"Okay." He leaned in and his lips grazed her cheek.

The acrid smell of charred wood and chemicals grew stronger as Hattie and Makarowicz approached the rear of the house.

"That your boyfriend?" Mak asked.

"Trae? No. He's, uh, he's the designer on the show. We had dinner earlier, and he was bringing me back here to pick up my truck when I smelled the smoke from the fire."

Makarowicz played the beam of his flashlight over the back of the container, which was now a blackened, hulking chunk of steel. The front hatch had been unlocked and a mound of unrecognizable cinders spilled onto the scorched ground around it.

"So that's where the fire originated?" the cop asked, walking closer. His steps made a sloshing sound in the puddles of water left from the fire hoses. He swept the light toward the house, and Hattie gasped softly.

A patch of the wooden siding nearest the house, roughly six feet by twelve feet, bore greasy black scorch marks, but the porch columns and planking looked untouched.

She walked up to the porch to get a closer look, and the cop's flashlight beam followed her. "It doesn't look too bad," she reported. "But I'm afraid to open the house to see if there's any water damage."

"Let it wait 'til morning," Mak advised. "Nothing you can do tonight."

"Guess not," she agreed.

He slapped at a mosquito on his arm and regarded her solemnly. "This might not be a coincidence, you know."

The thought had occurred to her as soon as she saw the knot of gawkers standing on the street in front of the house, but she hadn't wanted to voice the idea, for fear of giving it oxygen.

"You think somebody might have set this fire—intentionally?" she asked. "Could it have something to do with Lanier Ragan?"

"I'm not an arson investigator. It's been all over the news about the investigation into her disappearance being reopened. Maybe someone doesn't want you messing around with this house."

"Do you know Howard Rice? The city's code enforcement officer? He's issued us two different citations for code violations. *Someone* reported us to the city for cutting down what he says were mature trees. They weren't. Just a bunch of stunted scrub pines, palmettos, and weeds. That was a thousand-dollar fine. A couple days later, he came by to slap me with a two-hundred-dollar fine for violating the city's noise ordinance. He said neighbors had been complaining. But nobody's voiced any complaints to me."

"Don't know this Rice guy," Mak said.

"You don't want to. I'm just wondering if whoever ratted us out to Inspector Gadget might have gotten mad enough to set fire to the dumpster."

"You mean, as a warning?" Mak asked.

"They could have been trying to burn down the whole house. That firefighter told me if we hadn't seen the smoke when we did, this house would've burnt to the ground."

The cop was silent for a moment. "Who'd want to do something like that? And why?"

"I guess it could be a really pissed-off neighbor. Or maybe someone who's really pissed off that I bought his house 'out from under him' as he put it."

"You're talking about Holland Creedmore," Mak said. "Maybe it's time Junior and I had a discussion."

29

Almost Famous

- - - - - -

Mo was standing in the bathroom, shaving, when he heard his phone.

Da-dum. Da-dum, da-dum, dum, dum, dum. The ringtone was unmistakable. Every time he heard it he pictured Roy Scheider backing away from the hull of that fishing boat in the shark-infested waters of Cape Cod. But it was barely six A.M. in Savannah. What was she doing up at this ungodly hour on the West Coast?

"Rebecca?"

"Mo! You're a genius. OMG, these photos are priceless."

"What photos are we talking about?" He went back into the bathroom and unplugged the electric shaver, looked in the mirror. His face looked like an unmade bed. He tried to remember the source of the quote, but it was too early.

"On TMZ. Your stars. Hattie and Trae. Staring into each other's eyes, kissing, caressing each other's faces. Caught in action. These photos are perfection."

He put her on loudspeaker and typed "TMZ" into the search engine on his phone. Right below the stories of a spectacular Hollywood divorce and an even more spectacular story about a married US senator from a blue state being caught red-handed with a same-sex lover, he spotted the headline: DASHING HPTV DESIGNER GETS STEAMY WITH SAVANNAH COSTAR.

The photos had the blurry, sleazy tabloid quality that sold advertising and launched or sunk celebrity careers, depending on the public's mood that day. And just as Rebecca had said, they showed Hattie in a series of candid, candlelit shots, kissing and mooning at Trae Bartholomew, who was gazing at her with the look of a starving leopard considering a baby giraffe. From the look of the photos, they'd been taken at a local restaurant. And from the look of it, Hattie wasn't exactly fighting Trae off with a steak knife.

For a moment, he saw red.

"Fuck."

The accompanying story was breathless and riddled with hyperbole and sly insinuation. The gist of it was that Trae was shooting a new hit HPTV reality show called *Homewreckers,* and that he and his costar, a lovely but unknown local talent, were already getting along "like a house on fire."

"Mo! Are you looking at the photos? How did you even manage this?"

He closed the browser window. "It wasn't hard. You were right. The chemistry was there, all I had to do was light the match."

"That's the idea! Listen, I've already called Andrea in PR to alert her. We're going to pitch this story to every outlet in the country: *People, The Today Show, Headline Hollywood, Entertainment Weekly, Good Morning America . . .*"

"And don't forget *The National Enquirer,*" Mo said.

"Yes! Of course! Those supermarket tabloids aim squarely at our demographic."

"I was kidding."

"I'm not," Rebecca said. "Also, what's this about a fire at the house? You didn't actually start a fire as a publicity stunt, did you? I mean, I'm not saying that's a bad idea, but for insurance purposes . . ."

"What fire?"

She sighed. "Mo, don't you even have Google Alerts? There was some kind of fire there last night. All I got was a brief digest item, but I think it was on your local news there."

Mo walked into the living room and turned on the television, switching channels until he found one that wasn't talking about the capture of a ten-foot alligator in a local family's swimming pool.

"And up next, fire threatens the restoration of a historic home on Tybee Island." His eyes widened as he viewed orange flames billowing into the night sky. Another shot showed the Creedmore house from the front, with smoke pouring from the rear of the house.

The newscaster was the same guy with the slicked-back hair who'd showed up at the house after the discovery of Lanier Ragan's wallet. Aaron something.

"Fire officials say the blaze was discovered around nine thirty last night. It apparently started in a dumpster, and came dangerously close to the vacant hundred-year-old house. Fortunately, members of the Tybee Fire Department quickly brought the flames under control. The cause of the fire is under investigation. An alert neighbor sent us this video, but we'll be following up in our six o'clock news hour."

"Jesus! Rebecca. I gotta go."

"All right, but keep me posted. Honest to God, Mo, this story just gets better by the minute. I'll call Tony later, because I think this means we ramp up a major fall preview campaign."

He texted Hattie. No answer. He got dressed, found his car keys, went back into the bathroom to brush his teeth, and caught a glimpse of himself in the mirror. "Face like an unmade bed." He snapped his fingers. "Got it. Orson Welles."

30

After the Fire

It was Ribsy who nudged her awake just after six the next morning. He jumped onto the bed and began pawing at her back. When she turned over, he planted his entire body on her chest, resting the top of his head just under her chin.

"Ughhhh." She gently pushed his face away. "Dude, your breath!"

That's when she noticed her phone, which she'd switched to silent before falling into bed only five hours earlier. The screen was flashing with text notifications.

Two were from Cass, two were from Mo, and one was from Trae.

Cass: 5:42 A.M. OMG. Were you really swapping spit with Ashtray in public?

Cass: 5:45 A.M. What the hell? There was a fire at the house? Call me. NOW.

Mo: 5:36 A.M. Hey. If you and Trae are going to go viral, a warning would be appreciated.

Hattie sat up in bed after reading them. "Viral?"

Mo's next text, sent only five minutes before she woke up, echoed Cass's. *CALL ME*.

The phone vibrated in her hand. Mo.

"There was a *fire*? And you didn't think to let me know?"

Hattie rubbed her eyes. "How did you even hear about the fire?"

"Rebecca got an alert on her phone and called. And I just saw it on the news."

"It's on the news? Geez. It was in the dumpster. We caught it just in time, and the house is still standing," she said. "I didn't think you'd appreciate a call at one in the morning, which is when I got home."

"You can call me anytime if it's about the show," Mo said. "Just how bad is it?"

"Well, it was dark, so I couldn't really tell a lot. There was definitely some smoke damage to the siding on the back, and maybe on the porch. I didn't go inside last night."

"And you're okay, right?" he said. "I mean, you and Trae weren't inside the house making out when the fire started, right?"

"Not funny," she snapped. "Where do you get this whole making out and viral thing, anyway? We had dinner, he brought me back to the house so I could pick up my truck, and that's when I smelled smoke and called nine-one-one."

"Obviously, you haven't seen TMZ," Mo said.

"Until five minutes ago, the only thing I'd seen this morning was the inside of my eyelids."

She put him on speaker and typed "TMZ" into her phone's search engine. She felt the blood drain from her face when she saw the teaser headline: REALITY STAR TRAE BARTHOLOMEW GETS STEAMY WITH COSTAR ON SAVANNAH LOCATION SHOOT. Right below the headline was a series of fuzzy snapshots—Trae leaning across the table, staring into Hattie's eyes, Trae kissing her, Trae feeding her a bite of dessert. And yes, Hattie in the driver's seat of her truck, with her head buried in Trae's shoulder.

"Oh God," she moaned. "This group of women was at the table near ours. And then some chick just walked up to my truck while we were parked outside the house, waiting to hear from the firemen. Super fans. They must have sent in those photos. I'm sorry, Mo. It never occurred to me . . ."

"Don't apologize," he said, his tone brusque. "This is exactly what the network was hoping for."

"But it's so gross," she protested. "These pictures make it look like . . ." She shuddered. "Like we were ready to climb into bed together. And that's *not* what happened. It was one kiss."

"Listen, Hattie," Mo said. "Better get used to this stuff. The more eyeballs on you and Trae, the more eyeballs will be on the show in the fall. I gotta go now. See you at the house."

"Wait. Are we even going to be able to shoot today? I mean, it was a big mess when I left last night."

"Absolutely we're shooting today. Fire equals drama. Speaking of, now we gotta track down whoever shot that video of the fire that was on the news this morning."

"There's something else I need to tell you, Mo."

"What's that?"

"That cop, Makarowicz? He came to the house to talk to me last night, after the fire was out. He's wondering . . . and I am, too, if maybe that fire was intentionally set. By the same person who reported us to the city for code violations."

"You're talking arson? Who would do something like that?"

"Not sure. Maybe the guy whose family used to own the house?"

"Creedmore? C'mon, Hattie. That's a little far-fetched, don't you think?"

"I don't know," she admitted. "But Makarowicz said he's going to go talk to the guy."

"If it is Creedmore, maybe that'll spook him, and he'll decide to leave us the hell alone."

Mo disconnected and Hattie's phone beeped to alert her to an incoming call from Cass.

"Hello," she started.

"Are we best friends or not?" Cass yelled.

"Of course we are. I didn't call you about the fire because . . ."

"Who cares about the fire? I just saw on the news that nobody was hurt and the house is still standing. I'm talking about you getting hot and 'steamy' with Trae."

"It was one kiss!" Hattie protested. "We went to dinner at Sundae Café, and it so happened that there was a table full of pushy fans who took pictures of us. Calm down, Cass. I swear to God. It's not what it looks like."

"Who kissed who?" she demanded. "I need details."

Hattie got up and went into the kitchen with Ribsy following right behind. She popped a pod into the coffeemaker, and scooped some dry food into Ribsy's bowl.

"He kissed me," she said reluctantly. "What was I supposed to do? Slap his face?"

"Did you *want* to slap his face? Looking at those photos it kinda looks like you were enjoying yourself."

"I don't know," Hattie muttered. "Getting kissed by a gorgeous guy like Trae? It's not exactly torture. On the other hand . . ."

"What? You're afraid of what people will think?"

"Yeah." Hattie slid her mug onto the coffee maker. "What if Tug and Nancy see those pictures? How's that going to make them feel?"

"Honey? I got a news flash for you. Hank's dead. But you're alive. And it's been seven years now. Tug and Nancy might not exactly love the idea of you being with another man, but they're good people. They'll get used to it. The question is, will you? Hattie?"

"I'm here," she replied. "Look, Cass. The sun's not even

up yet. I can't get all existential with you before I'm fully caffeinated."

Cass disconnected, and Hattie sipped her coffee and tried to gather her thoughts. She looked down at the one remaining text message on her phone. The one from Trae.

I dreamed about you last night.

"That's it? That's the text?"

Ribsy looked up from his food bowl.

"What's that even supposed to mean?" Hattie asked him, dumping the rest of her coffee into the sink. She stopped and patted the dog's head. "Okay, boy. No offense, but I hate men."

31

The Show Must Go On

Hattie loaded Ribsy into the truck and started the drive to Tybee with her wet hair in a towel turban. Her phone was in the cupholder and it pinged to alert her to an incoming text. The message was from Cass. She felt a stabbing pain behind her left eye when she read it.

INSPECTOR GADGET IS BACK

The driveway was lined with vehicles, including a small white truck with the Tybee city seal on the door.

She parked her truck, jumped down, and made for the porch, with Ribsy bounding along behind. "Now what?"

Howard Rice was standing on the front porch of the house, clipboard tucked under his arm, nose to nose with Mo, who appeared to be having a spirited discussion with the code inspector.

She could hear his voice as she approached the pair. "This is harassment, pure and simple," Mo said. "Don't you have anything better to do with your time?"

"I have a fiduciary duty to the city," Rice replied, not backing down or away. "When a code violation comes to my attention, it's my job to enforce the law." He held up his

210   MARY KAY ANDREWS

clipboard and showed it to the producer. "This photo clearly shows that your dumpster was left uncovered. That's a thousand-dollar fine."

Hattie marched toward the porch and snatched the clipboard out of Rice's hand.

The paper was a printout of a color photo showing a dark green container similar to the one in the backyard, taken at night, probably with a flash. "Where'd you get this?" she demanded.

Ribsy positioned himself at her feet, alert for potential danger.

"A concerned citizen emailed it to me last night," Rice said. He reclaimed the clipboard. "Clearly, you can see the dumpster isn't covered, because there are boards and bits of tarpaper spilling over the side."

"Last night? What time last night?" A white-hot rage was boiling up from her chest.

"I'd have to check the time code on the email," Rice said. "Doesn't matter. It's a violation." He started to rip a citation from a pad clipped to the board, but Hattie stopped him.

"That dumpster is at the rear of my property. We both know it's not visible from the road. Whoever took that photo was trespassing on private property. I'm sure you're aware that we had a fire out there last night, which could have burned this house down. My crew and I were here working until around eight thirty, at which time I went to dinner. By the time I got back here shortly before ten, that dumpster was already blazing."

"What are you suggesting?"

"Are you blind and deaf?" Mo shouted. "She's saying your 'concerned citizen' is a goddamned arsonist who deliberately set fire to that dumpster."

Gadget had the good sense to take a step backward. "You don't know that."

"The hell we don't," Hattie said. She grabbed her phone from her pocket. "Stay right here. I'm calling Detective Makarowicz at Tybee PD. He needs to see this photo."

Rice ripped the citation from the pad and handed it to Hattie, who threw it to the porch floor and stomped on it.

"Super fun way to start the day," said Cass, who'd been leaning against the porch railing, watching Hattie's interaction with Inspector Gadget.

"My head already feels like it's going to explode."

She called the cell number Makarowicz had given her, but it went directly to voicemail.

"Detective Mak? It's Hattie Kavanaugh. Call me, please. It's important."

She disconnected and looked over at Mo Lopez. "How bad is it?"

He opened the front door and gestured for her to enter. "See for yourself."

The front of the house was untouched by the fire.

"The firemen cut power to the house last night," Hattie said.

"I found the main breaker and turned it back on when I got here," Mo said.

She heard voices coming from the kitchen. "The painters," Cass said. "Jorge and his guys feel awful. They heard about the fire on the radio and got here about the same time I did."

"But we don't know that it was their fault," Hattie cautioned.

"One thing we do know. It's a mess," Mo said.

Hattie's heart sank when she saw the pool of water seeping into the hallway.

Jorge and his son Tomas were inside the kitchen, using push brooms to sweep an inch of standing water toward the propped-open back door. A huge industrial fan was set up on the makeshift sawhorse worktable, and Jorge's nephew Eddie was dragging in a wet-dry shop vacuum. The whole back wall of the kitchen was coated with a fine, greasy black film, and all the cabinets, which had not yet been installed, were coated in the same soot.

Jorge looked up at her with mournful eyes.

"So sorry," he said. "We were careful, Hattie. Tomas says he had all the paint rags in a ten-gallon sealed bucket. It was on the back porch, but it's gone now."

Tomas nodded. "The can of mineral spirits we were using to clean brushes is gone too."

"Holy shit," Hattie whispered. "Someone really *did* set that fire on purpose."

"What happens now?" Hattie asked. "Will we have to shut down? Will the network give us more time to finish the house?"

They were standing on the front porch, sipping coffee, while the camera crews were busy documenting the fire damage for the insurance company.

"No, and no," Mo said calmly. "Rebecca called me as soon as I got off the phone with you. She was adamant. Nothing changes. We make the fire drama part of the story. Who doesn't love a good catastrophe—as long as it happens to someone else. Right?"

"That's crazy," Hattie objected. "That water in the kitchen was standing all night. There's a good chance those old wooden floors will have warped. And the back porch is a mess. I'm worried those columns might have more than just smoke damage."

"We'll have to figure a work-around. Trae can design something that looks close to or better. Where is he, by the way? It's almost nine."

"I don't know," Hattie said. "He texted me early this morning, but I haven't had time to text him back or call."

"Ooh, girl," Leetha said. "After I saw those photos of you two on TMZ I figured maybe the two of you would be strolling in here together this morning, looking all afterglowy."

Hattie let out a long, exasperated sigh. "How many times do I have to say it—it wasn't like that. We are not a couple. Okay? Are we clear?"

"Whatever you say," Leetha murmured.

Cass walked up, holding a paper plate loaded with fruit and muffins from craft services.

"Mom called the insurance company, and an adjuster should be here today."

"When can we have that ruined dumpster hauled away?" Leetha asked, helping herself to a muffin. "That thing is an eyesore."

"Not until the fire marshal comes back," Cass said. "Which should be this morning."

"I've left two messages for that Tybee cop," Hattie said. "I want him to hear what Jorge and Tomas told us about that missing bucket of rags and the mineral spirits."

"Who'd want to burn down this place, y'all?" Leetha asked. "Who'd you piss off?"

"Leave it to the cops to figure that out. We need to start filming," Mo said, crumpling his paper coffee cup. "With or without your new squeeze."

The film crew was set up in the hallway outside the kitchen.

Just as the cameras were beginning to roll, Trae arrived on the set. "Sorry," he said to Mo, who pointedly glanced at his wristwatch. "The valet guys at the hotel couldn't find my car, and then there was a train blocking the railroad tracks. For fifteen damn minutes."

Mo shook his head and turned his attention back to Hattie. "As soon as you're done here, we'll get Trae to talk about the cabinet situation. If he's not too busy."

Trae stood a few inches from Mo's face. "What's that supposed to mean?"

"It means I'm not interested in lame excuses," Mo retorted.

"Okay, you two," Leetha said, pushing herself between the men. "That's enough butt sniffin'. Can we go to work now?"

32

Suspicious Minds

- - - - - - -

Makarowicz parked his city cruiser at the curb in front of the address he'd found on the internet. The house wasn't what he expected of a man who was supposedly the scion of a wealthy old Savannah family.

It was the shabbiest house on East Forty-Eighth Street. A brick cottage with fading pale green paint with a scraggly yard and overgrown shrubs that obscured the front windows. But the pickup truck parked in the driveway looked fairly new and shiny.

He rang the doorbell and waited. "Who's that?" a man's voice called.

"Holland Creedmore? I'm Detective Makarowicz with the Tybee Police Department, and I'd appreciate a few minutes of your time." He held his badge up to the peephole in the wooden door.

"Shit," the voice muttered.

The door opened a few inches with the chain lock still engaged. Holland Junior had a high forehead, receding blond hair, and a thick handlebar mustache. "What's this about?"

"If you'll let me come in, I'll tell you," Mak replied.

Creedmore opened the door and motioned for him to

enter. "Okay, but you need to make this short. I've got some-place I need to be in thirty minutes."

"Understood."

"Sit there." Holland Jr. motioned toward a black leather recliner that faced a matching black leather sofa.

Creedmore took a seat on the sofa. He was barefoot and wore baggy khaki slacks and a navy T-shirt that did little to hide a roll of fat around his belly.

"I saw in the newspaper that they found Lanier Ragan's wallet at our old house on Tybee." Creedmore's tone was bel-ligerent. "We don't own it anymore, you know? Those TV people bought it out from under us."

"I'm aware," Mak said.

"All kinds of shady business going on out there at Tybee City Hall," Creedmore said. "You working for the police de-partment, I'm sure you see your share of the corruption."

"Nope," Mak said. "But I've only been on the force for a few months."

"Give it time," Creedmore said. "Those folks are crooked as a dog's hind leg."

"I'll keep that in mind." Mak took out his notebook and pen. "I understand you might have known Lanier Ragan? That schoolteacher who disappeared?"

"I played football at Cardinal Mooney for her husband, Frank Ragan," Creedmore said. "I saw her at games and stuff like that, but I don't have any idea how that wallet got there."

"Do you know if Mrs. Ragan ever visited your family's beach house?"

"My dad was head of the booster club for years, and my folks used to give parties for the whole football team and their families and the coaches. She could have come to one of those parties with her husband."

"Right. When was the last time you were in the house?"

"It would have been after the last hurricane. What was

that, Irma? So, 2017? We lost part of the roof after Hurricane Matthew in 2016. My dad is only part owner of the house. There's my dad's cousin who lives up north, he hadn't been down here in years, and then his cousin Mavis, who is a giant pain in the ass. We only just barely got the roof repaired when Irma blew it off again. And it turns out, Mavis had let the insurance lapse. My dad and I went out there to see how bad things were. And it was bad. My dad and Mavis had words, and next thing we know, she's locked us out. Of our own house."

"So, you're saying the last time you were physically inside that house would have been sometime in 2017?"

"Check the dates, but I believe it was in September," Creedmore said.

"Don't know if you heard, but there was a fire out there last night?" the cop said.

"Saw it on the news. Those dumb fucks almost burned down one of the oldest houses on the island. It's a crime what they're doing with that place."

"So you've seen the work they've done?"

"I've driven by a couple of times. I heard all our old neighbors are raising hell because of the traffic and noise coming from there."

"Someone reported Hattie Kavanaugh to Tybee's code enforcement officer. She's already gotten two citations and had to pay some serious fines," the detective said.

Creedmore laughed. "Serves her right, the stupid bitch."

"You know," Mak said, fixing Creedmore with a deadpan stare, "it kind of looks like someone is deliberately harassing her. And that dumpster fire looks like arson."

"So that's what this is about? You think I'm messing with her? Forget it. I've got better things to do with my time."

Makarowicz abruptly changed tack. "What do you think happened to Lanier Ragan?"

"How should I know?" Creedmore shot back. "I was just a kid. Ask her husband."

"Oh, I will," Mak said easily. "Just out of curiosity, when was the last time you saw Lanier Ragan?"

"I think we're done here. I've got an appointment to get to." Creedmore went to the front door and yanked it open.

33

Twenty Questions

– – – – – – –

The caller ID screen said "Unknown Caller." He picked up. "Makarowicz."

It was a woman's voice. "Detective Makarowicz? This is Deborah Logenbuhl, you left a private message on my Facebook page, asking me to call? I worked with Lanier Ragan at St. Mary's Academy."

"Yes. Thanks for getting back to me," Mak said.

"I was wondering if someone from the police would contact me," she said. "I saw on the news that Lanier's billfold was found in that house out on Tybee. I even thought of calling you myself, but I didn't want to be one of those crackpots calling the cops with some crazy conspiracy theory."

"Okay if I record our conversation?"

"Yes, I guess that would be all right."

He tapped the record button on the phone.

"I understand you were close with Lanier Ragan?"

"We were dear friends," she said. "Her classroom was next to mine. Lanier was a bright light. It was a huge shock when she disappeared. I don't think I've ever gotten over it."

"At the time, what did you think happened to her? Did she ever discuss the idea of leaving her husband? Or going away?"

"Going away? No," Deborah said.

"Was she unhappy? At home, or at work?"

The drama teacher considered the question. "I only realized it after she disappeared, but something was definitely going on with her that fall. She'd changed."

"How so?"

"She was . . . sort of closed off. Preoccupied, you might say. That fall, Lanier was always scurrying away to a meeting, or a conference, or a tutoring session. In the past, we'd meet up Saturday mornings for coffee, but she no-showed me a couple of times. The last time I saw her was at the faculty Christmas party. She was wearing one of those silly headbands with felt reindeer antlers, and a red foam nose. I went into labor the next morning."

"You said she did tutoring sessions?"

"Yeah. Lanier was tutoring some of our girls, prepping them for their SATs, and I know Frank had her tutoring some of the boys on the football team. Between that and Emma and the house, it was a lot, you know? And Frank wasn't around, because it was football season."

"Did she complain about Frank? Was the marriage okay?"

"She didn't have to complain. I saw it for myself. He expected her to be the perfect little wifey. Cook, clean, take care of Emma, help out her sick mom, plus be a saint in the kitchen and a slut in the bedroom."

"I take it you weren't a fan of Frank Ragan?"

"Hardly."

"Could he have had something to do with her disappearance?"

"Possibly. But I went into labor six weeks early, the week before Christmas, and I had a sick preemie in the ICU at Memorial. That time is just a blur to me now."

"But your baby was okay, right?"

"He's a high school senior, six inches taller than me."

"I'm glad," Mak said. "You said Lanier was tutoring some of Frank's players?"

"Two or three," Deborah said. "Big dumb lugs who didn't know a past participle from a forward pass."

"Do you remember the names of any of the guys she tutored? The football players?"

"Is it important?"

"It might be. We had a tip, that Lanier had been having an affair with a high schooler."

The drama teacher made a sound like the air escaping from a half-deflated balloon. "Ohhh."

"It might not be true," Mak admitted.

"I guess it's not *that* far-fetched an idea. Lanier was young—ten years younger than me, and she got so involved with the girls and their lives. Maybe too involved. So yeah, I guess it could have been one of the football players. But I wouldn't remember any of their names."

"What if I got a roster for the football team for that year?" Mak persisted. "Maybe seeing the names would spark a memory?"

"Sorry. I just never paid attention to sports. Not my thing."

"That's okay," Makarowicz said. "Thanks for getting back to me."

"This is Frank. You know what to do."

Makarowicz hesitated. He'd left three previous voice messages for Frank Ragan, none of which had been returned. He didn't have high hopes of hearing from the former football coach, but he'd give it one more shot.

"Mr. Ragan, this is Al Makarowicz of the Tybee Island Police Department. There has been a new development in the investigation into the disappearance of your wife, and it's urgent that I speak to you."

He spelled out his last name and left his number and disconnected. He was sitting in the claustrophobic cubicle that served as his office at the police headquarters on Van Horne Avenue.

Driving back to the island from his meeting with Holland Creedmore, he'd been thinking about the drama teacher's disclosure that Lanier Ragan had been tutoring high school kids, including some of her husband's football players, the fall before she disappeared. Could one of those "big dumb lugs" have been her secret lover? Holland Creedmore Jr. was on that team, but had he needed tutoring? Who else might fit that description?

He opened the browser bar on his desktop computer and typed in "Cardinal Mooney Catholic High Football team, 2004." There were dozens of citations. He learned that the Knights had gone undefeated and won the state championship that year, and that Frank Ragan had been named Georgia High School Coach of the Year, and that two of his senior players, André Coates and Holland Creedmore Jr., had been named to the all-state first team.

He found a photo of the team's two standouts, grinning and holding their all-state plaques. Coates was a beefy-looking defensive lineman, and Creedmore Jr. was, not surprisingly, a tight end. The article accompanying the story said that Coates was headed to Florida A&M, while Creedmore had signed to play at Wake Forest.

"Wake Forest, huh?" He studied the photo of an eighteen-year-old Holland Creedmore. His blond hair grazed his shoulders, and he was dressed in a white dress shirt, striped red tie, and blue blazer. Clear-eyed, handsome, every mother's son.

Makarowicz scrolled through other stories until he found an article from the *Savannah Morning News* extolling Cardinal Mooney's 2004 senior football players. Eight of the championship team's members had been seniors and were highlighted in the article. He printed out the story and read on.

Thirty minutes later, he had a folder of printouts and some thoughts. On his way out of the building he stopped by the office of the city's code enforcement officer, Howard Rice.

Rice was on the phone, so Makarowicz leaned in the doorway and scrolled through his phone messages. He'd already heard from Hattie Kavanaugh about her run-in with the man she referred to as Inspector Gadget, but he wanted to see the photo of the flaming dumpster for himself.

"Something you need?" Rice was off the phone now.

"I'm Detective Al Makarowicz," Mak said. "Only been with the force a few months, so I guess that's why we haven't met. I'd like to talk to you about that fire on Chatham Avenue last night. I understand someone sent you a photo of the dumpster yesterday?"

"That's right," Rice said. "A concerned citizen."

"Does the citizen have a name?"

"No," Rice said. "The citizen preferred to remain anonymous. We have a municipal tip website that allows citizens to directly report these kinds of violations."

Mak sighed. He'd dealt with this kind of self-important bureaucrat many times in his law enforcement career. They were almost invariably wannabe cops eager to demonstrate the power of whatever badge they wore.

"Can I see the photo you showed Hattie Kavanaugh?"

Rice hesitated. Makarowicz sensed he was trying to find a reason to refuse his request.

"I'm going to meet the fire marshal over at the house this afternoon. That photo could be evidence that the fire was deliberately set."

"This is a code violation—" Rice started.

"Not interested in code-breakers. I'm interested in arsonists," Mak said, holding out his hand. "The photo, please."

"Have you been avoiding me?"

Hattie was sitting on the edge of the seawall, looking out at the Back River. Mo had called for a lunch break, and she'd grabbed a sandwich and a bottle of water and was enjoying the light breeze barely ruffling the surface of the water.

She'd been contemplating walking out onto the dock to check out the dock house. The planking was decaying, boards missing and sagging in other places. Should she risk it? Was there enough money in the budget to rebuild the dock?

Trae sat down beside her and bit into a peach. "I'm definitely getting the keep-away vibe," he repeated. "Tell me if I'm wrong."

"You're not wrong," she admitted. "It's just . . . awkward. I thought our dinner last night—you know—"

"Are we talking about the kiss? Because it didn't feel awkward to me."

"You know what I mean. That was a private moment. But those photos on that website. Everyone has seen them. They're plastered all over the internet. It makes me feel kind of dirty. Like we were doing something shameful."

"It was just one kiss. Between consenting adults." With his fingertip, he traced the curve of her cheek, and Hattie shivered, involuntarily. "Although I think you know I wish it had been more."

"How do you stand it?" she asked abruptly. "And I'm being serious."

"What? Being young and semi-rich and semi-famous? I love it. I'm living my dream. I get to pick and choose my clients and my projects. I get to travel and see new places and meet new people. Like you. How is that a bad thing?"

"But I don't want to be famous," she blurted.

"What do you want?" He rested his chin on her shoulder.

"I don't want to be spied on. I don't want strangers gawking at me, or sticking cameras in my face. I don't want my private life out there on the internet. I want to do my work and make enough money to do . . . whatever I want."

Trae laughed. "In other words, you want to be rich."

"That's not it at all," Hattie said. But she couldn't tell him about what her life had been like before. Before her father got caught and went to prison. Before her family had been shattered. Before the mention of her maiden name made people snicker and whisper about her behind her back.

They heard rustling behind them and turned. Gage, one of Mo's production assistants, cleared his throat nervously.

"Hey, uh, Leetha and Mo sent me to look for you guys. They're set up for the after-the-fire shoot now."

Trae stood and helped Hattie to her feet. "Let's continue this discussion later."

Jorge and Tomas had changed into fresh white painter's pants and crisply pressed work shirts that had their company name embroidered over their breast pocket. A clearly nervous Jorge pointed to the fire-damaged porch and clapboard exterior wall.

"First, we are going to carefully clean up as much of this black soot as we can. We use a commercial degreasing product. Then, when we see how bad the damage is, we will figure out which part of the wall might need to be replaced."

Hattie ran the flat of her hand over the wall near the kitchen door and held her greasy palm up to the camera. "Yuck. Jorge, how long will it take your crew to clean up all this mess?"

"Four guys, we start this afternoon, work late. Maybe two, three days."

"In the meantime," Hattie said, sighing, "there's still plenty of work to do. The carpenters need to finish framing out the new stairway inside, and the plumbers are already working on roughing in the new half bath in the hallway."

Trae stepped easily into the frame. "Let's take folks inside and show them the progress we've made on the new downstairs master suite."

The claims adjuster was writing up his report in the kitchen when Hattie and Trae finished shooting at the front of the house. He was in his fifties, with silver hair and pale blue eyes behind silver-framed spectacles.

"And how soon can we get a settlement check?" Cass asked. "As you can see, we're on a tight deadline here."

"I need to get back to the office and check some numbers, but I think it should be early next week," the adjuster said. He glanced over at Trae, and then back down at his report, and then back again at Trae with a sheepish expression. "You're Trae Bartholomew, right? You probably get tired of hearing this, but my wife is a big fan. Huge fan. Loved that last show you did."

"Thanks," Trae said. "I never get tired of hearing from my fans. What's your wife's name?"

"Dani. Well, Danielle." He produced a sheet of paper from the back of his notepad and held it out to Trae. "Would you mind? I mean, if it's not too big an imposition?"

"Not at all. Tell your wife to be sure and watch *The Homewreckers*. That's the show we're filming here right now. It'll air in September."

"I'll do that," the inspector said. "*The Homewreckers.*

Got it." He looked at Hattie. "You should be hearing something from me about your settlement by early next week." He headed for the door and was about to leave, but then he doubled back. "Might as well get your autograph, too, young lady," he said, handing the paper to Hattie. "Who knows? Someday you might be famous, too, and this will be worth something."

The fire marshal's name was Steven Parkman. He was short and round and had a full, luxurious white beard and wore a black baseball cap with the Tybee city insignia on it. He and Makarowicz had been circling the dumpster, poking at it with a shovel, and snapping photos while Hattie was occupied inside with the claims adjuster.

"Hattie, this is Steve Parkman," Mak said, when she joined them outside.

"Mr. Parkman," Hattie said. "Thank you for coming." She noticed that both men were wearing thin, disposable latex gloves.

"Sparky," Parkman said. "Everyone calls me Sparky."

"Fire department humor," Mak said, not cracking a smile. He pointed at a misshapen lump that the two men had separated from the contents of the dumpster. "Your painter assured me that his son was storing oily rags in a bucket that was on the porch back here. We found what's left of it. In the dumpster."

With the toe of his boot, Sparky nudged a blackened rectangular object. "And here's your accelerant. A gallon can of paint thinner."

"We were right. The fire was deliberately set," Hattie said.

"Arson," Sparky said. "I've seen the photo of the fire taken by our anonymous 'concerned citizen.' I'll speak to

Howard Rice to see if he has any more information, but I'm guessing that's a dead end."

"What happens now?" Hattie asked.

The jovial-looking fire marshal's tone was grave. "We're going to find out who set this fire. And why."

After Sparky left, Makarowicz looked up at the painters, who were already scrubbing down the rear wall of the house. "How bad was the inside?"

"Come see for yourself," Hattie said. She and Cass led him into the kitchen. Two large industrial fans were aimed at the wooden floors, and one of Jorge's crew members was wiping down the new kitchen cabinets with a strong-smelling degreaser.

"Not a total disaster," Makarowicz said.

"Bad enough," Cass said. "We can't afford to lose these cabinets. If the smoke damage can't be mitigated, we'll have to order new ones. We really can't afford the delay."

"Damn shame," Makarowicz said.

"Have you found anything new about Lanier Ragan?" Hattie asked.

"Did you know a St. Mary's teacher named Deborah Logenbuhl?"

"Mrs. Logenbuhl," Hattie exclaimed. "How could I have forgotten about her? The flaming red hair and the wacky glasses and colorful outfits? She was like an exotic bird in a flock of gray pigeons."

"We talked on the phone," the detective said. "She was apparently good friends with Lanier."

"Right. They always ate lunch together," Hattie said. "Have you talked to her?"

"Yeah. She told me that in the fall of 2004 Lanier was busy, tutoring students, helping girls get their grades raised so they could get into the right college. And, she said, Frank Ragan got his wife to tutor some of his football players, too."

"Ohhh," Hattie said. "So, you think maybe what Molly Fowlkes heard was true?"

"Could be," Mak said. "Maybe Lanier was teaching more than adjectives and adverbs."

"Yeah," Cass said, "maybe she was helping some dude bone up on sex ed." Her tone was more bitter than funny, and Hattie did a double take.

"Sorry, not sorry," Cass muttered, leaving the room.

"Did Mrs. Logenbuhl know which football players Lanier was tutoring?" Hattie asked.

"No. All she knew was that Lanier was preoccupied."

"Can you get a list of all the guys on the Cardinal Mooney football team that year?"

Makarowicz reached into his hip pocket and pulled out a neatly folded square of papers. "For good or bad, the internet knows all." He unfolded a printout of an old black-and-white photo and placed it on the sawhorse worktable.

"Frank Ragan's football team won the state championship in 2004. Got lots of publicity." He tapped the photo. "I'm thinking one of this crew could have been teacher's pet."

34

Old School Ties

When Hattie got home, she took a long, hot shower, put on a pair of boxer shorts and a favorite old T-shirt, and warmed up a bowl of Kraft mac and cheese, which she ate sitting on her favorite chair in the living room.

Her eyes traveled to the rows of paperback mysteries on the bookshelves. After Hank's death, books, especially mysteries, had become her refuge. She liked the predictability, the unspoken promise that no matter how ugly, violent, or tragic things got in a mystery, by the story's end there would be some degree of closure. Justice would be meted out.

She was idly leafing through a battered copy of *Void Moon,* her favorite Michael Connelly novel, when she heard her phone ding to announce an incoming text message. She carefully stepped over Ribsy, who was asleep at her feet, and retrieved the phone from the kitchen. The message was from Davis Hoffman.

Hey. Heard about the fire. You okay?

Hattie sank back down into her armchair.

I'm okay. Just exhausted. And worried.

She watched the little bubbles popping onto the screen to indicate he was typing.

Anything I can do to help?

An image popped into her imagination, of the dignified, almost aristocratic Davis Hoffman rolling up his French cuffs to rip up mildewed carpet, or jackhammering a bathroom full of peachy-pink porcelain tile with those long, elegant fingers, the ones with the monogrammed gold signet ring and the bulky Cardinal Mooney class ring.

Maybe. But not with the house.

More bubbles.

???

Different topic. Didn't you play football at Mooney? For Frank Ragan?

If being issued a uniform and dressing out for practices count, yes, technically you could say I was on the team. Mostly I played left out.

Can you remember the names of any players Lanier Ragan tutored your senior year?

She scraped together the last bits of bright orange cheese from the side of the bowl and placed it in front of Ribsy's nose. He stirred, thumped his tail, then enthusiastically attacked the bowl with long, ecstatic licks.

Is this still about that wallet? What's that got to do with her tutoring jocks?

Ribsy was pushing the bowl across the floor with his nose, desperate to get at the last flecks of cheese. When he looked up, he had an orange spot on his black nose. She smiled and returned to her phone.

Cops are looking into a rumor that maybe Lanier had an affair with someone on the football team. Maybe a guy she was tutoring? Like a senior? Could have something to do with her disappearance.

Minutes passed. She opened *Void Moon,* losing herself to the story of a female cat burglar prowling through hotel rooms at Vegas casinos.

No idea who she might have been tutoring. Sorry not to be more help.

Hattie went into the bedroom and found the folded-up photo of the long ago Cardinal Mooney football team that Al Makarowicz had given her.

She smoothed the photo and read over the captions. Maybe this was a topic best discussed over the phone instead of text. She tapped Davis's phone number and he picked up immediately.

"Hey!" He sounded surprised to hear her voice.

"Hi. Is now a good time to talk? About football?"

"Honest to God, Hattie. My senior year, it's a blur. I was applying to college and working part-time at the store . . ."

"And dating Elise. I know. But I've got an old roster from the team. I was thinking if I read off the names, maybe you could guess whether any of them needed tutoring help."

"Don't you think you're taking this a little to the extreme?" he asked.

Was this his way of telling her to "calm down"? How many times over the years had men, including Hank and Tug, both men she adored, told her to "chill out" or "relax"? Which was really just a semi-polite way of telling women to shut up and smile.

"A week and a half ago, Lanier's wallet was found at the house I now own," she said, straining to stay civil. "It's the only clue the cops have found since the day after she disappeared. And since the news got out, someone has been harassing me. First, siccing the code enforcement guy on me, and now, setting fire to the dumpster behind the house. I don't think that's a coincidence."

"Arson? Are you sure about that?" he asked.

"The city fire marshal and the police seem convinced of it," Hattie said. "They found a can of paint thinner in the dumpster that they think was used to ignite it."

"Still seems like a pretty big stretch to me," Davis said.

"I've got an old photo of the team from that year," Hattie went on. "How about if I read you the names and you just tell me if you think there's a chance they were being tutored?"

"This is dumb," Davis protested. "I haven't thought of any of these guys in years."

"You don't go to any of the class reunions? Or alum nights at the football games?"

"No."

"Humor me."

She ran a finger down the photo caption and called out their names.

"Larry Albritton. Tommy Boylan. André Coates. Holland Creedmore, Matt Ellis . . ."

"Definitely not Ellis. He was a brainiac. I think he's a judge up in DC now."

Hattie continued with the roll call. "Braydon Jackson."

"Not exactly a rocket scientist," Davis said, chuckling. "He looked like he was thirty at fourteen, so he was always the guy we sent to Chu's to buy beer."

"I'll take that as a maybe," Hattie said. "Tyler Minshew?"

"Shew was a real straight arrow. Went to West Point. He was killed in action in Iraq."

"Anthony Sapenza?"

"Probably not Tony. He went into the seminary right out of high school."

Hattie looked back over the photo. She'd crossed through the names Davis had excluded. "What about Holland Creedmore?"

"I don't know, Hattie. I'm telling you, I hardly remember that year. What about good old Coach Ragan? Did the police ever clear him?"

Hattie looked down at the photo. Frank Ragan stood in the middle of the ranks of his team. He was tall, broad-chested, with chiseled features and a straight-ahead stare. "I'm not sure whether he was ever a suspect," she said.

"I get that you're curious, but if the cops haven't solved her disappearance after all these years, I find it hard to believe that any of this means anything."

"I guess we're just going to have to agree to disagree on this one," Hattie said, yawning.

"While I've got you on the phone, have you given any thought to my dinner invitation? Or are you too busy with your new costar? Looks like things have gotten pretty friendly between the two of you."

Her temper flared. "Don't believe everything you see on the internet, okay?"

"Whoops. Just kidding," he said hastily.

"Good night, Davis," she said.

On a whim, she decided to try one more name on that football roster.

She picked up her phone and scrolled through her list of contacts until she found his name.

André Coates had been a standout at Mooney and an All-Pro for the Atlanta Falcons, but after retirement, he'd returned home to Savannah and opened a successful car dealership. Two years earlier, tapping into what locals referred to as the "Mooney Mafia," otherwise known as old-school ties, André hired Kavanaugh & Son to rehab his parents' home.

André's voice boomed. "Hattie, girl, what up?"

"Hi, André. How're your folks?"

"Real good. They're loving the house, thanks to you."

"I'm glad. Give them a hug for me. Hey, André, have you been following this stuff about Lanier Ragan?"

"Oh yeah. That's crazy, you finding that wallet in the Creedmores' beach house. What's happening with all that?"

"The cops are investigating. Got a quick question for you.

Did Frank Ragan get Lanier to tutor you or any of the other guys on the team your senior year?"

"Sure did." He chuckled. "Coach wanted to make sure we did okay on our SATs. I have dyslexia, so reading comprehension was always a struggle. Ms. Lanier really helped me with that."

"Okay. Did she tutor any other guys?"

"For sure Tommy Boylan, and yeah, Holland Creedmore. Saturday mornings, she'd have us meet up at school to take practice SAT tests. Why?"

"Uh, well, a rumor has surfaced that Lanier was having a thing with one of Frank's football players, and maybe that had something to do with her disappearance."

"Ohhhh shit," André said. "Guess my mama knew what was up after all."

"How so?"

"She was real particular about me having my tutoring sessions with Lanier at the public library. You know, she didn't ever want anybody getting any ideas about what some Black kid was doing being alone with this pretty little blond schoolteacher."

"Your mama is a smart lady," Hattie said. "How about the other guys? Did they meet her at the library too?"

"You'd have to ask them," André said. "Tommy was okay, but I never was tight with Little Holl."

"Any reason you two weren't friends?" Hattie asked.

There was a prolonged silence from the other end of the phone. "Little Holl was trouble. The kind I didn't need. You know, he'd have these parties at that beach house. Girls, booze, weed. I needed to keep my nose clean if I was gonna get a scholarship. Different rules for guys like me. You know?"

"I get it," Hattie said. "Okay, well, thanks. You take care, André."

"Always!"

Hattie yawned. Ribsy was already curled up on the rug at her feet. She called Makarowicz to tell him what she'd learned from the night's sleuthing.

35

In the Still of the Night

- - - - - - -

Mo found a rusted aluminum beach lounger in the old boat shed at the edge of the property and dragged it onto the front porch of the beach house, positioning it in the darkest corner, under the roof overhang. He doused himself with mosquito repellant, stretched out, and waited.

It was his second, and, he'd already decided, last night on sentry duty.

The night was quiet, with the background thrum of cicadas, and the occasional sound of cars passing by on Chatham Avenue, and he was already beginning to regret this fool's errand.

Mo had been too embarrassed to admit his late-night mission to Leetha or Hattie or Cass, who would have ridiculed the notion that he might catch their arsonist on a return visit. He wasn't a cop, didn't have a weapon, except for a prybar he'd borrowed from one of the carpenters, and didn't think of himself as a vigilante. But the notion of someone deliberately setting fire to the place, and in the process risking someone's life, had been gnawing on him since the fire trucks departed.

The other thing that gnawed on him was Hattie's reaction to the fire. He kept seeing the tears streaming down her soot-smudged face as he watched her dreams going up in smoke. She hadn't really discussed her finances since buying the house, but he felt pretty sure that she'd staked every dime she had on the place, and it enraged him that some malevolent shitbag could take all of that away with the strike of a match.

As the soft, humid night settled over him like a cloak, Mo wrestled with his growing attraction to Hattie. She was nothing like any woman he'd ever known before; funny and fearless, prickly and pugnacious, but with a tender, vulnerable core that she rarely revealed.

He yawned and looked down at his phone. Just past midnight, and he was already feeling drowsy, despite the concentrated caffeine in the Red Bull he'd chugged.

Suddenly, he heard the crunch of tires on the driveway. He slid out of the chair and crawled over to the edge of the porch, where he peeked up over the porch railing, and spied a dark sedan, its headlights dimmed, rolling slowly toward the house.

Mo's pulse quickened. He had a small flashlight stuffed into his back pocket, and felt for it now.

The car continued past him, toward the rear of the house, and when it was out of sight he grabbed the prybar, opened the front door, and sprinted through the darkened house toward the back porch.

In his haste he banged his knee, hard, on one of the kitchen cabinets, and he whispered a curse. He opened the back door and crept onto the back porch. The sedan was parked a few yards away, under the shade of a live oak tree, its motor running. He heard the car door open and a slender, dark shape slowly emerged from the shadows. The stranger carried some kind of thick club in his right hand.

He inched toward the porch, shoulders hunched over, eyes focused on the uneven ground. Mo was moving now too; tiptoeing forward, he hid behind a huge, overgrown azalea and waited. He heard twigs breaking underfoot and ragged, uneven breaths as the stranger drew closer.

Mo felt sweat trickling down his back. Gnats swarmed around his face, and his heart thumped wildly in his chest. He peeked out from his shelter and saw that the intruder was within reach.

He took a deep breath and leapt out from his hiding place, knocking the stranger to the ground.

"*Aiiieeeeyyyyyy.*"

The high-pitched shriek echoed in the darkness. He grabbed his flashlight from his back pocket and shone it down on the intruder's face, shocked by what he saw.

It was an elderly woman, her face a mask of wrinkles and rage, with a black knit cap pulled low over her hair and forehead. "Get offa me!" she screamed, ineffectively flailing her arms and legs. "Owwwww, get offa me."

Mo rolled to one side, but kept his right hand clamped on her left arm. With his left hand he yanked the cap off her head, revealing a cloud of silvery hair. She swung hard, slapping him on the jaw and screamed, "Don't touch me, you sonofabitch!"

Suddenly, the back porch light snapped on, flooding the backyard in a bright yellow glow. "Who's out there? What's going on?" It was Hattie.

The old woman was sitting up now, scowling up at the two of them. She pointed at Mo. "This sonofabitch broke my hip! I will sue the two of you for every penny you've got."

"Mavis? Mavis Creedmore?" Hattie glanced over at Mo. "I don't understand. What are you doing out here this late?"

"I was waiting for her," Mo said, pointing at the old lady. "Only I didn't know it was her. I just figured our arsonist might make a return visit. I've been camping out, sleeping in a lawn chair on the front porch, for the past two nights. And sure enough, tonight, she did come back."

Hattie shook her head. "Come on, let's get her up and see if she's hurt."

"Of course I'm hurt," Mavis snapped. "This fool tackled me. Knocked me clean off my feet. I could have been killed."

Hattie and Mo each took an arm and gently hoisted the old woman to her feet.

"*Owwww,*" she moaned, when she was finally standing upright. She rubbed her bony hips and dusted sand from her baggy black knit pants.

"Mavis," Hattie said. "Why are you here? What are you up to?"

"I was checking on my house," Mavis Creedmore said, scowling. "No law against that."

Mo gave a snort of disbelief. "Checking? At one in the morning? In total darkness?" He pointed his flashlight at a wooden baseball bat lying near the spot where he'd tackled her, and picked it up. "With this?"

"I brought that for protection," she said. "And if I hadn't been sneak attacked, I by God would have laid it upside your head."

"This is not your house anymore, and you know it," Hattie said, her voice stern. "Your family left it to sit here and rot. And you didn't pay your property taxes, so the city condemned it and I bought it."

"That's a damn lie," Mavis cried. "Creedmores have owned this house for seventy years. My granddaddy left it to me, and I'll be damned if I let some pissant little girl like you steal it out from under me." Her lip curled into a sneer as she addressed Hattie.

"Hattie Bowers. You're a damned thief. You can change your name all you want, but everybody in this town knows who you are and who you come from. You're as crooked as a dog's hind leg, just like that thieving daddy of yours."

Hattie flinched and was silent for a moment, staring down at the old woman's loosely laced orthopedic shoes.

When she looked up again her voice was low but steady. "Mavis, I know you're the one who complained to the city about us. Now you need to get back in your car and drive away from here, right this minute, before I change my mind and turn you over to the police."

"You're letting her go?" Mo asked, incredulous. "She's an arsonist. Criminal trespasser and a vandal. She came out here tonight, probably intending to finish the job she started two nights ago."

"Arsonist?" the old lady sniffed. She poked a bony finger in Mo's chest. "If I'd a wanted to burn this house down, buddy, you'd best believe there would be nothing left standing out here. I didn't set no fire, and you can't prove I did."

Mavis snatched the bat from his hand and hobbled toward her car. She turned on the high beams, threw the sedan into reverse, backing over a shovel and a plastic bucket, then sped away down the driveway, kicking up a cloud of sand in her wake.

Hattie sighed. "Tug said this house has bad vibes. Cass said it too. I'm beginning to think maybe they were right."

"Bullshit," Mo said. He pointed at the sedan's red tail-lights. "Do you believe that old crone? Was she lying when she said she didn't start the fire?"

"I'm not sure what to think," Hattie admitted.

"Then, who else?" he asked.

Hattie shivered, despite the heat. Deliberately changing the subject, she lightly touched his jaw, which was already darkening with a bruise. "Did she do that to you?"

"Walloped me a good one," he said, his expression sheepish. "I'm just glad she dropped her bat when I jumped her."

"Mavis Creedmore didn't come to play," Hattie agreed. "Better put some ice on it when you get back to town."

36

Like Father, Like Son

The woman who answered the door at the gracious redbrick Georgian Revival on East Forty-Fifth Street peered at Makarowicz through the glass storm door.

Her silver-blond hair was slightly askew and her pale pink lipstick was smeared, but she wore a colorful pastel cotton dress and a tasteful string of pearls.

"Hello," she said, blinking and looking past him toward the street. "I wasn't expecting the Instacart delivery this soon. Can you bring it around to the kitchen?"

"I would if I were your Instacart shopper, but unfortunately I'm not," Mak said. He held out his badge. "I'm Detective Al Makarowicz with the Tybee police. I was hoping to have a few words with you and your husband."

She took a half step backward. "Oh. Well, um."

"Are you Mrs. Creedmore?" Mak asked.

"That's me. Dorcas. Holl isn't . . . I mean . . . right at this moment, he's not at home." She flashed an apologetic smile. "But I'll let him know you stopped by."

A pair of identical late-model silver Buicks were parked in the driveway. Both had Cardinal Mooney alumni stickers on the back window. The trunk of the car parked closest to the street was open, and a set of golf clubs was leaning against the bumper.

"Isn't that your husband's car parked right there?"

She opened the door and stepped onto the concrete stoop to get a look.

"Oh. I guess he must have just gotten home. Sometimes he goes straight out to the carriage house, where he, uh, has his office, without coming inside the house first."

"Good. Maybe you can let him know I'm here?"

A voice echoed from inside the house. "Dorcas? Who's that at the door? I swear to God, if you don't stop ordering crap off Amazon . . ."

She stepped back inside. "Holl! It's a policeman from Tybee. He wants to talk to us."

"What about?" the senior Creedmore appeared in the foyer. The resemblance to his son was uncanny. Same high forehead and receding hairline, jowly face, florid complexion, although the older man's posture was somewhat stooped, and the hair was completely gray.

"I'd like to discuss the home your family owns on Chatham Avenue," Mak said.

"Owned. The city sold it out from under us. Biggest land grab of the century," Creedmore said with a growl.

Mak was pretty sure the Native American nation might argue that point.

"Right," he said. "But the new owner's doing some work on the house, and they've discovered a billfold that belonged to Lanier Ragan, the schoolteacher who . . ."

"I know who Lanier Ragan was," Creedmore snapped. "Is. For all we know, she's dyed her hair black and is alive and well and living in L.A. I don't see what that's got to do with us."

"If you'd give me a few minutes of your time, I'd be happy

to explain that," Mak said. "You'd probably be more comfortable talking to me here than all the way out at Tybee. We do have a new station house, but it's a long ride, and I hate to inconvenience you like that."

Dorcas Creedmore opened the door. "I'll make coffee."

"No!" Big Holl placed his hand on her shoulder. "No, you won't. This isn't bridge club."

The living room was large and high-ceilinged. Prominently displayed over the fireplace mantel was a gilt-framed portrait of a young boy of seven or eight, dressed in a sailor suit with short pants. Little Holland back when he really was little, Makarowicz thought.

Dorcas Creedmore and her husband were seated as far apart from each other as humanly possible, she on the edge of an ornate French-looking chair, he on the far side of a tufted green silk sofa. Makarowicz took a wing chair near the fireplace.

"I'll just get right to it," Mak said. "The discovery of that billfold, after all these years, makes me wonder what connection Lanier Ragan might have to that house, and the family who owned it right up until a couple weeks ago."

"Connection?" Big Holland frowned. "What's that supposed to mean? Are you accusing us of something? Should I call my attorney?"

"Yes!" Dorcas piped up. "That's a good idea, Holl. We should call Web Carver."

Big Holl rolled his eyes. "Web Carver sold his practice and moved to Highlands three years ago, Dorcas."

"Right. I forgot."

"The only possible connection that young woman had to our family, or our house at Tybee, was that she was married to

Frank Ragan, who was our son's football coach at Cardinal Mooney," Creedmore said. "As president of the alumni association and the football booster club, I entertained the whole team multiple times over the years. There's a chance she accompanied Frank to some of those affairs, but I couldn't say for certain."

"Oyster roasts," Dorcas said. "We had an oyster roast the Sunday after Thanksgiving every year for the whole team and their families."

Mak scribbled a few nonsensical words in his notebook. He wondered if it was just his imagination, or whether Dorcas Creedmore was a little bit glassy-eyed. A little bit stoned.

"What difference does it make? This is all ancient history." The husband drummed his fingers on a spindly-legged glass-topped end table.

"It makes a difference because we've heard rumors that Lanier Ragan was sleeping with one of the members of Frank Ragan's football team."

Dorcas gasped and her husband shot her a dirty look.

"Rumors don't mean a damn thing," Creedmore said. "Cardinal Mooney usually dresses out about seventy boys every year. Are you tracking down all their parents and asking them these kinds of insulting questions?"

"I will if I have to," Mak said. "Naturally, I'm wondering how Mrs. Ragan would have gotten to know one of these teenaged boys that intimately. It's my understanding that Lanier Ragan tutored your son during his senior year."

"I don't remember that," Creedmore said.

"I hired her to tutor Little Holl," Dorcas said meekly. "Senior year, his grades had dropped a little. It was Coach Ragan's idea. She tutored a few of the other players too."

Creedmore shot her an annoyed look. "Nothing sinister about that," he said.

"Maybe not. I'm wondering, were you two aware of the parties your son used to have at the house on Chatham Avenue?"

Creedmore waved his hand dismissively. "Old news. They were high school kids. Didn't you ever have a few beers when you were in high school?"

"Oh, sure," Mak said. "But none of my friends' parents had a swell beach house like yours."

"I don't understand what you're getting at," Dorcas said. "These were all good boys from good families. They wouldn't have anything to do with this tragedy."

"What I'm getting at, Mrs. Creedmore," Mak said pointedly, "is that Lanier Ragan was last seen by her husband sometime before midnight on February sixth, 2005. Seemingly vanished into thin air. Her car was found, stripped, in a shopping center parking lot in a high-crime area of Savannah a few days later. Nobody was ever arrested. Now, all these years later, we find her billfold in the walls of an old house on Tybee. A home that was, until very recently, owned by your family. A home that you've already said Mrs. Ragan possibly visited more than once. And, as you yourself confirmed, Lanier Ragan did private tutoring for your son, who was a member of Frank Ragan's football team."

"I've heard about enough of this crap," Creedmore said. Grunting with the effort, he pushed himself off the sofa. "My wife and I are offended by your insinuations about our son. I suggest you don't repeat these slanderous remarks, because if you do, I'll be forced to retain counsel."

37

Dress Rehearsal

- - - - - - -

Da-dum. Da-dum, da-dum, dum, dum, dum . . . Mo flinched when he heard the ringtone. It was nearly midnight. *Da-dum, da-dum, da-dum.* He sighed and picked up. "Hi, Rebecca. What's up?"

"Mo, I have the most fabulous news. Jada Watkins has asked for an exclusive on the *Homewreckers* story!"

Mo rubbed the bridge of his nose. "Should I know who that is?"

"You *should,* but I guess I'm not surprised you don't. She's the East Coast correspondent for *Hollywood Headliner.* It's a huge get for us. Especially since she's coming on location to interview you and Trae and Hattie."

"You mean, here? To Savannah?"

"Of course. We had to move heaven and earth to arrange it, but she's flying in tomorrow, and will be on set with you on Friday."

Mo blinked. "Not this Friday. Right? Because that's impossible. I've just spent the past three hours juggling . . ."

"Of course this Friday. She and her crew will be there at nine A.M. She'll want to talk about the latest on the wallet-in-the-wall drama, and of course, the fire, and naturally, the 'smoldering romance' between Trae and Hattie."

"Rebecca, I don't think Hattie's especially comfortable talking about her personal life."

"Then you'll have to help her understand why it's important that she *get* comfortable with it, because I guarantee that's going to be the first topic Jada is going to address. Now, let Hattie know we're sending over a few things for her to try on tomorrow. Jodi in wardrobe will fit her and then we'll FaceTime and decide the best looks for her."

Mo winced, anticipating what Hattie's reaction would be to dressing by committee.

"What about Trae? Who gets to decide what he's wearing?"

"Aren't you precious? Trae has impeccable taste. We never have to worry about how he looks."

"Okay. But listen, since you're messing with our schedule here, you're going to have to extend the shooting timetable. All the exterior wood siding on the back of the house has smoke damage. And we won't know whether the kitchen floor is salvageable until it's completely dried out, which might be by Monday."

"Not possible," Rebecca said. "Tony wants everything in postproduction ASAP. *Homewreckers* has all the potential to be a major new hit, and we need everything wrapped up and ready to go so we can start talking to new sponsors."

"I just don't think it's going to be done by then," Mo objected. "We'll need another week. At least."

Rebecca stopped him. "Don't think. Just do it. Please, Mo? You need this show to be a hit, right? And that's the only way this happens. Right?"

"Right," he said. But she'd already disconnected.

Jodi picked the first hanger from the clothes rack and held it out for inspection. It was a floaty, floral chiffon sundress, deeply cut in the front with straps that crossed in the back.

"Nope." Hattie shook her head to underscore her reaction. "Not happening."

"Sweetie, this will be adorable on you," Jodi said. "With your coloring, and those great toned arms of yours . . ."

"Who wears a tea party dress on a construction site? I'll look ridiculous. Anyway, this thing is way too short. Do you want the whole world to see my cooter?"

"Your . . . cooter?" The wardrobe assistant giggled. "Does that mean what I think it means?"

"Yes. It means exactly that."

Jodi took a step backward. "Wow. Excuse my ignorance."

Hattie was immediately penitent. "Shit, Jodi, I'm sorry. That was uncalled-for. I'm just in a foul mood. The idea of that bitchy Rebecca picking out clothes for me, like it's my first day of kindergarten, it just gripes my grits."

"It rubs me the wrong way too," Jodi confided. "When I got here this morning, there was this gigantic box of clothes that was shipped from New York. Anyway, we've just got to suck it up and pick out something you don't hate."

She riffled through the clothes on the garment rack and pulled out what looked like a pair of indigo denim coveralls.

"That?" Hattie asked. "That looks like something you'd wear to work in a garage. It's the extreme opposite of that party dress. Can't we find something in the middle?"

"It's a jumpsuit," Jodi said. She pointed to the label. "This is LaLa Tarabella. She's, like, the hottest designer going right now. It might not look like much on the hanger, but try it on."

Hattie grabbed the jumpsuit and retreated behind a dressing screen. She studied herself in the mirror. The coveralls had an oversized orange industrial zipper front, accented in bright orange top-stitching, and puffy long sleeves. The waist was gathered. It wasn't . . . terrible.

"Come on out and let me see," Jodi called.

Hattie stepped out.

"Oh yeah," Jodi said. She pulled the zipper down another four inches, then rolled up the sleeves to elbow length. "Turn around," she ordered.

Hattie did a quarter turn. "Hmm. It kinda bags in the seat, but I can fix that easily enough," Jodi said. She grabbed a handful of pins and began pinning the excess fabric. "Turn again? That's better, but I think we'll take it in a half inch in the bust. That'll take care of the grease monkey look." She went over to a rack of accessories and plucked out an abstract patterned silk scarf in vivid hues of oranges, hot pink, lime green, and yellow. "Vintage Pucci," she said, giving Hattie a wink. "From my own collection." She knotted the scarf around Hattie's waist and stepped back again to study her handiwork.

"I love it," Hattie said. "The scarf really makes it."

"Well, you know what Dolly Parton says in *Steel Magnolias,*" Jodi reminded her. "The only thing that separates us from the animals is our ability to accessorize."

Hattie looked down at her bare feet. "You're not gonna make me wear some horrible spiked heels, right?"

"Nope." Jodi went back to the accessories rack and handed her a pair of stylish lime-green tennis shoes. "Lanvin," she said.

Hattie let out a deep sigh of contentment and threw her arms around the wardrobe mistress. "I feel so much better now. This outfit feels just right. It's me. Only more stylish. And cute."

"Great. Now take it off so I can get started on the alterations," Jodi ordered. "Once that's done we've got to Face-Time Rebecca so you can model the finished outfit."

"What?"

"I don't make the rules, I just make the rules look fabulous," Jodi said. "Be back here in an hour, okay?"

"Hmm." Rebecca's voice filled the small trailer. "What happened to the dresses we shipped down to you?"

Hattie started to speak, but Jodi beat her to the punch. "Way too short," she said. "And not enough fabric to let the hems down."

"What about those cute rompers? I was thinking we'd show off her legs."

"Hattie's got this weird body type. Short-waisted. They made her look like a puffin. Not flattering. At all."

"I don't hate the jumpsuit," Rebecca admitted. "Hattie, can you turn so I can see the back?"

Hattie obliged, turning her back to the camera just as she saw Jodi, out of camera range, shoot her a conspiratorial wink.

"The fit is decent," Rebecca allowed. "Turn again."

Hattie spun back around.

"Is this the LaLa Tarabella we sent down?" Rebecca asked. "It looks different from the one I saw on the website."

"I altered it slightly," Jodi said. "Took it in through the bust and butt, chopped the sleeves short to show off those tanned arms of hers, and then I did some machine-embroidered embellishments along the bottom of the pants."

Rebecca let out a long sigh. "This is probably as good as we're going to get on such short notice. Now, Hattie, I've already spoken to Lisa about your hair and makeup for tomorrow. She's going to go with a bit more eye drama than usual, because we don't want you looking like a sad little country mouse next to Jada Watkins. Good job, ladies. Bye now!"

Jodi clicked off the FaceTime app and turned to Hattie. "Sad little country mouse, my ass."

38

Lightning Striking Again and Again

"Detective Mak?" Emma Ragan's voice was soft, and cracking from emotion.

"Hi, Emma," he said. "Is something wrong? Can I help?"

"Y-y-yes. It's a long story. I'd feel better if we could talk in person."

"That's fine, Emma," he said, his voice soothing. "Tell me where and when. I'll meet you wherever you want."

"You know the square, downtown, with the big statue of General Oglethorpe? I called in sick today, could you meet me there in, like, an hour?"

"I'll see you then," Makarowicz said.

She was sitting in the shade of a huge oak tree, on the edge of a park bench, her pale, bony shoulders hunched over, feeding popcorn to a group of pigeons, looking remarkably like a wounded bird herself.

"Hi," he said, smiling at her as he approached. She looked up and he saw that she'd been crying, her eyes red-rimmed, nose runny. She wore a dress that looked like an old man's sleeveless T-shirt, what his daughter used to call a wife-beater, that accentuated her delicate build.

Makarowicz sat down on the bench and waited. Emma wiped her nose with a paper napkin she plucked from a bag she was holding on her lap.

"Are you really sick?" he asked. "I gotta say, you don't look so good."

"I told my boss I was on my period. Men never ask you any questions when you tell them that. I'm just super upset my dad showed up last night."

"You didn't know he was coming for a visit?"

"No! Get this. He broke up with the chick he was living with down in Florida, and he's been living in Richmond Hill. He rang my doorbell around eight last night, and said we needed to talk."

"About your mom?"

"Yeah. He knew all about that lady finding Mom's wallet in the house out on Tybee. And he said some cop had been leaving messages. He was really pissed about that."

"Why should he be pissed at you?" Mak asked.

"He doesn't need a reason. He just is. He wanted to know if I'd talked to you. Of course, I lied and told him I hadn't."

"Why lie to him?"

"Habit. I've been lying to my dad for so long, I guess it's just reflex. Me and him have been lying to each other, probably since the night Mom went away."

Makarowicz reached over and helped himself to a handful of popcorn from the bag sitting between them. "Maybe it's time for an honest discussion about that night?"

"Now you sound like my shrink," she said.

"Cops sort of are like shrinks. Sometimes," Mak said.

Emma was watching the pigeons. There were eight or nine of them, nervously pecking at the asphalt walkway where the dregs of the popcorn had been. She flung a handful of popcorn at them, and they excitedly swarmed in on it.

"I asked my dad what happened. The night she left. Of

course, he played dumb and told me he didn't know. That it was some big mystery." She waved her hands in a circle. "Woo-woo. Nobody knows anything. But I called him out. Finally. I fucking called his ass out."

She dusted her hands on the dress, leaving a greasy streak of butter on the fabric. She crossed her legs, and he noticed a tattoo on the inside of her calf that he hadn't noticed on their last interview. A large, jagged lightning bolt. Probably a Harry Potter thing, he thought.

Emma followed his eyes and pointed to the tattoo. "You like it?"

"Truthfully, I'm not much of a tattoo aficionado. But yeah."

She traced the ink with a fingertip. "You know, it was storming bad that night. Real bad. Lightning and thunder."

"The night she left? You can remember that?"

"Hell yeah, I remember. He didn't think I could," she said, her voice dripping with scorn. "But I did. About a year ago."

"Go on."

"All my life, I've been scared of lightning. Like, pee-the-bed terrified. This one time, when I was about ten, there was one of those bad summer storms. Lightning striking all around. I got hysterical. Hid in the bathtub, shaking and crying. Rhonda finally gave me one of her pills, to get me to shut up and calm down. That was the first time I had a Xanax."

Emma's eyes got a faraway look. "It was pretty magical. Like I was just floating in that bathtub, and nothing could touch me. Or hurt me." She looked up at Makarowicz, her blue eyes narrowed. "Pretty fucked up, huh? Your dad's girlfriend gives you a Xanax at ten?"

"Not exactly model parenting behavior," Mak allowed.

"My whole life, I never knew why I was afraid of lightning. Why it messed me up so bad."

She was watching the pigeons again. The largest of the flock, one with a paler coloration, aggressively pecked the smaller birds until they skittered away, or flew off.

Emma picked up a pebble and flung it at the bird. "Cut it out. Stop picking on them." The pigeon edged away but didn't leave. She picked up another pebble and threw it closer and the bird flew off.

"You were telling me why lightning scared you so much," Mak prompted.

"Yeah. I never knew why. Then, my first time in rehab, there was a bad storm, and I kinda went nuts. The counselor who lived in my pod—that's what they called our dorms— after I finally calmed down, she suggested I talk to my therapist about it. Why not, right? It gets boring talking about why you want to do drugs and why you want to harm yourself and why you hate your family all the time."

"And what did your therapist say?"

Emma rubbed the lightning bolt on her calf. "She asked me to talk about the first time I could remember being afraid. I told her about the bathtub thing, and she said, well, that's not the first time you freaked out, right?"

"Is that when you remembered that it was storming the night your mom went away? But you were only three years old at the time, right?"

"I was four, but no."

Makarowicz stared at her. "Back up. You weren't three when your mom disappeared?"

"I was definitely four," Emma said.

"All the old newspaper accounts I read gave your age as three," Mak said slowly. "Come to think of it, the initial police reports said the same thing."

"That's probably what my dad told them. Jesus! What kind of father doesn't even know how old his only kid is?"

"Maybe the kind who doesn't want the cops to question

that kid," Mak said. "Who wants people to believe the kid is too young to remember or understand what happened the night her mother disappeared."

Emma crossed and recrossed her legs again. "For a long time, I *didn't* remember. My therapist says it's called infantile amnesia. Because little kids' brains aren't physically developed enough to retain memories."

"That sounds about right," Mak said. "Emma, what *do* you remember about the night your mom went away?"

Her fingertips strayed to her right calf, picking at the scabbed-over tattoo. "There was a bad storm. The lightning woke me up. Usually, when that happened, my mom would come into my room and lay down on the bed with me. She'd hold me and sort of sing, and then I'd fall back asleep. But that night, she didn't come. So I went into their room. But nobody was there."

She glanced up at Makarowicz. "They were gone. I ran downstairs, and I went into the kitchen looking for my mom, but she wasn't there. He wasn't there either."

"You're sure of that?" he asked. "Maybe your dad fell asleep in the den, watching TV? I used to do that all the time, and my wife would raise hell with me."

She shook her head violently, and the tiny gold seashell earrings she wore swung against her white-blond hair like a pair of miniature chandeliers. "That's what he said, when he finally came into my room. He said I'd just had a bad dream. And he laid down in bed with me until I fell back asleep. 'Mommy and Daddy are here,' he said. 'You had a bad dream. That's all.'"

Emma stood, abruptly. The white pigeon was back, pecking at a smaller, darker bird. "Shoo! Shoo!" She waved her arms wildly in the air and all the birds scattered. She turned and scowled at Makarowicz. "I fuckin' hate a bully."

She slumped down on the bench, energy spent.

"You're positive your father wasn't anywhere in the house that night when you woke up?" Mak asked.

She nodded. "Yeah."

"When did you start remembering that night?"

"Bits and pieces of it started coming together the last time I talked to my therapist. We do video conferences now, because of my work schedule. That was maybe last year? I lose track of time. It was after another bad storm, and I'd had a panic attack. She asked me to keep a log, of what I associated with lightning. It was bad stuff. Darkness. Loneliness. Losing my mom."

"Is that why you got the tattoo?" He pointed at the lightning bolt.

"Uh-huh. My therapist said the best way to deal with my trauma was to finally start looking at it, instead of trying to forget. Or zoning out with drugs. I drew it, but it's in an awkward place, so my friend actually did the inking."

"You like to draw?"

"Yeah. I've been thinking, maybe I could take some classes at SCAD. A lot of students get ink from us, and they always tell me how cool my original designs are."

"So you started remembering that night about a year ago. That it was storming and there was lightning the night your mom went away. Is that all?"

"Yeah. There was nothing more specific, until I saw that story in the newspaper. About my mom's wallet. Something told me I should talk to someone about it. My therapist said I should call you. So that's what I did."

"But you didn't say anything to me about your memories of that night when we met up," Mak pointed out.

"I still hadn't put everything together. Also, I don't exactly have a great history dealing with cops. I wasn't sure I could trust you. After we met, I thought you seemed pretty cool."

"For a cop."

She flashed a rueful smile. "I sleep in their old bedroom now, you know. My parents' bedroom. The house is different now, because someone else bought the house when my dad sold it. But the night after I talked to you, things just started coming together. I went into the backyard, and I was on that swing, and it all came back—like *whoosh*! The storm, and waking up crying, and wandering around the house, looking for them. And then my dad, coming into my room. He was wet, his hair, clothes, everything. That's the first time I remembered that."

"And you realized it wasn't a bad dream?" he asked. "That it really happened?"

"I've been trying to figure out what to do about that. And then, last night, *he* showed up at the house. Out of nowhere. He's been fucking living forty-five minutes away from me for months now, but last night he comes to see me, because of you."

She pointed a finger at Makarowicz. "He's afraid of you, and he's afraid of what I might tell you."

Makarowicz's pulse quickened. That hadn't happened in a long time. Not since he'd left the APD and retired to Tybee Island, where the most exciting case he'd worked in months was locking up a porch pirate who'd been stealing Amazon packages from residents' doorsteps. Not since Jenny died.

"You said you called him out last night?"

"Yeah. Everything I just told you, I told him."

"And what was his response to that?"

"Typical Frank Ragan gaslighting. He said I'd never been alone that night. That he'd gone outside for like, a minute, because he thought he heard a crashing noise, and he was worried a tree had fallen on the house."

"Did you ask him where your mom was?"

"More bullshit. He said she was right there in bed. I was too young to remember anything."

Her eyes narrowed again. "He said my brain is fried from all the drugs, so nobody could believe anything I said anyway."

Makarowicz gripped the edge of the bench. Someday, he thought, in the near future, he would love an opportunity to kick Emma's father in the balls.

"And what did you say to that?" he asked.

"I kicked him out. Of *my* house. It felt awesome."

She reached into the bag of popcorn and flung a handful onto the pavement, then she stood up and dusted the remaining kernels off her dress.

"Detective Mak, I want you to find out what happened to my mom. If she ran off with another guy and left me behind, I can handle that. If she's dead, I can handle it. I can even handle it if my dad did it. Like you said, I'm a pretty tough customer. But what I can't handle anymore, is not knowing."

"Okay," he said. "I'll do my best. I guess the next step for me is to talk to your dad. Do you happen to have an address for him?"

"No. We didn't exactly end the night on friendly terms."

"That's okay," Makarowicz said. "I'll make some phone calls."

39

A Hail Mary Pass

- - - - - - -

Mak saw an incoming call from Mickey Lloyd, one of his detective buddies from the Atlanta PD, whom he'd called earlier that morning to ask for help in locating Frank Ragan.

"Mak? Looks like your football coach is living in a mobile home community in Richmond Hill," Lloyd said. "I'll text you the address and the phone number. My source says he's working at a store called Elite Feet in the mall down there."

Frank Ragan was easy to spot. He was the oldest employee in the sporting goods store. The rest of the employees, all dressed in their black-and-white-striped pseudo-referee shirts, were high school or college kids. The former coach looked to be in good shape. His hair was still thick, if dyed an improbable shade of auburn, but his belly was flat, and his biceps bulged beneath the sleeves of the ref shirt.

Makarowicz stood in the mall, just outside the store's entry, watching Ragan. He was obviously flirting with a customer while ringing up her tennis shoes. Ragan's eyes followed her as she left the store, checking her out.

Mak walked up to the cashier stand and addressed the coach, who was straightening up a display of protein bars.

"Frank Ragan?"

The former coach looked up, startled. "That's right."

Makarowicz kept his voice low and even. "I'm Detective Makarowicz with the Tybee Island Police Department. I've been trying to reach you without much success. Wondering if you'd have some time to chat."

"Sorry. I'm kind of busy at work here."

Mak looked around the store. "Doesn't look all that busy to me right now. Maybe I could ask your manager if you could take a coffee break?"

"Never mind. I'm the manager on duty. Just let me get someone to cover the register. I'll meet you at the Starbucks kiosk in five minutes."

"That's okay," Mak said. "I'll just wait here."

They took a two-top in a corner of the food court. Makarowicz had a coffee, Ragan had a green smoothie.

"Did Emma tell you where to find me?" Ragan asked.

"No. Your daughter pointed out that she had no idea of your address, or where you were working. I guess you two aren't so close, huh?"

"Her choice. I was as good a father as she let me be. You being a cop, you probably know how bad drugs can mess with a kid's head these days. I'm the one who about went broke paying for her rehab, you know. Bet she didn't mention that."

"I'm not here to judge your parenting skills," Mak said. "But I am kind of surprised that you haven't already asked me about your wife, or that you didn't bother to return any of my phone calls telling you there'd been a new development in the case."

"I follow the news," Ragan said. "If Lanier had turned up, I'd have gotten an alert on my phone. But she hasn't, has she?"

"No. But we have a couple of new leads I wanted to discuss with you. First, of course, I'm wondering why your wife's billfold was found in the wall of that house on Tybee."

"You got me," Ragan said. "If your next question was whether Lanier was ever there, the answer is yes. When the Creedmores owned the house, they had the whole team and the coaching staff and their families there for cookouts and stuff like that. I guess we were there at least four or five times over the years."

"Any idea whether your wife was ever there without you?"

"I don't know. I guess she could have been."

"I understand Lanier was tutoring a few of your players that fall? At your request?"

Ragan fixed him with a hard stare. "This shit again? Yeah, I've heard the rumors, that she was messing around with one of my players. I can't disprove it, and I can't prove it, because she's not around, is she?"

"No. She's not. I'd be interested in hearing your theories about what happened to your wife. Emma told me you once accused your wife of 'whoring around.' Is that accurate?"

"One time. I caught Emma sneaking in the house after she'd stayed out all night with her boyfriend. She was fifteen, for Christ's sake. I was trying to scare her. Maybe I got a little overly dramatic. I'm telling you, I don't know what happened to Lanier. We came home from a Super Bowl party. When I woke up the next morning, she was gone. That's it. Seventeen years have passed and that's still all I know."

"That's not exactly how Emma remembers things. She told me today that she woke up in the middle of the night—because it was storming, and she was afraid, and when she went to your bedroom, both you and Lanier were gone."

"No," Ragan said flatly. "Never happened."

"She ran around the house, looking for both of you, terrified and crying, because she was alone. And that's when you came into her bedroom. Wet. You told her something about hearing a tree limb fall on the house, and you told her to go back to sleep."

Ragan leaned over, his hands clutching the side of the table. "How come she's just now remembering that? Huh? All those years of school counselors and therapists—how come she's just now coming up with this fairy tale of hers? Emma was three when her mom disappeared. What kind of memory does a three-year-old have of anything? You tell me."

Makarowicz waited until Ragan had finished. "In all the old police reports, I saw that you told investigators Emma was only three when Lanier vanished. Emma herself says that at the time she was four. I checked with the state department of driver services, and she's telling the truth. She's a tiny little thing, isn't she? I'm betting the cops didn't question her at the time because she looked so young. And because you told them she was three."

"My wife had just disappeared!" Ragan said, his face growing red with rage. "Maybe I fuckin' messed up her age. Who cares?" He slapped the tabletop with the palm of his hand. "Do you know what happened to *my* life? *My* career, after Lanier disappeared? At first, everyone was so concerned. Poor Coach. Poor little Emma. There were search parties and prayer vigils. Casseroles. My God, I thought I'd never look at a noodle again. And then the rumors started. The next fall, my starting quarterback tore his ACL, two of my seniors got pulled over for DUIs and got expelled, and nothing seemed to gel. At the end of the school year, the headmaster called me in and told me I'd become a 'distraction' at the school, and my contract wasn't being renewed. I won the state championship just the year before. That same year three of my guys signed to play at Division One colleges and

I was prep coach of the year. But none of that meant any-thing, because I was a 'distraction.' I had to scramble to find another job—*assistant* coach and teaching driver's ed at a crappy public school the next county over. I've been hus-tling and scraping to keep it together for seventeen years. And why? Because my *wife*—the *sainted* Lanier Ragan— decided she didn't give a shit about me or our kid."

Ragan sat back in his chair, crossed one leg over the other, and let out a long breath. "Don't come to my place of business again, Detective. Don't leave messages on my phone. Leave me and Emma alone."

40

Mo Knows

- - - - - - -

Trae sat in the makeup chair, staring down at his iPad while Lisa fussed with his hair.

"You're up next, Mo," Lisa said, gesturing to the empty chair next to Trae.

Mo sat down and peered over at Trae's screen. "Is that a script?" he asked. "Movie or television?"

Trae abruptly closed the iPad's hand-stitched leather flap. "It's nothing, really. Just a concept I've been playing around with. But my agent thinks it has promise."

"Great," Mo said. "Hope it works out."

"Don't get me wrong, I still love being in front of the camera. It's my passion, but I've always thought to succeed in this business you have to write your own material."

Trae leaned over and lowered his voice to a near whisper. "I'd love for you to take a look at it, once I've got it a little more polished. You know, just share your thoughts."

"What kind of show are we talking? Home improvement, scripted reality?"

"Neither. It's a rom-com," Trae said. "About a guy who produces a scripted reality show, and he falls in love with his star, but there are complications, because *she's* in love with the hunky head carpenter on the show."

"Let me guess. You play the carpenter?"

Trae shrugged. "Who else?"

"All done," Lisa said, handing him a hand mirror. "See if you like what I did with the back."

Trae put the iPad on the countertop, held up the mirror, and studied his image. "Nice. What do you think about my brows? Could they use a little more shaping?"

"Your brows could win an Emmy they're so perfect. Now get out of here."

Lisa waited until Trae was out of the trailer. "Sounds like he's writing a movie about you, starring him."

"A little bit," Mo agreed. "Except for the falling in love with the star part."

Lisa squeezed a bit of moisturizer into the palm of her left hand, added a squirt of bronzer, stirred them together with her fingertip, then began massaging it into Mo's face.

"Mhmm," she said. "Never happens in real life."

According to Mo's research, Jada Watkins's great legs were her claim to fame. They were loooong and shapely, and exquisitely displayed beneath a very short, school bus–yellow sleeveless dress that seemed to be made out of a single piece of bandage material.

The *Headline Hollywood* star had a mane of glossy auburn hair and she had dark, almond-shaped eyes, a pronounced, beakish nose, and a generous mouth. He gave her a brief rundown of the *Homewreckers* premise before she moved on to the main attraction.

"You two," she exclaimed, taking Hattie's and Trae's hands in hers. "I hear you're the toast of Savannah! And I can't wait to hear all about the house, and of course, the missing woman angle."

Hattie seemed shy and ill at ease with Jada. She was wearing a kind of Rosie the Riveter getup, zipped low enough in front to expose some interesting cleavage, with a scarf worn as a belt. She somehow managed to look sexy and wholesome at the same time.

Trae was Trae, and he wasted no time sucking up to Jada Watkins. Maybe he was looking to cast her in his fantasy rom-com?

He had to admit that Jada seemed genuinely interested in the project, teetering around the house on backless spiked heels that made a clattering sound on the old wooden floors as she followed in Hattie's wake.

Hattie's jaw muscles ached from smiling. She'd been a dutiful television personality for close to two long hours, twinkling and laughing and chatting during take after take after take for Alex, the *Headline Hollywood* producer, and his star.

But now, the sparkle had definitely worn off, and she couldn't wait until the ordeal was over. After leading a tour of the house and discussing all the changes she and Trae had planned, they'd ended up in the kitchen, where the fire restoration team had wrought overnight miracles, sanding down the floors, scrubbing the worst of the soot from the walls, and making room for the camera crew.

Hattie gave a capsule synopsis of the wallet-in-the-wall discovery, and what it meant.

"Lanier Ragan was a beloved and respected educator in Savannah, and I felt her loss personally, because she was my favorite teacher. More importantly, she was a wife and the mother of a young daughter, Emma, who has been waiting for seventeen years for answers to her mother's disappearance."

Jada's animated face grew solemn. "Hattie, how do you think this perplexing mystery will be resolved? Where *is* Lanier Ragan?"

"I don't know," Hattie said. "But I don't think she would have voluntarily gone off and left her daughter behind."

"Cut!" Alex called. "That was perfect, Hattie. Now, one more interview question with you and Trae, and we're done here. I want you guys back out on the porch, okay?"

Hattie glanced at her watch. It was nearly noon, and she'd already lost a precious half day of work. But Mo, who was standing just behind Alex, gave her a subtle nod.

"Okay," Hattie said.

Alex directed her to sit in a rocking chair beside Trae, with Jada's chair facing them.

"Now, you two," Jada said, leaning forward and speaking in a hushed, conspiratorial tone. "I want to ask you about those photos we all saw burning up the internet this week—from the looks of it, you'd just shared a cozy, intimate dinner. So what about these rumors of an on-set romance?"

Trae gave Hattie a knowing, sideways glance. "All I can tell you, Jada, is that Hattie and I have developed an amazingly close working relationship these past few weeks. I mean, who wouldn't fall for someone like Hattie Kavanaugh? She's adorable and hardworking—and I never have to wonder what she's thinking, because she's not shy about telling me!"

"Aww," Jada cooed. "Hattie? What's it like, working with a heartthrob like Trae Bartholomew?"

Hattie felt her cheeks burn with embarrassment as she struggled to regain her composure.

"It's great," she managed. "But right now, I'm really focused on *Homewreckers,* and on working on this house. So I'm afraid matters of the heart are going to have to take a back seat until we reach the finish line."

"Hmm," Jada quipped, "I guess we'll just have to wait 'til *Homewreckers* premieres in September to see if those sparks can last."

"And cut," Alex said. "Great line, Jada. Great work, everybody."

Cass found her in the wardrobe trailer, peeling out of the jumpsuit. "Is the coast clear? Have the bad people gone?"

"Finally," Hattie said, pulling on her own jeans and a T-shirt. "What's going on out there? Why is everything so quiet?"

"The restoration guys are on break. You saw the truck got there to haul off the old dumpster, right? We knew it would make a hell of a racket during your shoot, so Mo bribed the driver with breakfast burritos."

Hattie finished lacing up her work boots. "Well, let's get our people back to work. We need that new dumpster. I don't want them dumping all that burnt siding on the ground. We've got enough of a mess as it is."

As they walked around to the rear of the driveway they heard the rumble of a diesel engine. Mo stood to one side of the drive, directing the truck driver as he backed his trailer down the sloping drive toward the ruined dumpster.

Hattie found herself watching Mo, intrigued. As uncomfortable as he'd been during his brief stint in Jada's interview, he was in his element here, juggling all the moving parts of a complicated production, with the assurance that came from a man who was totally comfortable in his own skin. Not cocky, she thought, confident.

The driver hung his head out the window, watching in his rearview mirror as he backed the truck up in halting, then lurching spurts, with black smoke spewing from the truck's muffler.

Mo kept waving and called, "C'mon. C'mon. Plenty of room! Keep coming."

When the semi gave one final backward lurch, Mo had to dive sideways to get out of the way. There was a thundering bang of metal on metal as the semi crashed into the dumpster, driving it backward until it finally slammed against the trunk of a huge live oak tree. Hattie let out an involuntary scream as the tree shuddered, then slowly toppled backward, landing in the yard.

"Jesus!" Mo exclaimed. He pulled himself to his feet and stood, trying to regain his bearings. He ran over to the cab of the semi, where the driver was slumped over the steering wheel, blood trickling from a gash on his lip.

"Hey, hey. You all right?" He opened the door and shook the driver's shoulder. The man looked up, dazed.

"Yeah, man. I'm okay. I think I hit my head when the trailer hit the dumpster."

He climbed out of the cab, leaning heavily against the door. "Something going on with the gas pedal. It like, stuck." A huge lump was already rising on his forehead, but he walked unsteadily around to the rear of his rig.

"Shiiiiiit," he muttered, clamping his hands on either side of his head as he surveyed the damage. "I'm fucked now."

The impact of the crash had caused the trailer to crumple in the middle. The dumpster had hit the oak tree at an angle, tipping the container on its side, spilling the contents onto the ground. Amidst it all stood the jagged stump of the decapitated oak tree. Oak leaves fluttered down onto the debris.

Hattie fetched a bottle of water from a nearby cooler and took it to the driver, who was dangerously pale and swaying on his feet. She uncapped it and handed it to him. "Here. Come on, you need to sit down."

He made a feeble attempt to resist, but finally allowed

himself to be led to the shade of the nearest tent, where Mo's assistant, Gage, was waiting with a first aid kit.

Hattie and Cass went to meet Mo, who stood staring down at the remains of the trailer and dumpster.

"Oh my God," Hattie said. "I didn't think things could get any worse, but they just did. What do we do about this mess?"

Cass pulled her phone from her pocket and scrolled through her contacts. "First we call the container company and tell them to hold off on that other dumpster. Then, I'm thinking we're gonna need a backhoe and a tree company." She gazed out at the fallen tree. "The good news is, you've now got an amazing view of the river from the back of the house. And with any luck, the insurance company will pay for that oak's removal."

"I'm gonna go check on that semi driver," Hattie said. "I'm worried he might have a concussion."

"What a clusterfuck," Mo said. "Yeah, let's make sure the driver doesn't die on our watch. We don't need one more thing today."

41

Trouble in the Air

- - - - - -

Tug Kavanaugh was not normally an excitable man, but this was an exceptional day.

"Jesus, Mary, and Fred," he exclaimed, taking off his baseball cap and slapping it against his knee. "Forty years I've been in this business, and in all that time I've never seen anything like this catastrophe. A fire, water damage, downed tree. What next? Lightning? Locusts?"

"You really don't like this house at all, do you?" Hattie asked. "But why not? The location is amazing. You'd never find a lot this big on the Back River, not even for ten times what we paid. And the house is solid. We can do this, Dad. You gotta believe in me."

"I do, but sometimes things are beyond our reach," he said sadly.

"My mom always said, 'The harder the delivery, the healthier the baby,'" Hattie said.

She could tell he was surprised by the reference to her mother.

"How is your mom? Have you heard from her lately?"

"I guess she's okay. She texts me once in a while. With her, no news is good news, right?"

"You think she'll ever marry the boyfriend?"

Hattie shook her head. "That's not something we ever talk about. But you still haven't told me why you're so opposed to this project."

He kicked at the tree trunk. "I never cared for those Creedmores. Big Holland was in my class at Cardinal Mooney. He was a bully and a blowhard. Still is, for that matter. Thought his family's money could buy him anything."

"So it's sweet revenge that they couldn't manage to hold on to a house they'd owned for generations," Hattie said. "You know what I'm gonna do?"

"Light a match and finish the job?" he said hopefully.

"I'm gonna go to that hippie-dippie herb shop in Midtown and buy a big old bundle of sage, and then we're going to have a cleansing ceremony to chase away the bad juju."

That got a laugh out of the old man. "Forever the optimist. That's my girl."

Hattie wasn't convinced she'd erased his doubts. "Come on. Spill it. What else is bothering you?"

"I don't like that fancy California designer," he said, his chin jutting out mulishly.

Hattie was mortified. "You saw those pictures on the internet, huh?"

"Pfft. I don't look at that crap. But Nancy saw them."

"Dad . . ."

"I don't think this guy is right for you, Hattie."

"You also didn't think Jimmy Cates was right when I dated him," she reminded him.

"At least Jimmy Cates can put a tight roof on a house," he retorted. "This Trae guy, what's he got going for him? As far as I can tell, he's just a snappy dresser and a fake smile."

"It was only a kiss," Hattie said, squeezing his shoulder. "Come on, let's walk down to the water. I want you to take a look at the dock."

It was low tide, and the beach sloping down from the

seawall was fully exposed. It was a clear day and they watched as a group of kayakers paddled out toward Little Tybee Island.

"This right here is what might sell this house," he conceded. "The dock house is okay too. Put some davits in and you could keep a couple boats out there."

He turned and started to walk toward the house, but stopped in his tracks. "You want to know what worries me the most about this house? I know you too well, Hattie Kavanaugh. You wear your heart on your sleeve. And what do I always tell you?"

"Never fall in love with anything that can't love you back," Hattie said dutifully. "But you're wrong this time. We're going to do *The Homewreckers,* fix this house, and then flip it for a huge profit. That's it."

By the time they'd trekked up from the beach, most of the crew was gathered to watch as the ruined trailer was loaded onto a new flatbed. Hattie held her breath until the process was completed and the wrecker was slowly rumbling down the driveway.

"One down, two to go," Cass said.

"My heart can't take all this excitement," Tug told them. "Zenobia called and needs me back at the office."

Cass watched him walk away, still shaking his head. "What's with him?"

"Nancy saw the pictures of me and Trae," Hattie explained. "He thinks Trae's a phony, and he never liked the Creedmores and thinks this house is a huge mistake."

"Typical Tug," Cass said. "The glass isn't half-empty, it's cracked and leaking."

Hattie gave her a grateful smile. "Tell me things are going to get better."

"They are. The container driver just called, he's parked out on the street waiting for trailer number one to clear the area. In fifteen minutes, the old dumpster will be gone, and shortly after that, we'll have a sparkly new one, and we can all get back to work."

"I can't stand to watch this." Hattie stood on the front porch and watched as the third trailer of the day inched up the driveway with a dumpster loaded on the back.

"I can," Mo said. He plucked his two-way radio from his waist and thumbed the on button. "Jack, get a camera set up to film it as they unload the new dumpster."

"Really?" Hattie wrinkled her nose. "Won't that be like watching paint dry?"

"No. People love to watch someone else's disaster. We can use all this stuff on social media to build anticipation for the premiere. In fact, I need you and Trae out there right now."

"But look at me," she protested. "I'm in my own grubby jeans and T-shirt. Won't Rebecca have a fit if you film me looking like this?"

"Keeping it real," Mo said. "Go!"

With the cameras rolling, Hattie stood just in front of the splintered oak tree. Trae was stationed alongside the cab of the truck. "Ready?" he yelled.

"Yeah, bring her back! But this time, let's take it slow."

Trae motioned for the driver to begin backing. "Straighten it out some," he called, walking alongside the driver. "A little to the left. That's good. All right. Now, straight back."

The trailer with the new dumpster inched backward, past the charred patch of land where the previous dumpster had stood.

"Keep coming," Hattie called, waving her arms over her head. "You've got another fifty feet."

"You're good," Trae told the driver.

"Ten more feet," Hattie called.

The trailer kept backing.

"Almost there," Trae coached.

"Whoa!" Hattie waved her arms over her head and stepped out of the way. The truck's brakes squealed as it halted. Hydraulic arms began lifting the container.

A sickening crack sounded as the earth beneath the trailer's wheels seemed to cave inward.

BOOM!

The container began to slide down the ramp and into a deepening pit in the grassy ground.

At first, Hattie was too shocked to move or speak. She took a few faltering steps forward, afraid that the earth beneath her feet would also collapse. The dumpster had come to rest, nose down, in some kind of concrete pit in the ground.

The truck driver was out of the cab now, and he and Trae stared at the scene in disbelief.

Mo's cameraman moved forward, too, capturing the scene as it unfolded.

"What the hell is that?" Trae yelled, pointing at the pit.

"That," the truck driver said, gingerly walking up to the edge, both hands clamped over his nose and mouth as he stared down into the abyss, "is a septic tank."

42

Buried Secrets

- - - - - - -

Hattie gagged and staggered away as an overwhelming stench filled the air.

"Oh, hell no," Leetha said loudly. "Momo, you know I did not sign up for this."

"Oh my God," Mo muttered. "And I thought this day couldn't get any worse."

The cameraman looked at him for direction and he signaled for him to keep filming. "Get in there, man. It doesn't get any grittier than this."

Mo pointed at Hattie, who'd pulled her shirttail up to cover her nose. "Talk."

Hattie dropped her shirttail and followed his direction. "That has to be the original septic tank on this property. I think the city ran sewer lines down Chatham Avenue years and years ago. At least we know it's not, uh, active." She turned to Cass.

"What do we do now?"

"Who knows? We've uncovered all kinds of weird, uh, shit, I mean, stuff, over the years, but I think this is the first time we've crashed a dumpster into an old septic tank."

She walked out of camera range and began working the contacts in her phone. In the meantime, the driver went back to the cab of his truck and retrieved his own phone and proceeded to walk slowly around the dumpster, documenting the carnage. "My boss ain't gonna believe this."

The trucking company supervisor's name was Milt. Hattie knew this because his name was embroidered on the breast pocket of his work shirt. He'd arrived at the scene prepared with a rolled-up T-shirt fastened around the lower half of his face, and now he was assessing the situation.

"Here's what happened," Milt said, turning, as Mo requested, toward the camera. "There was an old manhole cover right here." He stomped his foot on the ground to emphasize the point. "It was covered up with probably twenty years of dirt and leaves and what have you." He pointed to the dumpster driver, who stood uneasily at his side. "You managed to back the trailer with that dumpster over just this exact spot, and damn if the whole thing didn't collapse, manhole, rebar, concrete, and all."

Hattie had also been coached. "How are you going to get the dumpster out of there? And what do we do with the old septic tank once it's out?"

The T-shirt muffled Milt's laughter. "Well, ma'am. This old boy and me," he slapped the driver's back, "we're gonna reattach the winch to the front bumper of the truck and then we're gonna gun it and pray to the sweet baby Jesus that it will work."

"Oh." Hattie acted like this was exactly the response she expected.

"As to what happens after we get it out of there? Well, we'll reset the dumpster. But what you do with that stinky old septic tank after that? Not my problem."

* * *

They found Trae sitting under the catering tent, his face pale beneath the makeup.

"Gruesome," he said, when Hattie and Cass and Mo walked up. "Utterly gruesome." He shuddered to emphasize the point.

The other three sank down onto the chairs around the table. "This is the day that will not end," Mo said, as the others nodded in agreement.

"However, disgusting as this latest development is, we still have a full shooting schedule. I want to move upstairs this afternoon. Trae, is the upstairs bathroom ready for tile?"

"I still need to pick out the new faucets and showerheads, and we need a commode, too."

"I'll call Sandpiper, that's the plumbing supply showroom in town," Cass said. "They'll be expecting you. But Trae, you've got to pick something they either have in stock or can get right away. Nothing fancy, no custom finishes. And they close at four, so you'd better get going."

"What are we doing in those upstairs bedrooms?" Leetha asked.

"I've got my guys framing out two smaller closets on either side of the doorway. We could shoot that this afternoon. I've got two pairs of chippy old shutters we'll use for closet doors," Hattie said. "As soon as the closets are in, we can paint in there."

"What about the back bedroom?" Leetha asked.

"The guys have already cut the lumber and dry-fitted the new sets of bunk beds," Hattie said. "The lockers I salvaged from an old elementary school will go in there too. They just get bolted to the wall. With any luck, we could get to all that after they're finished with the closets."

"Luck?" Mo said with a snort. "What's that?"

* * *

Hattie and Cass stood on the back porch, looking out toward the river. The view, with the exception of the container truck, was now almost unobstructed.

Milt and his driver had successfully managed to extricate the trailer and dumpster from the old septic tank, and now both were standing at the rear of the trailer, looking down into the pit.

"Coastal Construction called. They're on their way with a Bobcat," Cass said. "Originally I thought we'd just get them to knock down the rest of the oak tree, but now, I'm thinking maybe we get them to fill in that septic tank. There's more than enough fill dirt on-site."

"The sooner the better," Hattie said. She pointed at the two men, who were now jumping up and down and waving their arms. "What's with those two?"

"I don't wanna know," Cass said. "Can't be good."

The younger of the two men met Cass as she was walking down to check. He was breathless and wide-eyed.

"Ma'am? You need to come look. I think there's a body in y'all's septic tank."

43

A Skeleton Crew

"Detective Mak?" Hattie Kavanaugh's voice sounded frantic. "We just found a skeleton in the backyard."

Makarawicz stood and walked out of his office. "At the beach house? Where?"

"In the old septic tank out in the backyard."

"Listen to me, Hattie," Makarowicz said. "Sit tight. Don't touch anything. Get your people away from that septic tank. Don't call anyone and tell them about this. I'm on my way."

Makarowicz called dispatch and asked for a patrol unit to be dispatched to the house. Then he called the Georgia Bureau of Investigation and the Chatham County coroner's office to inform them that skeletal remains had been discovered at a residence at 1523 Chatham Avenue.

He hit the rarely used light-and-siren switch on his dashboard and sped toward the Creedmore house.

Makarowicz shut off the siren as he rounded the corner onto Chatham Avenue. No use drawing the neighbors' attention to what was probably already a chaotic crime scene. He counted more than a dozen cars and trucks parked in the yard and driveway at the house.

Hattie Kavanaugh met him as soon as he stepped out of his car. Her television makeup was smeared, and she was pale and shaking. Her producer/director was with her.

"You okay?"

"Not really," she said, her voice wobbly. "I think it's Lanier, don't you?"

"Let's not jump the gun just yet," he said. "But yeah, I think it's likely her."

"What happens now?" Mo Lopez asked. "I went ahead and had our crews clear out of the area, although, you know, we've all been tromping around out there for weeks now."

"I've notified the GBI and the coroner's office, and they'll dispatch a crew to pick up the remains. There'll be an autopsy, and then the coroner will make a legal determination on the identity of the remains through dental records and anything else they recover."

"Have you got contact numbers for all your people who were here when the dumpster fell into the septic tank?" he asked.

"Yeah," Mo said. "You want me to send them home?"

"First, let's gather everyone up so I can have a word with 'em," Mak said. "I've got a patrol car coming to keep out sightseers, but until they get here can you send someone up to the street to wave off any busybodies?"

"I'll send my assistant, Gage," Mo said. "And I'll have everyone here in five minutes."

The television crew and construction workers gathered around Makarowicz.

"Y'all know we've found some skeletal remains here today, and that's serious business," he said, his expression stern. "The area around that septic tank is a working crime scene. We don't know whose body that is, but we're gonna treat those remains with the utmost respect. And I'd appreciate it if y'all would keep this discovery private until further notice. That means no statements to the press, and nothing, especially photos, on social media. We'll try to finish gathering evidence as quickly as we can so y'all can get back to work, but please be patient."

Donnie, one of the carpenters, raised his hand. "Hey, uh, do you think the body is that woman whose wallet we found?"

"Don't know yet," Mak said. "But that woman has a daughter, who has been waiting for answers for seventeen years. I wouldn't want her to hear from somebody's Instagram page that her mother's body was found in a septic tank. You wouldn't want that either, right?"

A murmur of agreement rippled through the crowd.

Hattie sat on the steps of the back porch, watching as a Tybee Island police cruiser pulled up, followed by an ambulance. Mo sat down, too, and offered her a cold bottle of water.

She uncapped it and took a sip. "I'm glad you sent everyone home. It seems . . . ghoulish to have people working while they bring up that body."

"Screws up our schedule in a major way," Mo pointed out.

"What's Rebecca going to say about that?"

"She's not gonna be happy. But there's nothing to be done. Hopefully she'll be appeased by the *Headline Hollywood* piece."

Hattie picked at the paper label on the water bottle. "Did you look? At the remains?"

"Yeah. I did. Really, all I could see was—"

She clamped her hands over her ears. "Please don't. I can't bear to think of her like that. If it's her. And who else would it be?"

"Sorry," Mo said. "You know, you don't have to hang around here if you don't want to. I'm gonna ask Makarowicz to keep someone posted there until I can get one of your guys to put up a temporary gate."

He paused. "If I'd done that two weeks ago, maybe we wouldn't have had a dumpster fire with thousands of dollars' worth of damages to the house."

"But then we never would have found Lanier Ragan's body," she reminded him. "I guess things happen for a reason."

Mo sighed. "This was not an accident. Someone killed her and put the body there."

"Someone who knew that manhole cover was there," Hattie said. "I sure didn't know it was there, and I've probably walked across it fifty times in the past two weeks." She shuddered as she considered the thought that she'd literally been walking across her old teacher's grave.

"Tell me more about the family that used to own this place," Mo said. "I know you said the son is a jerk, but is he capable of something like this?"

The crew members were packing up their gear and heading toward their vehicles. Hattie lowered her voice to make sure she couldn't be overheard. "Mak, I mean, Detective Makarowicz, has been looking into the names of the football players who were being tutored by Lanier that fall, including Little Holl."

"Huh. Is it possible it was one of the other guys?"

"There were a couple more names, but how would someone who wasn't familiar with this property know about that septic tank?"

"Didn't someone also say the family threw big parties for the football team out here?" Mo asked.

"Well, yeah. But can you imagine a party where 'hey, we've got an old septic tank buried out there' is part of the cocktail chatter?"

"Weirder things have come up with a bunch of testosterone-crazed teenagers," Mo said.

She cocked her head and appraised him for a moment. "You ever play a sport, Mo?"

"I ran track when I was a sophomore. I sucked at it. But my parents insisted I had to have an extracurricular activity that wasn't playing Dungeons and Dragons in the basement all day, so I joined the drama club."

"You wanted to be an actor? Really?"

"No, I just wanted to hang out with hot, loose chicks, and in my warped mind, that's who belonged to drama club."

"Did it work out? Did you get many dates?"

"That part of my plan failed miserably," Mo said. "But drama club got me interested in storytelling, which eventually led me to go to film school at USC."

"Storytelling?"

"That's what entertainment is, when you boil it all down. I liked to write, still do, but I'm more of a visual storyteller, so television is the perfect medium for me."

"How did you end up doing this kind of work?"

"Worked my way up. My first job out of film school was working as an assistant news producer at a local television station in Fresno. Then a friend told me about a job opening working on a pilot for a do-it-yourself craft show that never got off the ground, and while I was working on that, I dated a girl whose brother knew someone at HPTV, and he got me an interview. Later I left and started my own production company."

Mo slapped at one of the bloodthirsty mosquitoes that had been feasting on his flesh for the past hour. "Let's take this inside. Unless you want to leave? I mean, everyone else is."

Hattie stood and looked around. "I guess Cass must have taken off, too, huh? But I can't leave yet. It doesn't seem right to leave her there . . . in the ground like that."

"I'll stay too," Mo said. "Why don't we wait in your trailer?"

"Air-conditioning," Hattie said, nodding. "Great idea."

"I'm just gonna go check on Makarowicz, see if he needs anything, and then I'll meet you there," Mo said.

"Detective?" The crime scene technician ascended the ladder that had been dropped into the septic tank, peeled off his paper hazmat suit and booties, and rolled them into a ball as he walked toward Makarowicz, who'd been photographing every angle of the crime scene.

"Get anything good?" Mak asked, trying to breathe through his mouth.

"Long hair, a purple vinyl windbreaker, and a pair of tennis shoes say the victim was most likely a female," the tech said. "Looks like there was a fracture to the front of the skull." The tech took a step backward and shook his head. "Jesus, I gotta get a shower. I might never get the smell of that septic tank offa me."

"Any idea how soon we might know something?" Mak asked.

"Talk to the GBI," the tech said. He turned and pointed at a stretcher being lowered into the tank. "They're bringing her up now."

Makarowicz walked away. He'd seen enough. He didn't want her to hear this news from a stranger. He called the number Emma Ragan had given him. It went to voicemail, but before he could leave a message, he saw that she was calling back.

"Detective Mak? Do you have any news? Did you talk to my dad?"

"Hi, Emma," he said, deliberately. "I did talk to your dad. But that's not why I'm calling."

"Oh my God," she said. "You found her, didn't you? You found my mom."

"We found a body," he said. "Nothing is certain, but we believe the remains are a woman, and the circumstances of where we found it . . ."

"Ohhhh." Emma's voice trailed off, and she began to weep. "Mommy. My poor mommy."

"Are you all right?" Mak asked, alarmed. "Do you have someone who can be with you right now? Are you at work?"

"I'm . . . I'm . . ." Her speech was breaking up. "Hang on, please."

He heard her blow her nose and say something inaudible.

"Okay. My boss said I can take a break. I'm gonna go sit in my car for a minute and get my shit together. You won't hang up, right?"

"I promise I won't hang up," Mak said.

"Mak?" Emma's voice sounded steadier.

"I'm sorry to upset you this way at work, Emma, but I was afraid word might get out, after we discovered the body, and I didn't want you to hear it from anyone else."

"Thank you," she said tearfully. "What else can you tell me? Where was she?"

Makarowicz bit his lip. He did not want to tell this fragile young girl that her mother's body had been dumped in a septic tank. When he did tell her, it would be in person. "It might not even be her. But the location where it was discovered, seems to make sense."

She seized on that immediately. "On Tybee? Did you find the body near her wallet?"

"Yes," he said reluctantly. "On the same property."

"In that old house? That doesn't make sense."

"No. It was . . . buried."

"Oh." Her voice seemed to get smaller. "Can you tell how it happened?"

"Not yet. It might take some time. But listen, didn't you tell me you sent in a DNA sample of hers to one of those on-line ancestry sites?"

"Yeah," she said. "That detective did it a couple years ago, after they found some woman's body in the Okefenokee Swamp. Turns out it wasn't her."

"That might help move things along, if you still have that hairbrush. The GBI should have her DNA to compare to this body. And we'll get your mom's dental records, too."

"Good. Mak?"

"Yes?"

"Does my dad know?"

"I haven't called him. Do you want me to?"

There was a long silence, and then she was weeping again.

"What if it was him? What if he did this to her?"

"You don't have to decide right now, Emma. We don't know anything for sure. Why don't you think about it, and then let me know?"

"Okay. I'm gonna go now. I need to get back to work."

"Take care, Emma."

44

Suspicious Minds

- - - - - - -

"I brought us dinner," Mo said, holding out a foil-wrapped cylinder.

Hattie regarded the package with suspicion. "What is it?"

"Hot dogs. Courtesy of Chu's convenience store. Hope you like mustard."

"Love it." She unwrapped the still-warm foil and bit into the hot dog with such obvious enthusiasm it made Mo laugh.

"What? Do I have mustard on my face?" She swiped at her chin with a napkin.

"No. I guess I really didn't expect you to eat a convenience store roller dog. Not too many women I know in L.A. would stoop so low."

"I'm not from L.A.," Hattie said. "In case you haven't noticed." She took another bite and chewed. "And I missed lunch, so yeah, I'm starved."

Mo demolished his own hot dog in three neat bites.

"What's going on out there now?" Hattie asked, pointing in the direction of the grave site, where yellow tape encircled the pit. Crime scene technicians were still busy photographing and taking measurements under the glare of floodlights.

"They're about to remove the body."

Suddenly queasy, she pushed away the foil wrapper with the half-eaten hot dog.

"I can't stop thinking about her daughter, Emma. How she'll feel when she hears her mother's been found. After all these years."

"Maybe it will be a relief," Mo said.

"Unless she finds out her mother's disappearance had something to do with her father, or that her mother really was sleeping with a high school kid, and then that opens up another whole can of worms. Invariably, her family is going to get dragged through the mud." She made a sour face. "I know how that feels."

"That witch Mavis Creedmore said some pretty nasty stuff about your dad," Mo said. "Do you want to talk about it, or is it still too raw?"

Hattie fiddled with something on the tiny tabletop. "I still can't believe it's been almost twenty years."

She took a deep breath. "My dad was vice president of Integrity Bank. Ironic, right? Especially when you consider that he was also treasurer of the Community Chest, which is kind of like the United Way. Basically, Dad got caught with his hand in the cookie jar. He embezzled almost $1.2 million over the course of six years, until a new chairman—an outsider, no less—took over running the Community Chest. The new guy took one look at the accounting books and ordered an audit."

"And then what?"

"The board wanted my dad to quietly reimburse the money, because it must have been a 'misunderstanding' because my dad's family has been in Savannah forever, like, really, founding member of this and president of that. But the new guy didn't give a shit about my dad's pedigree and refused to sweep it all under the rug."

"And?"

"He was offered a plea deal. But he wouldn't accept because he was *that* sure he'd get away with it. He went to trial and all his dirty laundry got hung out to dry in public. It wasn't like he really needed the money. He and my mom always drove new cars. We lived in a nice house and I always went to private school. He stole money from orphans and widows and kids with cancer to pay for his mistress's new car, and 'business trips' to Bermuda and Napa and Palm Beach."

Mo offered a half smile. "How old were you when this happened?"

"Not quite fifteen. It doesn't compare to having your mom disappear when you're only four, but it rocked my world. During sentencing his lawyer got some quack to testify that my dad had schizophrenia, which is why he had this whole double life."

"Did you understand any of this while it was going on? I mean, it must have been a lot for a kid that age, even a smart kid like you."

"My mom told me nothing," Hattie said, her tone bitter. "Just that Dad was 'in trouble' and they were getting a divorce. Most of what I found out I overheard in the bathroom at school."

"Kids that age are brutal," Mo observed.

"Yeah. Private-school girls are absolutely lethal. Except for Cass. Anytime she thought I was being picked on she'd go into what she called 'demon mode.' Lanier Ragan helped too. She was genuinely compassionate. I can understand how maybe she took that too far."

"And what happened to your dad?"

"He did three years in federal prison. As soon as the divorce papers were filed, my mom changed our legal names to her maiden name and moved to Sarasota."

Mo got up and opened the RV's door. It was getting dark, and the chorus of cicadas outside was nearly deafening. "The ambulance is just leaving." He turned to address her. "You were having a tough time in school, so how come you didn't go with your mom? New name, new school, new life?"

Hattie got up and peered over his shoulder, just as the ambulance glided silently up the drive toward the street, bearing what was left of Lanier Ragan. She hadn't been inside a church since Hank's funeral, but now she sketched a quick sign of the cross.

"I was pissed at my mom. Always a daddy's girl. I was convinced she must have done something to drive him away from us. And for a fourteen-year-old, I guess, the hell you know is preferable to the heaven you don't. Cass went to her parents and begged them to let me stay with them, at least until school was out in May. Zenobia talks a tough game, but she's got the biggest heart. She never would have turned me away. May came, and I just . . . stayed."

"Where's your dad now?"

"Around. He lives at my grandfather's fishing camp, out on the Little Ogeechee River. He day-trades and spends his days worrying about his old enemies catching up to him."

"Do you ever see him?"

"Almost never. But I went to see him after I lost most of my investment in the house on Tattnall Street, and no bank in town would make me a loan. I borrowed fifty thousand from him, so I'd have enough cash to fix up this house." She took a deep breath. "Cass doesn't know. You're the only person I've told."

"Why is it a secret? He's your father, right?"

"Taking money from him, even a loan, feels . . . dirty."

Mo was intensely aware of how close they were standing together. So close he could smell the scent of her perfume. Close enough to put his arm around her shoulder and offer some kind of belated comfort. He wanted to do that, but he would not.

Hattie was still staring out the open door of the RV. Glowing fireflies flitted through the darkened treetops. The world was perfectly still, with the exception of the thrumming of the cicadas. Was she holding her breath?

"I should go home," she said finally. She gave a short, sharp whistle and Ribsy lifted his head from the bench where he'd been napping most of the day.

"Me too. You go on, I'll walk through the house and lock up. I want to get an idea of where we need to start in the morning. Assuming the cops don't shut us down."

Hattie's shoulders slumped. "I can't think about that right now."

"Go!" Mo said, pointing at the door. "Are you, uh, seeing Trae tonight?"

"No. Why?"

"I found his iPad when I was scrounging around craft services for food a little while ago. I just thought if you were seeing him . . ."

"I'm not. I'm going to go home and run a hot shower and wash off this *stink*."

Mo made a show of sniffing the air around her. "You don't stink. You smell like rainbows and . . . joint compound."

She smiled. "You know, Mo, you're not nearly as big an asshole as I thought you were when we met."

"Don't try to soften me up with all those cute flowery southern phrases, Kavanaugh. Tell me what you really think."

She patted his arm, then, on impulse, planted a quick peck on his cheek as she and Ribsy headed for her truck.

He cursed himself as he watched her go.

Mo's nerves seemed to crackle with pent-up energy. He went home to his carriage house, showered, and rummaged around in the fridge for something more substantial than a roller dog, but his erratic shooting schedule meant that his choices were limited to a wilting brown bag of salad and a rock-hard two-day-old bagel.

Savannah was full of great restaurants, he knew, so maybe, despite the late hour, he'd go get himself a decent dinner. He spotted Trae's iPad on the kitchen counter, and decided, on impulse, that he'd walk the six or seven blocks to The Whitaker, the pricey hotel where his *Homewreckers* budget was paying for his star to stay. He could hand off the tablet and grab a bite in the lobby restaurant.

He'd underestimated the heat and humidity of a summer night in Savannah. By the time he reached The Whitaker his hair was plastered to his head and his shirt was sticking to his back. He stood just inside the hyper-chilled lobby doors and looked around. He'd thought about calling Trae to tell him he was downstairs, but decided he'd really had enough of the pampered punk for one day.

Instead, he went to the reception desk and handed the iPad to the desk clerk, along with the request that it be delivered to Mr. Bartholomew.

Then, as a reward for his sweaty trek, he took himself to the lobby lounge, which was suitably dark and clubby-feeling, with leather booths and candlelit tables. He sat at the bar and ordered a New York strip, rare, with béarnaise sauce, pommes frites, and an eight-ounce pour of a Cabernet that the bartender promised was life-altering.

He was attacking the basket of warm bread when he heard a woman's familiar laugh echoing in the high-ceilinged hotel lobby.

Mo swiveled his barstool slowly around and momentarily froze. The earthy laugh was familiar because it was coming from the *Headline Hollywood* reporter who'd interviewed him, hours earlier, at the Chatham Avenue house. She wasn't alone. In fact, she was arm in arm with Trae Bartholomew.

He quickly spun his stool around before Trae could spot him spying. But he watched in the mirrored bar back as the two strolled to the elevator. When the elevator doors opened, they stepped inside, their bodies pressed closely together in an embrace so intimate Mo closed his eyes and took a slug of his Cab.

That pampered punk, he thought, would mess with Hattie's mind. Maybe break her heart. And there wasn't a damned thing he could do to stop it.

45

The Ring of Truth

– – – – – – –

Makarowicz was at his desk in his tiny home office at nine the next morning. Jenny had furnished the room with a desk and chair, and a daybed, for when their daughter came to visit. A cat the color of marmalade lounged on the bed, looking bored.

The cat had shown up on his porch the week after Jenny's funeral, and had displayed a remarkable talent for sneaking into his house every time he opened the door. Mak had never been a cat lover, but he did the responsible thing and had the damn thing fixed. The vet insisted the cat had to have a name, so now she was Agent Orange Makarowicz.

Technically, today was his day off. But what else did he have to do?

He leafed through the thick Lanier Ragan file he'd "borrowed" from the Savannah Police Department, until he found what he'd been looking for: Frank Ragan's account of the clothing he thought his wife might have been wearing the night she vanished.

Victim last seen wearing navy blue or black track suit, Nike running shoes, or possibly blue jeans and a red hoodie, the report said.

He checked it against the inventory of the items that had

been recovered along with Lanier Ragan's remains. Purple vinyl ski jacket, women's pink Nike tennis shoes, size four. Wedding ring found in pocket of jacket. The GBI had forwarded photographs of everything.

Mak gathered up the printouts of the photos. "Okay, Orangey," he said, addressing the cat. "You're in charge. Don't talk to strangers."

Emma Ragan said she understood when Mak told her he needed to question her father again.

"I need to show him some clothing items we found," Mak said. "The sooner that happens, the sooner we can positively identify the body."

"Okay," she said finally. "I get it."

Frank Ragan scowled when he saw the detective enter the sporting goods store. "I told you, I'm not talking to you again. Not unless you have a warrant or something."

Mak shrugged. "I thought you'd want to know that we found some skeletal remains yesterday, and we have reason to believe the body is your wife."

Ragan looked stunned. "You found Lanier?" His ruddy face paled and he swayed a little, grabbing onto a rack of running tights to regain his balance.

"Why don't we go someplace quieter to talk about this?" Makarowicz said. "Is there an office, or a back room?"

He followed Ragan through a stockroom and into a shoebox-sized office with barely enough room for a small desk and two chairs.

"Where . . . where was she?" Ragan asked.

"We'll talk about that later." Makarowicz opened his

briefcase and extracted the file folder he'd brought along, and tapped the record button on his phone. "Very little of the clothing we found was intact, except for a jacket and a pair of running shoes." He placed two photographs on the desk in front of Ragan. "Do you recognize this jacket?"

Ragan's hands trembled as he picked up the photograph. He stared at it for a long moment. "Yeah. This was Lanier's." He pointed at a small metal charm that dangled from the jacket's zipper. "I think that's a lift doohickey from when we went skiing in Beaver Creek, the year after we got married." He sighed. "Typical southern girl. She hated skiing, but loved drinking hot buttered rum in the ski lodge."

Makarowicz handed him the other photo. The running shoes were discolored, but the Nike swoosh on the side was still recognizable. "These look like hers," Ragan said, his voice breaking. "Size four. She had the tiniest little feet. Emma did too. Does too," he corrected himself.

He looked up at Makarowicz. "You're sure it's her? I mean, there's no chance it could be someone else?"

"The coroner's office will make the official identification, using dental records and DNA," Makarowicz said. "But there's one more thing I'd like to show you."

He handed Ragan another photo, of a platinum wedding band with braided bands of tiny diamonds. He'd looked up the style. It was called eternity.

"Oh my God." Ragan choked back tears. "This was Lanier's. It really is her."

His put his head down on the desk and his shoulders shook as he sobbed. "God, Lanie."

Makarowicz had never gotten used to this part of the job. Dealing with the next of kin was never easy, and it was even more difficult when the next of kin was still considered a viable murder suspect.

"I'm sorry for your loss, Mr. Ragan."

Ragan lifted his head and let out a long, ragged sigh. "I should call Emma."

"She knows," Makarowicz said.

The coach wiped his face with his forearm. "How did she take the news?"

"She was upset, of course. I promised to call her when the coroner makes it official."

"Okay." Ragan squared his shoulders. "Okay. Do you know, I mean, can you tell what happened?"

"Not really. After seventeen years, as you can imagine, all we have is a skeleton."

"Jesus."

"I still have some questions, if you don't mind," Makarowicz said.

"I didn't do this," Ragan said, his jaw tightening. "I might not have been a perfect husband. Our marriage might not have been perfect, but I would have never, ever hurt her."

"Okay," Mak said. "The best way for you to prove that is to be perfectly honest with me."

"I have been," Ragan said.

The detective picked up the photograph of the wedding ring and waved it at the coach.

"The only reason we were able to recover this ring is because your wife wasn't wearing it that night. She had it in the zippered pocket of that jacket. Why do you suppose that was?"

"I don't know," Ragan said. "I went to bed that night, and when I woke up in the morning, she was gone."

"Did you have a fight?"

"No!"

"What time did you discover her missing?"

"I don't know, man. Maybe six or so."

"I don't think so. Emma says she woke up in the middle of

the night because of the lightning and thunder. She went to your bedroom, but both of you were gone. You *and* Lanier."

"Never happened. She made that shit up. To hurt me. She was a little kid. She couldn't even tell time," Ragan said.

"She knew it was storming, and she knew that when she found you a few minutes later, you were wet. What happened, Frank? Was there a fight? Was it an accident?"

"Goddamn it, no! I'm telling you, I never touched her. I didn't do this."

"You're lying about something," Mak said. "I know you left the house that night, in the middle of that storm. Why not just tell the truth? Don't you want us to find the person who did this?"

Ragan twisted the large gold signet ring on his right hand. He was staring at a small framed photograph on his desktop. Makarowicz craned his neck to get a better look. The colors had faded over the years, but the image was distinct. It wasn't an old family photo, or even a picture of his only child. It was the Cardinal Mooney football team, posed in front of a banner that proclaimed STATE CHAMPIONS, and it was the only personal item in the cluttered, cramped office.

He picked up the photo and tapped the glass. "I had three seniors signed to Division A colleges that year. Two more walked on at respectable D-2 schools. You know what an accomplishment that is? How hard I worked? Practices, scouting the opposition, sucking up to the alums to get more money for equipment, buses, a decent weight room? From August 'til postseason, I was never home at night."

"Lanier resented your job," Makarowicz suggested. "Maybe she knew you were fooling around on the side. Maybe she was lonely."

"Maybe she was a selfish slut. Maybe she was a shitty mom. Nobody ever talked about that," Ragan retorted. "All the whispers were about *me*. About what Coach did to drive his wife away. Maybe Coach did it. My whole career was wiped out. Because she couldn't keep her legs together."

"You thought she was cheating." Makarowicz said it as a fact. "But with who?"

"I could tell something was up. I'd come home that fall and the babysitter was there with Emma, but no Lanier. She told me it was meetings at school, or drinks with a friend, or she was spending time with her mom. Her mom was having a rough time with the chemo, so I cut her some slack."

"How did you figure it out?"

"Her phone. Lanier was always leaving her phone around, on the front seat of her car, on the kitchen counter. Suddenly, though, she's super careful. I'd wake up in the middle of the night, and she'd be in the bathroom with the door closed, talking in whispers."

"Did you ever confront her?"

"I wanted to wait until I had proof. I think she sensed I was suspicious, because for a little while, things were back to normal. But then, right around Christmas, she was super moody, and secretive."

Makarowicz had one more photo left in the file folder. It was a shot he'd taken after the crime scene techs had brought up the skeletal remains and assembled them on a blue tarp at the edge of the septic tank pit. Now he placed it, faceup, on the desktop. He tapped the skull with his right forefinger.

"Someone bashed in your wife's skull. Was that you? Tell me about the night your wife disappeared. And no more bullshit, Frank. Because the more you lie, the guiltier you look."

46

Midnight Confessions

"Jesus!" Ragan turned the photo over and looked away. He swallowed hard, then dashed from the office. A second later, Makarowicz heard a toilet flushing nearby, then the sound of water running.

When the coach returned, he was mopping his face with a damp paper towel. He slumped down onto the chair, his breathing ragged.

"You can't show that to Emma," he whispered. "Please don't show her that."

Ragan twisted the signet ring around and around. Makarowicz realized it was his state championship ring. The symbol of the pinnacle of his professional career, which came crashing down not long after his personal life tanked.

"Okay. I did go out that night. Something woke me up, around midnight. Lanie was gone. I went downstairs, thinking maybe she was down there, finishing a load of laundry or something. But she wasn't in the house. Right about then, I heard her car backing down the driveway."

"Lanier's car."

"Yeah. I kinda went nuts. I grabbed my shoes and my car keys, and got in my car to follow her. There was a hell of a storm going on. Lightning and thunder, raining so hard my windshield wipers couldn't keep up."

"Did you have any idea where she was going?"

Ragan twisted the ring a quarter turn. "Not really. At first I thought maybe her mom was sick, but why wouldn't she wake me up to tell me she was going over there? Then, I realized she was headed in the opposite direction of her mom's house. She was on Victory Drive, headed east."

"Going where, Frank?"

"I honestly didn't know. I was kinda staying back, because I didn't want her to know I was following her. She rolled through a yellow light, at the intersection at Skidaway Road, and I started to go through too, but a car coming from the opposite direction was peeling through. I hit my brakes and hydroplaned. My car did a three-sixty, and honest to God, I thought I was a dead man. My car went up over the curb and I just missed a light pole. That's when I came to my senses. What the hell was I doing, leaving my kid home, alone? Whatever Lanier was up to, I'd settle it with her in the morning. I turned around and drove home. When I got inside, Emma was in our bedroom, crying hysterically. I finally got her calmed down and put her back to bed."

Ragan shrugged. "That's it. That's what happened. As God is my witness."

"Why didn't you tell any of that to the police?"

"I was ashamed," Ragan said. "And really, really pissed. At first, it never occurred to me that something bad had happened to Lanier. Then, as it got later in the morning, I started to panic. I called everyone she knew, drove around. I even backtracked to that intersection at Skidaway and Victory, thinking maybe she'd had a wreck or something. Finally, her mom started raising hell. She said if I didn't call the cops to report Lanier missing, she would. I didn't have a choice."

"And yet you still didn't tell the cops what you suspected," Makarowicz said.

"How would that have made me look?" Ragan asked angrily. "Like I couldn't handle my wife. Couldn't handle our marriage. I kept telling myself, wherever she is, she'll cool down, and she'll come home and we'll work it out."

Makarowicz plucked the photographs from the desk and placed them back inside the file folder. "You know, this story of yours sounds just stupid enough that I almost believe it."

Ragan massaged his temples with his fingertips. "It's the truth. But it doesn't change anything because I don't know who killed Lanier or why."

"Maybe you can help me figure that out," Makarowicz said. He took his cell phone out of the briefcase and placed it on the desktop.

47

Down by the Riverside

A Tybee police cruiser was parked at the Chatham Avenue end of the driveway when Hattie arrived the next morning.

"Hi, Officer," she said, when he approached the truck. "I'm Hattie Kavanaugh, the property owner."

He looked down at a clipboard he carried under his arm. "Okay. You're good to go."

She pointed in the direction of the house. "Everything okay down there?"

"As far as I know. Detective Mak just said to keep out the busybodies and tourists."

Mo had emailed everyone on the cast and crew about an eight o'clock meeting. Everyone was gathered around the craft services tent, sipping coffee and casting anxious eyes toward the backyard where the remains were discovered.

"Okay, everyone," Mo started. "For those of you who weren't here at the time, where do I even start to bring you up to speed about yesterday's events?"

He quickly rattled off the chain of events from the previous day, ending with the discovery of the body, and the likelihood that the remains were that of the missing school-teacher.

"I know it seems cold, but the network is adamant about not giving us an extension of our deadline."

He turned and pointed to Trae. "I need you and Hattie, in the kitchen, discussing the plans for the cabinets. Leetha can fill you in on what she wants. Later on, we'll film some stuff upstairs in the bedrooms." He turned to scan the crowd and his eyes settled on Cass, who stood at the back of the tent, looking shell-shocked.

"Cass, can you order some construction screening? Unfortunately, the cops don't want us backfilling that septic tank just yet, but I need it screened off, because it's a safety hazard, and also, pretty freaking creepy."

"Yeah." She took her phone from the pocket of her work pants. "I'll call right now."

Leetha stepped forward. "Okay, Hattie and Trae, I'm gonna need you in hair and makeup. We're gonna shoot some exterior stuff of the front of the house, but that can wait until after the kitchen shots. In the meantime, Cass, let's get your guys busy doing the tiling in the bathrooms, and maybe setting up everything to install the new fireplace mantel this afternoon?"

Cass nodded.

The somber-faced crew began to drift back toward the house, but Hattie noticed that Cass was run-walking in the direction of the river, giving a wide berth to the gaping hole in the earth.

She found her best friend sitting on the seawall, her shoulders hunched together, rising and falling with uncontrollable sobs.

"Cass?" In all the years Hattie had known Cassidy Pelletier, she'd never seen her in such a state. She sat down on the concrete abutment and put an arm around Cass's shoulders.

"You okay?"

"N-n-no," Cass managed. She buried her face in her hands. "I'll never be okay."

Hattie waited a minute. "What's going on?" she asked. "Can you talk to me?"

Cass shook her head, took a deep breath, and turned sorrowful, red-rimmed eyes toward Hattie.

"I can't stand this."

"What?"

"Lying to you. Lying to everyone. I'm such a fucking fraud."

"Hey!" Hattie tried to tamp down the alarm in her voice. "You're not a fraud, and you're not a liar. C'mon, Cass. This is me. You can tell me anything."

Cass used her shirt sleeve to wipe her eyes. "It's so awful. I don't know if I can."

"What?" Hattie said, trying to cheer her up. "Are you trying to tell me you killed Lanier Ragan?"

"No. But I think I know who did." Cass let out a long, shuddering sigh. "And that's just as bad. Because I never said anything. I never told anyone. Because I'm a fucking coward, and a fraud. You're gonna hate me, but not as much as I hate me."

"I could never hate you," Hattie said. "After all you've been through with me? The mess with my dad, and then, when Hank was killed? You and your family literally saved my life. I don't know what I would have done without you. So just talk to me. Please?"

Cass stared out at the river. "Holland Creedmore. Fucking Holland Creedmore Junior. I can't stand hearing his name. Hattie, I think he did it. I think he killed her. Jesus! What was I thinking?"

"Wait. Slow down. What are you talking about?"

"In high school. Sophomore year. I . . . hooked up with him." She turned and looked at Hattie, who gazed back in shock. "And I knew he was hooking up with her, too."

"How?" was all Hattie could manage.

"I went to a pep rally, with Sophie Dorman, and a friend of hers who went to Country Day School. Sarabeth something. I've blocked her last name. Sarabeth had a car, and said we should go to a party after, because all these hot guys would be there. It was like the second week of school."

"You went to a hot-guy party without me?" Hattie joked. "Now I really do hate you."

"The party was at some rich kid's house at Isle of Hope. The parents were out of town. They had a bottle of Captain Morgan rum. . . ."

"Oh God." Hattie felt sick. "I think I know where this is going."

"Sophie freaked out and called her brother to come pick her up. Lucky her. But I wanted to play it cool, so I decided to stay. I drank some rum and Coke, and this cute blond guy started talking to me. . . ."

"Holland fucking Creedmore," Hattie said.

"Yeah. I mean, he was the biggest stud at Cardinal Mooney. A senior, star football player. And here he was, talking to a lowly sophomore like me. Flirting with me. He had his own flask of Jägermeister, and pretty soon, we were sitting in his car . . ."

Hattie clutched Cass's hand. "Cass. Don't tell me he raped you."

"No." Cass shook her head violently. "He was a perfect gentleman. At first. Told me he'd noticed me from across the room. Liked my outfit. He had a can of Coke, and we were mixing it with the Jäger. I remember thinking nobody would believe it. Me, flirting and cutting up with Holland Creedmore. I kept drinking, and I felt dizzy, and I remember thinking, *I'm dizzy with love!*"

"More like drunk on Jägermeister. And Captain Morgan." Hattie shuddered.

"Yeah, but what did I know? I was fifteen and had never had anything stronger than communion wine," Cass said. "It got kinda late, and I guess I was sober enough to worry about how I was gonna get home, because Sarabeth whatever-her-name-was had disappeared. Holland said it was no problem. He'd give me a ride home."

Cass sniffled and wiped her nose again. "You can pretty much guess the rest. On the way home, he pulled into the parking lot at Daffin Park. He started kissing me . . . and touching me. And he wanted me to touch him. Said he'd never been with a Black girl, and all his friends said Black girls were the hottest . . ."

"Dear God," Hattie whispered.

"I wouldn't let him do everything he wanted, only because I was terrified I'd get pregnant," Cass said bitterly. "Afterwards, he told me I was beautiful and special . . . all the usual bullshit. The next morning, I felt so dirty, so ashamed. I would rather have died than let on to you. But then, a couple weeks later, he called me. I hadn't even given him my phone number, but he said he got it from Sarabeth. He wanted to take me to a movie. Me!"

"You weren't allowed to date when we were sophomores," Hattie said.

"Oh hell no, Zenobia wouldn't have let me go out on a date. Especially with a white boy like Holland Creedmore." She shrugged. "I told her I was going to Sophie's house to study. He picked me up there. And he had the bottle of Jägermeister again . . . we went to McDonald's, but there was no movie involved." She sighed. "Fifteen-year-old me was too dumb to know he didn't want to be seen with a Black girl. He just wanted to get *with* a Black girl. You know?"

"How long did this go on?" Hattie asked. "I swear, I had no idea."

"Maybe a month? Two more times for sure. I thought I was so damn smart. So damn cool. This one Friday night, it was after a football game, and Cardinal Mooney beat Country Day. You were with me that night, but I made up some excuse about going to a sleepover at Sophie's. Instead, I waited around, and when everyone was gone, I walked out to his car. It was parked way in the back of the stadium. I was gonna surprise him, you know? But the surprise was on me. He wasn't alone."

"Are you telling me he was with Lanier?"

Cass sniffed and nodded. "I hid behind another car and waited. I had to find out who he was with. After five minutes or so, she got out of his car and into her car, which was parked right beside his. I was so shocked, I almost died."

"You sure they were . . . ?"

"Definitely," Cass said. "His windows were all steamed up, and she was giggling and sort of pulling her clothes together. I knew exactly what that looked like."

"Oh honey," Hattie said, leaning her head on Cass's shoulder. "I'm so sorry you never felt like you could confide in me."

"I couldn't. I was so mortified. If anyone had found out? My folks? Zenobia would have killed me. And what would you have thought of your slutty best friend?"

"I would have thought that shithead Holland needed killing," Hattie said fiercely. "I would have keyed his car. . . . No. I would have slashed his tires.

"Wait," Hattie said, her eyes widening. "Were you the

one? The anonymous caller who told Molly Fowlkes that Lanier was sleeping with your high school boyfriend?"

"'Boyfriend' was a wild exaggeration," Cass said. "But I was drunk and I was mad, because I'd just read that tenth-anniversary story of hers. I kinda went a little postal."

Cass wiped her nose again, then held her hand over her heart. "But I swear, Hattie. I swear on the Blessed Virgin Mother, I never thought Lanier was dead. People were saying she ran off with a guy. I never thought *he* had anything to do with her disappearing. I just thought . . . I guess, I wouldn't let myself think, I mean . . . what does it say about me that I never told anyone? Not even my best friend, about what I did?"

"What *you* did? You were a fifteen-year-old little girl. He got you drunk and then he did what he wanted to you. It was statutory rape."

Despite the heat, Cass was shivering, rubbing her hands up and down her arms. "I should have said something when we found her wallet. I wanted to, but I just couldn't. . . ." She looked over her shoulder at the house. "I should have said something."

"Maybe," Hattie conceded. "But what difference would it have made? Makarowicz said her body has been there for years. Probably since the night she disappeared. Holland probably killed her and hid her body down there. Who else would know about that old septic tank? We walked over the manhole cover dozens of times, and didn't know."

"What do we do now?" Cass asked.

Hattie stood and reached out a hand to her best friend. "We call Makarowicz and tell him what you just told me. And we make sure Holland Creedmore pays for what he did to you. And to Lanier."

48

The Plot Sickens

-- -- -- --

The detective answered after two rings. "This is Detective Makarowicz," he said. "What's up, Hattie?"

Hattie glanced over at Cass, who nodded.

"Mak, I'm over here at the house with Cass Pelletier, who you've met. She just told me something about Lanier Ragan and Holland Creedmore that I think you need to hear."

"I'm listening," Makarowicz said. "In fact, I'm on my way over to pay the Creedmores a visit right now."

Hattie put the phone on loudspeaker and Cass leaned forward to recount the story she'd just shared. Her face was tense, her voice crackling with emotion.

"Fucker," Mak said, when Cass's humiliating ordeal was complete. "Motherfucker."

"Yeah." Cass's voice was toneless.

"I'm sorry, Cass, but I need to ask you a couple questions."

"Go ahead."

"Are you absolutely sure it was Lanier Ragan you saw that night, getting out of Holland Junior's car?"

"I'm positive."

"Any chance you remember the date this happened?"

"Not the date, but I know it was the Cardinal Mooney–Country Day game, because that was always the big rivalry. It was my sophomore year, so it would have been 2004."

"That helps," Mak said. "I can look that up, easy. Did you ever let Junior know you'd seen him with Lanier Ragan?"

"No!" Cass was emphatic. "I would rather have died. Anyway, he never called me again. I've been trying to bleach that nightmare out of my brain for the past seventeen years."

"Don't blame you," Makarowicz said. "Just one more question. Did he ever take you out to his parents' house on Tybee? The house y'all are working on now?"

"You mean the hookup house? No. I was strictly his parking lot sidepiece," Cass said.

"Good enough," Makarowicz said. "I'll need to get a written statement from you, but in the meantime, I appreciate your being straight with me. It can't be easy, dredging up this ugly stuff all over again."

"Yeah. It sucks," Cass said, rubbing at her eyes. "I just feel bad for Lanier's daughter."

"I've talked to Emma," Mak said. "She's had a bad time, for sure, but she's a tough little thing. A survivor. Kind of like you, Ms. Cass."

"We'll see," Cass said, her voice trailing off.

Makarowicz parked his cruiser in the driveway, behind Holland Creedmore Jr.'s car. He allowed himself a grim congratulatory smile as he traversed the cracked concrete sidewalk to the front door. It was just eight in the morning. A set of golf clubs was leaned against the wall, and a pair of golf spikes was sitting beside the doormat.

He rang the doorbell, and waited. No answer. He turned around and looked out at the quiet street. It was a weekday.

Most of the neighbors were at work, or inside, watching the news. At the house across the street, an older man trained a garden hose on a bed of wilted flowers. A mom pushed a stroller past, with a tiny, yappy dog trailing behind on a re-tractable leash. She stopped at the curb, waiting while the dog lifted a leg on the unmown grass.

Mak rang the doorbell again, then pounded on the door with his fist.

"Hang on, I'm coming." The door opened a crack, with the chain lock engaged.

"Mr. Creedmore," he started, but the door slammed.

"Not talking to you, asshole," Creedmore called.

Makarowicz leaned against the door. "Lanier Ragan's skeletal remains were found at your family's property yes-terday afternoon. You need to open this door, or I'll arrest you and drag you out in handcuffs in front of all your neigh-bors."

The door flew open. Holland Jr.'s eyes narrowed. "What did you just say?"

"We found Lanier Ragan," Mak repeated loudly. "Right where you put her, seventeen years ago."

Creedmore peered out toward the street. The old man across the street was leaning on the side of his car, unabash-edly watching the unfolding scene before him while his hose trickled water on the driveway. The lady with the stroller and the dog were paused too.

"You're crazy," he said. "I never . . ."

"You need to come with me right now," Mak said. "Or I can call the station and request a couple of cruisers to re-spond to this address with lights and sirens."

"Unbelievable," Creedmore muttered, shaking his head. "I had nothing to do with this shit." He was tucking his polo shirt into his pants. "Hang on. I need to find my phone. I need to call my lawyer."

Makarowicz gestured toward his cruiser. "Later. Right now we need to take a ride."

"You know I'm gonna sue y'all for false arrest, right?" Creedmore said, as they walked into the station house.

"Who said anything about an arrest?" Mak said. "We're just talking."

He ushered Creedmore down the corridor into a small interview room. He indicated one of the three chairs in the room and Creedmore sat, his back rigid. Makarowicz sat across from him at a small table. He placed his phone on the tabletop and tapped the record button.

"I'm Detective Allan Makarowicz of the Tybee Island Police Department, it's nine A.M. on May twenty-sixth, and this is an interview with Holland Creedmore Junior."

Mak crossed his legs and leaned back in his chair. "So, Junior. Tell me how a snot-nosed nineteen-year-old manages to seduce a married, twenty-five-year-old English teacher."

"Didn't happen," Creedmore said. "I don't know who you're listening to, but those are just old, bullshit rumors."

"I listened to a woman who saw Lanier Ragan with you, in your vehicle, late at night, after a football game ten weeks before she went missing," Makarowicz said. "On the date of November twenty-seventh, this witness saw Lanier emerge from your vehicle, laughing, adjusting her clothing, before getting into her own car and driving away."

Creedmore's eyes flickered. "What woman? Tell me her name. She's a liar."

"I don't think so," Makarowicz said. He leaned forward. "Lanier was supposed to be tutoring you in English. But who got schooled? How long had it been going on?"

"Didn't happen," Creedmore said.

"Her husband knew she was having an affair that fall," Makarowicz said. "Whispered late-night phone calls, mysterious 'meetings' at school. Only the meetings were with you, weren't they, sport?"

"Nope."

"Okay," Makarowicz said. "Explain to me how her body got in that old septic tank on your family's property. Nobody knew that manhole cover was there until yesterday, when a dumpster crashed down into it. And that's where we found her."

Creedmore stared down at his hands, which were clenching and unclenching.

"Who else knew about that abandoned septic tank?" the detective asked.

"I don't know. . . ." Creedmore's voice cracked. "I was just a little kid when my granddad had it pumped out." He wiped at his nose with the back of his hand.

"Lanier went to meet you that night," Makarowicz said. "Snuck out of the house after her husband and daughter were asleep. Met you out here at your family's beach house, right? What was it the other football players called it? The hookup house? Did your parents know what was going on?"

"I don't . . ." Beneath his unnaturally tan complexion, Creedmore's neck and cheeks were blooming a deep red.

"She was wearing a purple ski jacket, which her husband identified as hers. We found her wedding ring in the zipped pocket of the jacket. He identified that, too. And her sneakers. That was all that was left of your lover. Also, her skull was bashed in."

"Christ," Creedmore whispered. His forehead was slick with perspiration. His clenched hands left damp spots on the knees of his lightweight khaki slacks.

"I have enough right now to charge you with homicide," Makarowicz said. "But I'd like to hear your side of things. What made you kill her? And throw her into that septic tank?"

"I didn't," Creedmore said, his voice little more than a whisper. "I never would have hurt her. Never."

He stared straight at Makarowicz. "It had to have been Frank. I didn't do this."

"Talk to me," Makarowicz said. "I'm listening."

Creedmore licked his lips and looked around the room. "Okay, so yeah. We were, I mean, it wasn't a hookup. Not to me. I really loved her. I couldn't believe someone as beautiful and smart as Lanier would be interested in me. The first time, I thought, okay, this is just sex. And it was amazing."

"How long did it go on?" Makarowicz asked.

"It started in August. Frank wanted her to help me get my English grades up. I was being recruited by some D-1 schools, but my SAT scores were in the toilet. At first, we'd meet in the library at school, but she said it was too distracting. Anyway, I got the idea of coming out here, to the beach house."

"Did your folks know you were using the house?"

"Yeah. They were fine with it. Anything to help me get into a good football program. It was all they talked about."

"Keep going," Makarowicz said. "When did it turn sexual?"

Creedmore winced. "I'm telling you, it wasn't like that. It was gradual. This one time, I'd gotten a B on a term paper she helped me write, and I was psyched to tell her about it. She came into the house, and just sort of, hugged me, and then we started kissing. . . ."

"And pretty soon there wasn't a lot of tutoring going on?" Mak said.

"I guess. After that first time, she got pretty upset, said we could never do it again. We'd both get in trouble, she'd get fired. All that."

"But she kept on seeing you, and you kept sleeping together?" the detective asked. "At the beach house?"

"At first. But then my folks found out about the parties me and my buddies were having out there, and they changed the locks. After that, me and Lanier met in the dock house."

Creedmore twisted the ring on his finger. "It was crazy. But she was all I could think about. I'd text her, or leave notes in her car." Creedmore looked up at Makarowicz. "I would never have hurt her. Never. I'm telling you, Frank did this."

"Did she talk to you about him?"

"Hell yeah. She knew he was screwing around on her."

"Was he ever violent with her?"

Creedmore considered the question. "Not violent, but when he had a few beers, he was pretty shitty to her. A mean drunk, you know?"

"Did Lanier know Frank was suspicious about her?"

"Yeah. Toward the end, she got totally paranoid. A couple times, she thought he was following her."

"Was he?"

"Maybe."

"Talk to me about the night she disappeared," Mak prompted.

Creedmore pressed his fingertips to his eyes. The championship ring gleamed from the ring finger on his left hand.

He looked up at Makarowicz. "She broke up with me, you know? Said it had gone too far, and she was ashamed of what we'd done. She said I should be with a girl my own age."

"When was this?"

"After we won the state championship. She'd left me a

note in my car, but that night, after the game, I went over to her house, and waited outside. And we kind of got back together."

"Had sex, you mean," Makarowicz said. "Out here? At the beach?"

"No. In my car at a park around the corner from her house. And then she said it was the last time, and she really meant it."

"Classy," Mak muttered. "Talk to me about Super Bowl night."

He was staring down at the ring again, twisting it around and around. "For a while, after that, she ghosted me. I texted, left notes in her car at school, went to her house, but she wouldn't come out. Then, the day of the Super Bowl she texted me. She was pregnant."

It was Makarowicz's turn to stare. "And it was yours?"

"Yeah. Frank had a vasectomy. After Emma. I mean, what the hell? I was supposed to be going to Wake Forest, to play ball. I was fucking nineteen years old. What the hell am I supposed to do with that information?"

"So that's why you killed her. To keep anybody from finding out."

"No!" Creedmore shouted. "How many times do I have to say it? I didn't do it. She was supposed to come out to the house that night, so we could talk, but she didn't. I was waiting in the dock house, freezing my ass off, but she never fucking showed up. Eventually, I fell asleep. I woke up, drove home sometime before sunrise. And I never saw her again."

"You're lying," Makarowicz said calmly. "I know you were with her. Frank Ragan heard Lanier leaving the house. He followed her as far as Victory and Skidaway."

"See?" Creedmore shouted. "I told you it was Frank. He must have followed her all the way out to the house and killed her. He did it. I swear to God, I never saw her that night."

"Explain to me how Frank Ragan could have known about that septic tank in your backyard," Makarowicz said. He crossed his arms over his chest. "Go ahead. I'll wait."

Creedmore's head drooped to his chest. "I want my lawyer. Now."

49

A Mother Knows

– – – – – – –

Makarowicz went to the door of the interview room.

"Wait. What happens now?" Creedmore demanded. "What about my lawyer?"

"Call him, you piece of shit," he said. He opened the door and started to walk out of the interview room, leaving Holland Creedmore to, as his late mother would have said, "stew in his own juices."

"I don't have my phone."

"Too bad."

Makarowicz left the police station and drove directly to the Ardsley Park home of Dorcas and Holland Creedmore Sr.

This time Creedmore answered the doorbell. He opened the door, then started to close it again, but Makarowicz held out his badge. "Mr. Creedmore, you need to know that we have recovered skeletal remains at your property and they've been identified as Lanier Ragan. I am holding your son for questioning. You and your wife need to be forthcoming with me about what you know, or I will also take you into custody."

"Dorcas!" Creedmore bellowed.

She walked into the living room from the back of the house, wiping her hands on a dish towel.

"They found a body out at the beach house. It was Lanier Ragan."

She dropped the dish towel to the floor and sank down into the nearest chair.

Dorcas Creedmore glanced nervously at her husband. "We don't have to talk to him, do we?"

Makarowicz answered for him. "You don't. This is strictly a courtesy visit. I thought as upstanding citizens of this community, you might want to help us find who killed Lanier Ragan."

"How would we know something like that?"

"The body was found on property your family owned for decades. You told me yourself that she and her husband attended parties there. And then, there's the matter of your son, a teenager at the time, who was sleeping with Mrs. Ragan."

Dorcas gasped. "Where did you hear a thing like that?"

"Holland Junior told me himself. I picked him up this morning. He admitted to me that he and Lanier Ragan had a sexual relationship that was ongoing, up until the night of her murder."

Holland Sr. put out a hand, like a crossing guard directing traffic, as though to stop the questioning. "Who says she was murdered?"

Makarowicz sighed. "Sir, her skeleton was found buried in an abandoned septic tank. The skull had blunt force trauma. Common sense says she didn't bash her own head in and then bury herself and pull a heavy cast-iron manhole cover over herself."

"We don't know anything about any of that," Dorcas insisted. "And I can tell you that our son had nothing to do with whatever happened to that woman."

"Are you telling me you weren't aware that he was having sex with the wife of his high school football coach?" Mak asked, looking directly at Dorcas Creedmore.

Her husband answered for her. "We found out that Holland and some of his friends were having parties at the house, without our knowledge or permission. Typical teenaged boy stuff—drinking, and I suppose, they were smoking dope. Girls were involved too.

"As soon as we found out, we put our foot down. We had a talk with Holland, let him know we were disappointed, and that it had to stop," Creedmore said. "We changed the locks on the house, and we assumed that put an end to things."

"But you assumed wrong," Mak said. "Did you know Holland was in a relationship with Lanier Ragan?"

Dorcas grew agitated. "We should have had her arrested for contributing to the delinquency of a minor! Who do you suppose bought the booze? She was an adult in a position of authority. Holland was a minor. What she did was criminal."

"I understand he was nineteen at the time the relationship was initiated," Makarowicz said, "so technically, he wasn't a minor. You still haven't actually answered my question. When did you find out they were in a sexual relationship? And what did you do about that?"

"I found a roll of condoms in the pocket of his jeans," Dorcas said reluctantly. "I didn't know who the girl was."

"We were just glad he was taking precautions," Holland Sr. said. "Another boy we knew, the son of a family friend, he got a girl pregnant his sophomore year of college. He dropped out of school and married the girl. Holland knew the boy. We talked about what a mess he'd made of his life. My wife was upset when she found the condoms, but I told her I thought he was just doing the responsible thing."

Makarowicz was having a hard time keeping his temper

in check. "Again. When and how did you find out your son was sleeping with Lanier Ragan?"

Holland Sr. glanced at his wife. "Dorcas saw some text messages. On his phone."

"Mrs. Creedmore?"

"That whore! I couldn't believe the filthy things she was texting him. I wanted to call the school and have her fired, but Holl wouldn't let me."

"When did you find the texts?"

"Thanksgiving weekend," she said. "We were out at the beach house. For the oyster roast. Holland went out for a run and left his phone in his room. I knew something was going on, and I suspected that it had to do with a girl, so while he was gone, I went into his room and got the phone and went through the text messages. When I read what she wrote, I wanted to vomit. What kind of a woman sends those kinds of filthy messages to a teenaged boy?"

"Did you confront him?" Makarowicz asked.

"No."

"Why not?"

She pointed an accusatory finger at her husband. "His father wouldn't let me. I said we should put our foot down, do whatever it takes, but Holland absolutely forbid me to speak to our son about her."

Makarowicz blinked. "Excuse me?"

"Look. Frank Ragan did everything in his power to help our boy get recruited and signed to a Division One school," Holland Sr. said. "He took him to the right showcases, worked out a summer conditioning program for Holland. Stayed on him about his grades. He sent game films to every major school on the East Coast, at his own expense. He was responsible for getting Holland signed to play at Wake Forest. How would it have looked if word got out that Holland was messing around with Frank Ragan's wife?"

"So you did nothing?"

Creedmore shrugged. "We agreed that was the best plan. Holland never kept the same girlfriend for very long. We thought the affair would burn itself out."

"*We* agreed on nothing," Dorcas said with a withering sideways glance at her husband. "I told you that woman was trouble. I told you she would ruin his chances, ruin his life, but, oh no, the great and wise Holland Creedmore knew better."

"Dorcas?" Holland Sr.'s tone held a warning. "The detective isn't interested in hearing all this ancient history."

"Actually, what I'm interested in is knowing who killed Lanier Ragan," Makarowicz said. "And right now, unless I hear something different, your son is my prime suspect. He's already admitted he was at the house on Chatham Avenue the night she disappeared."

"He told you that?" Creedmore asked.

"Yes. He said Lanier texted him the day of the Super Bowl and wanted to meet up. Because she was pregnant."

Dorcas Creedmore's body sagged in the chair. She clamped a hand over her mouth and let out an agonized wail.

"Dorcas!" Holland Sr. said. "Control yourself."

She shook her head. "I c-c-can't. Enough. Enough, Holland! We have to tell what happened. We have to."

Makarowicz took his cell phone from his pocket, placed it on the small tea table beside him, and pressed record.

"You saw that text message, didn't you, Mrs. Creedmore?"

She nodded. "We had friends over. Everyone was watching the game. But I was watching my son. He kept texting someone, right as the game was starting. I knew it was her."

"Lanier Ragan?"

"Yes."

"Dorcas!" Creedmore said. "Not another word until I call our lawyer."

Makarowicz looked over at Holland Sr. "Mr. Creedmore, I'm speaking to your wife, here at your home, strictly as a courtesy. If you prefer, I can transport her out to the Tybee police station, and she and I can talk there, in private."

"You can't do that," Creedmore blustered.

"Actually, I can," the detective said calmly. "Your presence seems to be upsetting your wife. I'd suggest you find something else to do, in another room of the house, while we talk."

"This is my house," Creedmore protested, heaving himself out of his armchair. "You can't tell me what to do. In fact, I want you to leave my home, right now."

"If I leave here, I leave with your wife," Makarowicz said. "Is that really what you want?"

Dorcas placed a hand on her husband's arm. "Holl, please. I want to tell him what happened that night. I have to. Why don't you go out to your office?"

He brushed her hand away. "I'll go out to my office and call Web Carver."

Dorcas Creedmore waited until she heard the slam of the back door. "I need a drink," she announced, getting up and walking out of the room. When she returned she was holding a large glass tumbler with a straw protruding from it. The glass was full of a clear liquid that smelled like vodka. The ice cubes clinked as she walked.

"You were saying," he prompted her.

She arranged herself on the same little French chair near the fireplace, and sucked down a third of the drink.

"Mothers know when their children are in trouble," she began. "I knew something was wrong, that Super Bowl Sunday, and I knew I needed to see what that text was about.

I sent him into the kitchen to take out the garbage, and I grabbed his phone while he was gone."

"You saw the texts?"

She sucked down more vodka and nodded. "She told him she was pregnant. Little Holl texted her to meet him at the beach house.

"I didn't tell my husband about that text message from Lanier Ragan right away," she said. "I was beside myself, and I knew he'd say I was overreacting. Maybe if I had . . ."

"What *did* you do?" Mak asked.

"Little Holl left right before halftime. He said he was going to his friend Scotty's house, but of course I knew he was going to meet her. Our friends left too. It was starting to storm, and everyone wanted to get home before it got worse. I made some excuse to Holl. I can't remember what, and I got in my car. I didn't have a plan. I just knew I had to go."

Dorcas gulped down another swallow of vodka. The glass was nearly empty now. She looked down at it and shook the ice cubes, as though to wring out one last ounce of liquor.

"It was storming so hard. When I got to Thunderbolt, there had been an accident on the bridge. The police had the bridge closed down. Fire trucks and ambulances, and the state patrol. I had to sit in my car, waiting, for nearly two hours! I was absolutely wild with anxiety. By the time I finally got to the beach house, I saw Holland's car was parked in the driveway. The house was dark. I checked and it was still locked up tight. There was no sign of *her*. I sat in my car and waited for maybe half an hour."

"What did you intend to do?" Mak asked.

"Do? I was going to tell Lanier Ragan to leave my boy alone. He had his whole future ahead of him. I wasn't going to let him throw away his life for that little whore."

Makarowicz wanted to point out that nineteen-year-old

Holland Creedmore Jr. wasn't a boy. He was old enough to have sex with a married woman six years his senior. But he didn't want to put the "boy's" mother on the defensive.

"What time was this?"

Dorcas's face scrunched up. "I guess it was close to two by then. The longer I waited, the more worked up I got. Finally, I got out of the car and walked around toward the back of the house. I had a little flashlight on my key chain, and I was using that because it was raining so hard, and it was pitch dark."

Dorcas Creedmore shook the ice cubes in her glass. Without another word, she got up and left the room. When she returned, her glass had been refilled.

"I was walking out toward the dock. I thought . . . I don't know what I thought. I wasn't myself. At all. And then, I stumbled over something in the dark. I thought it might be a dead raccoon, or a feral cat. But . . . it was her."

Dorcas had done away with the straw. She took a gulp of vodka, holding the palm of her hand to her chest. She looked up at Makarowicz, who was waiting.

"It was her. She wasn't moving. I shined the flashlight and could see there was blood on her face. I touched her, and I knew. I knew she was dead."

"Where was Holland? Your son? Where was he?"

"I didn't know." She was crying now, her shoulders rising and falling with each sob.

"What did you do next, Mrs. Creedmore?"

"I . . . I called Holl. He was sound asleep. I told him something terrible had happened, and he had to come right away. I was hysterical. It was raining so hard. I unlocked the house, and I waited, in the dark, for Holl to get there."

"You didn't think to call the police?" Makarowicz asked. "You'd just found a dead woman, in your backyard, and you didn't call the police?"

"I told you, I wasn't myself."

"What happened next?"

"By the time Holl finally got to the house the rain had stopped. I showed him the body. There was nothing we could do for her. She was dead. So we, that is, Holl, moved her into the old boat house. She was a tiny little thing."

"Where was your son while all this was going on?"

"Turns out he was in the dock house. Sleeping. We found a nearly empty pint bottle of rum next to him. Holl said we should let him sleep it off. He'd spotted a car, I think it was a Nissan, parked behind some trees in our neighbor's driveway. The house was for sale, and it was vacant. Holl got a flashlight from the house and looked around and he found her purse, in some bushes near where we found the body, and the keys were in it. Holl said . . ."

"Dorcas!" Holland Creedmore stormed into the room. He saw the nearly empty glass of vodka she was clutching. "Goddamn it. Be quiet. I talked to Web. He's calling someone from his old firm. No more talking."

Dorcas raised her glass in a defiant gesture. "It's too late, Holl. I told him everything. He knows our boy didn't kill her. And we didn't kill her."

Creedmore sighed. "Goddamn it."

Makarowicz pointed at his cell phone, which was still recording. "Your wife is right. It's too late. There's no putting the toothpaste back in the tube now. I already know enough to arrest both of you in connection with Lanier Ragan's murder. I'd suggest you sit down and tell me exactly what happened next."

Creedmore didn't sit. He stood with his back to the fireplace, feet placed a few inches apart.

"We knew it looked bad for our son. He would never have hurt that woman, but there he was, passed out cold in the dock house, with her corpse a couple hundred yards away."

He rubbed his jowls. "I found the keys to her car. I drove and Dorcas followed in my car. We left the car at a shopping center. We went back out to Tybee, checked on Holland, who was still passed out—"

"I was afraid he'd been poisoned or something," Dorcas interrupted. "But Holl said . . ."

"Let him sleep it off," Creedmore said, picking up the narrative again. "We drove back home and waited."

Makarowicz was watching Dorcas, who was watching her husband recount their night of horror with chilling, detached clarity. He kept thinking of four-year-old Emma Ragan, being awakened by the storm that night, discovering her mother was gone; forever traumatized by the sound of lightning.

"Home?" he said now.

"Here," Creedmore said.

"Let me get this straight. You left your son, passed out in the dock house, and Lanier Ragan's body in the boat shed?"

"I covered it with a tarp," Creedmore said.

"And then you just . . . went home, and acted like nothing had happened?"

"It wasn't our fault," Dorcas said, her voice pleading, whining really. "We didn't kill her. And we knew Little Holl wouldn't have done it. But we had to save our son."

Makarowicz crossed and uncrossed his legs, struggling to maintain his composure.

"Okay," he said. "Tell me how Lanier Ragan's body ended up in that septic tank."

50

Nobody Knows Nothing

- - - - - - -

"We don't know," Dorcas Creedmore said. She turned to her husband. "Tell him, Holl."

"As God is my witness, I don't know how that body ended up there," Creedmore said.

"You don't expect me to believe that, do you?"

Creedmore started pacing around the room. "I went back out to the beach house the next morning, around eight. I wouldn't let Dorcas go with me. She was too upset."

Makarowicz was fascinated by the dynamic of this incredibly dysfunctional couple. The wife was skilled at passive-aggressive behavior, the husband was a controlling jerk. No wonder they'd managed to raise such a fucked-up, entitled son.

"What did you plan to do with Lanier Ragan's body?"

Creedmore's face took on a pained expression. "I didn't have a plan. I thought about putting her body in our boat, dumping her in the marsh. Doesn't matter now because when I got to the boat shed, she was gone."

"Gone, how?"

"She wasn't there, man. I swear, she was gone. I thought I'd have a heart attack when I opened the shed door and there was no blue tarp and no body."

"And where was your son while all this was happening?"

"Holl forgot to tell you that part. He'd sobered up, sometime in the middle of the night, and drove home," Dorcas volunteered. "I kept him home from school that day, obviously."

"Obviously, he was probably upset, having killed his pregnant girlfriend the night before," Makarowicz said, his voice dripping sarcasm. "Did you take his binky away and put him in time-out?"

"Don't you talk to my wife that way," Creedmore said, his fists balled up.

"Fine," Makarowicz said. "Tell me what you said to Junior when you saw him the next morning."

Dorcas looked at her husband, again, for guidance. "I didn't really say anything. Just gave him some aspirin and told him to take a hot shower."

"What did you do with the clothes your son was wearing?" Makarowicz asked.

"What's that got to do with anything?" Creedmore interrupted.

"Mrs. Creedmore?"

Dorcas looked down at her empty glass. "I think I threw them away."

"You think?"

She looked up. "Holl said I should get rid of them. I took them out to our backyard fireplace and I burned them."

"As one does when one wants to get rid of incriminating evidence," Mak said.

"I was trying to protect my son," Creedmore said belligerently. "You'd do the same thing if you were in my place."

"Wrong," Makarowicz said, pointing a finger at the older man. "If I thought my son might be falsely accused of a crime, I wouldn't destroy evidence that might prove otherwise. And if I thought he'd killed someone, I'd hand him over to the police myself."

"We weren't cops," Dorcas protested. "We were scared."

"Did you ask your son, point-blank, if he killed Lanier Ragan?"

Dorcas stood up, grasping her empty glass. She swayed slightly as she walked back toward the kitchen.

Watching her, Creedmore let out a long, martyred sigh. "Christ. Drunk and it's not even noon yet."

"Mr. Creedmore, did you or your wife discuss what had happened to Lanier Ragan with your son? Did you tell him you'd discovered her body the night before? And that you'd moved it?"

"No."

"So you actually have no idea whether or not he had anything to do with her murder."

"We know he couldn't have done it. He was never violent. Never been in any real trouble."

"That you know of," Makarowicz said. "The fact is, I've spoken to a woman whom he sexually assaulted, when she was fifteen and he was nineteen."

"I don't believe it," Creedmore said flatly. "Who is this person? Why is she just now coming forward with an accusation like this?"

"She was embarrassed. Ashamed, like most women who've been the victim of sexual assault. Her name doesn't matter. I find her credible, and she's the one who tipped us that your son was involved with Lanier Ragan, a fact which your son does not deny."

"What's that?" Dorcas Creedmore stood in the doorway, with another tumbler of what the detective assumed was vodka. "Are you calling our son a rapist?"

"It's more of this 'me too' bullshit," Creedmore said. "Probably some girl who had a crush on Holland and led him on. He was big man on campus. He wouldn't have had to 'assault' anyone."

"It's true," Dorcas agreed, slurring her words a little. "Our son could have had any girl he wanted. They were always calling him, showing up at football games, mooning over him."

"Tell me about that septic tank," Makarowicz said, abruptly changing the subject.

"The city ran sewer lines down Chatham Avenue back in the nineties, I think. My mother had someone pump out the old tank. She thought it was low class that those old houses were on septic tanks up until then," Creedmore said.

"Who knew that tank was still there?" the detective asked. "I walked all around that property after the billfold was found and before the body was found. That manhole cover was completely buried. So whoever dumped that body there knew of its existence."

"It was more than thirty years ago. I can't remember back that far," Creedmore groused.

"Your mother knew, but she's dead." Dorcas sipped her vodka with a slight smile.

"What about the rest of the family? Did Holland Junior know about it? Anyone else?"

"Little Holl was fascinated with the pump truck," Dorcas said dreamily.

"Dorcas!" Creedmore snapped. "Shut it."

"Well, he was. As a little boy, he was always fascinated with trucks, heavy equipment, whatever. I always thought maybe someday he'd go into the construction business."

"Anybody could have known about that old septic tank," Creedmore said. "The company that pumped it out, the landscapers my mother used for years to keep the grass mowed back there. Hell, even that crazy old coot Mavis knew all about it."

"You and your wife knew about it too, right?" Mak asked.

"Enough," Creedmore said. "We've cooperated with you,

told you everything we know, against the advice of our lawyer, I might add. We're through talking. Holland is through
too. I sent our lawyer out to your police station. We're not
saying another word."

51

The Camera Sometimes Lies

- - - - - - -

Trae breezed into the makeup tent as Lisa was taking the hot rollers from Hattie's hair. He squeezed her shoulder. "Morning, gorgeous."

Cass, out of Trae's line of vision, rolled her eyes. Hattie found herself blushing with discomfort.

"Did I say something wrong?" He set a mug of coffee on the makeup table and tied a cape around his neck.

"It's just . . . been a weird morning," Hattie said. "Makarowicz is going to pick up Holland Creedmore to question him about Lanier Ragan."

"Cool." Trae leaned forward to examine his image in the mirror. "I swear, there must be something in the water here in Savannah. I've never had problems with dark circles under my eyes in California."

"Oh, please," Lisa said. "Your skin is perfection. But if you want, I'll mix you up some concealer." She misted Hattie with hair spray, then turned her attention to him.

Trae closed his eyes while she applied toner, moisturizer, and concealer. "So, the police think that's the guy? He just killed this teacher, like, for the thrill of it, and tossed her in that old septic tank? Damn." He shuddered. "That's cold."

"Something like that," Hattie said.

"Hey, Cass," Trae said. "I think we're about done with the electrical and plumbing in the kitchen. Can you call for an inspection tomorrow? I want to get everything ready for the painters."

"Already?" Cass frowned.

"Oh yeah," Trae said. "We're humming right along. Today I'm going to get those lanterns of Hattie's hung over the island."

"I thought the new cabinets hadn't been delivered yet," Hattie said.

"We're going to salvage the base cabinets and paint them, so it's just the wall units we've got coming. The delivery guys texted me this morning, the cabinets should be here by noon. We'll get 'em installed, slap on the countertops and the sink and faucets today, then slide in the appliances tomorrow. Backsplashes get tiled tomorrow. Easy peasy."

"It's only easy if we don't hit any speed bumps," Cass pointed out.

Trae sat up and smirked at her. "They're your subs. I'm guessing you can push them to get it done on time."

"Let's wait 'til we know it's ready before we call for inspection," Cass said, her tone signaling what Hattie recognized as her code-red irritation level. "If Inspector Gadget shows up and finds one screw out of place, he'll flunk us, and God knows when we'll get him back over here."

"It's gotta get done before the end of the week," Trae said. "I want to get that new floor masked off and the diamond pattern painted over the weekend, when I won't have these dumbasses walking all over it and tracking in dirt."

Hattie allowed herself a small sigh. "Okay, Trae. *If* the cabinets get here by noon, and *if* the guys can get them installed and the sink and countertops done, we'll call for the inspection. But no promises. And no bitching and moaning if it doesn't get done on your time frame."

"That's all I asked for," Trae said. "And I don't need a side order of attitude to go with it."

Cass stomped out of the trailer.

"This is complete and utter chaos," Hattie told Mo, as the camera operators were setting up to shoot exteriors of the front of the house late that afternoon. "We can't schedule any of the subs like we would normally. Now Trae's got the cabinet installers working around the electricians and plumbers. Everybody is in everybody else's way. I don't get how that *Going Coastal* couple can finish even one project, let alone six a season with all this stuff going on around them."

"You get used to it. Besides, their projects are never as time-consuming as yours. They're dealing with new construction, and you're dealing with restoring a house that's nearly a hundred years old. And in the middle of a murder investigation, which was preceded by a fire."

"I guess," Hattie said, nibbling on a protein bar. "I've been working on old houses for more than fifteen years, and I've never had a project like this. Not even close. Every morning when I get up, I wonder what's going to happen next."

"Me too," Mo said. "Kind of keeps it interesting, don't you think?"

"I'd prefer boring. Safe and normal and boring would be just fine."

"You know," Mo pointed out, "if the show does well, the network's going to want to order another season, which means you're going to have to find another old house to restore as soon as you sell this one."

"*If* I can sell it," Hattie said. "Who's going to want to buy a beach house once they find out a body was buried in the backyard?"

Mo considered this. "You're just going to have to make it look so amazing, a buyer will be willing to overlook that."

"How do you think it's going? The show, I mean. And don't bullshit me, please."

"Rebecca likes what she's seen so far," he said. "And there's a hell of a lot of advance media buzz around this show, thanks to you and Trae."

"Ugh. I will never, ever get used to having someone stick a camera in my face," she said. "It feels like such an invasion of privacy."

"Better get over that, Hattie. I hate to say it, but once the news gets out about the body being found here, it's likely to be a media frenzy."

"Don't remind me," Hattie said, finishing her bar and crumpling the wrapper between her fingers. "I'm already dreading it."

"If we have to, I'll hire an off-duty cop to keep the press away from the house," Mo said. "Makarowicz seems like a good guy. I'm sure he'll do his best to keep it low-key."

Leetha appeared in the entrance to the craft services tent. "Okay, Hattie Mae. We're ready for you and Ashtray out front."

With the cameras rolling, Trae examined the vintage brass carriage lanterns that had been mounted on either side of the front door.

He climbed down the porch steps and stood a few yards away. "They're hung way, way too high," he announced. "They gotta come down at least six inches. Probably more like eight."

"But that's where you told the electrician you wanted them," Hattie protested.

"That was before I saw how dinky they are in real life. You only showed me a photo of them, without dimensions."

"If we move them now, it'll leave huge holes in the siding. And we'll have to repaint."

"Then find some larger lanterns," Trae said. "These don't look significant enough. They don't have the 'wow' impact I want at the entrance to the house."

Hattie felt herself grinding her back molars.

Trae flicked a finger against the front doorknob. "And while we're on the subject, we also need to replace this hardware. It reminds me of cheap builder brass from the eighties."

"This doorknob is original to the door, which is original to the house," Hattie said. "I took it off and stripped all the brass myself. It'll age fast in the salt air though."

"It might be original, but it doesn't look substantial," Trae repeated. "We need a chunky, oversized statement piece." He picked up his iPad and scrolled through some images until he found the one he was seeking.

"Like this," he said, showing a photo of a heavy-looking brass doorknob that was hand-engraved with an elaborate design of eagles and anchors. "I can call my supplier in California and get it overnighted."

"Eight hundred dollars? For a doorknob? Are you out of your ever-loving mind?" Hattie screeched. "We don't have that kind of money in the budget." She fixed Trae with a withering stare. "This doorknob stays. We are not buying bigger lanterns. And the only way *these* lanterns are getting moved is if you figure out a way to hide the holes in the walls where you told the electricians to drill."

"Have it your way," Trae retorted. The designer and the contractor stood with their faces inches apart, glaring at each other.

"Cut!" Leetha called. "That was great, kids. I could really feel the tension. So thick you could cut it with a knife."

"Me too," Hattie said. "I know we just staged that argument for the cameras, but Trae, you really can't move those lanterns now."

"I've got it all figured out," he said. "I'll have the finish carpenters cut me out some oversized shield-shaped backplates with fancy beveled edges from finish-grade spruce to cover up the first set of holes. We'll paint them out the same color as the siding, and it'll look like we planned it that way."

"You couldn't have told me that while we were filming?" Hattie asked.

"Nah. Like Leetha said, high drama makes for high ratings."

He flung an arm around Hattie's shoulder and turned to Leetha. "It's after six. Are we ready to call it a day yet? I'd like to take this lovely lady out to dinner."

Leetha shrugged. "I think we're done filming, but I don't know what all y'all need to get done in the house to stay on schedule."

"There's too much to do, and we're too far behind," Hattie said. "I rented a floor sander, and I was planning on knocking out the dining room and living room floors tonight."

"Tonight?" Trae shook his head. "No way. You've already been here for twelve hours. Let it go until tomorrow."

"I can't," Hattie said. "I want to get the floors sanded and covered up, so that, hopefully next week, the painters can come in and stain and seal them. I like to do at least four or five coats of poly on these floors, with a day between each coat, because I know they'll take a beating from all the sand people track in from the beach."

"That's nuts," Trae said. "Two coats are fine. This house is a flip, remember? The next buyer can worry about sandy floors. Your job is to make it look pretty. And that's it."

"No. My job is to do it right. All of it. Even the stuff that doesn't show on television. It's my name on the line. And Tug's."

"Okay, okay," Trae relented. "Guess I know where I'll be tonight."

52

The Floor Show

- - - - - - -

"You're really going to sand these floors yourself?" Trae kicked the bulky drum sander with the toe of his sneaker.

"Nope. *We* are going to sand these floors," Hattie said. "As in you and me."

She pointed at the rented power sanders. "Have you ever used one of these before?"

"Never. In California my people have people who do this kind of thing," Trae said.

"News flash. You're not in California. You're on Tybee, and out here, real men sand floors. And tile bathrooms. And anything else that needs doing."

Hattie retrieved the tool caddy she'd placed on the bottom stair landing. "Okay, since you're a newbie, I'll be the sander, and you'll be the detail man."

She handed him a putty knife and a claw hammer. "I need you to go around and remove all the shoe molding. Then, make sure we don't have any exposed nail heads anywhere that can rip up my sander."

Hattie produced a dusty boombox that a member of the framing crew had left behind. She punched a button and loud mariachi music flooded the high-ceilinged room. After a moment of fiddling with the tuning dial she found a radio station playing '90s oldies.

"Watch and learn," she said. She donned a set of goggles with an attached breathing apparatus and switched on the sander. She turned up the volume on the radio, flipped the sander's long power cord over her shoulder, then, lowering the drum until it touched the floor, she began making a slow, methodical, diagonal sweep across the scarred heart pine surface. When she neared the corner of the living room, she stopped and switched off the sander. "See?"

Trae was kneeling on the floor, attacking the baseboards with the putty knife and hammer. "You don't follow the grain of the wood?"

"Not at first. There's ninety years of old varnish on these floors. I'll do the diagonal passes first, then I'll go back and go with and against the horizontal grain of the planks, then I'll go back and do it again with a finer grain of sandpaper, until I get all the way down to bare wood."

"This is gonna take all night," Trae groused, sitting back on his heels. "I still don't get why you don't just let your subs do these floors."

"There isn't time," Hattie repeated. "My guys can be working on something else Cass and I don't have the skills to do, like finish carpentry. But anybody with a little muscle can sand floors. It just takes time, and willpower. Tonight, I've got both."

Two hours later, Hattie was making the next to last pass on the dining room floor when the sander suddenly stopped. She whipped around and saw Trae, standing a few feet from the wall, having unplugged the power cord.

"Hey!"

"Hey yourself," he said, shouting to make himself heard over the Spice Girls. "It's almost nine. Aren't you hungry?"

"Yeah, actually, I guess I am kinda starved. What did you have in mind?"

He turned the radio volume down. "What I had in mind was a quiet dinner in a white tablecloth restaurant downtown with a jazz pianist playing in the lounge. Maybe some pre-dinner cocktails, sea bass or poached snapper, a nice bottle of wine . . ."

"Too late now," Hattie said. "Would you settle for pizza and beer?"

He let out an exaggerated sigh. "Lighthouse or Huc-a-Poos?"

"Surprise me."

When Trae returned he had a large flat box and a brown pa-per sack that clanked as he walked. "Let's eat out on the porch," he suggested. "I'd like to get the taste of sawdust out of my mouth, if it's okay with you."

He spread the pizza box on the makeshift sawhorse table the carpenters had used earlier in the day, laying out paper plates and napkins. Then he lifted a bottle of Veuve Clic-quot champagne from the paper sack, followed by a pair of paper-wrapped glass flutes. Tiny beads of condensation had already formed on the chilled bottle.

"Champagne? With pizza?" Hattie raised a bemused eye-brow.

"Trust me." Trae walked off the porch and returned with a small cooler of ice he'd borrowed from the craft services tent. With practiced ease, he uncorked the champagne, poured some into each flute, and shoved the bottle into the cooler full of half-melted ice.

He took his phone from his pocket and scrolled through the apps until he came to the one he wanted, tapping an icon.

The mellow tone of a saxophone floated out into the thick night air.

"Nice," Hattie commented. He handed a glass to Hattie, then divvied up the pizza, placing a slice on each paper plate.

"Dinner is served," he said. He sat down on the top step of the porch and patted a spot beside him. "Be my guest."

She took a cautious sip of the champagne, and smacked her lips in appreciation. "Gotta tell you, I've never had champagne this nice. I usually go for the $9.99-a-bottle stuff."

Trae laughed. "Stick with me, kid. I'll teach you to appreciate all the finer things in life."

He took a bite of pizza and raised an eyebrow. "This is actually half-decent pizza."

"For Tybee."

"You took the words right out of my mouth," he admitted.

Hattie tried to pace herself, but the champagne was cold and fizzy and delicious and the pizza—well, the pizza was hot and cheesy and greasy, and the combination somehow worked.

She sighed and leaned back on her elbows. "Thanks, Trae. That was great. I guess I can never go back to the cheap stuff after this."

He leaned over and kissed her. "That's the general idea."

"That's what I was afraid of," she said, standing up. "Time to get back to work."

Trae groaned as he stood up and stretched. "I don't know how you have the energy to keep going. We've been at this for hours."

"We're almost there," she said, sounding peppier than she actually felt.

* * *

An hour and a half later, Hattie switched off the drum sander.

"We're done?" Trae asked.

"Sort of. I've got to get in the corners and edges with the other sander, but that won't take that long. I can knock it out first thing in the morning."

Without a word, Trae walked out to the porch and brought back the champagne bottle and flutes. "Time for a nightcap." He fiddled with the radio dial, which was still blasting raucous '90s hard rock, switching stations until he found one that claimed to be "the soul of the eighties."

"Much better." He poured her a glass of champagne and then one for himself.

She sipped the champagne slowly, allowing the bubbles to filter up through her nose.

"Oh, oh," Trae said, pointing to the radio, which was playing a song she vaguely recognized.

"What?"

"Only the best movie soundtrack song in the world," he said. "'The Time of My Life.' Bill Medley and Jennifer Warnes. The climactic dance scene from *Dirty Dancing*?"

"Oh yeah," Hattie said. "Now I remember. I think I might have watched that once, years ago, on late-night TV."

"Only once?" he said, feigning outrage. "How can that be? I saw it in the theater, then bought the DVD, so I could watch it whenever I wanted." He hesitated. "Want to hear an embarrassing-as-hell true confession?"

"Love to!"

He took a deep breath. "Okay. I bet I watched that finale, where Johnny and Baby are doing the dance they've rehearsed, with the lift, a hundred times. I even talked my high school girlfriend into doing it with me. The run, the leap, the lift and spin—we had it down to perfection. We were the hit of the prom."

"And then what happened?"

"What do you mean?"

"So, did you and the girlfriend take the show on the road, get a job at a resort in the—where did the movie supposedly take place?"

"The Catskills. No, we, uh, I guess, we drifted apart."

Hattie eyed him suspiciously. "You cheated on her, didn't you?"

"No! Well, not cheated really. More like, moved on. I was seventeen."

"Whatever."

"I still can't believe you've only seen *Dirty Dancing* one time."

"That whole eighties thing, it's not really my era," Hattie said.

"We should do it," Trae announced.

"Dude, that's the least sexy proposition I've ever heard. And I've worked with horny subs for the past fifteen years."

That got a chuckle from Trae. "I was referring to the dance. From *Dirty Dancing*." He pulled his phone from his back pocket and scrolled. Suddenly, Bill Medley's deep baritone voice filled the room. *Now, I've had the time of my life . . .*

"Oh yeah. That's also the song from *Crazy, Stupid, Love*. Ryan Gosling and Emma Stone. Now that one I've downloaded and watched a gazillion times."

He reached for the light switch and dimmed the overhead lights. "C'mon, let's dance." He pulled her into his arms as the music swelled.

"I feel stupid," she protested, but she reluctantly took his hand and allowed him to dip her backward, then slowly swing her around.

"*Whoooo!*" Hattie couldn't tell if it was the blood rushing to her head or the champagne, but suddenly she was definitely dizzy and light-headed.

He quickly brought her back upright. "Now, break forward with your left foot, rock back with your right, then quick left and break back right," he instructed. "Just a basic mambo."

Hattie found herself consumed with giggles as she attempted to keep up with his lightning footwork. "Are you kidding? I don't know how to do a mambo."

"Follow my lead," he repeated, and he drew her closer as he effortlessly swung his hips and shoulders to the music as they glided across the freshly sanded floor. After a moment, Hattie found herself relaxing, even singing the Jennifer Warnes verses.

"*You're the one thing I can't get enough of,*" Trae declared. He backed away and pulled her to him again. "Okay, now in just a couple more verses, you're gonna run toward me and launch yourself into the air."

"No way," Hattie said, still breathless.

"Way. Come on. You've gotta trust me."

"I saw where Emma Stone said they used a stunt double when she did this dance with Ryan Gosling."

"We don't need no stinkin' stunt double," he insisted. "C'mon. Just run, leap, and I'll catch you and lift you up and spin you around. You won't fall." He sang the next verse. "*I swear, it's the truth . . .*"

"Ohmygod, ohmygod, ohmygod," Hattie chanted.

"I'm counting you down," Trae said, still swaying to the music. "Three . . . two . . . one . . ."

"Go!" Hattie launched herself toward him and closed her eyes. His hands grasped her waist and she felt herself miraculously being hoisted into the air and spun around . . .

And suddenly, crashing toward the floor.

"*Aiiyyyyyyy!*" Trae's high-pitched scream drowned out

her own and frightened her as much as finding herself flattened on top of him.

She was motionless for a moment, with the wind knocked out of her.

"*Owwwww.*" She was conscious of Trae, moaning loudly. She slowly rolled to one side.

Trae raised himself up to a half-seated position. "That . . . didn't go as planned."

"Are you okay?"

He gingerly touched first one hip and then the other. He lifted his pelvis and groped his own butt. "My tailbone hurts like a mother."

"Do you think it's broken?"

"Maybe? I mean, I'm able to move, so that's probably a good sign, right?"

"Roll over and pull down your pants," Hattie said.

It was Trae's turn to raise an eyebrow. "Seriously, girl? If that's your idea of a proposition, we need to talk."

"I just want to look at your tailbone, to see if it's red, or bruised . . . or whatever."

He groaned, partially unzipped his fly, and rolled the waistband of his jeans down to his hips before turning onto his belly. "This is *not* how I envisioned the evening ending."

"Get over yourself," Hattie said, rolling his jeans and briefs down lower, until his tailbone was exposed.

She prodded his lower spine with her fingertips. "Does this hurt?"

His skin was smooth and tanned, and from what she could see of his butt it was just as fit and fine as the rest of Trae Bartholomew.

"It all hurts."

"Don't be such a man-baby." She walked her fingers down to his tailbone, which was slightly pink, but otherwise apparently intact. She gently prodded it with her thumbs.

"How about this? Shooting pains? Seeing stars? Ready to black out?"

"Uh, no."

She giggled and slapped his butt with the flat of her hand. "Good news. I think you're going to live."

He groaned again as he rolled over and zipped up his pants. "You're sure? Nothing's broken?"

"Sorry to disappoint, but no. I think if anything was broken, you'd be screaming in agony."

He sat back up again, resting his elbows on his bent knees. "You know, I've actually never had a broken bone."

Hattie stared. "Seriously? Never? Like, not even a sports injury?"

"Nope. Not even a sprain. I'm not really very sporty."

She considered this for a moment. "Hmm. A straight man who admits to not being athletic. That's a first for me."

"Now you're going to ask me if I'm sure I'm straight, right?"

"Pretty sure that's not an issue."

"Okay, good." He stretched out a hand to her. "Help me up, okay? It's the least you could do after jumping on top of me."

Hattie stood, grasped his elbows, and in one swift movement jerked him to his feet.

"*Owww.*"

She rolled her eyes, but didn't release her hold on his hand. She was loopy and she knew it, but didn't care.

"Which reminds me. Just how old are you?"

He considered the question. "Okay, I'll tell you, but this is strictly confidential."

"What's the big deal? Age is just a number, right?"

"Only someone your age—what, midthirties? Only someone your age would think that age isn't a big deal. In my business, it's a very big deal. I don't want people to think I'm old. Or irrelevant. But since you asked, I'm forty . . . two. Actually, since I'm being totally honest here, I'm forty-six."

"Seriously?" Hattie leaned in to examine his face. "I never would have guessed."

Trae placed his hands on either side of her face and kissed her forehead, and then her lowered eyelids. "Botox," he murmured.

"Hmm. Interesting. Tell me more of your secrets to eternal youth."

His lips traveled to hers. "Collagen fillers. Not something you'll ever need with lips like yours."

Her eyelids fluttered. "Really?"

He kissed her again, deeply. "Mmmm. These lips were the first thing I noticed about you. Very erotic."

His lips lingered there, and Hattie wondered which was more intoxicating—good champagne or being kissed by an expert like Trae Bartholomew.

Now he was kissing her earlobes, and then her neck.

"Neck cream," he whispered, his hands running along her shoulder blades. "People don't think about wrinkled necks, but it's a dead giveaway. Your skin is flawless, but start using it now. You'll thank me later."

As he kissed and caressed her, Trae was slowly inching her toward the living room wall until her back was pressed against the mantel. Her arms were wound around his neck and he pressed himself against her, his hands pushing his way beneath her shirt.

53

The Trouble with Bubbles

"What are we going to do about the body?"

Mo squeezed his eyes shut and massaged his temples with both hands. He had Rebecca on the speaker on his phone, and she'd been pounding him with questions about the latest development at the house.

"*We* are not doing anything about the remains," Mo said. "The police are handling it. I spoke to the police detective, and the family has tentatively identified the body as the missing schoolteacher. I understand they'll give some kind of press conference tomorrow."

Rebecca jumped on the mention of the press. "Will they mention *Homewreckers*?"

"I don't know. It's a homicide investigation, not a media junket. Anyway, do you actually imagine that the discovery of a body is good press for the show?"

"It's fabulous publicity," Rebecca said. "Everyone in the country has been following this story since that wallet was discovered. It's a real whodunnit. People are going to want to see the house where everything happened. In fact, I'm thinking we should move ahead with *Homewreckers* merch for the website."

"What kind of merch?"

"The usual. Branded coffee mugs, wine tumblers, hoodies, T-shirts, baby onesies, car magnets. Oooh. I know. Wallets. And tiny *Homewreckers* shovels."

Mo nearly spit out the mouthful of bourbon he'd been sipping. "Jesus, Rebecca. How ghoulish can you get?"

"Don't take yourself so seriously, Mo," she said, laughing. "What's happened to your sense of humor? You said yourself, the woman's been dead for seventeen years."

He mopped up the bourbon that had spattered all over the keyboard of his laptop. "I'll try to keep that in mind as I race to finish this damn house in the entirely too tight deadline you've given me."

"I'm going to rush those *Homewreckers* T-shirts into production and have them shipped down there to you," Rebecca said. "Maybe hand them to the local cops and firefighters on that island of yours. See if we can get *Homewreckers* trending on social media."

"Fine, whatever," he said wearily. "Anything else?"

"How's the romance between our two stars? Any new developments?"

Mo's eyelid twitched. He took another gulp of bourbon, then pushed the glass away because the thought of Hattie with Trae Bartholomew made him nauseous.

"You mean, have they hit the sack yet? Is there a timeline for that, too?"

"You really are in a mood tonight," Rebecca said. "I'm only thinking about the show and your career, you know. If it's a hit, that could go a long way with Tony."

"Right," Mo said. "I'll keep you posted. About all of it."

He went back to the endless emails on his computer, sorting, prioritizing, and deleting. It was nearly midnight, and his eyes were burning from staring at the screen for hours. But there was still more to do. He went to the small table near the kitchen door, where he'd made a habit of dropping his keys, sunglasses, and most important, his notebook.

He'd been using small, leather-bound Moleskine notebooks for years, to keep up with the notes, sketches, and doodles he produced over the stretch of every show he'd ever created. Mo wrote in the notebooks every day; to-do lists, reminders, ideas, even shopping lists. They were a time capsule of his television career.

But his notebook wasn't there. He went back to the dining room, searched the kitchen counters, went into the bedroom and checked the pockets of the shorts he'd changed out of after arriving home. No go. He fetched his car keys and went out to his rental, which was parked in the allotted slot in the lane behind the carriage house.

He searched the floor of the front and back seats, under the seats, even the glove box, although he knew he hadn't stashed the notebook there. For a moment, he sat motionless in the front seat, trying to visualize the last place he could remember taking notes.

He snapped his fingers. The beach house. The back porch just outside the kitchen door. He was sure it was there. And he was just as sure he couldn't risk leaving the notebook out in the damp ocean air.

He retrieved his billfold from the bedroom dresser and headed out into the night. Back to Tybee.

Thunder rumbled off to the east, and lightning zigzagged through the overheated cloud cover. Rain was in the air. He could smell it, almost taste it in the hot, moisture-laden air, and he sped up, hoping to reach the house—and the notebook—before the downpour began.

As he drove he mentally rewound the call with Rebecca.

He knew she wouldn't let up pressing him to exploit the trag-edy that had apparently played out at the Creedmore house, or the possibility of a made-for-TV romance between Hattie and Trae. At some point, he'd have to find a way to push back on her alternately ghoulish and voyeuristic instincts—without jeopardizing the show's chances at success.

There was no traffic this late; it was nearly midnight, and he reached Tybee in a record-for-him twenty minutes. The island was quiet.

The Tybee cop who was still posted at the entrance to the driveway nodded in recognition as he pulled off the street and into the drive. He'd only driven a few yards from the street when a series of high-pitched screams pierced the night air.

Mo floored the accelerator and sped toward the house. The house was dark, but he spotted Hattie's parked truck. He pulled in beside it, slammed on the brakes, and grabbed his flashlight.

His heart in his throat, he pounded up the porch steps and flung the front door open.

"Hattie! Are you okay?"

He played the flashlight around the room, its beam finally settling on Trae Bartholomew, who seemed to have Hattie pinned against the wall near the fireplace.

Hattie hurriedly straightened her clothes and gently pushed away from Trae.

"Christ," Trae growled, covering his eyes. "Turn that thing off."

Mo flicked on the overhead light. "What's going on here?" he demanded. "I heard screams clear up by the road. I thought someone else was being murdered."

Hattie could feel her cheeks growing hot with embarrass-ment. "It's fine. We've been sanding floors all night. Guess we got a little punchy. We were goofing around, and, uh, Trae fell."

"Why are you here?" Trae asked, dusting the sawdust off his clothes.

"I came back for my notebook," Mo said. He glared back at Trae. "I could ask the same of you, because I know you weren't sanding any of these floors."

"He was helping me," Hattie said lamely. Her jeans and shirt, even her hair, were flecked with sawdust.

Mo's eyes traveled from Hattie's disheveled clothes to her crimson face. "Uh-huh."

"What are you, her chaperone?" Trae looked over at Hattie. "I don't need this shit. I'm heading to town. See you in the morning."

As he passed Mo on the way out the front door, he added softly, "Fuck you."

Hattie sagged a little against the wall. "I need to get home too," she said, avoiding Mo's questioning gaze, which settled on the pizza box and empty champagne bottle.

"Are you okay to drive?" he asked.

"Of course," she said. "I'm fine." She looked around the room. "I just need to find my keys and my phone. And my dog."

"Ribsy? You didn't bring him to work today, did you?"

"Ohhh. Right. I gave Ribsy the day off. Lucky dog." She started to giggle, which turned into a hiccup. She walked somewhat unsteadily toward the kitchen and Mo followed her, switching on lights as he went.

"Here you are!" she said triumphantly, scooping her car keys and phone from the counter, then promptly dropping them onto the floor. "Whoops!"

Mo walked out to the back porch and found his Moleskine precisely where he remembered having seen it last. He tucked it into the pocket of his jeans.

"Hey," he said, touching Hattie's arm. "I think you should let me give you a ride home. It's late, and I get the impression you've maybe had a little too much champagne."

"Noooo," she started, and then sighed. "Okay. You're right."

He pulled alongside the cop, who was standing outside his cruiser, sipping from a foam cup.

"Thanks, Officer," he said. "The house is locked up tight, and nobody else should need to go back there tonight."

The cop nodded and gave him a thumbs-up sign.

Hattie sat in the passenger seat, looking straight ahead.

"I'm a grown woman, you know," she said abruptly. "What Trae and I do with our personal lives is none of your business."

"You were screaming bloody murder," he protested. "What was I supposed to think? The house was dark, I saw your truck parked outside. I thought someone was trying to maim you. Excuse me for being concerned for your safety."

"At first. And then you jumped to conclusions and got all weird," Hattie said. "Admit it. You hate the idea of me being with Trae."

Mo gripped the steering wheel so tightly his knuckles cracked. "It *is* none of my business," he said finally. "I have no opinion whatsoever about your private life."

"Good," she said, yawning. "Glad we got that straight."

Mo kept his eyes on the road, but after a few moments, he glanced over to see that Hattie's chin was resting on her chest. She was asleep, softly snoring.

Luckily, he remembered how to get to her house in Thunderbolt. He parked in the driveway, then walked around to the passenger side and tapped her on the shoulder. "Hattie. Wake up. You're home."

Her eyelashes fluttered open. She looked around and yawned. "Huh?"

"Give me your keys."

She handed them over and Mo took her arm and helped her out of the car.

"I can manage," she said, scowling and jerking her arm away. "I'm fine now."

"Well, I'm gonna walk you to your door, because that's what good guys do," Mo said.

"Fine." She took one step and stumbled on a crack in the concrete sidewalk. He caught her before she could fall.

"Just how much champagne did you have?" he asked.

"I don't know. I'm not drunk." She yawned again. "Just so, so tired. Long day."

When they reached her front door they could hear frantic barking from inside.

"Ribsy!" Hattie exclaimed. "Oh my God. The poor guy."

Mo unlocked the door and she stepped inside. The dog jumped on Hattie, nearly knocking her over, barking and wagging his tail and licking her face.

"Ribsy. Oh honey, I'm so sorry." She sank to the floor and gathered him into her arms. "Did you think I ran away from home and abandoned you?"

He ran circles around her, barking, and then stopping to lick her face.

Mo looked around the darkened living room. "Has he been inside all day?"

"No! There's a doggie door. But he gets separation anxiety. Plus, he wants his dinner."

"Where do you keep the dog food?" Mo asked. "I'll feed him." He walked into the kitchen and looked around. A plastic mat near the back door held Ribsy's water and empty food bowl, and on the floor nearby, a ripped-open bag of dog food. Bits of kibble were scattered all over the floor.

"Looks like he found what he needed," Mo muttered, picking up the now-empty bag. "Hey, Hattie. Where do you keep the broom?"

No answer. He walked into the living room and found Ribsy's mistress asleep on the floor, with the dog curled up beside her.

"I should leave you right where you are," he said. Instead, he leaned down and scooped her into his arms and deposited her on the nearby sofa. He went into the bathroom, wet a washcloth, and walked back into the living room.

Stepping over the dog, he knelt down and gently dabbed the cloth on her face, wiping away the traces of sawdust and dried sweat from her face and bare arms. "You're a mess," he said quietly.

Hattie stirred but didn't open her eyes. "Huh?"

He untied her work boots and slid them off her feet.

"Thanks," she murmured. "Sooo tired."

He went back to the kitchen, and found the broom closet. Mo swept up the dog food, depositing some of it in Ribsy's bowl, which he placed on the counter. He went back to the living room where Hattie was snoring again. He leaned over and tucked her hair behind her ear.

"He's not good enough for you," he said softly. "He should have driven you home himself, the chickenshit. He got you drunk and he should have made sure you were okay. I would never do you that way."

Hattie stirred slightly and turned her face toward his. "Kiss me," she mumbled. He hesitated, then dropped a kiss on her slightly parted lips.

"Mmm. Nice," she said with a sigh.

Mo lingered for a moment, studying Hattie's face, flushed with sleep, eyelashes still flecked with sawdust. He wondered what it would be like to wake up, every morning, to that lovely face.

Pushing the thought aside, he let himself out of the house, locking the door and depositing Hattie's keys in a planter of ferns on the porch.

She heard the click of the key in the lock and the departing footsteps. She touched her lips. Had she dreamed that kiss? She yawned and fell back asleep.

54

Alert the Media

Makarowicz stood uneasily before a microphone in the room that was usually reserved for Tybee traffic court hearings. He dabbed at his face with a handkerchief and checked the notes he'd hastily scrawled on an index card an hour earlier.

He counted eight reporters seated in the front row of the courtroom. Three were from local television news stations. One was from CNN, which surprised him, and there were four reporters armed only with notebooks and cameras, which meant they were from the print press. Molly Fowlkes sat squarely in the middle of the row.

Mak had lived up to his end of the bargain.

"We, uh, found skeletal remains, at a property on Tybee Island," he had said, when Molly answered his call. "It's her. There's a press conference at nine tomorrow, in the court-room at the police department."

Now he was surrounded by reporters and feeling seriously outmanned. He cleared his throat and tapped the mike.

"Good morning. I'm Detective Allan Makarowicz. Two days ago, at a property here on Tybee Island, a set of skeletal remains was discovered at the site of an abandoned septic tank on a privately owned property. Late yesterday they were identified as those of Lanier Ragan, a twenty-five-year-old

Savannah woman who went missing in February of 2005. The body was obviously badly decomposed, but it was subsequently identified through Mrs. Ragan's dental records. No cause of death until the coroner's office gives us that."

He put his hands in his pockets. "I'll take questions now."

Molly Fowlkes's hand shot up. "Has Lanier's death been ruled a homicide then?"

"Not yet."

He heard a ripple of camera shutters clicking.

Molly wasn't done. "Detective, you mentioned that the remains were discovered at a private property here on the island. Is that the same property where Mrs. Ragan's billfold was discovered recently? A house on Chatham Avenue that's currently being used to film a television reality show?"

Makarowicz shifted from one foot to the other. "Yes. That's correct."

"How was the body found?" Molly pressed.

Mak cleared his throat again. "Uh, a piece of heavy equipment that had been brought onto the property actually crashed through the manhole cover, and at that time the old septic tank and the remains were discovered."

The dark-haired male reporter from the local ABC affiliate followed up. "That home was owned up until recently by Mr. and Mrs. Holland Creedmore, a prominent Savannah family, right?"

"I believe so," Mak said.

"Have you questioned the Creedmores about how the body came to be on their property?"

"No comment," Mak said.

"How about the husband?" the reporter from the NBC affiliate called out. "Frank Ragan? Has he been questioned? Is he a suspect?"

"I can't comment about an ongoing investigation," Mak said.

"Detective, can you talk about when Lanier Ragan was last seen?"

Mak nodded. "She and her husband had attended a neighborhood Super Bowl party. Mr. Ragan has stated that when he woke up the next morning he discovered his wife was missing. He called friends and family members, drove around the neighborhood, and finally, when he could find no trace of her, he called Savannah police to report that she was missing."

The CNN reporter stood up. "There have been rumors that the Ragans' marriage was in trouble, and that she might have been involved with another man. Can you talk about that? Has that man been identified?"

"Those rumors have been investigated," Mak said. "But that's all I can tell you."

Mak looked up at the clock on the wall behind the judge's bench.

"That's all I have for now. Thank you for coming."

The reporters were still calling out questions as he made his way out of the room.

55

A Lightbulb Moment

"Have mercy!" Hattie sat up slowly and looked around. Her head was throbbing and her stomach was unhappy. Ribsy was curled up on the floor beside her, and she was flooded with guilt, again, on seeing how happy he was to greet her, even after the way she'd forgotten about him the previous night.

He jumped up onto the sofa and nuzzled her neck until she scratched his head, his ears, and his chin. "Good boy," she whispered. "Do you forgive me?" As an answer, he flopped onto his back to allow the administration of belly rubs.

She leaned her head against the back of the sofa, then groped around on the floor for her phone, which she found nearby. There was a text from Mo, sent the previous night. *Keys in planter.* It was nearly seven, and the sun was starting to rise. Time to get to work.

In the shower, she reflected on the previous night's surprising, and somewhat alarming, turn of events. She and Trae had come close, she thought, to doing the deed. It was clear from the way she felt now that she'd had way too much champagne. Had he deliberately gotten her drunk to have his way with her?

But she was a consenting adult, and she felt a powerful

attraction to her costar. She'd probably have given in to his charms anyway. Right?

She was blowing her hair dry when she thought about what Mo had whispered as he was tucking her in last night, when he obviously thought she was passed out. *He's not good enough for you.* And then there was that kiss. As kisses went, it was fairly chaste. There was tenderness, there, and she surely hadn't imagined that. But what else had he said? *I'd never do you that way*? It was all very confusing. Was Mo warming up to her? Was she warming up to him?

She was nearly dressed when it occurred to her that her truck was still parked on Tybee.

She tried calling Cass to ask for a ride, but her call went directly to voicemail. She considered, then immediately rejected the idea of calling Trae. Reluctantly, she called for an Uber, then leashed up Ribsy while they waited outside for their ride to arrive.

The Uber driver wasn't happy about it, but he finally agreed to let Ribsy ride shotgun, with his head stuck happily out the front passenger window, for an extra ten in cash.

"Headed to the beach?" the guy asked.

"To a job site," Hattie said firmly.

That was how she was going to think of the house on Chatham Avenue from now on, she promised herself. A job site. No more falling in love with a pile of lumber and bricks. This was strictly a business relationship. Wasn't it?

The off-duty cop was still stationed at the entrance to the driveway. She leaned out the window of the back seat and waved, and he gestured for the car to keep going. As she approached the house she noticed, with satisfaction, that it appeared all the subs were on the job, and everyone was busy.

The painters were on scaffolding, finishing the trim work on the façade. She saw that the plumbers, electricians, and HVAC trades were also present. Mo and Leetha were standing at the side of the house, talking to a man she didn't recognize.

"Just let me out here," she told the driver.

Trae waylaid her as soon as she walked into the house. "Can I see you for a minute?" He opened the master bedroom door. "In here."

When they were alone he stroked her cheek with the back of his free hand. "Can we talk about how things ended last night? I thought we were headed for some great sex until Mo parachuted in to defend your virtue."

Hattie had been debating that point ever since she'd awakened on the sofa earlier that morning.

"I'm not saying I wasn't thinking the same thing last night, in the moment. It seemed like we were headed that way. But the fact is, I'd had way too much to drink. My judgment was, uh, clouded. If and when you and I go to bed, Trae, I want it to be when I'm clearheaded. And Mo has nothing to do with that."

She didn't mention the thing that had been nagging at her all morning; the fact that Trae had abruptly left and driven back to town apparently without troubling himself about how she would get home in her impaired state.

"Let's continue this conversation over dinner tonight," Trae said, squeezing her hand. "I promise, we'll skip the champagne this time."

"Hattie!" It was Tug. She opened the door and stepped into the living room.

"Hey, Dad," she said. "When did you get here?"

"Hi, Mr. Kavanaugh," Trae said.

"Trae." Tug gave the designer a cursory nod.

"I just now got here. I need to show you something out in the kitchen."

"Leetha wants me in makeup because we're shooting upstairs," Trae said. "I'll talk to you later. Let me know about tonight, okay?"

Pete Savapoulis, their finish carpenter and Sheetrock installer, was standing beside her prized antique haberdashery counter that had been converted to an island for the kitchen. A stepladder stood on the marble-topped counter, and Pete's expression was a mixture of embarrassment and chagrin.

"Hi, Pete. What's up?"

"Tell her," Tug said, pointing toward the ceiling.

"Tell me what?" Hattie asked.

"Uh, well, Trae wanted me to get the ceiling in here Sheetrocked right away this morning, because he said Cass is going to call for an inspection, and the thing is, I found something that's not so good."

"Like what?"

"Like I was telling Tug, those old ship's lanterns up there, the way they're wired, they'd never pass inspection."

"Why not?" Hattie asked.

"Climb up that ladder there and take a look for yourself," Tug said, his jaw tensed.

He gave her a boost onto the counter and she climbed to the top of the stepladder, peering up at the ceiling.

"What am I supposed to be looking at?" she asked.

"Look at how those lanterns are wired," Tug said. "You see what's missing?"

Hattie craned her neck and immediately saw the problem.

"There's no junction box here," Hattie called down. "That's not right."

"No shit," Tug said. "Look closer. Can you see the scorch marks where those wires have sparked?"

"Oh God," Hattie said. "This thing is totally jury-rigged. It's a fire hazard."

"You bet your ass it is," Tug said. "Climb on down here. We need to talk."

Hattie leaned against the island, surveying the work that had been accomplished in the kitchen. The painters had worked miracles here, repainting the smoke-damaged cabinets and installing the new ones. Cabinet doors were stacked against the walls, ready to be installed.

"Pete, tell Hattie what you told me," Tug directed.

"Well, uh, when I was in here earlier, taking measurements to start hanging the Sheetrock, I noticed how those lantern things were wired up there. I mean, I'm no electrician, but I been around construction a long time, and I knew that wasn't right. Especially when I saw those scorch marks," the carpenter said. "I told Erik, one of the electrical helpers, about it, and he said Trae told him to wire those lanterns that way. He said there was no time to go back to town to get more junction boxes, because we need to get the ceiling dried in before inspection."

Hattie felt sick, even sicker than she had when she'd awoken on the sofa that morning.

"Thanks, Pete," Tug said. "We'll put off the Sheetrock in here until after Erik comes back and wires those lanterns properly. I sent him into town to pick up some junction boxes."

"Okay," Pete said. "I think Cass wants me in one of those upstairs bedrooms then."

When he'd gone, Tug crossed his arms over his chest. He was dressed in his favorite worn denim overalls, with pencil stubs sticking out of the bib pockets. "This ain't right, Hattie."

She sighed. "I know. I'll speak to Trae about it. He's just in a rush, because the fire put us so far behind. Is that why you came out here this morning?"

"Yeah. Cass called me as soon as Pete pointed out those fixtures to her. She said maybe you wouldn't listen to her, because you and Trae are kinda, what do they call it? Hooking up?"

Hattie's cheeks burnt with the shame of being called out by her father-in-law. She'd known him since her teen years, and his approval then, and now, meant more than she could explain to herself. She was a grown-ass woman, for God's sake, but feeling the sting of the old man's ire still made her want to crawl in a hole and hide.

"We are not hooking up. And of course I would have listened to Cass. She's the job foreman. I want things done right. You know that about me, Tug."

"I used to know it about you, but now I'm not so sure," he said. "I don't care if it's a TV show. We can't have shoddy work on one of our jobs. It's our reputation on the line, not that TV guy, and not Trae what's-his-name."

"I hear you," Hattie said. "I'll speak to Trae."

"You better talk to your friend Cass, too," Tug said. "You guys have been friends for too long to let some slick California creep come between you."

"I will," she said wearily. "Now, what else?"

"I don't know yet," he said. "I'm gonna walk all over this job, checking and double-checking." He shook his head and started to leave the room. "Oh yeah. Zenobia called. She says there's a woman waiting in the office to see you."

"Who is it? I'm not planning to go to the office, and I'm not expecting to meet anybody there."

"She wouldn't give Zen her name, just said she knew you'd want to talk to her."

56

The Ring of Truth, Again

- - - - - - -

"Hattie Mae!" Leetha caught up with her as she was walking out the kitchen door.

Hattie swung around to face the showrunner. "What now?"

"Whoa," Leetha said, taking a step backward. "Who peed in your Cheerios?"

"Nobody. I'm just . . . having a morning," Hattie said. "What's our shooting schedule like today?"

"That's what I want to talk to you about. We need to get your crew busy on the rear of the house, get all that siding finished, because we want to start shooting back there. And hey, what's happening with that nasty old septic tank pit? That thing gives me the willies every time I walk past it."

Hattie didn't bother to hide her exasperation. "You want me to pull the painters off the front of the house? I thought you said that was a priority."

"I did, but we've had a change of plans. The marketing people got a company that makes decking from recycled plastics to donate all the materials to redo that old dock but we need to start shooting the rebuild ASAP, because they want to use footage of the finished product in their upcoming commercials. Cool, huh?"

"For real? I didn't even have the dock repairs scheduled because I knew it wouldn't fit in our budget. That's awesome."

"But we need the back of the house to look great, because it'll be included in the shoot."

"Better talk to Cass about it," Hattie said.

Leetha raised an eyebrow. "Aren't you Cass's boss?"

"Talk to Cass, tell her you discussed it with me. You can also ask her to check with the cops to see if we can get the old septic tank pit filled. I don't like looking at it any more than you do."

"Cool."

"What's my revised call time for today?" Hattie asked.

"Not until late afternoon," Leetha said. "We'll shoot Trae in the upstairs bathroom and bedroom in a little while; they're too small for two people anyway."

"Good. I'm going to run into town, but I'll be back after lunch."

Zenobia Pelletier sat at her desk in the small Kavanaugh & Son office.

"Hey, Zen," Hattie said, approaching the office manager's huge metal tanker desk. "Tug said there's somebody here to see me?"

"Mhmm," Zenobia said, not pausing or looking up. "She's back there in his office. Looks like she's been sucking on a lemon."

"Great. Just what I need today. More confrontation."

Tug's office was little more than a glorified closet overflowing with detritus Zenobia wanted out of her eyesight.

The woman sitting in the chair opposite Tug's desk had her back to Hattie, but something in her erect posture and the way she held her head rang a faint bell of recognition.

"Hi," Hattie said. The woman turned slowly. She had

shoulder-length blond hair, a long, narrow, heart-shaped face with a pointed chin, and, as Zenobia had warned, a sour expression.

"Elise? This is a surprise."

Elise Hoffman's lips turned up slightly. Hattie hadn't seen Davis's wife in several years. She was thinner than she remembered, and much blonder. Maybe she'd had some work done around the eyes?

"Hi, Hattie," Elise said. "Listen, I just dropped by to have a little heart-to-heart with you."

"About what?"

"Davis."

"What about him? Is everything okay?"

"No, everything is not okay," Elise said. "My brilliant ex-husband somehow found a way to run his family's jewelry store into the ground. Turns out he sold our building to an 'investor' who since sold the whole block to a developer from Atlanta, who in turn has now tripled the rent on Heritage Jewelers. Davis is behind on child support and behind on alimony and God knows how much money he owes people that I don't know about."

"Oh my God," Hattie said. "I'm so sorry to hear that."

"Yeah. Me too. So, what I want to know, and why I came here to see you today is this—how the fuck does he write you a check for forty thousand when he can't pay for our child's preschool tuition?"

Elise picked up her Louis Vuitton pocketbook and fished around inside until she found what she was looking for. A single piece of paper. She waved it at Hattie. "And don't bother denying it. I've got the proof right here."

It was a copy of the receipt Davis had given her for her engagement ring.

"Where did you get this?" Hattie was stunned, then

furious. "This was a confidential business arrangement between Davis and me."

"I'll just bet." Elise crossed her legs and leaned back in the chair. "To answer your question, the judge ordered him to show me the books. One of the first red flags I see is a payment for forty thousand made to Hattie Kavanaugh."

"Stop it, Elise. There is absolutely nothing going on between your ex-husband and me. But even if there was, it wouldn't be any of your concern."

"If it has to do with money, it actually is my concern," Elise said. Even though she was frowning, her forehead and face remained immobile. Botox?

Hattie looked down at her ringless hands. They were clean, but she badly needed a manicure, unlike Elise, whose nails were flawless and painted a very pale shade of lavender.

"Okay. Here it is. I pawned my engagement ring. So that I could buy a house to flip."

"Ohhhh. Right. The old Creedmore house. Two doors down from Granny Hoffman's beach house. How very convenient for both of you."

"I'm telling you the truth. I needed cash. Davis appraised my engagement ring, and made me a fair offer of a loan, which I intend to repay as soon as I flip the house on Tybee."

Elise's upper lip puckered in disbelief. "Right. Like Hank Kavanaugh's shanty Irish family could ever afford a ring worth anything close to that kind of money. Just tell me this. How long has Davis been in your pants?"

"You're disgusting," Hattie said.

"I'm disgusting? Riiiight," Elise said. She crumpled up the paper and tossed it at the trash can—and missed. "Admit it, Hattie. Davis has always had a thing for you. Always."

Hattie blinked. "That's not true."

"My problem was, I was always too available. His folks loved me. God knows my mother loved him. He was from an old Savannah family, they owned a successful business. Speaking of engagement rings, did you know his mom picked out mine? She wanted to make sure I had the biggest rock in town. Which I did."

Elise leaned forward and fluttered her left hand in Hattie's face. It was true, the diamond solitaire in a platinum setting was approximately the size of a hubcap. A diamond as big as the Ritz.

"You were the one he had the hots for, not me. I was always second best as far as Davis was concerned. Being with me was convenient, that's all."

"I don't . . . I don't believe that," Hattie said. "But even if it's true, I never, ever did anything to encourage him."

"Just being unavailable was a turn-on. He wanted you because Hank had you. He was obsessed with Lanier Ragan because he knew she was getting it on with Holland Creedmore."

Hattie clutched the edge of the desk with both hands. "How do you know that?"

"Back in high school, Davis and I used to go out to the beach behind his granny's house and smoke weed and fool around. One night we were out there and we saw Holland, with a girl. They were skinny-dipping, jumping off the Creedmores' dock. We snuck over there, to try to see who the girl was. There was a clump of bushes right by the seawall. We hid there, and waited, and sure enough, after a while, they came running up to the house, both of them naked as jaybirds. I didn't know who the girl was, because I went to Country Day. But Davis said it was his coach's wife. He couldn't take his eyes off her, and when I looked down, he had the biggest boner I'd ever seen."

Elise's smile reminded Hattie of a crocodile's. "After that,

Davis started going out there on Friday nights, after the games were over. That's when the two of them met up, at the dock house, because the Creedmores figured out that all the football players were using their house to hook up with their girlfriends, and they changed the locks. He got off on watching them. He wanted me to go too, but even dumb as I was back then, I thought it was pervy."

"You knew Holland was sleeping with Lanier Ragan, and you never said anything after she went missing? All these years you just kept quiet?"

Elise clasped her hands on the top of her handbag. Hattie realized she was staring down at that diamond solitaire on her left-hand ring finger.

"My parents would have killed me, and his would have gone ballistic if they knew what we were up to out there. Anyway, everyone said that she'd run off with some other dude."

"And you believed that?"

"I did, right up until I saw on the news that they'd found her body this week. At Holland's house."

"Listen to me, Elise," Hattie said. "You need to talk to Detective Makarowicz, and tell him what you know. This proves it. Holland Creedmore killed Lanier Ragan."

"But what if it wasn't Holland?" Elise's pointed chin quivered, but her pale blue eyes stared directly into Hattie's.

"I don't understand."

"We were there that night," Elise said. "At Granny Hoffman's beach house. We stole a bottle of vodka from my dad's liquor cabinet and drove my Toyota out to Tybee. Davis wanted to fuck, but I wouldn't, because he didn't have a condom or anything. We had a huge fight. He called me a tease and all kinds of nasty names. I was so mad, I jumped in my car and left."

"This was the night of the Super Bowl?" Hattie asked. "The night she disappeared?"

"Yeah."

"You're sure?"

"Positive. We started watching the game, and drinking, and fooling around. I didn't know anything about football, but he was a big Patriots fan. We even had matching jerseys."

"Did you see Lanier Ragan that night? Or Holland?"

"I didn't see anyone. I went home right after the game started."

"What happened after you left? How did he get home?"

"He said he rode his bike back home that night. To Wilmington Island. He did that a lot in the summertime."

Hattie pulled her phone from her purse.

"Wait. Who are you calling?" Elise asked, suddenly sounding panicky.

"I'm calling Makarowicz. So you can tell him what you just told me."

"No way," Elise said, standing abruptly.

"If you won't tell him, I will," Hattie said.

Elise stepped over the wadded-up engagement ring receipt. "You repeat one word of what I just told you, and I'll tell everyone in town that you're a fucking liar. I'll make it *my* business to ruin you and your shitty business. And don't think I won't sell that alleged engagement ring of yours." She turned and walked out the door.

57

A Moment of Zen

"Who was that skinny-ass bitch?"

Hattie looked up to see Zenobia standing in the doorway.

"Remember Hank's friend Davis Hoffman?"

"The one whose family owns that jewelry store downtown? I remember him. That boy was kind of sweet on you way back in the day, wasn't he?"

"Way, way back. That was his ex-wife, Elise. She's under the mistaken impression that Davis and I have a thing."

Zenobia's braying laugh somehow cheered Hattie. "Haaaaah. He wishes." She took the chair Elise had just vacated.

"Something else is bugging you. You know I still need to mother my girls, even if you and Cass are grown and gone. What's going on out at that job site that's got you all twisted up—I mean, aside from finding a dead body buried in the backyard?"

"Oh, Zen," Hattie said with a weak smile. "I'm beginning to think Tug was right and that maybe the Creedmores' house really does have bad juju."

"And what's an old cracker like Tug Kavanaugh know about juju?"

"Okay, whatever you wanna call it. It seems like nothing is going right. First the code cops, then the fire, then the body—and not just any body. My favorite high school teacher."

"Well, yeah, that's real sad. Especially her poor little girl, wondering all these years what happened to her mama."

"Lanier Ragan helped me so much, after my dad went to prison and Mom left town. Aside from you and Cass, she was my biggest champion. Then I find out she had this whole double life. I mean—sleeping with a high school kid? One of her husband's football players?"

Zenobia shook her head. "Well that mess was all kinds of wrong. But there's good and bad in all of us, the Bible says. It doesn't mean your teacher didn't do some good in her life. Doesn't mean she deserved to get her head bashed in and buried in an old septic tank like she did."

"You're right, Zen," Hattie said.

"You still haven't told me how that Elise woman got you so upset."

Hattie made a face. "Can't keep anything from you, can I?"

"Worst poker face I ever saw," Zenobia said. "Spill it."

Hattie quickly sketched an outline of the secret that Elise Hoffman had just confided.

"So—the two of them were out there at the beach, the night Lanier Ragan went missing? And she says Davis had a thing for that woman?" Zenobia said. "And you're thinking maybe he had something to do with it?"

"Maybe. I begged her to call the detective who's in charge of the investigation, but she won't. And she made all kinds of threats if I call the cops."

"What are you going to do about that?" Zenobia fixed her with the same gaze she had leveled on both Cass and Hattie during their high school years—the one she'd leveled at them when inquiring about homework, curfews, boy troubles, and all other manner of teen dilemmas.

Hattie picked up her phone. "I'm gonna call him and tell him everything Elise just told me."

"Good. And then what are you going to do about the other stuff that's weighing you down?" Zenobia asked. "Because I know it's not just the house. You've worked on problem houses before. This is something different. Isn't it?"

Hattie bit her lip.

"Quit stalling. It's about a man, isn't it? That good-looking California designer?"

"Sort of. He, uh, wants us to have a relationship."

"And what do you want? He's good-looking and single, got money in the bank, I imagine. What's holding you back?"

"Trae's all those things you just said. But something is . . . off. Mostly little things. But today, we found out he told one of our crew to cover up a jury-rigged wiring job before the inspectors came out. Luckily, this guy noticed scorch marks around where the wires were spliced, and he pointed it out to Cass, who told Tug."

"And Tug had a fit, which he was right to do. Can't have substandard wiring. Don't need another fire out there."

"I agree."

Zenobia cocked her head. "There's something else, too."

"Yeah. I think . . . he's just not a good guy. Not for me, anyway."

"That's my girl." Zenobia stood up and patted Hattie's hand. "You got a moral compass, Hattie Kavanaugh. Didn't get it from your daddy or your mama, and I can't take credit for it, but you always did know how to do right. So go on and do it. Stop second-guessing yourself."

58

A Family Affair

Hattie called Makarowicz on her way back to the island. The call went directly to his voicemail, but he called back a couple minutes later.

"Hattie? How can I help you?"

"I, um, was wondering how your investigation is going. Have you questioned Holland Creedmore?"

There was a prolonged silence at the other end of the line.

"I'm not just snooping," she added. "Something's come up."

Mak coughed, clearing his throat. "This is just between us. Understand? I brought Junior in for questioning, and I talked to his parents, too. Junior admits he and Lanier were having an affair. Says she texted him that night, asking him to meet her at the beach house—and she told him she was pregnant."

"Oh my God," Hattie said.

"His story is that she never showed up."

"Do you believe him?" Hattie asked.

"I believe part of what he said," Makarowicz said. "His parents have a more unbelievable story." He filled her in on most of the tale the Creedmores had spun.

"Wait." Hattie gasped. "Are you telling me they found

Lanier's body, hid it, went back out to get rid of it, and it was gone?"

"Crazy, huh?"

Hattie was stopped at the light at Victory and Skidaway Roads. Her house was only a few blocks away. She wanted to go home and hug Ribsy and forget all about the ugliness Elise Hoffman had just spewed back in her office. But that damned moral compass of hers was pointing her back toward the beach.

"Hattie? You there?"

"I'm here. Unfortunately. I just had a visit from the ex-wife of an old friend whose family beach house is just two lots over from the Creedmores' and she has an even more un-believable story about that night."

"Does this mystery friend have a name?"

"Davis Hoffman. He owns Heritage Jewelers, downtown, on Broughton Street. He graduated from Cardinal Mooney with my husband, and played football with Holland Creed-more, for Frank Ragan."

"Go on."

"His ex-wife's name is Elise. They were high school sweethearts—just like Hank and me, but Elise went to Sa-vannah Country Day School. I went out with Davis a couple times, before Hank and I got together. Anyway, she says that back in the day, she and Davis used to go out to his grand-mother's Tybee house to fool around. And that's where they saw Holland and Lanier—together, uh, in the altogether."

"Interesting," Makarowicz said. "So these two knew Hol-land and Lanier were an item."

"Yeah. And Elise says Davis had the hots for Lanier back then. That he was obsessed with her. He got off on spying on Holland and Lanier when they met out at the dock house."

"Did this Davis ever act on his, uh, crush?"

"I don't know, and I'm not sure Elise knows either. She's

pretty bitter. Claims he owes her for back child support and alimony and has run the family business into the ground."

"So she's got an axe to grind," the detective said. "Why come to you?"

"Elise is under the mistaken impression that I'm sleeping with Davis, because she found the record of a forty-thousand-dollar loan he made me—when I pawned my engagement ring. That's the money I used to buy the Creedmore house."

"It always comes back to that goddamn house," Mak said.

"Seems like it," Hattie said. "Anyway, Elise says she and Davis were at his grandmother's beach house Super Bowl night. They'd smoked some weed and were drinking and got in a big fight. Elise got in her car and drove back into town."

"Without the boyfriend?"

"Yeah. Davis told her he rode his bike back to his parents' house that night. And she said they never told anyone about Holland and Lanier because they knew they'd get in big trouble for being in the wrong place at the wrong time."

"Did the ex say they saw Lanier that night? Or Junior?"

"No."

Another long pause from the other end of the line. "And you think, what?"

"I don't know what to think," Hattie admitted. "I've known Davis Hoffman for more than twenty years. Or at least, I thought I knew him."

"Interesting that those two were two houses away the night Lanier was killed," Makarowicz said. "Still doesn't tell us how she ended up in that septic tank. And I'm also wondering if the wife is so pissed at the ex, and has the goods on him, why tell you and not the cops?"

"He's still her baby daddy. And she's probably afraid of a scandal. It's a small town, you know. She threatened me when I said I'd go to the police."

"With what?"

"Not important," Hattie assured him. "What'll you do now?"

"I'm on my way to see the district attorney. I think I've got enough to get him to convene a grand jury and at the very least indict the parents for concealing a death and being party to a crime," Makarowicz said. "And I'm thinking maybe I'll go have another talk with Junior. And depending on what he tells me, I'll have a conversation with your friend Davis Hoffman."

"Please don't tell Davis how you found out he was on Tybee that night," Hattie said.

"I won't."

59

Deadline Drama

Mo had managed to avoid Hattie for most of the morning. He'd congratulated himself on his own smooth professionalism. And when he had to brief Trae on the morning's shooting schedule, he congratulated himself on not putting his fist directly in the middle of the asshole's smiling, perfectly arranged face.

At some point he would definitely rearrange those features, he promised himself. But not today. Today, he had to deliver the news Rebecca had shared with him while he was brewing his first cup of coffee.

"Good news," she'd said, calling him shortly before seven. "Everyone is loving what you're doing down there. But Tony wants to see the reveal ASAP."

"Why are you even awake?" Mo asked. "Where are you?"

"Oh, I'm in New York for sponsor meetings," Rebecca said. "So you understand—you shoot the reveal on Friday. The reveal, the listing with the real estate agent, Tony wants to see all of it by Saturday."

"That's only four days counting today," Mo protested. "We've still got a giant crater in the backyard here. The house isn't anywhere near complete. You're asking the impossible, Rebecca."

"For anyone else, yes," she cooed. "But not for Mo Lopez."

Mo worked out a new, warp-speed filming schedule on the drive to Tybee. He deliberately pushed aside his personal feelings for Hattie Kavanaugh. But now she was standing right there in front of him and there was no more avoiding her. If she had any memory of what he'd said to her the night before, any memory of that dumb kiss, she was too good an actress to reveal it.

"All right. The light's good, so let's go ahead and shoot the dock now instead of waiting until later as we'd planned. Here's what I need you guys to do," he said briskly, address- ing Hattie, Trae, and the crew. "I've had the guys test out the old planks on that dock. It's shaky but stable. It'll hold you guys, and the camera crew. You're gonna walk out to the end, to that dock house out there, and talk about the view to that island over there."

"It's called Little Tybee," she reminded him.

"Whatever. Hattie, you talk about what an asset the dock is to the beach lifestyle—you can keep a boat out there, kayak over to the island, fish, crab, blah, blah, blah. But the dock's gotta be replaced, and it ain't cheap. How much do you estimate that would cost—just materials?"

"We haven't done a dock in a long time, but I'd say at least forty thousand. More if you include the dock house," Hattie said.

"Great. Round it up to sixty thousand." Mo gestured to the stocky, balding man standing a few feet away. "This is Gary Forehand. His company, Lumberlyke, is providing all the materials for the new dock. He'll walk out there with you guys and you'll chat a little."

"Hi, Gary," Hattie said. "Thanks so much for the free stuff."

Forehand, who was dressed in sharply pressed khakis and a polo shirt with a Lumberlyke logo across the front, smiled and wiped at his sweaty forehead. "My pleasure. Uh, I've never done television before, so . . ."

"No worries," Hattie said, giving him a reassuring smile. "I'd never done it either, until Mo here recruited me for *Homewreckers*."

"What about me?" Trae asked.

Mo ignored him. "Gary, you're gonna talk about the dock material, what it's made out of . . ."

"Rot and weather resistant," Forehand said, suddenly animated. "And a lifetime guarantee. We're going to revolutionize this kind of application, which is especially great in coastal areas."

"Great," Mo said, looking down at his notes.

"Hello?" Trae repeated. "What am I going to be doing in this shot?"

Mo gave him his best deadeye. "You'll walk out to the dock house and come up with some pie-in-the-sky, totally unrealistic ideas for improving it. . . ."

"First off, raise the roof. Then we screen it in, maybe build some low cushioned benches with storage underneath. A sink with running water and an under-counter mini fridge. I designed something similar for a lake lodge in Montana. Overhead we do a very cool retro ceiling fan . . ."

"Is Lumberlyke donating materials for any of that?" Hattie asked, her face impassive.

"Oh no, we're strictly providing the raw building materials," Foreman said, sounding alarmed. "I thought that was understood."

"It is," Mo said.

Hattie nodded. "We rebuild the dock. We can raise the roof of the dock house, and if there's any money in the budget, we can talk about screening, but that's about it, Trae."

The designer shook his head in disgust. "Not even a kitchen sink?"

"I saw an old stainless-steel sink in the boat shed," Hattie said. "Maybe you can design a counter thing out of the Lumberlyke material. Also some benches." She flashed her winning smile at Gary Forehand. "That'd be okay, right?"

"Absolutely." He beamed at her. "In fact, our company just bought a firm that makes lawn furniture from recycled plastics. Adirondack chairs, tables, things of that nature. You'd swear the pieces were cedar. Or even teak. I have a catalogue if you'd like to see some. . . ."

"Plastic furniture?" Trae asked. "I don't think so."

"Wait," Hattie exclaimed. "Are we talking about TikiTeak? I love that stuff. I ordered a couple chaises for the pool house we did in Ardsley Park last year."

"Yes, that's right. TikiTeak is our newest subsidiary," Forehand said.

Mo turned to Leetha, who'd been making notes on her iPad. "How's the back of the house looking to you?"

"We're good to go," Leetha said. "We'll just make sure we keep tight shots on the area around the kitchen door and back porch. The painters cleared out of there half an hour ago."

"In other news," Mo announced, addressing the assembled camera crew and construction workers, "on Friday, we film the reveal."

"What?" Hattie squawked. "You said we had six weeks. It's barely been four. We can't get everything finished by Friday. Not after the fire and everything else . . ."

"Gotta happen," Mo said. "The network's breathing down my neck to get everything in the can so we can go to post-production. We'll need it furnished, too. You can do that, right?"

"No," Trae said. "Furnish this whole house, from scratch,

while we've got painters and carpenters still working? It can't be done. I'm a designer, not a magician."

"They've got furniture stores in Savannah, right?" Mo said. "The good news is, we'll just shoot the living and dining room, the kitchen, and the master suite. Concentrate on the downstairs rooms. It's a beach house, so it doesn't have to be fancy."

"Unbelievable!" Trae said loudly. "Fucking insanity."

Mo ignored the designer's tantrum. He pointed to Trae and Hattie. "Let's do it. I want you to re-create that whole little tableau you two just acted out, right down to the cute little lovers' spat over the furniture. Gary, you ready?"

"Lovers' spat?" Hattie glared at Mo.

"Squabble?" He walked away, smiling to himself.

Hattie sat on the back porch, dabbing at her melted makeup. The trailer with the Bobcat had arrived shortly after filming halted for the day, followed by a dump truck full of sand, and now the bulldozer operator was running his equipment back and forth, scraping and smoothing the earth above the filled septic tank pit. Cass had given her the news that a truck full of sod would be delivered early the next morning. Soon, all signs of the spot where Lanier Ragan had been entombed for seventeen years would be erased.

She couldn't bear to watch, so she averted her eyes, and finally got up and walked rapidly toward the seawall and the river.

She'd been thinking about Elise Hoffman off and on all afternoon, and in her mind, reliving what might have happened here on that stormy Sunday night all those years ago.

Pushing past an overgrown clump of palmettos and oleanders, she walked along the seawall, pausing to inspect the house to the north of her property, which was also undergoing a dramatic transformation. Formerly an unfortunate rendition of a seventies cedar A-frame, the house had been lifted up on jacks and rebuilt on top of a concrete foundation. Hattie knew the builder-designer, Liz Demos, who'd made a specialty of buying small flip houses in gentrifying in-town Savannah neighborhoods, and was interested to see what she'd do with a project on this scale. Rumor was that Liz would ask north of a million dollars, once the remodel was complete.

Whatever she did, Hattie hoped the project would help with the comps on her own property. She stood on the seawall for a moment, looking out toward Little Tybee. A boat roared past towing a bright orange inner tube bearing two waving bikini-clad teenaged girls.

A dock jutted out from the seawall on the next lot. The tide was out, revealing a thin strip of sandy beach dotted with clumps of seaweed and oyster rakes.

Hattie turned and looked up at the house she knew belonged to Davis's family.

The Hoffmans' beach house had been designed in the 1960s by a famous Atlanta architect who was better known for his high-rise hotels and resorts. Made of poured concrete and painted gray, it resembled the prow of a ship, pointed directly toward the river, bristling with iron-railed decks and expanses of plate-glass windows and sliding glass doors. On the bottom level, a tiled deck featured a narrow lap pool surrounded by huge potted palms. Locals referred to the house as "the Titanic."

She heard the clatter of a lawnmower and watched as a man pushed the mower around from the side of the house toward the back. His face was shaded by a baseball cap and he was dressed in a long-sleeved T-shirt, shorts, and sneakers.

For a few minutes he seemed oblivious to her, but then he stopped to empty the mower's bag of grass clippings and looked up, obviously surprised to see that he had company.

"Hattie?"

She'd assumed the worker was part of a landscape crew, but to her shock it was actually Davis Hoffman.

Her stomach lurched as he walked toward her, grinning. "Howdy, neighbor," he said. "Good to see you."

"Oh, hey," she said, hoping her voice didn't sound as jumpy as she felt. "Didn't expect to find you out here today."

"I didn't expect to find me here either, but my mother called in a panic because we've got family coming in from out of town to stay here this weekend, and her yard man has a bum knee." He wiped his perspiring face with the back of his arm and she noticed that his right hand was wrapped in a wide gauze bandage.

"What happened there?" She pointed at his hand.

"Oh." He stared down at his hand as though just discovering it. "So stupid. I was getting ready to grill some steaks last weekend and I guess I got a little carried away with the lighter fluid. I jumped back, but obviously not fast enough."

Hattie felt herself freeze. Davis's eyebrows were singed too. And she spotted an angry blistered spot just above the neckline of his sweat-soaked T-shirt. Whoever had torched the dumpster at her house could have gotten a similar burn. Temporarily tongue-tied, she struggled to keep her voice light.

"That must hurt. I have a terror of being burned. Which is why I haven't used my grill in years."

"It looks worse than it feels," Davis said. "How's it going over at your place? I've been riding my bike past there, but you can't see much from the street. Especially with that cop posted at the driveway."

"The network's deadline is looming, and I'm starting to panic," Hattie admitted.

"I'm sure you'll make it, and the house will be great," Davis said. "Are you going to live there yourself, or will you sell it?"

"I can't afford to keep it," Hattie said. "I've got to get my money out of it so I can repay my loans. And get my engagement ring out of hock."

Davis's sweaty face flushed. "No hurry on my account."

"Elise came to see me at my office today," Hattie said. "She made some pretty nasty accusations."

He wiped his brow with the back of his arm again and grimaced. "Sorry about that. For some reason, she's got a real bee in her bonnet about you. Her asshole lawyer got the judge to let her examine the books for the jewelry store, and I guess you know the rest."

"She told me the jewelry store is in trouble," Hattie said.

"Jesus! It will be if she keeps going around town spouting that kind of bullshit," he exclaimed. "We hit a bumpy patch, that's all. My accountant gave me some bad advice, and I sold the building to an investor, who sold it to a developer and now he's tripling my rent. I just have to move some money around, that's all. Believe me, Heritage Jewelers is not about to go broke."

"Glad to hear it," Hattie said. The conversation felt weird and awkward. Davis was studying her face, just as she was studying his. Who was he, really? Had he guessed what else his ex-wife had confided in her?

"Gotta go," she said, swatting at a mosquito that had been buzzing around her face. She started to walk away, but Davis reached out and caught her by the elbow.

"Hattie? Is something wrong?"

"No," she lied.

His fingertips tightened on her arm. "You sure? We go way back, Hattie. You know me. You're not gonna believe any of that shit Elise is slinging about me, right?"

"Right." She felt a droplet of sweat running down her back, and then another. Stay calm, she told herself. Be cool.

"Good." He released his hold. "Call me, okay? I really want to see what you've done with the house. Who knows? Maybe I'll buy it myself."

"I'll do that," she said, hoping the slight tremor in her voice didn't betray how spooked she felt. She had to force herself to walk, not run, back along the seawall.

60

Ladies' Night

- - - - - - -

By the time she got back to the job site, the crews had dispersed for the day. Hattie climbed into her truck, closed her eyes, and exhaled. Her mouth was dry and her pulse was racing after her encounter with Davis Hoffman. Had there been something faintly threatening about the way he grasped her elbow, some lurking malevolence that she'd been blinded to over the years of their friendship?

"Hey." She jumped at the sound of Cass's voice, and actually clutched at her chest.

Her best friend leaned against the side of the truck. "Something wrong?"

It was the second time she'd been asked that question in just a few minutes. "I'm not sure," Hattie said.

"Well, you look like you just saw a ghost. Where'd you run off to after we finished shooting? Trae was looking all over for you."

Hattie hesitated. "What are you doing tonight?"

"I'm gonna go home and chill."

"You wouldn't want to come over to my place and chill, would you?" Hattie asked.

"Really? You don't have plans with your new squeeze?"

"Don't call him that," Hattie said, her voice sharper than

she intended. "Sorry," she said, shaking her head. "I'm just tired. And on edge. And to tell you the truth, I'm spooked."

"You?"

"Yeah. So what do you want to order in? Thai? Mexican? Burgers?"

"Let's do healthy," Cass said. "I'll pick up something at Whole Foods and meet you at your place."

"Healthy? Who are you?"

"I'll explain when I get there," Cass said.

By the time Cass arrived, Hattie had showered and changed into a pair of frayed gym shorts and one of Hank's ratty old T-shirts.

Cass unpacked cardboard cartons of kale salad, fruit salad, and grilled chicken as Hattie set out plates and silverware on the kitchen table.

"I brought a bottle of wine," Cass said, but Hattie waved her off.

"I'm on the wagon. At least for a couple of days."

"Intriguing."

The two women ate in companionable silence with Ribsy crouched beneath the table waiting for handouts.

"I've missed this," Hattie said, spearing a chunk of pineapple with her fork.

"Me too," Cass said. "But you've been kind of busy these past few weeks, so I'm not complaining."

Hattie thought about that for a moment. "I think I might have broken the best friend commandment. Hoes before bros."

"You kinda did," Cass agreed.

"I just . . . got swept up in the moment," Hattie said. "Literally swept off my feet."

"I get it. Trae Bartholomew is a pretty irresistible force,"

Cass said. "You know, if you like your guys tall and sexy and charming."

"Ugh. What a lethal combination." Hattie slipped a sliver of chicken to Ribsy.

"I take it the charm has worn off? Does Trae know?"

"No. I'm such a chickenshit. I avoided him as much as possible today."

"Anything happen in particular?" Cass asked.

Hattie looked around the kitchen. For the first time she noticed the broom and dustpan standing in the corner of the room. Had Mo actually swept her floor the previous night, while she was passed out on the sofa?

"I think it was a combination of things. I won't bore you with the details, but while we were sanding the floors last night, I drank a lot of really good champagne—way more than I meant to, and things got pretty steamy."

"Oooh. How steamy?"

"Very. But then we were horsing around—did I mention I was totally drunk? And I kind of fell on top of Trae, and I might have screamed, really really loudly, and then the next thing we know, Mo charges in from nowhere, thinking I'm being murdered or something . . . which pisses off Trae. So he up and left."

"Okay. You've lost me," Cass said. "You were drunk. Was Trae also drunk?"

"Nope."

"He just left you at the house? Drunk? How did you get home?"

"Mo drove me. I must have nodded off on the way, but he got me into the house and loaded me onto the sofa. I'm pretty hazy about the details, but I'm pretty sure that before he left, he leaned down and kissed me."

"Like, a brotherly peck on the cheek?"

"Definitely not."

"You're sure you didn't dream it?"

"Nuh-uh. I touched my lips and they were still damp."

"You probably just drooled on yourself," Cass reasoned. "You tend to do that when you pass out drunk."

"I'm telling you, Mo kissed me," Hattie insisted. "He was muttering about how Trae wasn't a good guy. And then he kissed me and said he'd never do me that way. And he left. But first I think he maybe swept the kitchen floor."

"What do you think that means?"

"The sweeping? Maybe Ribsy made a mess in here? Or he's a clean freak?"

"You know I'm talking about the kiss," Cass said.

Hattie sighed and looked away. "It was sweet. And . . . nice. I woke up thinking I wish I'd kissed him back."

"Maybe you should."

"Definitely not. I don't need that kind of complication. Things are bad enough with Trae as it is. I can't believe he deliberately tried to cover up that shitty wiring job."

"That's the least of what he did. While you were in town, Tug and I discovered a soggy spot in the new sink cabinet in the kitchen. Somehow, while they were installing the new dishwasher, someone punctured the drain line, and water's been leaking into the cabinet. We caught it in time, or the whole cabinet would have had to be replaced. When one of the carpenters pointed out the leak, Trae told him it wasn't that big a deal."

"Oh, God." Hattie pushed her plate away. "I feel sick. How could he do that?"

"As long as it looks good, and he looks good, Trae doesn't care. He's got no skin in the game. Tug started raising hell with him and Trae just laughed and walked away."

"Did you guys find anything else he covered up?" Hattie asked.

"That was enough," Cass said. "What are you going to do about Trae?"

"What can I do? I've got a contract. We've got four days to finish and then the show's over, and Trae Bartholomew and I are history."

"What if the show's a hit and the network wants a second season?"

"I can't think about that right now," Hattie said.

"How do you think he's going to take the news?"

"His heart's not going to be broken. I'm pretty sure he never meant for me to be anything more than a summer fling. More like a drive-by fling."

"Pretty sure?" Cass asked.

"Maybe I flattered myself—at first—that I was more than that to him. But now? The blinders are off." Hattie tossed another piece of chicken to Ribsy, who leapt up and caught it in midair.

"You know what else? Trae never even called to see if I was okay."

"He's such a douche," Cass said. "Mo, on the other hand . . ."

"I thought you didn't like Mo."

"It's the damn house I don't like. But you have to admit Mo is super bossy."

"Takes one to know one," Hattie said.

Cass got up and fetched a bottle of water from the fridge and sat back down again. "You still haven't told me what freaked you out so bad today, back there at the house."

"It started with that damned septic tank pit. I can't stop thinking about Lanier. . . ."

"By tomorrow morning you'll never know it was there," Cass said.

"I'll always know. And now, I know way more than I wish

I did." Hattie ran her hands through her hair. "Elise Hoffman dropped in at the office to have a 'chat' with me today."

"Who?"

"Davis Hoffman's ex. Skinny blonde, went to Country Day?"

"What did she want?"

"She wanted to make sure I'm not sleeping with Davis these days."

"Eew. Gross. Where'd she get an idea like that?"

Hattie filled her in on the Hoffmans' marital woes, and the $40,000 loan.

Cass's eyes widened. "You pawned your engagement ring? To buy the house?"

"I had to get the money from somewhere." Hattie looked down at her plate, out the window, anyplace but directly at her best friend's unflinching gaze. "I even hit up my dad."

"Shit. Why didn't you tell me?"

"I was embarrassed. To admit the lengths I'd go just to prove a point to Tug. And the world. That I could make a success of something, after the debacle at Tattnall Street."

"That wasn't your fault. Nobody blamed you."

"Tug did. He lost a lot of money on that house, money he and Nancy can't afford."

"What are you talking about? Mom says they're loaded, and she oughtta know cuz she does the books. He owns like, a dozen rental houses around town, and a strip shopping center in Pooler."

"That can't be. He hasn't bought a new truck in a decade, and he and Nancy still live in the same house they bought when Hank was a kid. He brings a sack lunch to work most days!"

Cass howled with laughter. "That's because he's tight as a tick. The Kavanaughs live that way because they want to."

"Well, damn," Hattie said. "Here I've been worrying my screwup would put them in the poorhouse."

Cass cocked her head. "It's always about proving yourself to other people, isn't it? You're the smartest, hardest-working woman I know, Hattie, but nobody has a poorer opinion of you than you."

Hattie tipped the contents of her plate into Ribsy's bowl, and he pounced.

"When did you turn into such an armchair psychiatrist?"

"Funny you should ask. I've started seeing a therapist."

"Since when?"

Cass began boxing up the leftovers. "It's been about six months now."

"Does it help?"

Cass nodded. "I think so. It was Mom's idea, actually."

"Zen sent you to a shrink?"

"After my last disastrous relationship with that guy I met on Tinder who turned out to be married, she sat me down and asked if maybe I was deliberately sabotaging my own life."

Hattie smiled. "I just hate it that your mom's always right."

"Not all the time," Cass said. "Remember the time she used that home hair-straightening stuff on me? Or that mini-van she bought herself when we were seniors?"

"Who could forget the grocery grabber?"

"Worst car ever. But let's get back to Davis Hoffman. What made Elise automatically assume you were sleeping with her ex?"

"She says he's always had a thing for me, going back to high school."

"I gotta say, I never really liked Davis Hoffman. It always felt like he was watching you and Hank when you two were together—like a housecat waiting to pounce on a wounded chipmunk," Cass said.

"Nice image," Hattie said, recounting the rest of what Elise had told her—about Davis's finances, and about the two of them being at the Hoffman family's Tybee house—two doors down from the Creedmores', on the night of Lanier Ragan's death.

"Did you tell that to your detective friend?"

"I called him on my way back to Tybee. Cass, this thing keeps getting crazier and crazier. He's been grilling Holland and his parents, and he finally got Holland to admit that he and Lanier had been meeting up that fall at the beach house. He said the night she disappeared, Lanier texted to say she was pregnant and wanted to meet up with him there."

"Oh my God," Cass whispered.

"This next part I'm not sure I understand, but somehow Holland's mom figured out what was going on and she drove out there too."

"To save her innocent baby boy from the evil school-teacher."

"Here's where it gets really screwy. Holland swears he went out to the dock house, and waited, but Lanier never showed. He proceeded to get drunk and fall asleep. In the meantime, his mom gets out to Tybee, and she's fumbling around in the dark and finds a body—which turns out to be Lanier."

Hattie repeated the rest of the Creedmores' fantastical account of finding, hiding, and then losing the schoolteacher's corpse.

"They're fucking lying," Cass said, slapping the table-top with the palms of her hands. "Junior killed her, and his parents literally covered it up. Think about it, Hattie. Who knew that septic tank manhole was there? We sure didn't. It had to have been them."

"You're probably right," Hattie said. "But what if it wasn't them? What if Holland and his parents really are telling the truth? What if someone else was out there that night? And what if that someone also had a thing for Lanier Ragan?"

"That's a lot of what-ifs," Cass said.

Hattie leaned across the table. "You wanted to know why I was so creeped out this afternoon? I'll tell you. I went walking down the seawall, just to see if the Creedmores' dock house was visible from the Hoffmans' house. And Davis was there. Mowing the grass."

"So? What's creepy about that?"

"He had a big bandage wrapped around his right hand, and I could see a place on his chest that was blistered. He said he'd had a grilling accident. But Cass, I think he was lying. I think he got burned when he started that fire in our dumpster."

Cass opened the bottle of chardonnay she'd stashed in the fridge and poured a glass for herself. She gestured with the bottle toward Hattie. "Hair of the dog?"

"God, no."

Cass sat back down opposite her friend. "Why would Davis set that dumpster fire?"

"To scare us off or make us abandon the project. As long as the Creedmores owned the house, he probably thought his secret was safe. No chance they'd go poking around back there, and if they did somehow discover Lanier's body, they'd never broadcast that fact because they were complicit in her death. And it could be tied back to Holland."

Cass sipped her wine. "That's a huge supposition you're making."

"Not really. Davis has called me twice—out of the blue—to ask about our progress on the house. He as much as offered to buy it from me and said if he'd known it was going on the market, he'd have bought it himself. And he's asked me to dinner twice. Why? After all these years?"

"Face it, kid, when you're hot, you're hot."

Hattie snorted, pointing at her damp, unruly hair and the outfit that was one step away from the rag bag. "Riiight."

"Okay, suppose Davis did set the fire and suppose he did kill Lanier. How did he hide the body in that septic tank? How did he even know about it?"

"That's what Makarowicz needs to figure out," Hattie said. "He told me he's going to ask the district attorney to take the case to a grand jury."

"I hope they indict the whole family," Cass said. "Including that old witch Mavis."

"I'm sick of thinking about them," Hattie said. "Let's go in the den and eat junk food and watch some trashy TV."

Slowly, a mischievous smile spread across Cass's face.

"Hey. Did you know you can still watch all the old episodes of Trae's last show? They're streaming online. My favorite part is the finale, when he loses."

"Brilliant!" Hattie said. "We can hate-watch *Design Minds* while we figure out how to get this damned house finished and sold in a little more than a week."

61

The Clock Is Ticking

The next morning, Trae stopped Cass as she was walking through the dining room toward the kitchen.

"Hey," he said, grabbing her arm. "Hattie's giving me the cold shoulder, and I think it has something to do with you. I bet you tattled to her about those goddamn kitchen lights."

Cass pried his fingers loose. "Your relationship with Hattie is none of my business, but this house—and the quality of the work being done here—*is* my business. Now I've gotta worry about what else we didn't catch before our final inspection."

"No worries there," Trae said. "I took care of things."

Cass took a step backward. "Are you saying you bribed the inspector?"

"That's how stuff gets done," Trae said. "You grease some palms and suddenly you don't have to order more kitchen cabinets and wait for them to be installed. You don't have to tear down light fixtures and wait for some idiot to run into town to buy junction boxes. You need to wise up, Cass. It's done all the time."

She shook her head emphatically. "It's not how we do things. One bad wiring job, this whole house—which is made of hundred-year-old heart pine, which is essentially kindling—could go up in flames. What if someone was here when the fire started? It's our reputation on the line, not yours. And what happens when that sleazeball inspector decides the only way he'll pass our next inspection is if we pay him off? Again and again?"

"Not my problem," Trae said. "My job is to make this place look fabulous, despite all the fuckups by you and your lamebrain crew."

He started to walk away, but the door to the hall bathroom opened, and Hattie walked out, wiping damp hands on the back of her jeans.

Her face was still, but her voice crackled with barely suppressed anger. "It *is* your problem, Trae. Now I'm going to have to get Erik's guys to pull down every single light fixture you had them hang and do it over the right way."

"No! That'll totally screw up everything," Trae protested. "We've got the walk-through in less than forty-eight hours. You take those fixtures down, every ceiling will have to be patched and repainted. I've got furniture being delivered, window treatments to install, and art to hang. I can't have electricians on ladders in the middle of all that."

"That's your problem," Hattie said, her tone icy.

Trae stared at Cass. "Could you let Hattie and I have a little privacy here, please?"

"Gladly," Cass said. "I've gotta go fix your screwups."

When they were alone, Trae clasped Hattie's hands between his. "Look, Hattie. This is just a little snag we've hit here. It can be worked out. I know you're pissed, and okay, maybe that was the wrong way to handle things, but I was just thinking of us, of getting the house done and hitting a home run with the network."

"There's no us," Hattie said. "There never really was."

"What about the other night?" He nodded his head in the

direction of the living room. "What was that about? You're telling me that wasn't real?"

Hattie turned around and looked at the living room, where one of the electricians was on a ladder, removing the ceiling fans that had been installed only a few days earlier.

"That was about you getting me drunk so that you could get laid," she said. "And when Mo busted in on us, interrupting your plan, you walked off and left me here. Did it occur to you to wonder how I'd get home after you drove away?"

"You weren't *that* drunk. I figured you'd get an Uber or something. You're a big girl. I knew you could handle yourself."

Hattie gave him a grim smile. "I *was* that drunk. Mo had to pour me into and out of his car, and then I passed out on my sofa when I got home. After he did what you should have done yourself. But nothing is ever your fault, and nothing is ever your responsibility. You really are a big fucking manbaby, Trae. You and I both know you only pursued me to get publicity for *Homewreckers*. Mission accomplished, right?"

He opened his mouth to protest, and then closed it again.

"That's what I thought. Now that the air is cleared, let's get back to work. I need to get this money pit fixed up and sold."

Construction workers swarmed over the house on Chatham Avenue. A tractor-trailer load of Lumberlyke planking had arrived and was unloaded, and Hattie's framing crew set about rebuilding the old dock. The electricians removed, rewired, and reinstalled four more light fixtures with faulty wiring. The painters repaired and repainted the ceilings.

As soon as the kitchen fixtures were replaced, Trae shut himself off in the kitchen. On his hands and knees, he measured and taped off the checkerboard diamond pattern he'd designed for the wooden floors.

Hattie and Cass spent an entire day working with the finish carpenters to complete the upstairs bedrooms and bath, installing new baseboards and window trim, and painting the heavily scarred wooden floors with a coat of milk-white deck paint.

"Amazing," Cass said, standing in the doorway of the guest bedroom, where the afternoon sunlight cast warm streaks of light on the pale, gleaming floors. "I think this was the smelliest, gloomiest room in the whole house. Now, I just want to move in."

"It looks and smells a lot better now that the roof isn't leaking, and the ceiling has been replaced. And look at the view out those windows," Hattie said, pointing to the bay windows on the east side of the room. "Can you imagine lying in bed in here, watching a Tybee sunset?"

"I can't imagine lying in bed, period," Cass said, groaning and clutching the small of her back. "I feel like I've been working nonstop for the past eighteen hours."

"That's because you have."

They moved down the hallway and the stairway, pausing to take in the living room below. The new mantel had been installed, and the brick fireplace with its light coat of limewash gave the room a mellow dignity. The floor had received two coats of matte polyurethane. "Looks awesome," Hattie said. "We'll come back later and give it another light sand and a couple more coats. We'll just have to warn anybody who walks through here to take off their shoes."

They moved downstairs and opened the door to the new bathroom that had been tucked under the staircase. "What else are we doing in here?" Hattie asked. "It looks so bare."

The floors were covered in a vintage-looking gray-and-white basket-weave tile, and a painted wooden wainscot extended halfway up the walls, with unadorned Sheetrock above.

Cass leaned against the doorjamb. "I've been meaning to talk to you about that. Trae ordered some fancy custom wallpaper, but he waited until yesterday to tell me it hasn't shipped yet."

Hattie sat down on the closed seat of the commode and glanced around. She'd found an old pine dresser with a marble top to use as a sink vanity, but the rest of the room was bare.

"It definitely needs something," she mused, and then snapped her fingers.

"Nautical charts. I bought a whole barrel full of them at an estate sale down in Brunswick last year. They're great colors, and a lot of them are of the South Atlantic coast. We'll glue them right to the walls with wallpaper paste."

"Sounds good." Cass picked up one of a pair of antique unvarnished brass sconces that had been laid out on top of the vanity. "Trae found these out in the boat shed, beneath that old farm sink. They'll look good in here, right? But what should we do for a mirror? He said that hasn't shipped either."

"Didn't we save a dresser mirror from one of the upstairs bedrooms?" Hattie asked. "Seems like that would be about the right size."

"But it's mahogany. Don't you think it's too fancy with this primitive pine piece? What if we wrapped the frame with rope?"

"I like it. No, I love it," Hattie said.

"What'll Trae say about us taking over his design decisions?" Cass asked, raising one eyebrow.

"Who cares? Get 'er done. That's my new mantra."

The two women spent the rest of the day measuring, cutting, and gluing nautical charts to the walls, and even the ceiling of the bathroom. They were almost finished when Leetha arrived to check on their progress.

"Ooh, I like it," the showrunner said. "Thinking outside the box. I just came from the kitchen. Saw Ashtray down on his hands and knees taping those floors." She held up her cell phone. "Had to take a photo to commemorate the occasion."

"Did Trae say when he thought he'd be done?" Hattie asked.

"He swears it'll be done by morning," Leetha said, looking dubious. "Said he's going to paint it himself, because he doesn't trust y'all's painters not to muck it up."

"Good," Cass said. "Our guys already have enough to do fixing his screwups. Let him spend the whole night crawling around on the floor."

62

Quel Scandal

Mo was sitting at the bar at The Whitaker, nursing a bourbon and water, going over his notes. He'd ordered dinner and was savoring the opportunity to relax and clear his mind after another chaotic day of homewrecking.

Two more days. His stomach growled. He'd had a stale bagel from craft services for breakfast and couldn't remember having lunch. The Chatham Avenue set was chaos, as Hattie and Cass and even Trae raced the clock to finish work on the house.

He'd been back to this hotel several times since the night he'd dropped off Trae's iPad. The place had grown on him. He liked the clubby ambience, and the food and excellent selection of bourbons. But mostly he liked that he wasn't eating his own fairly dismal cooking.

To Mo's surprise, Savannah had started to grow on him too, despite his best efforts to resist its charms. He didn't care for the heat or humidity, or the damned no-see-ums, but the city itself, with its wide streets lined with moss-draped oaks, the quiet green squares surrounded by elegant nineteenth-century town houses, the languid pace, and the quirky friendliness of most of the natives? He'd succumbed to all, dammit.

And what about Hattie Kavanaugh? He'd grown more attached to her than he wanted to admit. He found himself watching her before and after the shoot. She was dogged, determined, funny, smart, and yes, sexy. In the evenings, he found himself watching the day's footage, but mostly watching Hattie. The way she unconsciously twisted her ponytail when she was anxious, how she bit her lower lip when she was concentrating on something. He found everything about her slightly intoxicating. But the show would wrap in just a few days. What then? It could be months before the network decided if it wanted to order another season of *Homewreckers,* and in the meantime, he needed to begin thinking about another concept for another show.

Mo was torn. He was sick of *Homewreckers,* the drama and the overwhelming amount of work. But if the network liked what they were seeing? And ordered another season? Maybe he would stay in Savannah and see if something developed with Hattie.

Mo jiggled the ice cubes in his glass and glanced up at the television mounted over the mirrored back bar. It had been turned to the local news when he'd sat down, but now he recognized the opening montage for *Headline Hollywood.*

The volume was on mute, but the male half of the anchor pair, Antonio Sorrels, a former quarterback for the Oakland Raiders, seemed to be talking about the breakup of an entertainment industry power couple, because the cameras flashed on photos of the couple, with a jagged rip through the photo. Then came a police blotter photo of a former '90s child star, who'd been arrested for assaulting a bouncer at a trendy Manhattan nightclub.

And then Jada Watkins was on-screen, seated on one of the *Hollywood Headline* director's chairs, followed by the grainy photo of Trae Bartholomew and Hattie, caught kissing at dinner only a couple weeks earlier. And another photo, which Mo recognized as one of the publicity stills the network had shot.

HOMEWRECKERS STAR HAS REAL-LIFE DRAMA, read the chyron streaming across the bottom of the screen.

Next came a film clip, footage of the Chatham Avenue house, either taken from a very long lens, or more likely, a drone camera, showing the Chatham County coroner's van parked beside the gaping septic tank pit, with another streaming chyron line—MURDER MYSTERY DEEPENS AT HPTV SET.

"Hey, miss!" Mo called to the bartender. "Could you turn up the television volume, please?"

The bartender pointed the remote control at the television, clicked it, and moved on down the bar to wait on another customer.

Mo leaned forward to listen.

"The long-unsolved missing person case involving a popular Savannah, Georgia, private school teacher was cracked wide open last week, when the woman's skeletal remains were discovered at a home undergoing renovation for the upcoming HPTV show *The Homewreckers,*" Jada Watkins said, in a hushed, serious tone. "The show pairs heartthrob L.A. designer Trae Bartholomew, best known for his hit show *Design Minds,* with television newcomer Hattie Kavanaugh, a Savannah contractor whose company specializes in historic restorations."

Jada crossed her long, slender legs. "The schoolteacher, Lanier Ragan, vanished on a stormy night seventeen years ago, leaving behind a grieving husband and three-year-old daughter. But last week her tomb was discovered—in the cavity of a long-disused septic tank pit at the *Homewreckers* house, and the mystery deepened."

She turned to Sorrels, seated on the director's chair next

to hers. "Antonio, the making of this new HPTV show has more twists and turns than one of those winding staircases in one of Savannah's famed historic mansions."

"So it seems," Sorrels replied.

"What a stiff," Mo mumbled to himself. "And whoever scripts this clichéd pile of crap should be fired."

"The murder has rocked the *Homewreckers* shoot, where insiders say that Trae and Hattie, who've become romantically involved during the shooting of the show, have recently quarreled over the design direction on the home renovations," Jada said.

"Insiders tell me that the discovery of the body is only the latest in a series of incidents that have caused turmoil on the Tybee Island set. Local authorities have cited Hattie Kavanaugh's company for numerous building code and noise ordinance violations, and a fire of suspicious origin did extensive damage to the hundred-year-old historic beach house. Law enforcement authorities are calling the fire arson."

"Wow, a fire, a dead body, what next?" Sorrels said, trying to look concerned but only managing to look slightly constipated.

"Well . . . our sources tell me that there is significant friction between Trae Bartholomew and the show's creator slash producer, Mauricio Lopez, whose most recent HPTV series, *Killer Garages,* was canceled after one disastrous season."

"Disastrous?" Mo yelped. "Who's feeding this bullshit to these two?"

A petite brunette, who was sitting two barstools down, looked at him and just as quickly looked away. "Sorry," Mo muttered. Although he wasn't.

"In the meantime, network execs are reportedly alarmed by recent revelations concerning Hattie Kavanaugh's family. *Headline Hollywood* has learned, exclusively, that her father, Woodrow Bowers, once a prominent Savannah banker, was convicted in 2002 of embezzling millions from a local nonprofit which he chaired at the time."

"Oh wow," Sorrels said.

Jada crossed and recrossed her legs again. "At trial, Bowers admitted that he stole from the charity, money designated for sick children and homeless families, to fund expensive vacations and buy a condo for his mistress, who worked at the same bank."

"Jesus Christ," Mo exclaimed. Out of the corner of his eye he saw the brunette take her umbrella drink and move to a table near the window.

"Hmm," Antonio Sorrels said. "What's the network have to say about this news?"

"I called the VP of HPTV programming, Rebecca Sanzone, earlier today, and she declined to comment specifically on the revelations about Hattie Kavanaugh, but we do know that cast members on shows like *The Homewreckers* are routinely asked to sign what's called a morals clause, which would allow the network to cancel their contract for cause if the personality was accused of behavior that would cause shame or embarrassment to the network," Jada said.

"Rebecca Sanzone said she was unaware of Hattie Kavanaugh's family history," Jada went on. "Antonio, we'll be following this story as it develops."

"There is no story," Mo growled. He looked down to see that his dinner, a rare cheeseburger and garlic-sprinkled pommes frites, had materialized while he was engrossed in watching *Headline Hollywood*. He pushed the plate away and summoned for his check.

63

Kiss and Tell

Hattie was dozing when Ribsy began barking. She'd arrived home shortly after nine, sweaty and exhausted, and after showering and dining on a bag of microwaved popcorn, she'd stretched out on the sofa, intending to continue reading *Void Moon*.

But now Ribsy was barking, so she staggered to the door and snapped on the front porch light. She saw Mo Lopez bounding up the front steps.

She unlocked and opened the door, poking her head out. "Mo? Is something wrong? Did something else happen at the house?"

"Not at the house," he said. "Can I come in for a minute?"

Hattie glanced down at herself. She was dressed in a tank top and a loose-fitting pair of shorty pajama bottoms, and her hair was knotted on top of her head.

"Uh, yeah. Let me just grab a bathrobe."

Ribsy followed Mo to the armchair opposite the sofa, and when Mo sat down, he thrust his snout into Mo's crotch.

"Ribsy, no!" Hattie said, tying the belt of her robe as she emerged from the bedroom.

Mo gently pushed the dog's nose away, distracting him with an ear scratch.

Hattie sank down onto the sofa, her legs curled beneath her. "What's up? It's kind of late for a social call, isn't it?"

"Sorry," Mo said. "It's, uh, kind of important. Did you watch television tonight?"

"God, no. I only got home about an hour ago. Why? What was on?"

Mo cleared his throat. "I don't know how to tell you this, so I'm just going to say it. Remember that reporter from *Headline Hollywood*?"

"Jada whatever? What about her? Did she run another story about us?"

"Yeah, but Hattie, it was a hit piece. She talked about how there are all kinds of problems on *Homewreckers,* about the murder, of course, and the code violations and the fire—all of that—plus what she called tension between you and Trae, and me and Trae. I can't believe you didn't see it—or that nobody called to tell you about it. Not even Cass?"

"My phone," Hattie said, feeling around on the sofa cushions. "I don't know where it is." She got up and lifted the cushion she'd been sitting on. "It's not here."

"I'll call you," Mo said, pulling his own cell from his pocket. He tapped her name on his contact list and they heard a faint buzzing coming from the direction of the bedroom.

Hattie followed the buzzing and emerged from the bedroom holding the phone. "I left it in the pocket of my jeans, on the bathroom floor." She studied the call log.

"Uh-oh. Four calls from Cass, one from Zenobia." She looked up at Mo. "And one from my father, who never, ever calls me. What the hell?"

"Someone told Jada about your father. About the embezzlement thing, and how he went to prison."

Hattie's face crumpled. "She brought up my dad? On television? What's that got to do with anything? And how did she find out about it?"

He got up and sat beside her on the sofa. "I'm sorry. If I'd known she was going to do a piece like that, I never would have allowed her on the set. Honest to God, I thought she was working on a puff piece, about you and Trae. . . ."

"What else? What else did she say about me?"

She looked back down at her phone. "Wait. Cass sent me the link to the show."

"You don't want to watch it," Mo said quickly. "I'll give you the nitty-gritty. Jada Watkins apparently called Rebecca and asked for her reaction to the thing about your dad. Because of the morals clause you signed in your contract."

"*My* morals are just fine," Hattie said. "I was fifteen when he stole that money. I had nothing to do with any of that. Why, Mo? Why would someone deliberately trash me like this?"

"I honestly don't know."

"Have you talked to Rebecca?"

"I called her on my way over here and left a message."

"Is it true? Can the network fire me? Can they enforce that morals thing?"

"No," Mo said quickly. "I'm the only one who can fire you, and that's not happening."

"Can they cancel the show?"

"They won't. They've given us a primetime slot and invested a lot of their own money in *Homewreckers*. They've already begun promoting it on the network."

"I just don't get it," Hattie said. "It's horrible. Who would do this to me?"

Ribsy whimpered, jumped up on the sofa, and started licking his mistress's arm in consolation.

Mo patted her back awkwardly. "I know this sounds sick, but even bad publicity is good publicity as far as the network is concerned."

"It is sick," Hattie said. "I'm going to quit the show. None of this is worth it. Let Trae finish the house. Maybe then we can sell it, and I can give you and the network what you've invested in it."

"Don't do that," Mo said sharply. "I know you're upset, but listen to me. If you quit *Homewreckers,* people will believe you have something to be ashamed of. I don't give a flying fuck about the show or the network. But I do care about you."

"You do?" She searched his face for confirmation. "Really?"

"Yeah," he said softly, his lips grazing hers. "I really do."

"You've got a funny way of showing it," Hattie said.

"I was trying to avoid that whole casting couch thing. Falling for your leading lady? It's such a showbiz cliché. And it seldom works out in the long run."

"I don't know," Hattie mused. "What about Tracy and Hepburn?"

"There's that," Mo said, kissing her deeply this time. "And also Bogie and Bacall."

"Mmmm, my fave," Hattie said, kissing him back.

She pulled away for a moment. "You know, the other night when you brought me home? Just before you left, I could swear you kissed me. . . ."

"Because you told me to," Mo said.

"Me?" She looked perplexed. "I was so out of it, I wasn't sure I didn't just dream it."

"I distinctly heard you tell me to kiss you, so I did."

He kissed her again. "Did you want it to be a dream?"

"No," she admitted, tracing the stubble on his jaw. "I wanted it to be real. And I wanted there to be more."

She placed her hands on either side of Mo's face. "You're a really good guy, aren't you?"

"I try."

She kissed him deeply, then stood, holding out her hand to him. "Come on, then. If we're going to do this, I want to do it in my nice, cushy bed instead of this lumpy old sofa."

Mo's face lit up. "*Are* we going to do it? In your bedroom?"

Hattie smiled and tugged him to his feet. "Much better than a casting couch, don't you think?"

Ribsy scrambled off the sofa and followed them to the bedroom door. Hattie bent down and scratched the dog's neck. "Sorry, kid. It's grown-up time." She gently closed the door.

"Hattie?"

Mo placed his lips near her ear. After they'd made love, she'd promptly fallen asleep, snuggled in his arms. She smelled like that pink baby lotion his little nieces liked to slather on themselves after a bath, but on Hattie, it was sexy as hell.

"Hmm?" She stirred slightly.

"Your phone. I can hear it buzzing in the other room."

Her head was on his chest, and he stroked her bare shoulder. This was nice. He'd forgotten what it was like to be with a woman who cuddled after lovemaking.

"What time is it? Morning?"

He reached for his own phone, on the nightstand, and chuckled. "It's not even eleven."

She yawned and stretched. "Is that all?"

"I think I tired you out."

She raised her head and grinned at him. "We tired each other out. But in a good way. Right?"

He kissed her. "Very good. Do you need to answer your phone?"

"I guess." She sighed and sat up, clutching the sheet to her chest. She rubbed her eyes and looked around the room. "Clothes. I know I was wearing clothes when we came in here."

Mo felt around on the floor beside the bed and came up

with his own polo shirt, which he handed to Hattie. "Be my guest."

She pulled the shirt over her head and padded over to the door. Ribsy came bounding into the room and leaped onto the bed. He planted his head on Mo's chest in the exact spot Hattie had just vacated.

"I think he's jealous," Hattie said.

When she came back a moment later, her face had a sour expression. She held up the phone. "It was my dad again. He texted and called. He's super pissed about the *Headline Hollywood* story."

Mo sat up in bed and reached for her. Ribsy growled and moved exactly eight inches, toward the foot of the bed. "Are you going to call him back?"

Hattie shook her head. "What's there to say? Get this. He never watches television. He only found out about the story because his ex-girlfriend Amber called him up and read him the riot act because Jada referred to her as his quote 'mistress.'"

She curled up beside Mo. "I texted Cass to tell her I know about the hit piece, and she texted back that she thinks Trae leaked the story to Jada Watkins."

Mo hesitated. "I wasn't going to tell you this, but I think he and Jada had a fling while she was in town filming."

"You think?"

"Okay, I'm pretty sure of it. Trae left his iPad in the craft services tent that day, so I took it to his hotel to drop it off at the front desk. While I was there I decided to stay and have dinner in the lobby lounge and I spotted Trae and Jada strolling in, arm in arm. Very, um, friendly. Last thing I saw was them kissing, after they got in the elevator."

"Oh."

"He's a piece of shit, that guy," Mo said angrily.

"You don't know the half of it." Hattie told him how she'd overheard Trae bragging about bribing the city inspector.

"He was proud of himself," she said. "But why would he leak a story like this to Jada Watkins? How did he even know about my father?"

Mo groaned and slapped his forehead. "Oh shit. Shit. Shit. Shit. I think maybe he figured it out from something I said."

Hattie went very still. She felt the burn of bile in her gut. "You told Trae about my father?"

"Not all of it." He gave Hattie a pleading look. "It was after we first started shooting at the house, and he was raging about you—like, 'Why does she always have such a stick up her ass about following the rules?'"

Hattie jumped up and began pacing the floor. "And so, what? You just blurted out what I told you—in confidence, about my father?"

"No! I . . . mentioned that it might have something to do with your dad. Because he'd gotten into some kind of trouble with the law when you were a kid. That's all I said. I swear."

"You told him enough, though. And now everyone in the goddamn country knows my father is a jailbird who stole money from widows and sick kids and homeless people."

She grabbed the hem of the polo shirt and ripped it off over her head, throwing it at him with shocking fury and accuracy.

Hattie stood in the middle of the room, her arms folded across her bare breasts. "This was a mistake. Tug always tells me, 'Hattie, don't get your honey where you get your money,' or 'Don't ever dip your pen in the company ink.' And you know what? He was right."

"Hattie," Mo said, his voice pleading. "I'm sorry. I never meant to hurt you. It was a stupid mistake. Please believe me." He reached for her hand, but she brushed it away.

"You should go," Hattie said, pointing to the door.

64

The Succession Plan

Tug called Hattie first thing the next morning, as she was getting in the truck.

"How are you, sweetheart?" he asked.

"I'm . . . hollowed out. I take it you saw *Headline Hollywood* last night?"

"I don't watch that trash, but other people did. Where are you now?"

"I'm just getting ready to leave for work."

"Stay right there. Start the coffee. Nancy made sausage and biscuits."

"Dad, no. I need to get to the house. We're so far behind as it is. . . ."

"Cass can handle it. You stay where you are and have my coffee ready."

Twenty minutes later her father-in-law walked in the front door with a foil-wrapped package that smelled of hot biscuits and sage-spiked sausage.

"Come here," he said, opening his stubby arms and enveloping her in a hug. She was half a head taller than the old man, but somehow his bearlike strength made her feel safe and childlike again.

He released her without a word, and she poured him a

mug of coffee with two teaspoons of sugar and a huge dollop of cream, and they sat down at the kitchen table.

Hattie opened the packet and bit into one of Nancy's biscuits, dabbing at the honey that dripped from the corner of her lips.

"Have you heard from your old man?"

His question startled her.

"He called. Twice. Mainly he's mad that the story referred to Amber as his mistress."

Tug chuckled and sipped his coffee. "Did you call him back?"

"No. I think he just wanted to vent. He doesn't exactly have a lot of friends."

"What a terrible thing that woman did, dredging up something from your past that you had no control over."

"Yeah, well, it's out in the world now. Again."

"That's what I wanted to talk to you about this morning. I don't want this crap to derail you or make you ashamed. You've done nothing wrong. In fact, you've done everything right."

"No," Hattie said, shaking her head vehemently. "The house, the stupid show, Trae Bartholomew? It was all a mistake. You tried to warn me, but I wouldn't listen."

"You were right not to listen to me. I've been too hard on you. Listen, the Chatham Avenue house, what you and Cass and our subs have accomplished over there, it's nothing short of a miracle. I was dead set against taking it on, but I was wrong. You don't grow and learn by doing what you've always done in the past. Sometimes, you've gotta take a leap of faith, like you did signing on to this *Homewreckers* outfit."

Hattie nibbled at the edge of her biscuit. "That's sweet, Tug."

"Dammit, don't you call me sweet," he insisted. "The only shame in making mistakes is if you don't acknowledge them and learn from 'em. You taught me that, Hattie. I'm proud of you."

"Me?"

He reached for a biscuit and took a bite, chewing slowly while crumbs cascaded down the front of his worn bib overalls. "I'm just a hardheaded old man, and I know that. Maybe it's time for me to retire and hand the business over to you and Cass."

"You can't retire, Dad. I won't let you. You are Kavanaugh and Son. You've forgotten more about building and restoring old houses than I'll ever know. All our subs, our clients? You're the one they trust. The one they respect."

"Nah. You've earned their respect, Hattie. Besides, I can't keep up working like this forever. Nancy says she wants us to travel, before she has to push me around in a wheelchair. She says I need to fix all the things that are wrong with our house, instead of somebody else's."

He dunked the edge of his biscuit in the coffee and looked up. "Maybe we need to work out some kind of a timetable, what's that called?"

"You mean a succession plan?"

"That's it. You know, I'm eligible for social security now, but I thought I'd wait 'til I'm sixty-five. In the meantime, there's no reason you can't take over bidding out the jobs. Cass can keep up with the scheduling. And of course, Zenobia runs the office. She's really the brains of the operation, but don't you dare tell her I said that."

"Dad, I'm not sure I'll have the resources, even three years from now, to buy you out. The trucks, the equipment, the office? Property in Midtown, on Bull Street, is hot right now. I can't even imagine what it would sell for today."

He allowed himself a smug smile. "I'll tell you a little secret. It's not just our office. I own the whole strip of storefronts, bought it for peanuts back in the seventies. Anyway, the price is immaterial because I'm not selling it."

"You shouldn't. That's your retirement fund right there."

"I'm giving it to you," Tug said.

Her coffee mug made a loud clatter as it hit the tabletop. "Me?"

"Who else am I going to give it to? Nancy's good-for-nothing nephews? My niece? Who never even bothered to send a mass card when Hank was killed?"

"I don't know what to say," Hattie started.

Tug finished his biscuit and lumbered to his feet. "You don't have to say anything. You're our family. Have been since the day Hank laid his eyes on you. Family takes care of family."

"Thank you," Hattie said, blinking back tears. "I'll never forget the way you and Nancy have taken care of me all these years."

"Go on then," Tug said, pointing toward the door. "Get yourself out to Tybee. Finish the job the way I know you can. Hold your head high, and don't take no shit off of nobody. Especially that fancy-ass designer."

"Especially him," Hattie agreed.

65

The Coldest Shoulder

- - - - - - -

Trae Bartholomew pounced the minute she parked her truck in the driveway at the Creedmore house.

He opened the driver's side door and reached his hand in to help her out.

Hattie recoiled. "Don't touch me. I have to work with you until we're finished with this house, but unless the cameras are rolling, I don't want you to speak, or even look at me. You're dead to me. Understand?"

"I had nothing to do with that *Headline Hollywood* piece," Trae protested. "I had no idea Jada knew anything about your family history. Hell, I hardly knew anything myself."

"Right," Hattie said, slamming the truck door. "Are you telling me you didn't sleep with Jada Watkins when she was in town, filming that piece? Was that your idea of pillow talk?"

Trae's handsome face flushed beneath the tan. "How did you . . . ?"

"Doesn't matter," she said. "Nothing you say matters to me. 'Cause now I know that if your lips are moving, you're telling a lie."

"Whoa!" he said, running to keep up with Hattie as she strode up to the house. "Aside from the fact that I did not, repeat, did not, tell Jada anything about your father, please explain why you think I would do anything that would negatively impact this show? We need this show to succeed, Hattie. We both need it."

Hattie stopped and took a deep breath. "Actually, Trae? This morning I realized I don't need this show to succeed. I want to finish this house and make it the best thing I've ever done, so that I can sell it and move on with my life. But even if the network hates it, I'll be okay."

"Keep telling yourself that," he said under his breath. Then he hurried away.

Cass was waiting for her on the front porch. "What'd you say to Trae just now? I saw the look on his face. He took off away from you like a scalded dog."

"Let's just say we have a new understanding," Hattie said.

"Something tells me this was about that *Headline Hollywood* story. Did you get my messages last night?"

"Yeah," Hattie said, sheepish. "Sorry I didn't call you back. I fell asleep on the sofa almost as soon as I got home, and by the time I dragged my butt to bed and saw you'd called, I figured you'd be asleep."

Her account of the previous evening wasn't a lie, Hattie rationalized. She was just choosing to omit the part where Mo had joined her in the bed, before she accused him of betraying her and kicked him to the curb.

"It's okay," Cass said. "Sucks, though. You should have heard what Mom had to say about that Jada Watkins bitch. Child, please!"

"Nobody messes with Zenobia's girls, right? So, what's going on inside?"

"Trae must have stayed late finishing the kitchen floor, and if he wasn't such a man skank, I'd tell him how great it looks. Hate to say it, but everything in that kitchen is perfection now. The island, those brass ship's lanterns, all of it. The glue's dried on our nautical charts, so I hung the mirror when I got here this morning, and the electrician is in there hanging the sconces as we speak, so we can check that off the list. The backyard has been sodded. No more septic tank of doom. We have landscaping! And the carpenters have started tearing apart the old dock house. They're moving right along."

"That's awesome, Cass," Hattie said, walking into the living room.

"Mo got here even before I did," Cass said. "He was asking if I knew where you were. He wants to shoot you and Trae talking about the kitchen this morning. Lisa's waiting to do your hair and makeup."

Hattie frowned. "There's nothing on the call sheet. I was supposed to do a walk-through with the Realtor, Carolyn Meyers, to talk about what price we want to list the house for."

"Did you check your email this morning? Mo sent a revised call sheet at one thirty-two A.M. Guess he had a sleepless night."

Hattie bit her tongue.

Lisa had Hattie's hair up in hot rollers while she applied Trae's eyeliner and mascara. The silence in the room was deafening.

"Not much longer now, huh?" Lisa said, glancing between the two stars. "Two more days?"

"That's what I hear," Hattie said.

"I'm really gonna miss this gig," Lisa said. "And Savannah."

"Where are you from, Lisa?" Hattie asked, mostly to fill the silence in the chilly space.

"Originally? L.A. But there's so much film work in Georgia now, my boyfriend and I moved to Atlanta a couple years ago. He's a sound engineer. I wouldn't mind staying right here on Tybee. That's the one thing I miss about California. The beach. Do you guys think the network will order a second season of this show?"

"I don't know," Hattie said.

Lisa looked at Trae, who merely shrugged.

The RV door was flung open and Leetha poked her head inside. "Ten minutes, y'all."

"I'm ready," Trae said. Then, he bolted.

"Seems like things have kind of cooled down between you and Trae, huh?" Lisa asked.

"Yes."

"Hey, uh, I saw that nasty *Headline Hollywood* piece last night," Lisa said, removing the rollers from Hattie's hair. "I can't stand that Jada Watkins. And I really hate those garbage extensions she wears. They need to fire whoever's doing her hair."

She patted Hattie's shoulder. "Don't worry about any of that stuff she said about your father. Nobody cares about shit that happened twenty years ago. Hell, my father did way worse stuff than that. One time he set fire to my stepmother's mobile home. While she was inside!"

Hattie gave a half-hearted laugh. "Thanks for the pep talk, Lisa." She peered in the mirror. "Am I all set? I gather Mo's in a mood, and I don't want to be late for my call."

Lisa picked up a tube of lipstick. "Let me give you some color on your lips."

They were on the third run-through of the kitchen scene, and tempers were on edge.

"Come on, guys, this is flatter than day-old seltzer," Mo

snapped. "You've gotta pretend to like each other—at least while the camera is rolling. Give me some energy here."

"It's a kitchen floor," Hattie said. "Not *The Last Supper.*"

"Yeah, it's only a fabulous one-of-a-kind hand-stenciled, hand-painted floor that took me eighteen hours of backbreaking work," Trae countered. "And don't forget what this room looked like before I waved my magic wand. It was dirty, dark, cramped. . . ."

"Let's not forget that the island made out of the antique store counter was mine, as were those antique ship's lanterns," Hattie said. "All the things that give this kitchen character were my ideas."

"Say that," Mo said. "But make it funny. Hattie, you sort of disparage all his hard work, but in a jokey way, and Trae, you come back with what you just said. It's called banter. Now let's go. We don't have all day for this scene."

Cass caught up with Hattie at lunch. "What's going on with you two?"

Hattie had piled a bowl with salad and was eating in the shade of the front porch, away from the rest of the crew. "I don't know what you're talking about."

"You and Mo. Last I heard, he was playing Prince Charming to your Sleeping Beauty. Today, you're at each other's throats. I know sexual tension when I see it, Hattie Kavanaugh, so don't even bother trying to lie your way out of this."

Hattie glanced around to be sure they couldn't be overheard. A huge moving van was cruising slowly down the driveway toward the house. "Thank God. That better be Trae's furniture."

"Talk," Cass repeated.

"Mo came over last night, after he saw the *Headline Hollywood* thing. He said he knew how upset I'd be."

"And?"

"And he told me the only thing he cared about was me. And like the idiot I am, I fell for it, hook, line, and sinker."

"And?"

"Use your imagination," Hattie said. "I was upset, vulnerable. . . ."

"Horny."

Hattie didn't deny it. "Afterward, he told me that he'd seen Trae with Jada Watkins, making out in Trae's hotel lobby, and headed upstairs in the elevator. Of course, I assumed Trae told Jada the stuff about my dad, but I couldn't figure out how Trae knew about it, because I sure as hell don't go around talking about it."

"Almost never," Cass agreed.

"And then, Mo admitted he 'might' have mentioned something about it to Trae, back when we first started working on the show."

"Nooooo. Why would he do that?"

"He claims it was just an offhand remark, and that he never told Trae any of the real details. But how else would Trae know?"

"Did you confront Trae about it?"

"As soon as I got here. He denies everything, but we both know what a liar he is. I mean, who else knows that much about the big, ugly skeleton in my family closet?"

Cass tapped her forehead with her forefinger. "Oh, I don't know. Maybe someone who's lived in Savannah their whole life? Someone with a festering grudge against you? Who probably even called the code enforcement cops on us, and then threw the whole sins-of-the-father thing right in your face—to your face? Who'd love to slime you, just for the sport of it?"

"Oh. Oh my God," Hattie said. "I bet you're right. I bet

it was Mavis Creedmore. Oh damn, damn, damn. This one time, Trae was actually telling the truth."

"Which means that probably none of this was Mo's fault," Cass concluded.

"I'm an idiot," Hattie said.

"Took the words right out of my mouth. Now what are you going to do about it?"

"I can't do anything about it right now," Hattie said. She pointed at the gleaming white Mercedes SL convertible that had followed in the wake of the moving van. The driver parked near the porch. "There's Carolyn Meyers now," Hattie said. "Show time."

66

The Price Is Right

- - - - - - -

Carolyn Meyers removed her sling-back pumps and left them at the front door. She was wearing white silk pants and a black halter top that showed her sinewy tanned arms, with Gucci sunglasses tucked into her pale blond hair. "Wait," she said, stepping back to shoot a photo of the door itself. "I want to have it photographed professionally by our in-house guy, but I can use these to give him a shot list. Hattie, I can't believe it's the same house."

"Me neither," Hattie said, opening the door to allow the real estate agent to step inside.

"We put the paper down so the movers don't mess up the floors we just refinished."

"Good," Carolyn said. "All original hardwoods, up and down?"

"Yes," Hattie said.

"Was that the furniture in the moving van that just pulled up?"

"I certainly hope so. Trae, our designer, has been having a fit because the network moved up our deadline by a week. He's not sure all the furniture he ordered will be in on time."

The agent frowned. "It's going to show much better with furniture, so maybe we wait to have the house shot until you've got it styled and staged."

"Well, it's just stunning," Carolyn said, when the tour was over. They were standing in the kitchen, which, Hattie would never admit out loud, had undergone the biggest transformation. "You've done a magnificent job here. It's crisp, it's classic, it's the house equivalent of a good white dress shirt that will never go out of style. This kitchen is the chef's kiss. I mean, that floor is to die for."

"Trae's idea and Trae's handiwork," Hattie said. "So, bottom line, what do you think we can list it for?"

Carolyn pulled a large folder from her handbag, and withdrew a computer printout. "Here are the comps I pulled. Lucky for you, there's not that much competition for a waterfront house on the island right now. Liz Demos's house is a couple months away from completion still, but it got listed for $1.2 million, and she's already accepted an offer."

Hattie's eyes widened. "And that house doesn't even have a dock like ours. The dock house will be done today, and then it's really going to be spectacular."

Carolyn sighed and pointed out the window. "Liz's house also doesn't have a body that was buried in the backyard. I'm not going to soft-soap it, Hattie. This thing with Lanier Ragan has gotten a ton of publicity, and I'm afraid it's going to scare off a lot of potential buyers. People don't like the idea of having a crypt on their property."

"I get it," Hattie said. She'd been anticipating something like this, but hearing her real estate agent say it, out loud, was a gut punch. "But this is a much bigger lot. And the house . . ."

"Is one of a kind. You've done an amazing job with it, as always. I just want you to be prepared for buyer reluctance. Under other circumstances, I'm confident that the house would easily appraise at $1.4 million."

"But at this time?"

Carolyn fiddled with the thin gold necklace dangling in her cleavage. "I think we get aggressive and list it at $890,000, but be prepared to negotiate down."

"Okay," Hattie said, her shoulders sagging.

"Didn't someone tell me you got it for a steal after the city condemned it? Even at that price, you're going to make a nice profit."

"We did get it for a great price, but we've poured so much time and money and effort into it. I've got loans to pay back, and the bills are piling up. . . ."

"But you won't be losing money, right? Who knows, maybe my instincts are all wrong. With all the attention your show is getting, people are definitely fascinated by this place and the story behind it. Maybe after we get it styled and the listing photos go live online, we'll get in a bidding war. I've seen it happen before."

"Right." Hattie swallowed hard. "Let's price it at eight-ninety, then."

Carolyn beamed. "I've got all the listing documents in my car. I know you're on a tight deadline. Why don't you fill them out and then drop them by my office? And let me know as soon as we can get the photographer in here."

The kitchen door was flung open and Trae stepped inside, followed by two men, each carrying plastic-wrapped bundles. "Coming through," he called. He stopped for a moment and shot the blond Realtor his most beguiling smile. "Hi, there."

Trae's smile was really his most potent weapon. His teeth

were so straight and dazzlingly white. Hattie was still self-conscious about her own slightly crooked teeth. She'd been scheduled to get braces as a teenager, but then her father went to prison. . . .

"Trae, this is Carolyn Meyers, my real estate agent. Carolyn, this is Trae Bartholomew, the designer. . . ."

"Oh, I know who you are," Carolyn said, extending her hand to his. "Loved you on *Design Minds*. I understand this kitchen is your handiwork. It's spectacular."

"Thanks, Carolyn," Trae said, brushing a stray bit of hair out of his face. He gestured toward the bundles the movers had just set down and winked. "Wait 'til you see the killer rattan barstools I ordered to go around the island."

"Carolyn was just leaving," Hattie said abruptly.

"Can't wait to see the place when you're done," Carolyn said, recognizing her cue.

"That was pretty rude," Trae commented. "Even for you." He turned to the movers, who were waiting for directions. "You can set those down right here, but then start bringing in the rest of the stuff through the front door, okay?"

When they were gone, Trae began ripping the paper from the barstools.

"It's just a reflex with you, isn't it?" she asked.

"What?" He balled up the paper and started on the next chair.

"Hitting on pretty women. I bet you don't even realize you're doing it."

"Oh, I realize it. You know the old saying, right? You don't shoot, you don't score." He looked up and flashed her the same grin. Briefly.

"Don't waste the wattage on me," Hattie said. "That ship

has sailed. Tell me about the furniture. Did everything you ordered arrive?"

The grin faded. "No. I haven't done a real inventory, but a lot of the stuff is still backordered. I mean, the case goods and upholstery are here. The living and dining room furniture, most of the bedroom stuff, and soft goods. But I don't have lamps or art, or rugs, or any accessories. And since all of this stuff is on loan from vendors who're doing this as a favor to me, I can't really call 'em up and bitch about what wasn't on the truck. So I'm kind of screwed."

A part of Hattie wanted to gloat about his predicament. But there was no time. They had just one more day before Mo's crew would shoot the big reveal, and the only way the house would be ready was if they worked together.

"Okay, let's put what you do have in place in each room. Do you have a list of what you still need? And rug sizes?"

"I can make one," Trae said. "But what good will that do?"

"There are two kick-ass consignment shops in Savannah, and I'm friends with the owners of both. I'll call and see if they'd be willing to loan us stuff for the shoot."

He looked at her with obvious suspicion. "Didn't you just tell me this morning, in no uncertain terms, that I was never to speak or look at you again? Why would you want to help me out like that?"

Hattie took a deep breath. "As Carolyn just pointed out, the faster we get this house styled and photographed and listed, the faster I can get my money out of it. So give me your list, okay? And leave Carolyn alone. She's married. Also, I think I owe you an apology. For the Jada Watkins thing. It looks like I jumped to the wrong conclusion."

"Wait!" Trae cupped a hand to his ear. "Could you repeat that last part? A little louder? I want to make sure I heard it correctly, because it sounded like you, eating crow."

Hattie leaned in. "I said, 'Fuck you, Trae. Fuck you very much.'"

Five minutes later, she tracked Trae down as he was hauling a mattress and box spring up the stairs. "Okay, so I think we can get everything we need at Clutter. And Leetha wants to send the camera crew along to shoot some B-roll. How soon can you leave?"

"Leave? Are you nuts? We've barely started unloading the moving van. I'll be at least another two hours."

"No good," Hattie said. "They usually close at five on Fridays, but Lynn agreed to stay open longer, in return for on-screen credit. It's now or never. If you want, I can go without you."

"You?" His expression was incredulous.

"Yes, me. I've been staging and styling houses for years, Trae. But if you're not willing to rely on my taste, that's okay." She started back down the staircase.

"Wait!" He set the edge of the box spring down on the top stair tread. "Okay, I'm out of options. The list is on the island in the kitchen. Text me pictures of what you're getting, okay?"

"Beggars can't be choosers, Trae. You're just gonna have to trust me this time."

67

The Disappearing Act

Detective Makarowicz pulled into the driveway at the Chatham Avenue house as Hattie was about to turn onto the street. He backed up until his driver's side window was parallel to hers.

"What happened to our off-duty cop?" Hattie asked, gesturing toward the shoulder of the road where the patrol car had been parked on previous days.

Ribsy, who was riding shotgun, clambered onto her lap and stuck his head out the window to greet the cop.

"Good boy," Makarowicz said.

"This is Ribsy," Hattie said. "Now, what about our cop?"

"It's summer, you know. Tourist season. Chief wants every man on duty, which means we can't spare anyone for this. Anyway, looks like the sightseers have all lost interest in you."

"Was that what you were coming to see me about?"

"No," Mak said, his expression troubled. "Your friend is in the wind."

"Which friend?"

"Davis Hoffman. I've been trying to track him down for questioning, but he's gone. Not at the jewelry store, not at his house. I'm running out of places to look."

Hattie felt the skin on the back of her neck prickle. "Have you talked to his ex-wife?"

"Elise Hoffman claims she's been looking for him too. He's not answering his phone."

"What about his mom? When I saw him a couple days ago, he said she'd asked him to come out to their house here to cut the grass."

Makarowicz had a pained expression on his face. "Mrs. Hoffman was not what I'd call forthcoming about her son's whereabouts."

"Yeah, that sounds like Sylvia."

"Thought I'd ride over here and see if you have any idea of where he might go," the detective said.

Hattie pointed in the direction of the pale gray house two doors down. "Did you check the Titanic?"

"Mrs. Hoffman refused to give me permission to enter the house, but I walked down the driveway before I came here, just to see if his car was there. I looked around outside. No sign of him."

She felt another ripple of dread. "Up until I went to see him about buying my engagement ring, I'd mostly lost touch with Davis over the past few years. He was more Hank's friend than mine. I don't have a clue where he might be."

Makarowicz nodded. "Any chance he bolted after you talked to him the other day?"

"I don't know," she admitted. "I tried to act nonchalant after I saw those burns on his hand and chest, but maybe he saw how spooked I was. Can you search his house or something?"

"Not without a warrant, which I can't get because I don't have enough probable cause yet. But his ex-wife has a key, and she says there's nothing out of place in the house."

"Davis knows you want to talk to him, right?"

"I left messages for him at the jewelry store and on his cell," Mak said.

"Do you think he's like, dangerous?"

"I've never met the man. You tell me."

Hattie bit her bottom lip. "I'm starting to think I never really knew him either. Davis was always such a nice guy. He was . . . there. Not in the center of things, but maybe on the periphery. Cass says he was always watching, waiting for a chance to pounce, but I never saw that in him."

She heard a horn toot from behind and looked in the rearview mirror. "Oh, Mak, that's my camera crew. We're headed into town."

"Let me know right away if you see or hear from Hoffman," Makarowicz said.

"I will," Hattie promised. She felt that icy ripple start at the back of her neck again, but then Leetha, who was in the truck with the guys, beeped the horn again.

Lynn, the owner of Clutter, roamed through the tightly packed aisles of the consignment store, plucking lamps and paintings from displays, with Leetha and her camera crew squeezed in between a mountain of rolled-up Oriental carpets.

It was too hot to leave Ribsy in the truck, so he crouched near the front door, watching the goings-on with interest, thumping his tail every time Hattie spoke.

"Just don't leave that door open," Hattie warned. "He's a flight risk."

She pointed to an oversized pair of blue-and-white ginger jar lamps. "I want those for the console table in the living room."

Lynn unrolled the corner of a jewel-toned Heriz rug and Hattie gave it a thumbs-up. "That'll work in the dining room. What do you have for the living room? Trae's looking for something big and bold to make a statement." With the toe of her shoe, Lynn pointed to a lumpy bundle of reds, greens, and blues. "This is a palace-sized Kashan. The fringe is worn, but it won't matter under a sofa."

"Let's do it," Hattie said, consulting her list. "We need bedroom rugs, too. Blues and greens, and more earth tones for a larger nine-by-twelve. Do you have any dhurries?"

"Over there," Lynn said, pointing to the front wall of the store. "I'll get Johnny to take them out to the parking lot so you can unroll and choose which ones you want."

"Good. Now. Art. Need a large statement piece to go over the fireplace, and maybe four or five other pieces for the living room."

"Contemporary? Abstract? Traditional?" Lynn gestured toward the paintings and prints hung, gallery style, on every inch of wall space in the consignment shop.

"Knowing Trae, maybe something more oversized and contemporary for the fireplace."

"We just got a huge new Bert John marsh scene," Lynn said, pointing to a canvas leaning against the cash stand. "Really dreamy."

"If this was my house, I'd totally buy that," Hattie said. She turned to Leetha. "Can the guys shoot that? It's my favorite piece I've seen."

"We already did," Leetha said.

"How about a grouping of these Chuck Scarborough collages?" Lynn asked. "He paints on the canvas, then adds bits of ephemera. His new series is beach-themed."

"Definitely," Hattie said, bending down to examine one. "These three will work in the dining room."

"I've got a great Bellamy Murphy of palmetto fronds," Lynn said, pointing to a large-scale canvas hanging on the back wall of the shop. "Just came in."

"Fabulous," Hattie said. "Someday I'll own one of her pieces for my own place."

"What else?" Lynn asked. "Accessories?"

"I need lots of books. Leather-bound if possible, but I'll take whatever you've got. Coffee table books. Hmm. Maybe some giant hunks of coral or big specimen seashells? Candlesticks? Maybe some blue-and-white transferware platters for the walls above the bookshelves?"

Hattie read Trae's list and within an hour they'd assembled a huge stack of goods and checked off almost everything.

"Six thirty," Lynn announced. "Time to lock up and go home."

Hattie gave the shop owner a quick hug. "You're a lifesaver. You know Zenobia, our office manager, right? Will you send her an inventory of all this stuff we've borrowed?"

"Thirty days, correct? I can't afford to have this much inventory out for any longer than that, Hattie."

"Hopefully, the house will be sold much quicker than that, but yeah, it all comes back here by the end of next month."

The drive back to Tybee took nearly an hour. Hattie spent the time thinking about how wrong she'd been to fly off the handle at Mo the previous night. But as wrong as it was to assume he'd leaked the story about her father, she decided she was right to regret sleeping with him.

Whether or not the network picked up *Homewreckers* for a second season was immaterial. She wasn't at all sure she should repeat the experience again. Sleeping with a business associate was always a bad idea. Even if the business associate was kind and funny and loyal and a great kisser. Especially if he was a great kisser, because then, who knew—you might be tempted to keep sleeping with him and making the same mistake over and over again.

Her phone was in the truck console. She considered calling Mo. She could admit that she'd been wrong to accuse him of talking out of turn. Much easier than telling him that to his face. Just as she reached for the phone, it rang.

Jinx. The caller was Mo.

She hesitated, then tapped accept.

"Hey," she said.

"Hey. Where are you?"

"Headed back to the house with the rest of the stuff Trae needs to finish up. Leetha and the crew are right behind me. Why? What's going on?"

"Not much. I, uh, wanted to talk to you. About last night. But every time I looked up today, there were too many people around."

Hattie looked in the rearview mirror and saw the van with Leetha and the crew was two cars back. "I'm alone now."

"First off, I would never purposely do anything to hurt you."

"I believe you."

"You do?"

"Yeah. Mo, I'm sorry I jumped to such a stupid conclusion. I should have known better."

"Well, yeah. Good. Glad we got that straight."

"Anything else you wanted to tell me?" Hattie realized she was holding her breath, waiting for the other shoe to drop.

"It'd be better if I could tell you this face-to-face," Mo said.

"I should be back at the house in fifteen minutes unless traffic gets worse."

"Yeah, but I'm on my way to the airport. Rebecca decided to 'surprise' me by flying in tonight. She wants to be on hand for the reveal tomorrow."

"Oh." The word hung there.

"It's kind of a command performance. Probably won't be

much time to talk privately tomorrow, and, uh, I just wanted to tell you that I don't regret last night. I know you think it was a bad idea, and I'm sorry you think that, because I think it was pretty great. Even if it was just that one time, I don't regret it. I think you and I could work. . . ."

"No," Hattie interrupted. "We're not Spencer Tracy and Katharine Hepburn. We're too different. We want different things."

"We're not that different," Mo insisted. "I'm passionate about my work. I'm stubborn as hell, but I'm loyal, and I'll never lie to you." He sighed loudly. "Look, we can't resolve this over the phone. I'll see you in the morning. In the meantime, think about what I said. Please?"

"I gotta go," Hattie said. She disconnected before he could.

68

House Beautiful

- - - - - - -

As soon as the van pulled into the driveway behind the truck, Leetha jumped down from behind the wheel and directed the camera crew to start shooting. "The light's great right now," she enthused.

Trae had enlisted one of the finish carpenters to stay and help unload the truck and van, and he was obviously eager to critique all the things Hattie had borrowed.

"That rug is way too faded," he sniped, as the helper unrolled it in the living room.

"That's the Tybee look," Hattie said. "Faded and worn but beautiful."

"Like me," Leetha quipped from off-camera.

Hattie picked up the blue-and-white ginger jar lamps and placed them on the console table at the far end of the room. "They're obviously not old," Trae said. "But it's a good look."

"Help me with this," she ordered Trae, picking up one end of the huge Bert John abstract and propping it on the wall above the mantel.

"Okay, the paintings are great. This one especially. We'll leave it leaning like this. More casual." He grabbed a pair of large, seeded-glass hurricane lamps Hattie had unloaded and placed them on either side of the painting, then stepped back to admire the effect.

"All right," he said. "Yeah. Now I'm seeing the vision. You done good, Hattie Mae."

Hattie lifted an eyebrow. "Good?"

"Okay, great. Now let's get this place styled up."

"Where's Cass?" Hattie asked.

"I sent her into town to pick up the porch furniture. The stuff I ordered wasn't on the moving van, so we arranged to borrow some from her mom's house."

"Good idea," Hattie said. "Zenobia's got an awesome collection of old, dark green–painted wicker. Is Cass coming back out here tonight?"

"No. She said she'd be here first thing in the morning. She's going to stop at that nursery on Victory Drive and borrow some palm trees and plants for the porch."

As soon as her rented van was emptied, Leetha called a halt in the shooting. "We've got way more footage than we need," she said. "Trae, reveal first thing in the morning, right?"

Trae yawned widely. "No way. We've got window treatments to hang, the bookshelves have to be styled, and then the kitchen and bathrooms and porches still need doing, and the beds have to be dressed. If you're quitting, I'm quitting too. It's way past cocktail time."

"I've still got some gas left in my engine," Hattie volunteered. "If you'll lay out where you want everything, I can knock that out before I leave."

"Don't stay too late," Leetha warned. "You've got an eight A.M. call tomorrow." She snapped her fingers. "Damn. Almost forgot. I was supposed to text Mo photos of today's progress. Can you do that before you leave?"

"Probably wants to impress Rebecca while he's wining and dining her tonight."

Leetha grimaced. "Ugh, don't remind me."

*   *   *

With the house to herself, Hattie turned on her Pandora playlist, a mixture of classic '90s rock and current country music. She sped around the house with Ribsy following close at her heels, styling bookshelves, hanging art, making beds, and unpacking dishes and kitchen accessories. She documented her progress by taking cell phone photos of each room. It was after ten o'clock by the time she dropped down onto one of the rattan barstools, and looked around.

Carolyn Meyers had said the kitchen alone could sell the house, and while Hattie actually thought the porches, especially the upstairs one with the view out to the river, were her favorite features here, she had to admit the kitchen was stellar.

She was already having seller's remorse, for sacrificing this great old cabinet for the island. And she'd probably never again find a matched set of oversized brass ship's lanterns like the ones hanging here.

It was always like this for Hattie when she finished rehabbing an old house; a mixture of pride, exhaustion, and regret. She shrugged it off and reminded herself that there would be more old houses and more salvaged house parts.

Hattie picked up her phone and began texting the photos of the house to Mo.

Ribsy went to the back door and began scratching.

"Oh yeah," she said. "I guess maybe you do need to pee. Let's do that, then we'll call it a night. Big day tomorrow, right, pal?"

She found his retractable leash and clipped it to his collar. Her phone rang as she was opening the back door. It was Mo.

"Hey. You're not still at the house, are you?"

Ribsy was straining at the leash, desperate to get outside.

"Yeah. Hang on. I'm just taking Ribsy outside to pee."

She closed the back door and walked off the porch, letting out enough leash to allow the dog to make it to the nearest oak.

The sun had been down for hours now, and a breeze ruffled the oak leaves and rustled the sawgrass palmetto fronds. As she inhaled, the scent of salt water and marsh mud filled her lungs. The moon was nearly full, and Hattie stood for a moment, drinking in the vision of the silvery white orb reflected on the dark waters of the Back River. She'd been so busy these past few weeks she hadn't taken the time to stop and appreciate the luminous beauty of this stretch of the island. But the view didn't impress Ribsy, who was intently sniffing at something in the clump of azaleas at the foot of that oak tree.

"The photos look fantastic," Mo said.

"I hope Rebecca approved."

"She hasn't seen them. I dropped her off at her hotel and then went straight back to my place because I had a call with a guy out on the coast." He hesitated. "I'm working on putting together a proposal for another project."

"Good for you." Hattie wasn't interested in hearing about Mo Lopez's next project. He'd be on the next flight to California as soon as they wrapped up *The Homewreckers*.

"Is Trae still there with you?"

"You're kidding, right? He left along with everyone else. Said it was past cocktail hour."

"Asshole," Mo muttered. "So you're there by yourself? Jesus! It's nearly eleven. You've got an early call tomorrow, you know. There's something I need to talk to you about. . . ."

Suddenly, Ribsy lifted his head, sniffed, and bolted toward the boat shed.

"Whoa," Hattie shouted, nearly dropping the phone. "I'll call you back. Ribsy's on the run."

69

The Pit and the Pendulum

- - - - - - -

Ribsy tugged at the leash, and Hattie let out some more slack. This was typical of Ribsy. If she let him out in the backyard by himself, he was content to trot away and do his job. But put him on a leash, and he'd wander and explore, especially here at the beach, where there were so many strange and enticing things to discover.

"Come on, dude," Hattie called. "Let's get this over with. Mom's ready for bed."

Ribsy lifted his snout and sniffed, his ears pricking up at the same time. Then he bounded away, running out the slack in the line while Hattie ran to keep up. "Ribsy! Stay!"

The dog ignored her, racing toward the seawall and yanking Hattie along in his wake.

"Ribsy! NO! Back! Back!"

Ahead, she saw a flash of white streaking from beneath a huge clump of ferns, and realized her dog was hot on the trail of one of the hundreds of feral cats that populated the island.

"Ribsy! Ribsy!" she screamed. A sane person would have let the dog go, but Ribsy, when motivated, was a speed demon and natural-born hunter and she couldn't bear to think what would happen if he caught up to his quarry.

So she hung on for dear life, panting and swearing as he ran north along the grassy strip abutting the seawall. He tore through the cluster of oleander bushes that marked the boundary line between her property and the next house over, and Hattie plowed through too, wincing as the lance-shaped leaves whipped at the flesh of her face.

Ribsy veered away from the seawall now, in the direction of the looming mass of the nearly finished house next door. Piles of lumber, concrete block, and pallets of brick were stacked around on a sandy patch of earth that had been graded in preparation for a patio, or maybe even a pool.

Ribsy paused then. He stood stock-still, with his snout in the air, and Hattie stopped too, grateful for the pause in action. Her arms ached and her lungs burned.

"Come on, boy, you've had your fun. Let's go home," she coaxed. But in the next second, he was off again, running toward the darkened ground-floor level of the house which had been raised on concrete pillars, but not yet enclosed.

He was out of her view now, but Ribsy began barking furiously, yanking harder on the leash, the barks becoming high-pitched yelps. Had he cornered the poor cat under there? She pulled hard on the leash and could tell by the up-and-down motion that the dog was pitching himself against something.

"Ribsy!" she called, walking closer. Now she was directly beneath the house, and she had to strain to see in the dimness. From the corner of the room, obscured by another stack of bricks, Ribsy let out a low, guttural growl. Her neck prickled with a cold chill. She was reaching into her pocket for her phone to turn on the flashlight app when a man's voice stopped her in her tracks.

"Hi, Hattie."

Davis Hoffman stepped out from behind a five-foot

stack of concrete blocks. He had a small penlight, which he pointed at her, then carefully set on top of the stack.

"Jesus, Davis!" she exclaimed, clutching at her chest. "You scared me."

The dim light revealed a man she hardly recognized. The old Davis Hoffman, even in high school, was always immaculately dressed and groomed. But this stranger's dark hair was lank and unkempt, and his lower face was covered with graying stubble. He was hollow-eyed and dressed in a dingy gray T-shirt and jeans.

Ribsy was crouched four feet away, his eyes trained on this stranger, ears pricked, on alert.

Her heart was racing and her mouth was dry. She was still clutching the handle of Ribsy's leash, but her palms were damp and slippery. "What are you doing here?" she croaked.

Davis glanced around. "What do you think I'm doing?"

"I . . . don't know."

"Come on, Hattie. You know I'm hiding out from the cops. You sent them looking for me. After Elise came to see you. After you saw me cutting the grass at my mother's house. You knew how I got those burns." He looked down at his bandaged hand.

"You did it," she whispered. "You set that dumpster on fire. And you killed Lanier Ragan."

"It was an accident. I just wanted to talk to her. She was going to meet Holland, in the dock house. I saw him walking onto the dock earlier that night, in the storm, with the lantern. That fucking freak! I wanted to warn her, tell her what he was really like. I reached out to stop her, and she started to scream. I put my hand over her mouth to quiet her down, but something happened. It was raining so hard. Her foot must have slipped. She tripped and hit her head on the concrete. There was a lot of blood, but she was still screaming . . . I was afraid Holland would hear her."

"Davis," Hattie said, her voice pleading. "You have to go to the police. Tell them how it happened. An accident, like you said."

"No. They'd put me in prison. You know what that'd do to my little girl? You know what that's like, right, Hattie? Everyone talking about you, pointing at you. The humiliation. The shame. I can't put Ally through that."

He took a step toward Hattie, and Ribsy growled a warning. Davis pulled a pistol from the pocket of his jeans and looked at it, as though he were seeing it for the first time. His hands shaking, first he brought the gun to his head, then pointed it at her.

"Davis, no," Hattie yelled.

Ribsy leapt at Davis and the leash handle flew from her hands. He threw himself at the stranger, his barking frenzied and high-pitched. Davis batted at the dog with his free hand, and Ribsy snapped at him, running around him, jumping onto his back, ripping at his shirt. Davis slapped ineffectively, making contact with the dog's flank, and Ribsy circled around, wildly flinging his body at his attacker.

Davis stumbled briefly, his feet tangled in the leash wrapped around his legs, regained his balance, and then, struck at the dog with his gun hand. Hattie screamed again, and Ribsy sank his jaws into his attacker's bandaged hand. Davis screeched in pain and as though in slow motion, he tripped and fell onto the floor.

Hattie stared in horror as Davis sat up and raised the gun and pointed it at Ribsy. She looked wildly around. A wheelbarrow with sacks of concrete mix stood nearby with a shovel balanced on top of the stack. She grabbed the shovel and blindly struck out at him with the back of it, raining blows at his head, his shoulders, and his abdomen. When he tried to shield his face with his arms, she slammed him again. Davis howled, and the pistol flew across the room, skidding a few feet away from Hattie.

She lunged for the gun, then stood and pointed it at him. "Don't you fucking touch my dog again."

"Ribsy, come!" Hattie said. He was crouched by Davis's feet, growling. The dog looked back at her, hesitated, then trotted over to her side. She reached down and scratched his ears, keeping the gun trained on Davis.

Her legs were wobbling badly. She spied an empty five-gallon bucket of joint compound near the wheelbarrow and collapsed on top of it. Then she pulled out her phone.

Davis was moaning softly, cradling his bleeding hand close to his chest. "What are you doing?"

"Calling the detective who's been looking for you."

But before she could do that, her phone rang. It was Mo.

"You were supposed to call me back," he said. "I was worried. Are you okay?"

"I am now," she said, her voice cracking with emotion. "But I need to hang up and call the police."

"Hattie? Where are you?"

"At the house next door. I'll call you later. I swear."

"Call nine-one-one. I'm coming out there."

She ended the call but instead of dialing 911, she called Makarowicz.

"Hey," she said, keeping the gun trained on Davis. "I found your guy."

"You mean Hoffman? You found Davis Hoffman? Where are you? Is he still there? Are you okay?"

"I'm at that house just north of mine. The one under construction. I think he was hiding out here. Anyway, he pulled a gun on me, but then Ribsy jumped him, and I kinda beat him up with a shovel. Davis, I mean, not Ribsy. How soon can you get here?"

"On my way," Makarowicz said.

"I would never have shot you," Davis said. "You know me, Hattie. I would never."

Hattie stared at him. Her thoughts flashed back to their early teen years. She remembered halcyon summer days at the beach, or out on Davis's boat, the three of them, Hattie, Hank, and Davis.

"No. I don't know you at all. I thought we were friends. You, me, Hank."

"Truthfully? It was never about Hank. I just wanted to be close to you, Hattie."

"What about Elise?" she asked.

"Elise was always the consolation prize. She knew it, I knew it. She wanted a kid; we both thought it would fix things. It didn't. Nothing can fix me because I'm broken."

His liquid brown eyes were pleading. "I came out here to kill myself. But there were too many people around. So I hid over here. Waiting for the right time. Tonight was the night. You should have let me do it."

"Let you take the easy way out? Not on your life," she said. Her hands were trembling so badly she had to prop her elbows up on her knees and grip the pistol with both hands.

"Will you tell me something?" she asked.

He rubbed at his forehead with his good hand. Even in the dim light she could see a huge lump forming. "Depends on what you want to know."

"How did you know about the septic tank?"

"When we were nine or ten, Holland and I used to play army. We were best friends, played together all the time back then, when I was at my grandmother's house, and he was at his. This was before I realized what a psycho he was. His grandmother had workers over there, draining the tank. Holland tricked me. He said I could be the American soldier, and I should jump down in the foxhole, and he'd be the Nazi, and then I should just pop up and shoot him. Next thing I know, he's dragging a big sheet of plywood over and covering the pit. I was trapped. I couldn't push it away. It was summertime and I was crying and begging him to let me out, and all the time, I could hear him up there, laughing his ass off. I don't know how long he left me there. An hour? Eventually, he came back and let me out. But he told me if I ever ratted him out to my parents he'd sneak into my house and cut my throat with a knife. He was a sick little bastard, even then, and he grew up to be a sick, horny teenaged bastard."

Hattie felt a twinge of sympathy for nine-year-old Davis, being bullied by Holland Creedmore. But then she remembered Lanier Ragan's fate, and she felt the cold fury burning in the pit of her stomach.

"If it was an accident, how did Lanier's skull get bashed in? You said she was screaming after she fell. The fall wasn't what killed her."

Davis was silent then. He dropped his head to his knees, and she saw his shoulders rise and fall as he wept.

She waited.

When he raised his head, tears glinted on his cheeks. "I was afraid he'd hear her. Holland. He'd been signaling her, with that stupid lantern. 'Hurry. Hurry.' We taught ourselves semaphore with an old book we found. Did you know that?"

"You haven't answered my question. How did you kill her?"

"There was a big rock, like an old piece of coral or something. I kind of went crazy. I grabbed it. And I hit her. And then she was quiet."

"You mean she was dead, Davis. You killed her. Then what? You ran away and hid?"

"No! I was trying to figure out what to do next. It was raining so hard. I went back to our house and waited for the storm to stop. After a while, I snuck back over there. I saw Holland's mom. She had a flashlight, and she found the body. I kind of hid behind those big oleanders by the seawall and waited to see what would happen next. Pretty soon, old man Creedmore showed up. I watched them get a tarp from that shed in the backyard. They wrapped her up in it and put her in the shed. Then they left and they took Lanier's car. It was parked in the driveway over here."

"When did you move the body?"

"As soon as it was light outside. Holland must have left earlier. I saw his car was gone. I was afraid the Creedmores would come back and call the cops. I thought, if nobody knew where Lanier's body was, they might think she ran away. Then I saw the big metal manhole cover back there. The rain had washed away a lot of the dirt that had been on top of it. I found a crowbar in the shed, and somehow, I jacked it open. I put her in there, then I got a rake and smoothed the dirt back on top of it, and then I went back to my grandmother's house. I still had some weed, and there was some vodka left, so I got drunk and then I got stoned, and I guess I fell asleep."

From off in the distance they heard an approaching police siren. Ribsy raised his snout in the air and began to howl.

Davis lowered his head to his knees and covered his ears with both hands.

70

Blue Light Special 2.0

- - - - - - -

The flashing blue lights of four police cruisers lit up the Tybee night. Makarowicz read Davis his rights. A uniformed officer led him away, in handcuffs. "I need to see a doctor," Davis protested. "My hands are bleeding and I think I'm concussed."

"Just as soon as you give us a statement, we'll take you to the ER," Makarowicz called. He looked over at Hattie, who was still holding onto Ribsy's leash. "I know it's late, and maybe you're in shock or something, but I need to get a statement from you, too."

"Hattie?" Mo's voice cut through the darkness as he walked up from the seawall. He rushed over to her, and she leaned gratefully into his arms. "Are you okay?"

"Yeah," she managed. "Tired, but okay."

Mo looked over at the detective. "Can I take her home now?"

"Afraid not. She needs to come back to the station with me."

Hattie allowed herself to rest her head on Mo's shoulder for a moment. "What did he say?" Mo asked. "Did he admit to anything?"

Hattie managed a weak smile. "He confessed to everything, including killing Lanier Ragan and dumping her body in the septic tank pit. Also, he had a gun."

"Did he hurt you?"

"No. I'll explain the rest later." She leaned down and scratched the dog's ears. "This guy's gonna get the biggest steak they've got at the IGA tomorrow."

"But in the meantime," Mak said, gesturing toward his police cruiser.

Hattie closed her eyes and sighed. Mo wrapped an arm around her waist. "Can I go with you to the police station? I won't say anything. I just don't want you to be alone."

She looked to Makarowicz for approval, who nodded. "Okay. That would be nice," she said.

Hours later, Mo tapped her gently on the shoulder. "Hey. You're home."

She managed to drag her eyelids open and yawn. "This is the second time this week that you've had to come to my rescue, Mo."

"My pleasure."

Hours later, she sat up and glanced frantically at the bedside clock. It was after nine. Ribsy was asleep at the foot of her bed and sunlight shone through the thin slats of the bamboo blinds. She staggered into the bathroom and splashed cold water onto her face. She looked a hot mess.

"Hey," Mo's voice called from outside the door. "Are you okay in there?"

"I missed my call time," she said, opening the door and peeking out. "Did you stay here last night?"

"Yeah. I couldn't see leaving you alone. That sofa of yours sucks, by the way."

He handed her a mug of coffee. "I talked to the boss, which would be me, about this morning's shoot and explained. This one time, you get an extension. Are you hungry?"

"Starved. But I gotta get out to the house. There's still so much left to do."

"Let Trae take care of it. He owes you. How about breakfast?"

"Let me grab a shower first. Can you let Ribsy out and then feed him?"

"On one condition."

"Name it."

"After you shower, you let me borrow a toothbrush."

They drove Hattie's truck back to Tybee, then waited in line at The Breakfast Club for ten minutes before taking the last two stools inside at the bar.

When Mo ordered shrimp and grits, Hattie feigned shock. "Are we finally turning you into a southerner, Mo Lopez?"

"We have grits in California," he said. "But they don't taste the same." He gave her a sidelong glance. "Want to tell me about last night?"

In between sips of coffee, she gave him a recap of the night's events.

"What happens now?"

"According to Makarowicz, Davis will be charged with murder, arson, and attempted kidnapping. And whatever else the district attorney can come up with."

"I was on the phone with Rebecca while you were in the shower," Mo said. "Makarowicz held a press conference this morning to announce Davis Hoffman's arrest. Of course

Becca's already finagling how to turn this thing into ratings gold. She wants us to shoot an extra episode, sort of like an epilogue, with a true-crime kind of twist to it."

Carefully, Hattie put her coffee mug down on the countertop. "Okay, but I want script approval. We do this my way, or not at all."

"Seriously?"

"Very seriously. I've been through some drama in my own life. I don't want this story to be sensationalized any more than it already has been. And I'll only do it if Emma Ragan gives it her blessing. I won't exploit her misery."

The food arrived and Mo attacked his breakfast with a vengeance. Hattie picked at her omelet and nibbled at a piece of toast. "Well?"

"Okay," Mo said. "Seems fair."

71

Show Time

- - - - - - -

Hattie stood in the front yard at the Creedmore house and beamed. "It's not even the same house. I don't have words."

Looking at it in the light of day, the transformation was startling. The formerly sagging, rotting porch stood proud, with a row of fluffy green fern baskets hanging between the columns, and huge iron urns filled with red geraniums and trailing ivy flanking the newly painted front door. The brass lanterns had been polished and gleamed in the sunlight.

She turned and looked at the camera. "The first time I saw this place it was boarded up with plywood. The city had condemned it. The house is a hundred years old and was showing its age."

Cass joined her on the front porch and Hattie turned to her. "Cass, you had a pretty dramatic reaction to the house, didn't you?"

"At first, I wouldn't even get out of the truck, the place was that bad. It was so overgrown, you couldn't even tell there was a house back there. I told her, no way we can save this place."

"It was gruesome," Trae said with an exaggerated shudder.

"The second floor was sort of tilted," Hattie said, as they

climbed the porch steps together. "It looked like an old lady who had put her hat on crooked."

"Look at this," Trae said, pushing the door open. "Remember that nasty wall-to-wall carpet? I really didn't think there could be anything worth saving here."

"But I knew there would be hardwood floors. Most of these old Tybee raised cottages were built from heart pine. Sanding and refinishing these floors took a lot of sweat equity, but look how it paid off," Hattie said, gesturing at the living and dining rooms. "And look how great the fireplace turned out."

"I love the whitewash paint finish we used to mellow it out and make it look like local Savannah gray bricks," Trae said. "And that huge oak beam you had milled from a fallen tree really works well for the mantel."

The cameras trailed them as they moved from room to room, explaining the process of rehabbing the old beach house. Finally, Hattie and Trae stood in the kitchen.

"This room looked like something out of a crack house," Trae said.

"I'd hoped we could salvage some of the original cabinetry, but in the end, the only original element in here are these wood floors," Hattie said.

"Which I sanded, taped off, and painted with this checkerboard design," Trae said, rubbing at his back. "It was literally a pain in my butt. Of course, the floors are my favorite thing in the kitchen. Hattie, I think I already know what you're proudest of."

Hattie pointed to the island, which was styled with a primitive wooden dough bowl filled with Meyer lemons from a tree she'd discovered in the backyard, and a cut-glass pitcher of lemonade. "My favorite is this work island. For years, I'd been hoarding this antique display cabinet that came out of an old haberdashery on Broughton Street, in downtown Savannah. We put a new marble top on it, and then, continuing the vintage Savannah theme, we hung these old brass ship's lanterns as pendants. You know, Trae, Carolyn Meyers, our real estate agent, says this kitchen is the sizzle that's going to sell this steak."

Carolyn walked into the kitchen on cue, holding a leather folder. "I can't wait to get this listing online, you two. The house is going to show beautifully, and I truly believe we'll have no problem getting our list price. In fact, I predict a bidding war."

Trae held the back door open, and the threesome walked out onto the back porch.

Hattie pointed at the view through the trees. The new sod was a bright green, and in the distance, sunlight sparkled on the water and pelicans glided by in formation.

"That's the real star, right there," she said. "This view of the Back River and Little Tybee. That's what beach-house living is about. Can't you just picture yourself kayaking out there on a spring day? Or dropping a fishing line or a crab trap off the end of the dock?"

"What about just hanging out in that dock house, sipping an adult beverage or grilling the day's catch? There's even a dining area out there," Trae said. "And this huge property could accommodate a swimming pool and a guesthouse if the buyer wanted to really gild the lily."

Hattie spotted Mo standing behind the camera operator. He nodded and gave her a thumbs-up.

Hattie linked her arm through Trae's. "In the meantime though, Trae, our work here is done. This old beach house has been thoroughly and successfully homewrecked. Thanks for watching!"

"Bye, everybody!" Trae waved.

"Cut!" Mo stepped out from behind the camera. "Wrap party starts in thirty minutes!"

A food truck from Papa's Barbecue had been parked at the rear of the house for the *Homewreckers* wrap party. Members of the production crew and the construction crew mingled around inside and on the porches, eating chopped pork, coleslaw, potato salad, Brunswick stew, and banana pudding. There were coolers full of iced-down local craft beers, and drink dispensers filled with sweet iced tea.

Rebecca sat on a folding chair on the front porch, dabbing at her sweaty forehead with a paper napkin and looking down, with distaste, at the plate of barbecue she'd just been handed.

"Sooo," she said, looking over at Hattie and Cass and Mo and Trae. "That went well, don't you think?"

"Well?" Mo took a swig from his beer bottle. "That's kind of faint praise, isn't it?"

"Don't get me wrong," Rebecca said. "I'm sure you'll do wonders with it in postproduction, but I just thought the big reveal was . . . I don't know. Kind of quiet?"

"We took a falling-down piece of crap and in less than six weeks transformed it into a showplace," Mo said, his voice rising as his annoyance grew. "The before and after shots are going to be amazing. We've got a ton of drama in this season, Hattie buying the house with a sealed bid, then the discovery of that billfold . . ."

"We literally uncovered a skeleton *and* solved an old cold-case murder, Becc," Trae added.

"Well, yeah, I guess that does up the suspense," Rebecca admitted.

"And don't forget our makeup and breakup," Trae said, pointing at Hattie. "Think of all the publicity that generated for the show. I can't leave my hotel room in downtown Savannah without someone stopping me to ask when Hattie and I are getting engaged."

"That would be never," Hattie said quickly.

Cass pointed her beer bottle at Rebecca. "Y'all, the vibe I'm getting here is that she's trying to tell us something. And it's not good. Right, Rebecca?"

Rebecca dipped a plastic spoon into the cup of banana pudding, then scraped most of it off before tasting.

She dropped the spoon and grimaced. "Why is everything so sweet down here? I'm amazed everyone doesn't go into diabetic shock from just looking at this food."

"Rebecca?" Mo pressed. "Why are you here? Has Tony seen any of the raw footage I've been sending you?"

"I was hoping we could discuss this someplace more private," Rebecca said, looking around at the faces focused on hers.

"Obviously, Cass is right. You've got bad news. So just tell me. Us. All of us have a stake in this show. What's the deal?"

"Tony has seen a bit of the early footage. He's incredibly busy right now. What I can tell you is that he wasn't bowled over. I told him, 'Tony, just wait. Mo's team has done an incredible job with this house,' but he isn't buying in. The thing is, we're just not sure this concept is going to win us the demographic we're looking for."

"Which means what?" Mo demanded.

"Okay, we're definitely going to honor our commitment for six episodes, so no worries there."

Mo's expression relaxed a little.

"But not on Wednesday night. Tony got an early look at Byron's new show, *Haunted Hideaways,* and honestly, Mo, it just hits all the sweet spots for the new direction the network is headed in. It's dark, it's gritty, it's going to bring us that elusive eighteen- to thirty-year-old male demographic, and it's a new kind of storytelling. We're incredibly excited about it."

Mo closed his eyes and leaned his head back for a moment as he digested Rebecca's bombshell. Finally, he leaned forward, his jaw muscle so tight it twitched.

"*Haunted Hideaways*? Isn't your network called Home Place TV? Give me a fucking break, Rebecca. You think a show from the guy who dreamed up *Bulldozing Bayonne* is going to win you Wednesday nights? What have you people been smoking?"

Rebecca stood up and smoothed the fabric of her very tight pencil skirt. She dumped the plate of food in a plastic trash barrel. "I knew you weren't going to take this very well, but Tony was insistent that I be the one to tell you, and in person. As I said, we'll honor our commitment. Right now, the plan is to do test screenings as soon as you're done with postproduction. Barring any major surprises, we're holding a slot for *The Homewreckers* on the Sunday afternoon lineup."

"What? Following reruns of *Mobile Home Makeovers*? Or as a lead-in for *Garage Sale Mayhem*?"

Rebecca's large black crocodile handbag began emitting a series of insistent beeps. She reached inside and glanced at her phone. Moments later, a black town car came bumping down the driveway toward the house. "There's my ride. Mo, we can discuss this later. Hattie, Cass? Wonderful job. Our marketing people have ideas for some promotional events you two could do in support of *Homewreckers* this fall. Trade shows, county fairs, like that. We'll be in touch. Trae—see you next week. Right?"

Trae smiled. "I'll just walk you to your car and see you off."

Hattie watched the two of them stroll toward the waiting

car. "County fairs?" Hattie said, peeling off her fake eye-lashes. "That's a hard pass."

Cass reached up and began unfastening the extensions Lisa had so laboriously pinned into her hair earlier that morning. "Trade shows? Hell, no."

Mo took another sip of beer, then tossed the bottle into the recycling bin. "I'm sorry about this, you two. We all put our heart and soul into this show. And we've just been officially shafted. Guess I should have known better."

"But she said *Homewreckers* will still air. So that's good news, right?" Hattie asked.

"Yeah, but the time slot they're giving us is a graveyard," Mo said. "Realistically, unless we work some kind of miracle, it looks like *Homewreckers* is gonna be one and done."

"There goes my show-biz career," Cass said, unbuttoning the lacy scoop-neck top wardrobe had outfitted her in, to reveal a black tank top with the words MAMA TRIED printed across the front. She tossed the blouse over the back of one of the front porch rockers. "Who wants more banana pudding?"

72

Bye-Bye, Love

- - - - - - -

Hattie and Mo sat on Zenobia's borrowed wicker rocking chairs on the screened porch. They were alone in the house. The last van full of rented film equipment had pulled away hours earlier. Crew members hugged and exchanged contact information and promised to keep in touch. Cass and Trae had given each other chilly, cursory nods of farewell before parting ways.

They'd snagged half a bottle of wine from the party left-overs and climbed the stairs to the second-floor porch.

The sun was setting over the Back River, staining the sky in gentle swaths of cobalt, violet, copper, and yellow, leaving the treetops of Little Tybee in stark silhouette.

"What happens now?" she asked.

"You mean with us?" He reached for her hand but she linked only her pinkie with his.

"I meant with the show."

"Oh. We start postproduction in L.A. next week. And then, I've got some irons in the fire . . . HPTV ain't the only network doing my kind of programming. In fact . . ."

"I've got to sell this house," Hattie interrupted. "I wake up in the middle of the night, panicking about it."

"You will. I bet it'll be sold before the first episode of

Homewreckers airs in the fall. So. You still haven't answered my question. What about us?"

Hattie stalled by sipping her wine. Here was the moment she'd been dreading since filming had ended hours ago. Why hadn't she left along with the others? Why stay behind and subject herself to uncomfortable questions and impossible scenarios? She mustered a diversionary response. "You'll be in L.A. dreaming up a new project, and I'll be back here in Savannah, demo-ing another stinky old bathroom and crawling around under rotten kitchen floors."

Mo looped his fingers through hers. She didn't pull away. "Maybe I'll drop in and see you."

It took a moment for her to get the reference to his chance meeting with her at the Tattnall Street house. She gave a rueful laugh. "That seems like a lifetime ago."

"But it's only been two months. A lot has happened," Mo reminded her. "Let's see where this thing takes us. Okay? The lease on my Airbnb isn't up yet, which gives me a few days of downtime. I was thinking we could . . ."

"No," Hattie said.

"Let me finish," he protested. "We could spend some time together. Just the two of us. Maybe get out of this blast furnace you call summer in Savannah. I did some research. We could go to the North Carolina mountains. To Cashiers. I hear it's a lot cooler. There's an inn, with a spa, and terrific food. Do you like to hike? It's pet-friendly, so we could take Ribsy."

She dropped his hand, and was staring out at the darkening sky, her arms crossed over her chest, a defensive mechanism, as though she had to shield her heart from the potential of losing it to this stranger who'd literally come crashing into her life.

Finally, she turned to him. "You said it yourself. You're going back to L.A. What did you call *Homewreckers*? One and done, right? That's us, too, Mo. One and done."

Mo stood up so quickly that his chair rocked violently before tipping over backward.

"What's going on with you, Hattie? You're the most utterly fearless person I've ever met, man or woman. I've watched you deal with dry rot and termites and crooked inspectors and backyard burial pits, and arson and vandals. Last night you single-handedly disarmed a gun-toting maniac. So why are you such a chickenshit when it comes to being with me?"

"I'm not!" she protested.

"Then prove it. Go away with me."

She shook her head. "What's the point?"

He flipped the rocker back upright. "I care about you and I think you care about me. That's the point. But you won't even give us a chance."

"Because we don't stand a chance," Hattie said sadly. "Our lives are literally a continent apart. Suppose we do run away for a weekend? What happens after that? You have a business, and family in L.A. You're inevitably going back there. And I'm not. My roots, my life, are here in Savannah. Tug told me this week that in the next two years he wants to turn the business over to me. I'm not like you, Mo. I can't just 'take a meeting' in New York one day, then fly out to L.A. the next."

He knelt down on the floor in front of her and grasped both her hands. "I'm not asking you to do anything like that. Honest. I'm not. I've got this great idea, and I think I can make it work, but only if you're a part of it."

Hattie bit her lip and gazed down at him. She wanted to run her fingers through his dark hair, experience more kisses, take a long, sunset walk on the beach, and then spend a Sunday morning in bed with him, but she knew these could only be fleeting moments.

Giving up Mauricio Lopez might be the hardest thing she'd ever have to do. Losing Hank had been the worst, but she hadn't had a choice in that, had she? He'd been taken, in an instant. It had taken her seven years to find a man as good, and decent, and kind as Hank Kavanaugh. And now she had to let him walk away.

"I can't," she said, disentangling their hands. "You say you work in reality television? But we both know it's all a lie. Interior decorators in designer jeans swinging sledgehammers for the camera. Jury-rigged light fixtures. And phony romances. That's your reality. But it can't be mine."

She pushed herself up from the rocking chair and took one last look at the sky outside. Only the faintest fingers of orange were visible on the horizon.

"Go back to L.A., Mo," she said wearily.

"I'll go, but I'm coming back, Hattie," he said. "And when I do, you'll have to listen."

73

One Week Later

- - - - - - -

Hattie closed the lid of her computer and rubbed her eyes. She'd been looking at real estate listings all morning, but the pickings were slim.

"Find anything?" Zenobia asked, walking past to drop a stack of invoices on her desk.

"Nothing we can afford," Hattie said. She leafed through the bills. "Damn. All these vendors want their money from the Creedmore job ASAP."

"Looking at over twelve thousand for the windows alone," Zenobia commented. "Lumber's another eight thousand, and that's after I talked Guerry into giving us a deeper discount. Scotty Eifird wants his money too."

"I thought we got the HVAC in exchange for promotion," Hattie protested.

"Yeah, but Scotty's guys don't work for free, and we only got the units donated. Not the ductwork. So that's another six thousand."

"Damn," Hattie said.

Her phone rang and she picked it up. It was Al Makaro-wicz.

"Hi, Al," she said. "How are things out on Tybee? Got any crime sprees going?"

"Oh, yeah, doing a booming business in jaywalkers and bike thieves. And yesterday I nabbed a guy who tried to run out of the IGA with a twelve-pack of Natty Lite shoved down his sweatpants. I'm headed into town and thought you might want to take a ride with me."

Hattie looked around the office. It was nearly noon. Tug was in his office, with the shade pulled down. Probably taking a nap, she surmised.

"Want to tell me what this is about?" she asked.

"You'll see."

She was waiting on the sidewalk in front of the office when Makarowicz pulled up in his cruiser.

"Long time, no see," she said, sliding into the front seat. "Anything happening with your case? I saw that big story Molly Fowlkes did in the *Morning News* on Sunday. I guess it's good news that Davis is going to plead out, right?"

"It'll save the county and the city a bunch of money," Makarowicz said. "And he'll escape the death penalty. The district attorney is asking for life without parole."

"Part of me hopes he rots in prison. But I still feel bad for his little girl," Hattie said. "What's happening with the Creedmores?"

"Big Holl and Dorcas recanted their statement, as soon as we got Davis Hoffman locked up. But I've got 'em on tape, and Hoffman signed an affidavit that he saw them move Lanier Ragan's body. If I've got any say in the matter, they'll do time."

"What about Holland Junior? He just goes free?"

"I don't like it any better than you do, but the best we can do is hope the grand jury indicts him, along with his parents, for concealing a death and hindering the apprehension of a criminal. The concealment carries a ten-year sentence, hindering apprehension is twelve months."

Hattie looked out the window of the cruiser. They

were headed south on Bull Street. He turned left onto East Fifty-Seventh, crossed Abercorn Street, and on the next block, pulled to the curb in front of a redbrick cottage with wrought-iron burglar bars on the windows, and a plaster statue of the Virgin Mary on the front porch.

"What are we doing here?" Hattie asked.

"I thought we might pay a visit to Mavis Creedmore," Makarowicz said. "I just want to clear up a couple last details that have been bothering me."

"What makes you think the nasty old bat will talk to you?" Hattie asked.

Makarowicz pointed to the badge clipped to his belt. "Her generation generally has at least a begrudging respect for law enforcement."

The detective rang the doorbell and waited. "Who's that?" The old woman's voice was muffled by the thick wooden door.

"Tybee police, Miss Creedmore."

The door opened a crack and Mavis peered out, eyes as hard and black as coffee beans behind thick-lensed glasses. "I don't live on Tybee and I didn't call no police."

"No, ma'am, but this is in regard to the property you formerly owned there."

"What about it?" Mavis opened the door wider, but glared when she saw her other visitor.

She pointed a bony finger at Hattie. "That one stole my family's beach house out from under us. She's got no business standing right here on my porch. I'll talk to you, but not her."

"I've got as much right to be here as you did when you snuck onto my private property," Hattie shot back. "You're lucky I didn't call the cops on you that night."

Mavis Creedmore scowled, but she opened the door and stepped out onto the concrete porch. Her sparse white hair had been teased into a pouf that revealed patches of pink scalp. She wore a white short-sleeved blouse, navy-blue slacks, and lace-up black walking shoes.

"What is it you want, then?" she asked Makarowicz. "Be quick about it. I don't want my neighbors thinking I'm some kind of a criminal like those low-life cousins of mine."

"It's about Lanier Ragan's wallet," Makarowicz said.

"Never met the woman."

"But you did find her wallet at your beach house, isn't that right, Miss Mavis?"

"Not saying I did, not saying I didn't."

Makarowicz shook his head. "Miss Mavis, this is serious police business, concerning a homicide that occurred on property owned by your family. Now, would you like to answer my questions here, or would you prefer that I handcuff you and put you in the back of my cruiser, in front of all your neighbors, and take you out to Tybee for questioning at the police station?"

Mavis took a step backward. "You can't do that. Can you?"

He tapped the handcuffs snapped to his belt. "Would you like to find out?"

"Fine," the old woman snapped. "Yes. I found that billfold. Might have been a year or so after that girl went missing."

"And you didn't think to report it to the authorities?"

"No."

"And why was that?"

"I found it in the boat shed when I was looking for a crab trap. Holland and them always did leave things in a mess after they'd been out there. My grandfather would have had a conniption if he'd seen the condition they left that house in.

How'd I know how it got there? I had no idea what it meant. I took it in the house to look at it, and right then, here comes Big Holl and that useless woman he married. Dorcas. Wasn't even their weekend to be out there. Didn't want them to see what I'd found, so I stuck it in that old razor slot in the bathroom wall. And I didn't think no more about it."

Makarowicz stared at her in disbelief. "You didn't think any more about it after her body was discovered? You didn't wonder how that body got there and who put it there, or how someone would know about that long-disused septic tank?"

Mavis looked down at her shoes, which suddenly seemed more fascinating than the disapproving stare of the police detective.

Hattie couldn't restrain herself. "Seventeen years, Mavis! For seventeen years Lanier Ragan's daughter has agonized over what happened to her mother. And for most of that time, you knew. You're a horrible person, you know that? And you're just as bad as those low-life cousins of yours. How do you even look at yourself in the mirror every morning?"

"Get off my porch," the old woman said with a snarl.

With the toe of her shoe Hattie tipped over the plaster Virgin Mary. It broke into four or five large chunks.

"Oops."

She was sitting in the front seat of the cruiser, still fuming, when Makarowicz returned a few minutes later.

"You should have hauled her bony ass off to jail like the rest of her miserable family," Hattie said, as Mak started the car and turned the air-conditioning to the max.

"I'll admit, it would have felt good, but the truth is, no judge or jury in this town is going to convict an octogenarian white lady for being a spiteful old hag. Sometimes, just knowing the truth has to be enough."

"How do you do it?" Hattie asked, glancing over at the detective's calm demeanor.

"You mean dealing with people like her?"

"Yeah. All of it. People stealing, lying, raping, killing. How do you stay sane?"

"It's not all bad stuff. Some days I get to return a kid's stolen bike, or lock up a dirtbag who's been abusing his wife. Crimefighting 101."

He looked over at Hattie. "Do you have time for one more stop? It's not far."

"Sure."

They picked up iced coffee at the counter at Foxy Loxy, then walked out to the courtyard. The young woman was sitting at a table under an umbrella, reading a book. She was a tiny, blond sprite, with tattoos.

"Detective Mak," she exclaimed, standing up and giving him a hug.

Makarowicz blushed, and gestured to Hattie. "Emma Ragan, this is Hattie Kavanaugh."

Hattie felt suddenly shy. "Hi, Emma," she said. "It's nice to finally meet you."

"No, it's nice to meet *you,*" Emma said. "I hear you knew my mom."

"She was my favorite teacher," Hattie said, sitting down at the table. She cocked her head. "You look like her, you know."

"I get that a lot."

Makarowicz handed Emma a manila envelope. The girl opened it and pulled out some photos. She spread them out on the tabletop. One was obviously a school picture of a little girl dressed in a frilly blue dress, another was a family photo, a handsome young couple and their daughter.

"That's me. Wearing my favorite dress," Emma said, tapping the picture. She shuffled the pictures. "Me on the swing in our backyard." Another photo showed Lanier Ragan cradling an infant in a baby blanket. "I've never seen this one," she said.

"They're copies, and not very good ones," Makarowicz said apologetically. "I can't give you the actual pictures from her billfold until all the court stuff is done."

Emma nodded. "My mom's wedding ring?" she said hopefully.

"It shouldn't be long now. Davis Hoffman's lawyer wants to spare his family the spectacle of a long, drawn-out trial."

"But they'll all go to prison for what they did to my mom, right?" Emma asked. "Even the Creedmores?"

"The district attorney assures me that he's going to ask for the max for all of them, but then it's up to the judge. You're willing to give a victim impact statement, right?"

Emma lifted her chin. "Absolutely. My dad will give one too."

She turned to Hattie. "Now that it's all over, I'm going to have a service for her. He wants to come. Do you think I should let him?"

Hattie thought of her fractured relationship with her own father, how it had grown colder and more distant with the passing years. Would things have been different if he'd reached out to her earlier? If he'd expressed remorse? She'd probably never know. Her last visit with him had reinforced the wideness of the gulf. It was too late.

"I don't know, Emma," she said, answering the girl's question. "He's the only family you've got, right?"

"Yeah."

"I can't tell you what's right or wrong. But, if he wants to see you, and you think he can change, or if you can find a way to forgive him, maybe give him another chance."

Emma slid the photographs back into the envelope. "That's what my therapist said too."

She looked over at Makarowicz. "Thank you for these. I don't have many photos of her. Or of us together as a family."

The cop coughed, clearing his throat. "You know, just because you've lost someone you loved, that doesn't mean you have to stop living yourself."

"I get that now," Emma said softly. She stood up to leave, tucking her book and the envelope into her backpack.

"You take care of yourself, you hear?" Mak said. "And keep in touch."

Hattie felt a pang of guilt as she watched Lanier's daughter walk away.

"Emma?"

The girl came back to the table, waiting.

Hattie brought her change purse out of her bag, unzipped it, and removed the green scapular.

"This was in your mom's wallet, along with the photos. I knew it was wrong but for some reason, instead of turning it over to the cops, I kept it."

She held it out. "Here. This is yours."

Emma took the scapular and pressed it into Hattie's hand, gently folding Hattie's fingers over the square.

"You keep it. You gave me back my mom. I think that's a fair trade."

74

Icebreakers

- - - - - - -

Two weeks passed. Hattie was back at her desk at Kavanaugh & Son, trying to find a new old house to rehab. Cass
rolled her desk chair up next to Hattie's. "Can we talk?"

"Yeah. What about?"

"A couple things. First, I went over to the district attorney's office today and gave a victim impact statement. About
Holland Creedmore, and, you know, what he did to me."

"That's great, Cass," Hattie said. She glanced over at Zenobia, who was on the phone, and lowered her voice. "How
did it go?"

"Don't worry about Mom. I finally told her everything last
night. She fussed at me a little, for keeping it bottled up all
these years, but then she pointed out that I was just a kid, and
kids do dumb things. We both cried."

"I'm glad you finally told her."

"It was my therapist's idea. Anyway, today I met with a
woman at the DA's office who prosecutes sex crimes. She's
pretty cool. About our age, not at all judgy. The bad news
is, the statute of limitations has already run out, because I
didn't report it within seven years of the time of the sexual
assault. So Junior can't be prosecuted for what he did to me."

"Well, damn," Hattie said.

"It's okay. The assistant DA says my statement can be included in the sentencing file they give to the judge. It might not make a difference, but at least I made the effort. And you know what? The minute I walked out of that office, I felt like a huge burden had been lifted. No more guilt, or shame. Literally, I felt lighter."

Hattie hugged her best friend. "Cass, I'm so proud of you."

"I'm kind of proud of me too."

"We should have a girls' night tonight, to celebrate," Hattie said. "We could do Mexican, and if you're nice, in between margaritas, I'll let you help me finish tiling my kitchen backsplash."

"You're working on your kitchen again? What brought that on?"

"Boredom, maybe? I was so proud of the kitchen we did over at Chatham Avenue, I thought, what's stopping me from doing that in my own damn kitchen? We had a couple boxes of tile left over, and I already had the granite for my countertops, it's been sitting in the backyard since . . ."

"Since Hank died," Cass said gently. "The clocks stopped at your house the day he died."

"They kind of did," Hattie agreed. "I didn't see any point in fixing up the house just for me. But this past week I've had this crazy surge of creative energy. Anyway, so you'll come over tonight, right?"

"Actually, I might already have plans."

"Might? What kind of plans?"

"That depends. There's a guy I think I kind of like, and he asked me out, but I need to clear it with you first."

"Me? I'm not your mom. You don't need a permission slip from me to go on a date."

"I kinda do," Cass said, looking guilty. "The guy is Jimmy."

"Jimmy Cates? Our roofer?"

"Formerly your Jimmy Cates," Cass said. "I won't go if . . ."

"Of course you'll go," Hattie said. "We only dated for, like, five seconds. Jimmy's nice, but turns out he was a . . ."

"Icebreaker?"

They both got a laugh out of that. "It was never gonna work out for us," Hattie said. "But you two? I can totally see you together."

"You really don't mind?"

Hattie's cell phone rang. She glanced at the caller ID.

"It's Carolyn Meyers," she said. "Fingers crossed she's got good news."

"Hattie!" the Realtor exclaimed. "We've got an offer on your house."

"Thank you, baby Jesus," Hattie said. "I'm at the office with Cass and Zen. I'll put you on speakerphone so they can hear."

"Hi, ladies," Carolyn said. "We have an all-cash offer on Chatham Avenue. Which means no appraisal, no mortgage approval, and a quick close."

"What's the offer?" Hattie asked.

"Eight seventy-five," Carolyn said. "I know it's less than we hoped for, but they can close immediately, with no stipulations."

"Do they know the, uh, history of the house?"

"They know, and they don't care," Carolyn said, chuckling. "They live in Michigan now, but the husband grew up here. He's Holland Creedmore's first cousin."

"Ahhh. The despised Yankee cousins," Hattie said.

"Exactly. He'd given up trying to deal long-distance with Mavis and Holland Senior. And he was fit to be tied when he found out the city condemned the property and sold it to you. He's been following your progress on social media. He called me after he saw the listing photos."

"That's incredible," Cass said.

"I just got off a long phone call with him," Carolyn said. "He and his wife are ecstatic about having the house back in the family. They love how you brought the place back to life, and what they love most is the prospect of never having to deal with their Savannah cousins again. So, what do you say?"

Hattie had been taking notes during the conversation, underlining the sale price and adding exclamation marks.

"The answer is yes. Absolutely. I accept."

"Great. I'll write up the contract and email it as soon as we get off the phone. Sign it, and shoot it back to me. What's a good closing date for you?"

"How's tomorrow?"

Carolyn laughed. "That's maybe a little premature. I know they're planning on flying down this weekend. Let's see if we can do the walk-through and closing next Friday."

"That works for me," Hattie said.

Hattie disconnected the call and grabbed Cass's hands. "Sold, sold, sold!" Hattie sang out, as they did a clumsy ring-around-the-rosy waltz around the office. "We sold the house! We sold the house!" They danced over to Zenobia and coaxed her into joining them. "Sold! Sold! Sold!"

"All right, y'all, that's enough foolishness for me," Zen said finally, extricating herself from the other two women. "I got work to do."

"Promise you'll call me first thing tomorrow," Hattie whispered to Cass. "I wanna hear all about your date with Jimmy."

* * *

"Looks like it's just you and me again, Ribsy," Hattie said. She fed him a bite of steak from the burrito she'd picked up at her favorite Mexican restaurant on Victory Drive, and tried not to feel sorry for herself.

"Better to be alone than with the wrong guy, right?" she asked the dog, who wagged his tail in response.

She ran her hand over the granite countertop, which she'd bribed two of her painters into hauling into the house and installing earlier that afternoon. It was white with pale gray flecks and gleamed in the harsh light of the naked lightbulb overhead.

"Should have kept those brass lanterns for my own kitchen," she groused. "But hey, now I've got an excuse to hunt down some more." She picked up a tile from the box on the counter and finished the row she'd laid out. "Time for mortar mix, right, sport?"

Instead of answering, Ribsy's ears pricked up and he dashed through the house toward the front door, barking as he ran.

As soon as she opened the door Ribsy launched himself into the visitor's arms. Mo laughed and dropped to the floor of the porch as the dog wriggled and wagged and licked his face with a series of ecstatic yips.

Mo looked up at Hattie. "At least somebody's glad to see me."

She was momentarily speechless. "Mo? What are you doing here?"

"I've got news. And I tried calling, but as usual, got no answer. Do you even know where your phone is?"

"Oh. Damn. I guess I left it in the pocket of my work pants again after I got out of the shower," she said.

"I did warn you that I'd be dropping in again," Mo said. "Are you going to invite me inside?"

"Want something to eat?" she asked, gesturing toward the foil takeout container on the kitchen counter. "There's some black beans and rice, and some chips and guac."

"No, thanks," he said, gazing around the room. "Looks like the cobbler's children are finally getting some shoes."

"Yeah," she said, feeling suddenly shy. "I couldn't let that tile left over from Chatham Avenue go to waste. Hey—guess what? We sold the house. Carolyn called to tell me this afternoon."

"That's great!" Mo said. "Did you get your asking price?"

"We came close," Hattie said. "Close enough that I said yes. It's a cash offer. We close on Friday."

He raised an eyebrow. "That's fast. Do they know about the body?"

"They do. Turns out the buyer is actually Holland Senior's much-despised Yankee cousin. Carolyn says the feeling is mutual."

Mo leaned back against the counter. He was wearing faded blue jeans and a Dodgers T-shirt that had seen better days. He needed a haircut, and there were dark circles under his eyes, but he smiled that slow, lazy grin as he let his eyes wander over her body and Hattie's stomach did an involuntary little flip-flop.

"I've missed you, Hattie," he said.

Keep it casual, she told herself. "Want something to drink? A beer or a glass of wine?"

He tilted his head.

"I was hoping you'd say you missed me too."

She got a bottle of wine from the fridge and poured two

glasses, hoping her shaking hands wouldn't give her away. She handed him a glass and tried to gather her resolve.

"I didn't."

He set his glass down on the counter and pulled her to him. He put his arms around her waist and kissed her.

"Liar," he murmured. He cradled her face between his hands, then kissed her again, parting her lips with his tongue. His kisses were warm and sweet and she realized that trying to resist Mo Lopez was futile.

"Okay, maybe I missed you a little." His hands roamed under her shirt, and she felt herself melting into him.

"I wanted to call you as soon as I got the news today, that the house was sold."

"But you didn't. Why not?"

"This will never work. . . ."

He stopped kissing her. "Could you just listen? First off, I've thought a lot about this 'don't get your honey where you get your money' theory. And it's bullshit. Lots of successful couples work together in this business. Hell, you're already working for your father-in-law, and your best friend and her mom."

"That's different. They're family."

"Not *that* different. Besides, we're good together, Hattie. Admit it. We piss each other off sometimes, yeah, but that's what happens on any creative project."

Mo pressed his lips to her ear. He kissed her earlobe, then moved slowly down her neck, lingering when his lips were on her collarbone. "You know what makes us so good together?" He'd managed to unsnap her bra and now his thumbs grazed her nipples.

"Sexual tension. You can't deny it. It's always in the air when we're together. Like those damned no-see-ums."

His fingers worked lazy circles around her nipples and then he was kissing her again.

She struggled to find a reason to pull away, when all she wanted was to get closer.

"Your news?" she managed.

She felt his lips widen into a smile. He pressed his forehead to hers.

"Remember that show I originally pitched you—right after we met at Tattnall Street?"

"*Saving Savannah*?"

"Yeah. HPTV didn't want it, but I knew it was a great concept. The whole time we were working on *Homewreckers,* I kept tinkering with the proposal, and my agent and I pitched it to another network. I wanted to tell you about it after the wrap party, but you wouldn't let me. You chased me away."

"Yet here you are again."

"Lucky for you, I'm a very persistent guy. Earlier this week, we met with the head of programming at Apple. Hattie, they want it!" He grasped her shoulders. "They want to buy *Saving Savannah*."

"So . . . you'd shoot another series here? In Savannah?"

He rolled his eyes. "Yeah. It won't work if we shoot it in Omaha."

"I didn't know Apple did reality television," Hattie said.

"They do now. And here's the thing. It won't be just a weekly streaming series. They'd want us to do a weekly podcast, and maybe some spin-off DIY videos as we progress. It's called vertical integration. I'm gonna need a host, too, someone who lives and breathes historic preservation. And who really understands Savannah. Know anyone like that?"

"I do, but I doubt you could afford her."

Mo touched her chin. "I hear she's expensive, but worth every penny. So what do you say? Are you willing to dip your pen in the company ink? Will you work with me?"

"With you?"

"As a partner. You'd host and get executive producer credit. We'd have complete creative control with *Saving Savannah,* and a big-time budget. No more Rebeccas pulling the strings. Oh, and Cass could be your cohost on the show. They like the idea of having Tug on camera too if he'd be comfortable with that."

"No L.A. designer? No phony romance angle?"

"Definitely no L.A. designer. And the only romance angle would be ours." He kissed her again.

"What happens to *The Homewreckers*?"

"I own the franchise," Mo said. "If, in the off chance it manages to survive the first season, and HPTV wants to re-up for another, they'll have to buy me out. Unless, of course, you're looking for a reunion with Trae Bartholomew."

She shuddered. "No, thanks."

Hattie reached for her wineglass and took a sip. "Can I think about it?"

"You really enjoy breaking my balls, don't you?" Mo said plaintively. "I drive all the way here from L.A. to tell you my news, and you still need to think about it?"

"You *drove* here?"

"It seemed like a good idea at the time, but I'll admit when I hit Amarillo I started having second thoughts. I pulled into a truck stop and got a solid five hours' sleep. I was gonna stop in Oklahoma City, but then I got my second wind and just kept going."

"That's insane. Why would you do that? You didn't even know if I'd say yes. I don't even know if I'll say yes."

"I need you to believe in me, Hattie. Believe in us. Can you do that?"

She took a step away, needing some distance from this man who somehow kept drawing her into his schemes and his dreams.

"I wish I could," she said. "But what if none of this works? Mo, I finally got to the point where I think I could be okay with my life as it is. Earlier today, Cass told me that all the clocks stopped in this house the day Hank died, and she was right."

Mo looked around the room, at the bucket of mortar mix on the floor, and the box of tile on the granite kitchen counter. "The last time I was here you had plywood countertops. That's progress, right?"

"Yeah. I'll probably never not miss Hank, but I'm done grieving him. I've got my work, my dog, friends. And that's enough for me. But it'll never be enough for you. You'll shoot a show and then you'll be on to your next great project. And I'll be here, alone, another broken clock." She shook her head violently. "I can't do that again. I won't."

He raked his hands through his hair, then grabbed her hand. "Okay, that's it. You're coming with me."

"Where?" Hattie asked, alarmed, as he steered her through the living room, with Ribsy following behind, barking in excitement. Mo opened the door and pointed at the dog. "You stay here."

They were on the porch and then standing in the driveway, where a silver Audi was parked. Mo opened the passenger door and the dome light flickered on.

Hattie leaned forward to peer inside. The seat was full of taped-up boxes. His messenger bag was tossed on the floor along with a jumble of tennis shoes. He pointed to the back seat, which was loaded with golf clubs, suitcases, a garment bag, more boxes, and a slightly wilted potted palm tree.

"What's all this?"

"This is approximately half my life, or all of it that would fit. The rest is in storage. I've leased my condo to a guy, with an option to buy."

He reached for her, sliding his arms around her waist.

"This is me, telling you, Hattie Kavanaugh, that I am all in. It's me promising you no more fake drama and no more stopped clocks. It's me promising more bickering, more impossible deadlines, but also more fun. And more great sex." He kissed her forehead, the tip of her nose, and then, finally, his lips found hers again.

Hattie thought about what Makarowicz had told Emma Ragan, about love and loss and finding a way to keep on living. She hooked her thumbs through the belt loops at the back of Mo's jeans like it was the most natural thing in the world, and she caved. Standing in the driveway of the house she'd shared with her first, lost love, she discovered, to her wonderment, that she'd found love again, right here.

"Okay," she said, when they'd paused kissing, because they could hear Ribsy inside the house, barking to be let out. She laced her fingers between his. "Okay. I'm all in too."

Acknowledgments & Thanks

- - - - - -

Writing and researching a novel is always hard work, but doing so during a pandemic seemed a Herculean task. Which is why I'm so grateful to the following for their advice and expertise; G. M. Lloyd, Gwinnett County Chief Medical Examiner Dr. Carol Terry, Gordon Center, Billy Winzeler and Bob Timm, Anita Corsini, Alyssa Kaufman Kopp, Brittany Bailey, Scott Efird, and Carolyn Stillwell. Any errors or misunderstandings of facts are mine alone.

This year (2022) marks my thirtieth year of being a published author, and *The Homewreckers* is my thirtieth book. I'm so blessed to have had this career, and to have had the support of family, friends, and my publishing team.

Stuart Krichevsky is still the best damn literary agent on the planet, so thanks to him and his co-workers at SKLA. Meg Walker at Tandem Literary is a marketing superhero and a dear friend/sister. I'm forever grateful for the entire team at St. Martin's Press, led by the indomitable Jennifer Enderlin, whom I'm lucky enough to have as publisher *and* editor; for the publicity prowess of Jessica Zimmerman and the marketing mojo of Erica Martirano; and of course, for another fabulous cover from Michael Storrings.

Huge thanks to my Friends and Fiction sisters, Patti

Callahan Henry, Kristin Harmel, and Kristy Woodson Harvey, who let me lean on them when the going got tough, and to our 60,000-strong Friends and Fiction community.

To say that the past year was a challenge would be a laughable understatement. No way could I have done any of it without the love and support of my amazing family. Tom Trocheck is my rock and my refuge, and Katie and Mark, Griffin and Molly and Andy are always the light of my life.

And thanks, as always, to my dear readers, for allowing my childhood dreams to come true and for allowing me to keep spinning stories for all these thirty years.

Turn the page for a sneak peek at
Mary Kay Andrews's new novel

Summers at the Saint

Available soon in hardcover from St. Martin's Press

"Got a minute?" Traci Eddings looked up from the spread-sheet of doom that she'd been studying. Her GM was stand-ing just outside her office doorway, and from the pained expression on his usually sunny countenance she knew the news wasn't good.

Charlie Burroughs had worked at the Saint since the age of fourteen, and he was in his early sixties now. His face, wreathed in wrinkles and sun blotches, was a roadmap of all the disasters he'd witnessed: the 1972 hurricane that had peeled the roof off the main lodge; the food poisoning de-bacle in the men's grill in 1988; the drought of 1996, when temperatures had hovered in the nineties for thirty-seven days straight and a watering ban had burned every blade of turf on the golf course. He'd seen the Saint through stuff nobody talked about, stuff that still made Traci shudder. Charlie had been there the summer of 2001, when the red tide had caused a massive fish kill resulting in three tons of dead fish washed up on the beach, and of course, the plane crash four years ago that had claimed the life of Hoke Eddings and transformed her into a widow at the age of forty.

Charlie had been a tower of strength to Traci in the years that followed.

Traci pushed her reading glasses into her hair and waved him inside, pointing at the chair across from Hoke's desk. Well, her desk now.

"Do I even want to know?" She rubbed her forehead and closed her eyes.

"Mehdi's leaving us," Charlie said as soon as he was seated. "Accepted an offer at that new resort up the coast."

"Nooo," Traci moaned. "Not Mehdi."

"Afraid so. And of course, Sam is going with her."

"Which means I'm out my guest relations director, as well as a chef who went to culinary school on our dime," Traci said. She looked over at Charlie. "Is it definite? I mean, could we offer them both a raise, some kind of incentive to persuade them to stay on?"

"No. Mehdi showed me their offer. It's stupid money and she'd be stupid not to take it. Hell, I'd take it if they were looking for a washed-up old grouch with a bad knee."

"You're not that old," Traci said. "But don't kid yourself. I happen to know you can't cook for shit."

"Memorial Day is only a month away," Charlie said gloomily. "We were already shorthanded, and now we're losing two of our best."

"So we'll hire some more help," Traci said unconvincingly.

"From where? The spring hiring fair was a bust. High school kids don't want to spend a summer sweating their balls off as lifeguards or caddies or housekeepers."

"Like you and I did," Traci put in.

"The locals are all going to tennis camp in Florida, or doing TikTok videos for an energy drink that costs eleven bucks a bottle. Have you seen all the businesses in the village with HELP WANTED signs in their windows? Everybody's hiring but nobody wants to work."

"Maybe we need to try something different," Traci said. "Can we recruit from farther away? We're a beach resort, Charlie. Who doesn't want to spend the summer at the beach?"

"We could, but where are these kids from Sumpter or Jacksonville going to live? It ain't like it was when you were growing up here. Do you have any idea what the rents around here are now? Folks who used to rent to our summer help have turned their cottages or garage apartments into short-term vacation rentals."

She swiveled her chair around and stared out the office window at the postcard-pretty view of the Saint Cecelia, the venerable beach resort and country club that had been founded by her late husband's grandfather in the Roaring Twenties.

Nestled on a tiny private island off the Georgia coast, the Saint, as it was known locally and formally, had been a mainstay destination for generations of upper-crust families who'd flocked there for over a hundred years. If Traci squinted, she could see the pink-and-white candy-striped cabanas that lined the beach. And if she leaned out her office window, she might spot white-garbed players whacking croquet balls on the "village green" that had been added to the resort in the postwar years. One thing that had changed little over the decades was the presence of designer-clad moms watching as their little darlings splashed in the pool, while dads sipped martinis and plotted business deals après-golf at the Watering Hole lounge.

The golf course was lush and green, and just beyond the beach club and pool was a wide, sandy strip of shore and the shimmering green Atlantic.

If she closed her eyes she could almost picture walking along the beach, hand in hand with Hoke, after their first real date. Even at twenty-nine, he'd been so awkward, so tentative, bumbling even, in an adorable way, as he pulled her behind a palm tree for a kiss. Reliving the moment, she felt the inevitable lump in her throat and was glad her back was to Charlie.

"Traci?" Charlie's voice brought her back to her present-day problems.

"I'm thinking."

"About?"

"Housing. What if we turned the old golf cart barn into a sort of dorm? Like the one everybody stayed in back in the day."

"The one from back in the day that was a firetrap? That the county would have condemned if your father-in-law hadn't paid off the inspectors?"

"Not like that," she said firmly. "There are bathrooms in the cart barn, right? One for caddies and one for guests?"

"There *were*. The roof on that barn is falling in, Traci. The electrical wasn't up to code when it was built, so it sure as hell ain't gonna meet code now. It wasn't fit to house golf carts, which is why we built a new one, and it sure as hell ain't fit to house our summer help."

"We'll put a new roof on it, bring the electrical up to code, get some of those splitter heat and air units, like the ones we put up in the cottages by the lagoon."

Charlie shook his head. "You want all that done in less than a month? You know what that'll cost? In materials and labor?"

"You know what it'll cost if we have to delay—or even cancel opening up by Memorial Day? How much money we'll lose? You remember the pandemic? We're still bleeding red ink. Now, we've got an almost fully booked summer season ahead of us, Charlie. We can't afford to take that kind of a financial hit."

His mouth opened to protest, but then he thought better of it.

"What's the absolute minimum number we need to be staffed up?" Traci pressed. "How many more bodies do we need?"

"Nine would be ideal. But I guess, if we offer overtime, and maybe come up with some decent signing incentives, we could do with seven. But no less than that."

"Some of the hotels out by the interstate are offering

signing bonuses to new employees, or current employees who recruit someone new," Traci said. "Maybe we could try something like that."

"I can make some calls," Charlie said. "Chefs come and go all the time. We can find somebody in the kitchen, but as for the front desk . . ."

She swiveled back around. "I'll talk to Parrish."

"I don't know if that's a great idea," Charlie said slowly. "How will it look to the rest of the staff if you install your niece in a high-visibility job like that?"

"It'll look like this is a family-owned company and she's family," Traci said.

Charlie clearly wasn't in favor of the idea. "Didn't I hear something about her spending the summer in Europe?"

"I'll talk to her," Traci said firmly. "But if you see Ric? Don't mention it, understand?"

"Got it." Charlie didn't need to ask any more questions. He'd worked for the Eddings family all this time; he knew where all the bodies were buried. Literally. Like her, he'd grown up in the business. Traci knew he'd do whatever it took to keep the Saint afloat. Just as she would.